Love Changes

A NOVEL

SHERRY LUCILLE

Inspiring Destiny

MADISON, WISCONSIN

Published by:
Inspiring Destiny Press
C.O. - S. Lucille
Madison, WI 53725
www.sherrylucille.com

Cover art by Heather Biederman.

Cover and book design by:
Calluna Graphic Design, LLC
202 E Garfield St., Mt. Horeb, WI 53572
(608) 237-6737, www.callunagraphics.com

Current ISBN-13: 978-0-615-33252-9

Originally published by Goblin Fern Press, Inc.

Original ISBN-13: 978-1-59598-038-0   ISBN-1-: 1-59598-038-5

LCCN: 200692892

Library of Congress Cataloging-In-Publication Data

Lucille, Sherry.
Love changes : a novel / by Sherry Lucille.

p. ; cm.

ISBN-13: 978-1-59598-038-0   ISBN-10: 1-59598-038-5

1. Love--Fiction. 2. Chicago (Ill.)--20th century--Fiction.
3. Nineteen fifties--Fiction. 4. Nineteen sixties--Fiction. I. Title.

PS3612.U25 2006   813./6   2006928924

Printed in the United States. Second printing.

To God, who gave me wings,
my pastor, Alex, who taught me to fly,
and my husband, John, who said, "No matter how high!"

Greg, Cassy, JIV

Christine DeSmet

In Honor of:
Mabel B. Gaines
Mrs. Willie Bryant

Special thanks to:
Laurel Yourke, Wanda Tapp, Victoria Woodward,
Valencia Mayfield, Mark Kramer, Emily Auerbach, Lilada Gee,
Theresa Dillard, Viola Edmonds, D.L., David Glenn Edmonds,
Martina Smith, Pamela Payne, Cynthia Woodland,
Akilah Beyah Shakur, Carolyn Renee Laine, Laura Dettinger,
and Evonne Higgins.

Prologue

1931

"Twenty-five, forty-one Rhapsody Way, a good place to visit, a better place to stay." The Kennedy twins made up the song, and all of the neighbor kids sang it. The long winding driveway and the rolling hills gave one the sense of approaching an enchanted castle. And the trees—oak and walnut, with branches that reached into the depths of the blueberry sky—made you want to climb and never come down. All the children thought Jake Schultz was the luckiest boy in the world to live in such a marvelous house. He'd feel lucky right now if he could just get out of this house before Maxine could make her way down the hall. Her footsteps would be muted at first by the kitchen linoleum; then they would become clicking and hard as her heels hit the lacquered floor. Jake's stomach lurched. He was almost there. He padded quickly down the few remaining stairs and past the potted palm.

"Jacob!" his father's shrill voice rang out from the opposite direction.

Jake walked faster, his heart beating quickly.

"Jacob!"

Sweat caused his hand to slip off the cold metal doorknob. He had almost made it outside where he could be free and just plain Jake.

"Yes, Father," he answered.

"Come here."

Jake's shoulders slumped. Hanging his head, he walked slowly toward the sound of his father's voice. Black and white portraits of the Schultz family lined the walls. He had seen these men, grim and stern, looking down from their lofty perches many times before, all disapproving of him, all disowning him. His father said that Willow Wood, Illinois, was an excellent place to live, a place where he could do his work in peace and a place where "they" hadn't come yet. Jake thought it could have been a pretty house except it lacked color and life. Fear and despair hung from the rafters, a kind of gloomy gray that weighed him down.

"Have you done your chores?"

"Yes, Father."

"And where are you going?"

Jake looked down, letting his black wool jacket slide off his broad shoulders which hunched up in response to his father's question. He could almost see his reflection in the brown varnish shine of the wood floor, sad. He looked really sad.

"Don't shrug at me, boy!"

"I wasn't going anywhere." In response to his father's look of annoyance, he continued, "I...I mean out to play."

Jake felt the whip of Maxine's skirt as she rounded him to stand behind her husband. She leaned against the wall drying her damp hands on her cotton apron. He searched her face for some hint of sympathy, but there was nothing, as usual. Jake raised his face. At the age of ten he was already equal to his father in height, Jake being quite tall like his mother and his father being rather short.

"Join me," his father ordered as he walked toward the dreaded conference room. It was where his parents held their meetings. It wasn't a small room, but when Jake was in there he found it hard to breathe. He looked toward his mother again. Her hard blue eyes were unyielding. A quick jerk of her head told Jake to get going. He wouldn't be scared this time. He just wouldn't look at the pictures posted on the walls or read the articles lying on the tables. He'd listen to what his father had to say and get out as fast as he could.

Jake's gait was slow as he followed his father, Maxwell Schultz, to the door. How had Max and Maxine found each other? Were these even their real names? His father's bony hand clutched the knob. "Dad, do I have to…" Noting his father's expression, he corrected himself, "Father, do I have to go in…"

"Jacob, you are not a little boy anymore. Come."

Chapter One
Thirteen years later —1944

A shrill wind nearly took Jake Schultz's breath away as he lifted the right-facing window of the bay trio in his living room for air. Chicago wasn't called "The Windy City" for nothing. He was an early riser, and he loved this house of his because the breeze blew right through it, waking him so he could get ready for his day. He looked up and down Maple Street. Great old trees stood sentinel between the houses. The sidewalks were clean and the people plain. They mostly stayed to themselves, but Jake thought they could be counted on if he really needed them. Life was uncomplicated. This was the way it had always been and the way Jake wanted it to stay. Max and Maxine had raised him to abhor change. He could remember vividly his father sitting him down as a child saying, "Son, this country is devolving into a place of decay. The lesser races will soon take over if we don't stop them. Your mother and I intend to take action. People who think the way we do will stop this onslaught of darkness." Jake didn't have much use for his parents, but even Uncle Thomas said that coloreds and whites didn't belong together. And Uncle Thomas was the best man Jake had ever known. Still, change was bound to happen. He was well aware of that, but wasn't there anyplace in the Midwest where a white man could live in peace?

For seven years he had been proud to call this place home. Good people living together peacefully; what was so wrong with that? Nothing. Jake allowed a heavy sigh, rubbed the back of his neck and wondered why folks couldn't leave well enough alone. His neighbor, Clem, said a Puerto Rican man and his wife had moved in a couple of blocks away. They had to know they weren't welcome. That was just the beginning, Jake knew. And he didn't like it one bit.

As with most things, however, even change could be good. Jake Schultz, proud father and abandoned husband, was about to be reunited with his son. The thought of holding his boy again was overpowering. His last memory of Mark was stroking his chubby cheeks as he lay snuggled soft and content in his handcrafted cradle. Jake remembered being sure the blue blanket that Irene bundled the baby in would cut off his circulation, but she fretted about Mark being chilly, so as usual he gave in. It was while making that cradle for his son that Jake discovered his talent for woodworking. He made it sturdy to hold his big baby but delicate so that Irene would feel confident it was suitable for her infant. Jake felt that Mark could sense the affection in the craftsmanship, so well did he sleep when he was laid in the thing. How Irene could have kept Mark away from him for so long was beyond his understanding. She knew how much he loved the boy. Was she that offended by his parents when they visited with them all those years ago? Their behavior was harsh but was it enough to make her leave him and break up their family? Did Irene really think he'd turn out to be like them? If only he knew for sure, maybe there was still something he could say or do. No, she wouldn't listen to him now. It was as if there had never been any love between them. But they had been happy. If only he had followed his gut and not taken his family to his parent's home.

Sitting in her dilapidated black Plymouth, in front of the large stone house that had once been her home, with the engine running,

Sherry Lucille

Irene read and re-read the letter that Jacob sent to her in care of Mr. Namio. She had lived above Nick Namio's restaurant briefly, and Jacob's hunch that she maintained occasional contact with him was right.

> *Dear Irene,*
>
> *I will never understand why you left me and took my son away. You must know how much I love you both. I'm not a man who writes complicated words, but you are my life. Please, if you have any care for me, let me know where you and Mark are. Whatever my parents said or did to you, or if I've done something, I'll make it right.*
> *Love you, honey,*
> *Jake*

Irene crumpled the letter in her fist. She used the back of her hand to wipe the unrelenting stream of tears that fell from her eyes. God help him if he didn't mean what he was saying about Marky. For almost three years she had managed to keep herself and her son away from her husband. She would never forget what happened that night, but it was out of her hands now. She had to believe that Jacob would take care of his son. He had declared his love for Mark. It had better be true.

All of the time that she had been away, Jacob had continually sent investigators looking for her. She had managed always to evade them, to stay one step ahead of them. But when the sheriff showed up serving papers and threatening her with jail, she knew she had to allow Jacob visits with his son. If she ended up in jail she could lose all rights to Marky. She was forced to take this chance, and God help Jacob if she was wrong.

Irene pushed at the door of her old automobile. It stuck. Giving it a hard shove with her shoulder, the hinge released suddenly and she toppled onto the street. Steadying herself, she walked quickly around the front of the car's coffin-black, broad hood. Pulling the passenger door open, she helped her young son onto the running board and down onto the sidewalk. Holding his cool hand, she marched him up the stairs to Jacob Schultz's house.

With a tight grip on his mother, the boy looked up at the closed door. "Be a good boy, Marky," she whispered, giving her son a sympathetic look. "Don't give that man any trouble." She then bent down to pull the wrinkles out of his navy blue jacket, stroked his dimpled cheek and dusted the dirt off his chubby knees.

"Be good now."

"Poppy bad, Mom?"

"Let's just say he can be a mean S.O.B." Irene regretted her words. She had to believe that Jacob would not intentionally hurt her son. "You won't understand what I'm saying now, but just remember this: you mustn't believe everything he says to you; he gets confused."

"Poppy 'fused, Mom?"

"Yes, Poppy's 'fused, son. Now be good. I'll be back in a couple of hours." She kissed his head, rang the bell and ran down the stairs.

Jake thought for sure he had worn a path in the living room carpet pacing to and from the window. Irene was an hour late, and he couldn't make himself do anything but wait in this room. And what an agitated wait it was. If he heard a car slow, he'd jump to the window seat. He had pulled the curtains back with such vigor he feared ripping them from the rod. For a while he stood leaning in the open doorway trying to be casual. He looked so unnatural that several neighbors stopped to ask him if he was okay. So here he was, like a prisoner in his own home, checking every stray sight and sound. A car stopped with a lurch. He parted the curtains once more, carefully this time.

It was her, his Irene. He was immobile, transfixed by her presence. Her body had lost some of its robustness and her skin some of its color, but to him she was as beautiful as ever. Her lustrous black hair and misty brown eyes still enchanted him. He could drown in those eyes. He watched the way she moved. Her poise was still apparent. And the way she talked to the boy, all of her gestures were tender, meant to reassure.

She was such an antithesis to him. He was a bulky blond with blue eyes. He had been called handsome, but no one could compare to his wife.

It was too late for them, but the years of searching had paid off. The courts were requiring that he be permitted to see his son.

*A*t the first sound of the bells' shrill chime, Jake, in a burst of excitement, pulled the door open. Irene flew down the stairs, her black coat flying in her wake, shielding her from his desperate glimpse. Before he could set one foot on the porch, she was safe in her sputtering Plymouth. It was a wonder it still worked. He had hoped, rather than expected, he'd be able to speak with her, but he'd easily settle for just his son. The longing almost overtook him. The boy stood before him, stocky and strong. He was decked out in blue navy shorts, a matching short-sleeved jacket and a blue and white bow tie. His arms were down at his sides as he peered expectantly up at his dad.

"Hello, Mark."

Little Mark turned his curly brown head to look over his shoulder, "Where?"

"Where?" Jake questioned, at first not understanding. He picked his son up and squeezed him tightly, "What's your name then, boy?"

"Marky."

"God!" He said it as if it were a swear word, "Who the, who named you that, son?"

"Mommy, 'course," Marky replied, giving his dad a quizzical look. His mouth twisted causing one side of his cheek to dimple. It was such an odd mix of humor and curiosity.

Jake's hardy laugh shook both he and his son. "And do you know who I am?"

"'Course."

When Marky didn't elaborate, Jake peered directly into his bright eyes, "Well, who am I?"

With a big grin and in his loudest voice yet, he yelled, "Poppy!"

To this, Jake did swear. He wasn't about to be anyone's "Poppy" or "Pop." What was wrong with just plain old "Dad?" Only a woman seeking revenge could have come up with names this irritating. She had to remember that he liked things simple.

"Poppy?" Marky reached up and squeezed Jake's nose when he didn't answer right away. Jake looked down into his wonderful son's face, and "Poppy" it was. Out of the corner of his eye, Jake watched Irene watching him. He turned to move toward her. She twisted the key in the ignition, shifted the gears and floored the gas.

She hates me, Jake thought, but he wasn't about to let anything ruin this day. He turned his attention back to the bubbly little boy in his arms. He thought his heart would burst.

With a bit of effort, three-year-old Mark climbed up onto the beige, red and blue plaid cushion of the window seat. He rested his chin on his fleshy palms and his elbows on the windowsill. Then he peered out the broad open windows as he had seen his father do every morning when he was there. The smell of ham sizzling on the stove wafted from the kitchen and across the narrow hallway into the living room. "Umm, 'mells good," Mark said to no one in particular. He breathed in. A choking gust blew his dark curls away from his face. He squeezed his eyes closed, and when he opened them he saw something wonderful. "Look, Poppy. See the baby?" Mark yelled.

His dad was busy under the sink unplugging the drain. "No, Marky, Poppy doesn't see the baby. Poppy's working and cooking."

"She's cute, Poppy. Oh, ooo," Mark turned excitedly from the window, jumping up and down on the bouncy cushioned seat. "She fell, Poppy. Poppy, come see, come see!"

"Where?" Jake said, dropping tools in his wake as he walked quickly toward Mark.

"Peter's house."

"That's Peterson's, son, and they moved." Jake scooped Mark up and leaned with him to get a better look out the window. "Good god, niggers!"

"What's niggers, Poppy?"

"Forget it," he said, "and don't you be callin' no nigger cute."

Mark sniffed the air and scowled. "Something stinks."

"Good god, the ham!"

seven years later — 1951

Eight-year-old Shelly felt like a pretty big girl. After all she was being trusted with big girl responsibilities. Her grandmother, Mama Rose, who, by the way, had sewn her lovely yellow and white cotton dress for her, was letting her go to the store alone. Shelly had walked about five steps before taking the time to smooth her hand down the wide bell of the skirt. The pocket was so large that she was sure she'd be able to fit a whole bag of potato chips into it. She couldn't wait to try. And her sandals, these had to be the most beautiful ones anybody had ever owned. They were white leather with clear diamonds on the ankle strap. The straps were a bit loose, but she didn't want to wait for Mama Rose to add more holes for a tighter fit. Besides, her ankles would grow into them, and Mama Rose had already spent a lot of time gluing the diamonds into place. Her grandmother said she was a princess, and the diamonds would help her always to remember that. Yes, she was dressed for having a grand adventure on this walk, and she couldn't wait to get started.

It seemed like you could see more when you weren't trying to be sociable, like: the little old lady with the limp who wore flat brown shoes and thick white stockings, her cane hardly touching the ground as she shuffled along; or the mother in the red dress pulling her son away from the ice cream cart; and the men looking all sporty, tipping their hats as the ladies passed by. Yes, it was fun to watch the people, but Shelly didn't like them watching her back, especially when they looked at her as if she had two heads. What was so exciting about brown skin anyway? She certainly didn't find white skin all that thrilling. Mama Rose was right when she said they was just ignorant. Chicago was going to be integrated all over sooner or later. Maple Street was no different and people might as well get used to it. Just be decent and straight and nobody can complain. Shelly didn't understand all the stuff Mama Rose said, but she figured she was decent enough and she thought she walked pretty straight, too. Summer was a lazy time; even Mama Rose took a little rest in the summer. It wasn't hard at all for Shelly to talk her into letting her make this trip to the variety store.

Oh no, the bad boys are back. They had come from between two houses across the street. They were walking fast and talking loudly. Shelly pretended not to hear.

"Hey, Mike, is it true what they say...the blacker the berry the sweeter the cherry?"

"I don't know, David, maybe we ought to see for ourselves." Their pace quickened as they crossed the road to catch up with her. "Hey, Shell, is that your name, Shell?"

Shelly looked around; there were three of them, no, four. The dazzling light made their blond heads shine. The redheaded boy looked like he was on fire.

"Hey, Shell, how's about a little taste," the lanky one named David teased.

She froze in her tracks as they approached. Sweat beaded up at the nape of her neck. She could almost feel her baby hair curling and twisting. *Too many,* she thought as she turned and walked away. Her feet slipped in the loose-fitting white leather sandals she wore. The sun was blinding. She headed straight into its brightness.

As she became more nervous, her fast walking turned into a trot, and the trot into a run. The boys pursued hard on her heels. *Please help me, Lord. What do they want? Why can't they just leave me alone?*

Oomph. A crashing force caused Shelly to stumble backwards. Twisting at the waist, she turned and fell forward hard. Her palms and knees stung, but her bare foot caused her immediate concern. Her sandal was missing. Fear was temporarily replaced by worry for Mama Rose. She had spent her hard-earned money on those shoes. It wouldn't be right if she had to buy new ones. Shelly searched the cement walk for the missing sandal. As she crawled about, the biting scrapes on her knees throbbed. She looked down and noticed crimson smears on the sidewalk.

"I'm bleeding," she shrieked. Tears obscured her view. An ominous figure loomed above her. All she could make out were black tennis shoes with white laces. The feet were huge.

"He looks mean," said one of the blond boys, leaning with his hands on his knees. He shook his head hard as if trying to drive the sweat from his brow.

"Is he going to help her?" questioned the redhead, his chest heaving, as he stopped in his tracks.

"I'm going home," said the first. With that, Shelly's tormentors disappeared. She plopped down on her bottom, took a deep breath, surveyed her new dress and allowed her eyes to follow the sound of the voice now speaking to her.

"Get up," the evil-faced, big foot demanded.

" I can't," she winced.

"Yes, you can." He reached down to grab her arm.

"Don't touch me!" Shelly yelled at the big boy.

He tilted his head. Their eyes met. His lower lip turned subtly up. "Get up, Shelly. Let me help."

"You know me?"

"Of course. You're the only nig...err, colored family on the block."

"You were going to say nigger. You're Mark; you belong to that mean man, Mr. Schultz."

Mark shrugged. "Yeah, he's my dad but he's not really—"

"You have to say that 'cause he's your dad." She got up with a limp.

"Here," he said, taking her arm and wrapping it around his waist. "Hold on to me."

"Why would you help a nigger?"

"'Cause you're people, too, least that's what my ma always says."

She leaned on his arm. "You got a mom? I never seen no lady at that house."

"She doesn't live here; neither do I. Well, I stay here sometimes."

"Oh, your mom and dad separated, like mine."

"Yeah, I guess."

"Ugh." She let out a sigh noticing more blood oozing.

"Look, old man Wilson's sprinkler is on. Sit here in the grass."

"Why?"

"Just trust me," he continued, firmly gripping her hands and gently assisting her to a soft grassy patch.

The pain kept her from arguing. Mark pulled the hose over to where she was sitting. She shook her legs because they were starting to stiffen and burn.

"I know," he said. It wasn't the words but the look in his heavily lashed, glistening brown eyes that made her calm. She stopped shaking her legs and just looked as he examined them for injuries and gently rubbed away bits of gravel.

"Where were you going?"

"Goldberg's."

"That's a Jew store."

"A what?"

"You know a..."

Shelly looked up at him as if he were not speaking English. She then boldly stated, "I like Mr. Goldberg. He's a nice man. Me and Mama Rose go there all the time."

Mark looked as though he was thinking that over. "Are your legs better?" he asked, letting the cool water wash away any remaining dirt. He then lifted each leg, gently rubbing and soothing away the pain.

"What are you looking at?" Shelly asked as Mark stopped rubbing and stared intently.

"The bottoms of your feet are almost white and the tops are brown. Your knees look almost black when your leg is straight, but the brown evens out when it's bent."

"So?"

"I just never saw…"

Shelly shook her head. "Why did those boys run away?"

He smiled, "I don't know, but my mom says I can be intimidating, like my dad."

"I like your smile. You're cute…for a white boy."

"What does that mean, 'for a white boy'?"

"I don't know. It's what Mama Rose always says. You wanna be my boyfriend?"

"No!"

Shelly crinkled her nose. "Oh, it's because—"

"Nooo," he stated, jutting his neck forward, "I'm too old for you."

"You are?"

"I'm ten."

"I'm only eight." Suddenly she felt sad. She thought Mark looked sad, too.

Chapter Two

1953

June in Chicago can be a tricky venture. Jake had misjudged the weather badly. When he left for work the wind was blowing. The allure of a crisp day was hard to resist. But the day was not crisp. Leaving his work site, Jake was starting to count the black lines that separated the cement squares of the walk. Every three-leaf clover and fledgling weed commanded his attention. A mile and a half lay between Market Street, where the new houses were going up, and his own home on Maple Street. Jake's carpentry and repair skills had been his means of support for as long as he could remember. When he wasn't overseeing projects for his own modest company, builders like Dunn and Sons contracted with him to work on theirs. Such was the case today. Ted Dunn paid well, but working on these tiny, wooden, cookie-cutter houses, each one exactly like the next, was uninspiring. They weren't substandard, but they were certainly not as substantial as the other houses in his South Side neighborhood. Jake wondered about the trend; would it continue? Would his comfortable surroundings become "assembly line"? What kind of people would this type of neighborhood attract?

Lifting his reddened and stiff left hand, he noticed blistering and decided to forego shifting his heavy metal toolbox to it. Perhaps starching his work shirt had also been a mistake. The collar was rubbing and chafing the back of his neck. The walk stretched on. Earlier clouds had winnowed and waned the sun's raw rays. But now the bulbous stretch of fluffy cover was scattering, leaving a gaping hole through which at least eighty-five degrees of unadulterated hot escaped. Blond curls, undoubtedly looking a bit brown now, matted down on Jake's forehead and clung to the tips of his ears. Droplets of sweat pooled between his shoulder blades, giving him a sticky sensation that started there and streamed down the center of his back. Jake felt as if he were the direct target of the blaze-red assault. Yes, walking today had been a bad idea. At any rate he'd be home soon.

His own neighborhood lay before him like a bastion of peace: Goldberg's where he knew Mark and his friends purchased plastic bow and arrow sets for five cents, the dry cleaners on the corner, and the houses. Jake liked the houses best. Each had its own distinct character. Raised porches were the only common feature, but every woman on his block had added touches to make hers unique. A vine, a wreath, or an ornate welcome mat served to make their houses home. Mama Rose's house was a classic example. It was as if her living room had spilled out onto her porch. It was delicate, flowery and bright. It was like she wanted people to feel her presence before they ever set foot on her first step.

And here was his own house: stone and sturdy. In a few short minutes he'd have a quick bath, check on Mark, eat, and go back to the work site. He'd drive this time.

Jake trudged up the stairs, heaving boots, heavier now than when he started out this morning. He clutched the doorknob to the wooden screen door, turned his key in the entry door and stepped over the threshold.

"Whew!" A pungent odor assailed his nostrils: a crude mix of burnt toast and overcooked bacon with eggs. He ventured cautiously toward the kitchen, dropped his toolbox and scanned his surroundings. The room looked okay. A plate, saucer and water glass sat on top of the otherwise clean surface of his oak dining table. His view shifted left. An iron skillet lay half on and half off the stove burner. Congealed grease with bits of fat held in suspension caught his attention. A saucepan in the sink had remnants of fried egg plastered to the handle. Toast too charred for consumption lay piled on a serving plate; another of Mark's forays into cooking gone awry. Jake smiled, thinking that this display dashed all hopes of Mark having inherited his mother's knack for cooking.

Yesterday Mark had asked about money for the movies. Kevin, a seventeen-year-old neighbor, had seen one of those new 3-D pictures. He said wearing the glasses made Vincent Price and the other actors come out of the screen. One girl in the audience was convinced that a woman on the screen had reached out and stroked her neck. In her agitation, she tossed her popcorn all over the patrons in the row behind her.

Nothing about this mess left Jake in the mood to advance Mark money from his allowance. Mark had stayed almost exclusively with Jake over the last few weeks, Monday through Friday. Irene wanted him to give Emerson School a try. The timing was odd given that there was only a month left before summer break, but Jake wasn't about to question her motives. He was happy to have his son under any circumstances. And Jake was learning more about Mark's habits than he ever did during his sporadic summer visits. Mark, usually neat, wasn't when he was excited. Jake wanted to be furious, but all he could think of was Mark's angry scowl when he realized that in his haste he hadn't given himself enough time to complete the task. He was harder on himself than Jake could ever be.

Jake unbuttoned his shirt and rolled up his sleeves. He carefully parted the canary yellow curtains above the kitchen sink. The contrast between the roughness of his palm and their fancy lace edging intrigued him. Irene had put her touch to the store-bought curtains he'd purchased from Woolworth's. He could still see her smiling up at him as her delicate fingers worked the sharp slender needle, weaving it in and out of the yellow cotton. Only she could make something as mundane as sewing seem poetic.

Grabbing the faucet, Jake turned the handle to cold. He splashed the refreshing wet over his face and through his hair. He leaned forward, squinting. Was that Mark crossing the street? No, it was another boy about his size. Jake pulled a fresh drying cloth from the oak drawer.

Laying it on his face, he inhaled the lemony detergent scent before running it over his dripping hair and neck.

It was becoming obvious that he would be the one to clean up the mess left by his son. With a turn of the faucet handle, the water gathered steam. He plugged the drain with a rubber stopper, poured in powdered white flakes and leaned over his wide porcelain sink, watching the ivory suds rise and spread. He submerged Mark's glass, lingering to savor the silky feel of the mingling soap and water. It assuaged the aching of his fingers, palms and wrists. Outside, clouds were converging, forming a welcome barrier. Jake watched the leaves of the tree-of-heaven swaying. As he opened the window, a soft pouting breeze sucked the stiff curtains in and blew them gingerly out.

"Give Emerson a try." She had to be worried about Mark going to school in her neighborhood. It was quite a walk from their apartment to the school, and that particular neighborhood was no walk in the park. The more he thought about it, the more he suspected that worry was the real reason Irene wanted Mark to try out Emerson. Darren Drive, where her building was located, was deteriorating fast. A South Side pocket, concealed partially by the railroad tracks above, it had become a hub for drug users and derelicts. Irene had lived there about two months. It was a sure sign that her financial situation was desperate. She said she was looking for a new place. Maybe it wasn't going so well. She wouldn't take any help from him, so it was what it was.

The suds bubbles were becoming small and translucent. A shiver replaced the soothing heat. Jake unplugged the stopper, allowing the tepid water to escape. More warmth would be needed to clean this mess.

Perfection was not a quality Jake would ever claim, but he was responsible. He had taken care of himself since the death of his Uncle Thomas, some sixteen years ago. At age seventy, Uncle Thomas said he needed some help with the little things. When Jake sat on the sofa, he knew it was stable because he had replaced the front wooden leg. The screen door didn't fly in the wind because he had replaced the hinges. And the fussy sink drain rarely jammed any more because he had replaced all the pipes just two years ago. Yes, he was handy; Uncle Thomas saw it and used it to make him feel that he could contribute something meaningful to this household. But Uncle Thomas was not feeble or needy. It wasn't until the last year of his life that Jake noticed any frailty. Cancer was eating away at his uncle. His broad frame became slight, his complexion sallow.

Unlike Jake's relationship with his parents, his relationship with Uncle Thomas was good, really good. Uncle Thomas was always grateful for anything Jake did, giving him big hugs and sometimes even kissing his cheek as a reward. Jake really didn't appreciate the kissing part.

Then there were the talks, the things Uncle Thomas felt Jake needed to know. "Your parents are extremists, son; one of these days they're gonna do some real harm. My niece wasn't always the way she is now" —Jake found that hard to believe— "but I tell you at times I think she is as full of hate as your father."

Jake didn't like hearing these things. He suspected they were true, but hearing Uncle Thomas say them made them undeniable.

It soon became harder and harder for Jake to be home. On the night of his tenth birthday, his father invited him to one of their clandestine meetings. It was held in the private parlor. Jake's legs wobbled and shook from the knees down while he tried desperately to keep his thighs from rumpling the gray-green tweed throw that covered the couch. An ornate royal red velvet album was placed in his hands. He caressed it tenderly. Wonder filled his mind. Did it contain treasure? His finger moved carefully to the leather edging, smooth against rough. Hesitantly he opened it, wanting to fully experience the mysterious contents. His eyes searched. There was no color. He soon became thankful for this. Instead of normal photos, he remembered newspaper-like pictures, historic clippings. Vague recollections of children wearing tattered clothes clutching their parents' pant legs and skirt tails invaded his mind. Others showed adults, Negroes. Their eyes were wide with terror. At ten he really couldn't make sense of it all. His reaction to seeing them must have displeased his father. Even now he could feel the dragging and pulling inside his gut causing a sickening burning in the pit of his stomach. Bile rose in his throat at the same time that tears raced to form reservoirs in the corners of his eyes.

All of this preceded his father's blistering speech: "You're weak, boy. I've known it for sometime now."

His mother, a tall, big-boned woman, stood silently hunched in the background. Jake thought she might have been crying.

"You don't have what it takes," he said, tightening up his gaunt face. Jake would never forget his sneer. "When the revolution comes, you'll be crushed like all of the other nigger lovers. We will get rid of them all. And I am not just talking about the black ones, either; I mean all of them: the slanty eyes, the Jew pigs…"

A hailstorm of insults and curses spewed from his absurd mouth. By now Jake was on his feet, his eyes flying wildly from side to side, desperately seeking his exit. His feet were heavy and planted, though every other part of him quivered and quaked so that it scared him. If he were to run, where would he go? This house was comfortless, starkly furnished, only what was necessary. Color was minimal and Jake had always thought their living room should have been called the dying room. He felt like dying whenever he was subjected to one of these talks.

Hit me; please hit me. Knock me out or better yet, make me so mad I'll kill you. Jake didn't feel brave, but he had such anger that he thought he really could kill his father. He was such a short, narrow man. His slick black hair and piercing blue eyes made him look like a wet weasel. And did the man ever eat? Uncle Thomas said an ill wind would blow him to smithereens, whatever that meant. He wanted to laugh. The feeling didn't last long.

"Get out of my sight, you good-for-nothing…" Jake didn't wait to hear the rest. He ran as fast as he possibly could from the horrid room.

Once in his own room, he sat on the side of his bed, a muted plaid covering spread beneath him. All of his furnishings bespoke necessity. He had a hard wooden desk and chair for study and a bed for sleeping. He had his own bathroom, which he was to keep meticulously clean. His fun toys were hidden under the drape that ran the base of his bathroom sink. As long as his area was neat, he didn't have to worry about them trespassing. Minutes turned into hours, and there he sat trying to remember what he really wanted to forget. The pictures, the frightful pictures. Why had his father insisted on showing them to him? Blank walls stared back at him. They had no answers to give. A single chandelier hung from the ceiling. It gave no light of revelation. The bed he sat on, with its single pillow and cover cinched tight, did not engulf him. It offered no snug cushion to soothe away his weariness. And the people—the invited guests—why had they all stood around him, wide grins plastered on their faces? What had they expected him to say or do? There were no answers to be gleaned, so Jake attempted sleep.

A glaring white light shone in his face. He shielded his eyes with his right hand. Angry and sad children tugged at his pant leg. They were crawling on the ground. He couldn't see them as much as sense them. He shook his leg, trying desperately to get away. The smell of sweat, pain and blood crept up his pant leg and encircled his waist. When bony fingers clutched at his throat, he bolted upright.

"Mom? Mom!" he cried.

The tears that earlier had begged to spill now came in abundance. She wasn't coming. She never did; thought she was toughening him up for the revolution. She was so pretty, Jake used to think: tall and blond. At first he couldn't understand what they had in common, his mom and his dad. Finally it dawned on him: as ugly as Max was on the outside, Maxine was on the inside. If she was crying earlier, it was because he was weak, not because she was concerned for him.

When Uncle Thomas said he could stay, Jake never looked back. Even while Uncle Thomas's cancer was taking him away, he was making provisions for Jake. The house was left to him. Jake was only sixteen but his parents permitted him to stay there alone. He had always been a hard worker, and now that his survival depended on it, he worked two jobs and sometimes three. Whatever it took not to have to go back home was more than worth it.

At eighteen, he met Irene Mills. And before he was nineteen they were married. She was a timid girl who didn't trust easily. He promised never to hurt her and he thought he never would. For eighteen glorious months, Jake thought he had vanquished all his demons and God had granted him sanctuary.

Clouds moved away to reveal a brilliant yellow sun, effectively jarring Jake from his musings. This morning he had sought solitude, and now he was glad to be roused from his thinking. His past was too strange a place to dwell long. His arms now felt like spaghetti. How long had he been daydreaming this time? The water was cold; soap and grease were forming a nice comfortable partnership. And where was Mark?

"Boy's gonna push me too far one day. When I was his age..." He stopped, thinking that sounded exactly like Uncle Thomas. But Mark should be here by now. He turned to look over his shoulder. The wall clock said 4:30. Mark was now officially an hour late.

*M*ark knew his dad expected him to be considerate and responsible and he usually was, so a quick stop here at the park would be forgivable. Michael's Memorial Park was between school and home, and today the lush emerald grass called to him. He had to stop. It was one of those days that only came around once in a while. The perpetual blue of the sky was interrupted only slightly by puffy silver and white clouds, which shifted back and forth to let the sun's fluorescent rays shine through. If all of this wasn't enough, the wind cooperated beautifully, tenderly caressing Mark's face, causing his curly hair to lift and sway. All of the elements were in perfect union. Only a swing was needed for Mark to join this perfect dance of nature. He'd soon be flying, cruising the atmosphere to places far and near.

There was one left. He pounced on it. He sat on the leather strap and held onto the chains. Walking backward until the chains were strained tight, he leaped into the air. The first cycles were low. He went back and forth, the breeze brushing his face and causing his eyelids to flutter. Before long he was cutting a path in the wind. Swinging was one of those solitary pleasures, a thing to be enjoyed and savored. It was as close to being like a bird as a human could get. He loved it.

His ride was interrupted by a familiar voice.

"Hey, Marky," she was yelling his name over the din of the squeaking, squawking metal play yard.

"Don't call me that, Shelly," Mark yelled back.

"Why not? It's what Old Man Schultz calls you."

"Don't call him that."

"What?"

"God, Shelly, you can be dense."

"What's that?" she said, curling her lips into a smirk. He smirked back, knowing now that she understood him fully.

"Can I swing?" she asked.

"Do you see any empty swings?"

"No, but I can ride with you."

"No way."

"Pleeese, Marky."

"Okay, but only if you stop callin' me that."

"What?"

"Get on, Shelly," he said as his heels dug into pebbles, pushing up sand and dragging the swing to a sudden stop. Shelly ripped off her sneakers and tore off her socks. She quickly placed one foot on each of Mark's thighs and started to pump. After several minutes her energy waned.

"Hey, Mark, I need to sit down."

Mark looked up at her face. He had a hard time refusing her anything. "Okay."

She sat hard with a bounce. Her long brown legs encircled his waist. He had seen girls swing like this: two together, facing each other, but he and Shelly? Something didn't seem right. Before he could voice his objection, she started to pump her legs. He pumped his. Higher and higher they soared.

"Man, this is fun," they said simultaneously.

Brilliant and glittering greens formed a sea beneath them. Fragrant lilac enveloped them. The housetops seemed a thousand miles beneath them. Mark looked up. Clouds like galloping ponies moved away. The blinding sun peeked through. Mark squinted.

Shelly looked at him as if searching for his pupils. Deeper and deeper she looked. What was she looking at? She was kind of pretty, for a colored girl. Her skin was the color of dark honey or light syrup and her hair was a wavy mass of velvet black with dark sandy streaks, and she had the biggest, brownest eyes he'd ever seen.

"Shelly, squooch over. You're crushing me."

She wiggled her bottom a little bit forward. That didn't help.

"Get off me!" he yelled.

"What I do?"

"Just get offa me!"

"I'm going, and quit poking me." She looked down at his lap, then immediately back at his face.

He felt humiliated. He quickly dug his heels into the sand, causing Shelly to bump her forehead into his and then yank her torso back with a hard force.

"Get off!" He felt his head throbbing from an emerging lump.

"Okay!" Shelly yelled back and squirmed off him as fast as she could. At first they stood there transfixed, chests heaving, tongues thick. Shelly was the first to recover. She turned stiffly and marched away from where he sat saying nothing.

For a while she walked. Then she glanced back at his face. His eyebrows arched, his nostrils flared and his mouth twisted. It was the worst evil look he had ever done. Near tears, she began to run.

Gasping for breath, Shelly's legs carried her with a speed she had not known before; every part of her was tingling. She had never really feared Mark, and she didn't really think she feared him now, but her stomach was all twisted in knots. Just before Mark got mad, she was resting her hand on his chest. The steady beat beneath his shirt made her hand pulse. She wanted to lay her head there and listen to the rhythm. Stupid boy, he had to go ruin everything.

She was hardly aware of the block and a half she had covered getting from the park to her house. However, her legs were beginning to simmer from the constant pounding on the pavement. A few more steps, up the stairs and through her door, safety was in her grasp. Ignoring the bell, she pounded on the door with both her fists.

Mama Rose yanked the door open. "What's wrong, girl? You're actin' as if the hounds of hell is after you."

Shelly rushed past her, knocking the antique floor lamp against the wall, causing an indentation in the plaster.

"I'm sorry, Mama," she said, bursting into tears.

"I said, what's wrong with you, girl?" Mama Rose questioned while clutching Shelly's arm as she flew by.

"Mark, Mark's mad with me."

"That all. He'll get over it."

"No, he won't. I hurt him, on the swing." With that she snatched away and sped up the steps to her room.

*E*very step Mark took toward his house begged a new question, a quasi-revelation, mind-bending confusion. Waves of steam flounced and floated above the cement: reflections of his thoughts, too many to number. One thing was certain: they all had something to do with what happened on the swing. Was Shelly responsible? He could still remember how her hair looked when the rubber band on her ponytail broke, releasing a glob of rippling curls: funny and wild but pretty at the same time. His personal had gotten hard before, especially at night. But this time it definitely seemed to have something to do with Shelly. Mark watched the fabric of his heavy denim pants; each step seemed to weigh him down.

"What you thinkin' 'bout, boy?" Mama Rose shouted from her honey-colored wooden porch. The ivy, lacing its way up the support post, momentarily obscured his vision, causing her voice to be disembodied.

"Nothing," Mark replied dryly.

"I've seen a lot of people thinkin' 'bout nothing and none of 'em looked at all like you," she said, walking toward him.

"Can I ask you a question, Miss Rose?"

"Call me Mama Rose, boy, everybody does."

"I can't, my pop, he wouldn't—"

"I know all about your pop, boy." She straightened to her full height of five foot three and propped her hands on her waist.

"What do you know?" Mark could feel his agitation rising.

"I know what he thinks, or thinks he thinks 'bout black folks, and I know what he thinks 'bout you."

"My dad loves me," he snapped.

"Oh, I know he does that."

Mark paused to formulate his question. "Miss Rose—"

"Mama."

"Okay. Mama Rose, is Shelly…well, is she okay?"

"She will be. But you have something else on your mind, don't you?"

"Yes, Ma'am, it's kinda personal." His timbre was low. He could hardly hear his own voice.

"Well, come on in, boy. We can't be discussin' personals outside on the street."

"My dad, he won't…"

"Does he have to know everything? Run on in, let 'im know you're home, then come back when he leaves for work."

"All right, but just for a minute."

To say it had been a long day didn't begin to describe Jake's experience. After an exhausting nine hours at the site of the new houses he was working on and the long, hot walk home, he waited for Mark to arrive, which he eventually did. He didn't have time to question the boy or even express any annoyance. As soon as he saw Mark he said, "Hi," and "See you when I'm done at the site." And now, when he should be preparing for sleep after an utterly exhausting day, he was standing at his closet, finger-filing through shirts looking for the one that would complement his gray suit the best. Unless he missed his guess, this action would most assuredly draw his son's attention. Mark didn't miss much.

"Here we go," Jake said, pulling a sparkling white shirt from the closet. He heard Mark slowing his gait as he approached the bedroom door. Jake picked the crisp shirt from the closet rack and pulled the sleeves over his arms. He straightened, admiring his reflection in the mirror while fastening the buttons down the front. Opening the drawer to his sturdy red wood dresser, he removed his lapel pin and cufflinks. It was then that he spied the inquisitor practically dragging his feet as he passed the bedroom door.

"What you getting all dressed up for, man?" Mark asked as he walked casually in and took a seat on his father's enormous bed. Hand-carved posts supported each corner. Heavy and highly stylized, they looked like something Paul Bunyan would have crafted. "Fit for a giant," as Mark was known to say. Beige wallpaper lined the walls above the waist-level molding, meeting the crown molding of a very high ceiling.

"I got a date, boy, and who you callin' 'man'?"

"Poppy?" To his dad's accusing look, he amended, "Pop, why did you and Mom break up?"

"I've told you the story before. Weren't you listening?"

"I was, but I didn't get it," Mark said, drawing his legs beneath him as he sat squarely in the middle of the bed. He was now resting his chin on his hands as he peered up at his dad from the plush maroon-colored blanket.

"I'm not sure I get it, Mark," Jake was adjusting his shirt collar and sneaking another peek in the mirror.

Jake could tell that his son admired him, thought he was "pretty hip." This was a sort of ritual they shared, Mark watching him carefully as he got ready to leave the house. It didn't matter if he was getting ready for work or an occasional date, as was the case this evening. Mark said that Shelly thought he was handsome, said he looked just like Mark. Jake figured he should be flattered but instead found himself wishing that Mark didn't put so much stock in what a ten-year-old colored girl had to say.

"Tell me one more time, Pop. I promise I won't ask you again." He made this statement while turning onto his back and letting his head hang off the edge of the bed, giving him an inverted view of his dad.

"Okay, Mark," Jake said, lifting a brush to organize his curls, "but I've got to make this quick. I don't plan on being single all my life. It happened something like this: you were about five months old when Max and Maxine requested, for the umpteenth time, that I bring you and your mother to meet them."

"And you didn't want to go, right?"

"Right. My parents are strange. They hate all niggers." Noting Mark's grimace, he proceeded more gingerly, "Blacks, browns, all of 'em. And I don't think they liked me a whole lot either."

"But they loved you?"

"Yeah, sure," Jake answered, more for Mark's sake than the truth's. "Are you gonna let me tell this story or what?"

"'Course, go on."

"This time your mother wanted to go. She left foster care at sixteen and never really knew her mom or dad. She thought you should have some grandparents. I didn't agree, but my parents were askin' so much I hoped they might have changed some. When we got to the house, Maxine answered the door.

"'Come in, Jake, and this must be…Irene? Let me see the boy. Max, come here,' she belted in one breath while removing the blanket from your face. My dad suddenly appeared wearing his signature black three-piece suit. It was faded and somewhat threadbare. You know, somehow I never noticed he had a limp but he did, and it suited him.

"'Oh good, I see Jake and…come over here, girl, let me look at you.' He adjusted the shade of the floor lamp to direct the beam at your mother, 'My, you're dark.'

"He actually said that. That was the first thing he said to your mother. She was a trooper though. If we hadn't broken up so soon after, I wouldn't have thought any of that stuff bothered her." Jake looked at Mark to see if Mark had noticed his anguished expression. He hadn't seemed to.

"Next thing you piped up, 'Waah, waah!'"

"No, I didn't," Mark yelped, pitching forward as he sat up.

"Yes, you did."

"Okay, go on," he said, now on the edge of the bed, eyes wide and twinkling.

"'Bring the boy to me,' Max demanded with the superiority of a king. I remember the planks of the floor creaking as Irene walked forward. I was starting to shake, but she was brave. It all seems silly now."

"But you didn't think so then."

"No, I didn't. I was actually getting sick. What time is it?"

"Please, Pop."

"Okay, but no more interruptions. Max and Maxine, the terrible two-some, looked at your beautiful round face and looked horrified. I guess your mom could feel the slight. She said you needed a diaper change and stepped into Max's parlor. I hadn't been in there since I was ten."

Jake stopped for a minute to shrug off a chill. "Neither Max nor Maxine tried to stop her, so I figured it was okay. Before Irene could get the door closed, she bolted back out. Maxine was in the middle of asking me if you were mine. And Max was asking me if your mother was part…"

"Part what? You never told me this before," Mark stated quickly, his voice rich with excitement.

"Sorry, time's up. Gotta go." He moved toward Mark, gently gripped his shoulders and gave him a playful hoist out the door. *Thank god I caught myself,* he thought. Jake sat down on his lumpy mattress. What else had he blocked from his memory?

*R*ose didn't believe in wasting time, day or night. And since she was having some sort of nightmare about cymbals clanging and drums pounding on her head, she decided to get up. 12:30 A.M., her clock had read as she raised it to the night-light. She swung her legs over her thick quilt, slipped her feet into her cushiony house shoes, and removed her robe from the metal rail frame at the foot of her bed. A brief stop in the bathroom to wash the sleep from her eyes and she headed down the steps. Were the walls vibrating? Her vivid dream was proving more real than imagined. *Girl can sleep through anything*, Rose thought as the loud music wafted through her open windows, a quick gust causing her curtains to flap. It's not like Jake to be so loud.

Rose padded across her living room and into the kitchen to get a drink of water. A few steps into the kitchen and her foot caught on the linoleum. Unable to lift her fuzzy purple slipper, she leaned onto her free foot and flicked on the light. Remnants of orange ooze stained the floor. The Kool-Aid Queen had struck again. Rose had half a mind to wake Shelly and make her clean up her mess. That would take too long and the poor thing might not get back to sleep. She'd mop it and give Shelly the required lecture later. Yesterday had been a scorcher, but late into the evening, the wind started blowing and now in the morning's wee hours a robust gust was picking up. If she mopped now, the breeze would dry the floor in no time.

Mama Rose drew a large metal bucket of simmering hot water, poured in some detergent and started to mop the sticky floor. Once done ,she gathered the cotton strands of the mop into her strong hands and squeezed the dirty water into the sink, after which she proceeded to wash it with bleach and scalding hot water. The porcelain gleamed from its scrubbing. With her work finished, she turned to walk toward the couch. It was small but very comfortable. She'd sit a moment before putting the mop away and going upstairs to bed. Walking wearily toward her resting spot, she thought she heard something.

"Sure is late for visitors," Mama Rose said aloud, moving closer to her front door, about to place her ear next to it.

A slight banging on the door ended her inquiry.

"Mama Rose, can I come in for a while?"

Rose could just hear Mark's whispered plea. "That you, boy? What you doing here so late at night?"

"I don't like the people in my house," Mark was saying as Mama Rose pulled the front door open, causing him to topple from his squatting position.

"Who's in your house, boy? Talk slow." She extended him a hand up from her looped-yarn welcome mat.

"Miss Ann and some men. One of them came to my bed and tried to… I killed him, Mama Rose, and he let me go. I think he was drunk." By now Mark was on his feet, shoulders back, head up.

"Killed him, are you sure?"

"No, but he fell awfully hard, and he didn't move."

"He ain't dead. Why are these people at your house, boy?"

"I told Pop I was big enough to stay alone, but he asked Miss Ann to come and she invited some men over. They had lots to drink and maybe some other stuff; it smells funny."

"You stay with me until your dad gets home. You'll be safe here. Mama'll make you a pallet," she said, gripping his shoulders to reassure him.

"Do we have to tell Pop?" Mark questioned, leaning on the end table next to the closet.

"Yes, but let me worry about that." She smiled at the boy she now had to look up to.

Mama Rose went over to the extra closet and pulled out one of her hand-sewn quilts.

"Here, boy, make yourself comfortable." She handed him two blankets and a couple of pillows to go with the quilt.

"Your mother made this." Mark ran his hand over the puffy blues, yellows and oranges set in Fat Mama's signature pattern.

"She did."

Both of their heads snapped toward a hard rap on the door.

"Who is it?" Mama Rose questioned as she walked hesitantly toward the door. Unfortunately the caller stepped in as she approached.

"Who are you? And what are you doing in my house?" Her entry light glowed above the man's head, illuminating all too clearly his spoiled and inebriated appearance.

"I came for the boy, saw him run out. When I couldn't find him, I noticed your open door." The stranger advanced on Mark.

"No," Mark shouted, his voice squeaking.

"If you touch one hair on that boy…"

The man screwed up his face trying to get a better look at her. "You're Rose, ain't you?" he snorted, his feet shuffling in an effort to remain standing. Reaching past Mama Rose, he made an unsteady grab for Mark.

She intercepted the man's forearm.

"Why you're one uppity black…"

Rose cut him off with what Shelly affectionately called her "killer look" while grinding her nails deep into his arm. It worked. The man turned with a growl and left.

*T*he warmth of the night wasn't quite as hot as Jake's date with Jennifer. The windows of his sleek, 1950 Oldsmobile 88 were rolled all the way down. His tie was fully loosened and his dark gray suit coat lay strewn over the passenger seat. He could still taste the sweetness of her pouty red lips. It had been a terrific evening, a perfect end to a tiring day, a quick dinner at Mistel's: roast beef, so tender chewing felt like an option, served with roasted red potatoes. Mrs. Mistel's secret herb blend made them the house favorite.

After the meal, Jennifer demanded the obligatory dance, and with that done, they were off to her place. She had drenched herself in his favorite perfume, Flora-Lorna, a heady mix of citrus and spice. Jake leaned his head into the curvature of her neck and breathed in all of her. Overly scented women sometimes turned him off. But he was too flattered by her attempts to woo him to let a little overuse interfere with their date. When he was buttoning his shirt and raking his hand through his hair in order to regain his appearance, she nudged her body up against his. Self-control; he'd have to add that to his list of attributes. She wanted him to stay over. She didn't know him yet. She'd soon discover that his only bed was the one he left hours ago. It was the one he'd return to every night while his son was a minor. Still, it was fun letting his dates try to dissuade him from his chosen course of action. And, truth be told, he was weary. Only a short drive and a quick check on Mark lay between him and sweet slumber.

Jake was a quarter of a block away from his house when blisteringly loud music overtook him. It was past 1:00 A.M. Who would be playing records and keeping up such a racket at this hour? By the time his car was parked, he was steaming for a whole new reason. He couldn't imagine what Ann could be thinking. He slammed his car door and raced up the stairs. Not only was his door unlocked, it was ajar, and the stench emanating from the house was intense.

"What's going on here? Mark, Mark? Where's my son?" he roared.

Ann was roused from her drunken state. "He, hee's…" she waved her hand with a wilted flourish toward the stairs, "Junior wanted to check on…" She slumped back onto the sofa.

Jake's heart thundered as he took the steps two at a time, "I'm coming, son." Jake stomped on the man who was apparently Junior sprawled out next to Mark's bed on the floor. *God, please let my son be okay.* He never prayed but if God would save his son today, well, he was desperate.

Jake pulled the mound of covers off Mark's bed, yelled for him, looked in the closets and the bathroom. Rushing back to door he wailed, "Son, where are you?" He covered his eyes with the heels of his hands, unwilling to let the mist gathering in them cloud his vision. He struck out into the hall checking each room as he passed the doors.

"I'm here, Poppy," Mark yelled from the bottom of the stairs as he and Mama Rose made their way up.

Jake started down the hall. Bleary-eyed, he nearly knocked Mark over. Lifting his son into his arms, he smothered him with kisses.

"Pop," Mark squirmed. "Mama Rose," he said, pointing in her direction.

"Thank you, Miss Rose. I know you saved my boy." He grabbed her hand and squeezed so hard it looked as though she would cry.

"He saved himself, Mr. Schultz. This boy of yours is some kind of fighter. He grabbed a trophy from his nightstand and hit a man over his head who was trying to get after him. Then he came to my house."

The man growled and groaned on cue. "I 'spose that's him." She was pointing to a man now slumped in Mark's doorway rubbing his head.

"Wait here," Jake commanded.

Jake slapped Junior hard on the face, once, twice, then three times, "Wake up, dog!" Jake barked.

"Pop!" Mark lurched forward, grabbing his dad's elbow. The man's face was already ripe red and swollen.

Because of Mark's pleas, Jake slowed himself, grabbed Junior by his sweater and dragged the semi-conscious man down the stairs, taking no care to avoid his head banging against the banister railing. One man was already gone by the time they reached the main floor. The one who had come looking for Mark almost ran Mama Rose over trying to get out before Jake noticed him. Mark stuck his foot out as the man passed, causing him to fall against the sharp edge of the coffee table. His lip split and immediately oozed blood.

Rose had seen enough. With a shaky hand, she reached for the telephone and dialed. She waited impatiently for the rotary to roll back into position so she could complete the number to the police. She had to be worried about Jake ending up in jail for murder if they didn't come soon. Once Jake was on his porch, a great toss landed Junior solidly on the concrete pavement. Whatever consciousness Junior had regained slipped away. So he lay there arms and legs sprawled in unnatural positions, his clothes pulled and ripped.

Jake re-entered the house. Ann was perched on the couch, her legs in a most unladylike position and a bottle of booze dangling precariously from her small hand. Jake gave her an unceremonious hoist as he dragged her toward the door. The bottle fell from her hand, spilling over his black wing-tipped shoes. She mumbled something, and it was all Jake could do not to slap her across her thin pink lips.

Jake saw the squads coming as he gave Junior one last kick and was thankful he hadn't killed anyone that night. Red and blue lit the night sky as the cars raced toward them. Just as the first officer's leather shoes hit the walk and his hand gripped the car door to give it a hard push to close, Jake leaned and gently kissed Rose on the cheek. Astonished is the word that came to Jake's mind. She looked it. He felt it.

Mark and Mama addressed Jake together.

"Pop?"

"Mr. Schultz?"

Lowering his head, Jake said, "Mama Rose, if I can ever..."

She placed a gentle hand on his shoulder and turned toward her house. No wonder Mark had gone there. The place resonated with warmth and comfort, broad pillows on a pale pink bench, flowers reaching as if to express welcome, and cozy throws offering respite to the lonely or troubled.

"Just remember that God's children come in all colors. Just remember that for me," she said in parting.

Jake wondered if he could.

$\mathcal{L}$ater, sitting in the dark on Mark's bed, rocking an already sleeping twelve-year-old as if he were a baby, Jake's rage began to quake him. Shadows eased in and out of his consciousness. Ominous, ugly shadows invaded his reason. The knuckles on his left hand became white from squeezing the covers on the side of the bed as he thought about what could have happened to his son. It was amazing that booze could turn a perfectly respectable woman like Ann into a slut. Or maybe he was just too quick to believe the best of some people, while automatically believing the worst of others.

He had no use for alcohol himself. The last time he remembered having anything to drink was after that awful visit with his parents. As soon as his car started to wind its way up the road leading to his childhood home, a feeling of dread came over him. The trees he had played in — when he was fortunate enough to escape his parents' watch — looked twisted and gnarled. A heavy black sky loomed over them. Everything in him was screaming, "Don't go on." No sooner had they arrived, poor Irene and Mark became targets of Max and Maxine's ferocious barbs. He wanted to forget the whole thing, their insinuations and the queasy feeling that lingered long after he, Irene, and Mark had left.

The visit didn't last long. For the life of him Jake couldn't figure out how his parents could still make him feel so small and insecure. Mark made precious few sighs as he lay snuggled in his soft woolen blanket cuddled close to his mother's breast. His raspberry-colored mouth curled in a restful smile. Jake looked on the two, almost like an outsider not allowed in on a private moment. The last few miles of the trip home went quickly.

Before he realized it, the car was pulling to the curb. He noticed that his hands were shaking as he opened the door for Irene and the baby. As they walked through the front door, the side of his temple started to throb. Irene brushed by him and headed straight for the baby's room. She was mad at him. He could feel it. She hadn't said a word to him on the ride home. He went to the bathroom to get aspirin from the medicine cabinet. He stood there for several minutes staring blankly at his reflection. *Oh yeah, the aspirin,* he remembered as he twisted the knob to the cabinet. The small door opened. They were out. Perhaps a beer instead, that would mellow him.

The kitchen was dark. Nobody had bothered to turn on the overhead light. He reached for the metal handle of the fridge and pulled. The bright white cast an eerie glow against the darkness. Jake set the two beers on the heavy oak table and stared at them for several minutes before retrieving the bottle opener and popping the caps off. He sat and drank them slowly. Nothing changed; he could still feel the creeping pain of his childhood closing in. He decided to walk to the corner store for something stronger. Scotch; he had tried it one or two times before. Tonight seemed a good time to have something with greater powers of persuasion. He unscrewed the cap and stood by the counter. No, that wasn't right. He sat down at the table. Just as he was wondering if he was up to a plunge into hard liquor, they came again: the bony, outstretched, accusing finger of his father and the stinging insults. He thought he was done with all that; thought he could face his father and stand toe-to-toe with him. He couldn't. After all these years, he was still that sniveling kid who refused to speak up. Filling a heavy, ornate drinking glass to the brim, he lifted it and watched the glistening liquor swirling as he attempted to steady his hand. Darkness filled him. After a moment's hesitation, he threw back his head and gulped. An absurd urge to laugh would have spewed the accursed burning fluid from his jaws and all over the floor. Instead he swallowed. An overwhelming melancholy consumed him as the fire burned first his mouth, then his throat and stomach. The second glass went down faster. He was beginning to lose himself in a midst of forgetfulness when Irene entered the room. He vaguely remembered getting to his feet with an alcohol-induced swagger. She looked different to him, strange. His father's words flooded his mind: "part nigger"? He was trying to wrestle them from his thoughts when the baby started crying. He had yelled, swore and maybe even threw something.

Jake could now remember Irene's bewildered, no, frightened face as he shouted at her. What was he saying? He rubbed the back of his neck struggling to remember, "Bring that baby here, Irene." No, that wasn't it. Damn, why was it so hard to put all of the pieces together. What exactly had he said to Irene? "Bring that baby"…no, "Bring that bastard…" God no, yes. "Bring that bastard here, Irene. You been screwing around on me? Is he some kind of nig…?"

Jake pressed his fist against his mouth to stifle an emerging howl. He remembered it all now, her eyes wild with searching like she was trying to find her husband buried beneath the brute before her. That was the last time he had seen her. She left and took their only child with her.

Poison: the sins of the father and all that. He didn't want to be like them, yet he was. All this time Jake had blamed his lunatic parents for Irene's sudden disappearance and all this time he alone had been the one at fault. Would he ever be able to forgive himself?

*I*rene had said he was getting older and things would be changing. Mark wasn't sure what that meant but she was letting him try out a new school, the one near his dad's place. He had stayed there every school day for the past few weeks. However, school would be over soon and he would be back on his normal schedule, Mom's most of the week and Dad's on the weekends, with some extended periods since it was summer.

Mark loved his mother dearly, but staying at her apartment was becoming unbearable. Darren Drive was the worst street in their area. It was considered the near South Side because of its 51st address, closer to downtown Chicago than addresses with larger numbers. But in symbolic terms it couldn't have been further from downtown. It was a slum. Mark's dad had tried on several occasions to get in to see what the place was like, but his mother knew if he ever did, she'd lose custody for sure. The courts would never think that living here was as good as living at his dad's. And Mark hated it. He wasn't used to being uncomfortable anymore. This was by far the worse place they'd ever lived, and for the first time in a long time he was hungry.

Sitting on the one cushion that the pea green sofa still had, Mark wondered where his mother was this time. He ran to the window and pulled the thin tattered drapes to one side. Gray; everything was gray: the old man sitting on the stoop, the wads of trash blowing down the street and the night sky. There was no sign of her yet. The efficiency, with its mildew smell and faded blue walls, seemed much smaller this time. Was she going to bring something home for dinner? The refrigerator was empty of everything except moldy leftover TV dinners. The stench that came from that underused appliance still irritated Mark's nose.

Tired of waiting, he marched over to the cabinet and reached up over the greasy stove. His toes strained to lift his body a bit higher. He had seen Irene push some cans to the back for a rainy day when they first moved in. Extending his arm, he reached further and further into the hollow space. His underarm and side ached from the arch. He knew there was something back in the depths of the cabinet. Finally he fingered what felt like a soup can. Inching it closer, closer, "Yuck!" He yanked his hand back. A roach scurried down his arm and the can came crashing down on his head. "Arrggg," he yelped as he went to his knees.

Frantic rattling at the door drew his attention. His gaze was fixed on the knob. His heart thundered. "Who, who?" The door flew open.

"Mom," Mark sputtered, irritation, frustration and pain causing unshed tears to well in his eyes.

Irene ran over to his side. Kneeling on the sticky unwashed floor, she grasped both his hands and looked into his eyes. "What happened?" Pulling him into her chest, she smothered his head with kisses. "I'm sorry, Marky."

He pulled away. "Mom, can I go..." Noticing the hurt in her face, he pressed his lips together, willing himself not to complete his statement.

Living with Irene was like living with a ghost. She floated in and out of their dingy apartment like a spirit. Often, when she was there, she sat on her thin metal chair with the ripped seat cushion staring at their small television. "Hit it again, Mark," she'd mutter from time to time or she'd get up and adjust the hanger they used for an antenna. When she wasn't watching television, she'd sprawl out on the dingy beige carpet and pour over one of the many library books or discarded newspapers she continually brought home.

Her tastes seemed to run in extremes. One day Mark would pick up a book and read some stuff about transcending the natural realm, and the next time she'd have stacks of books about housekeeping and the marital relationship. Mark wanted to ask her why she didn't try a little living rather than always reading about things. But she looked so deflated and so sorrowful that he couldn't bring himself to add one more burden to her life. And given her minimal attempts at conversation, Mark thought she favored living in her head.

For all of Irene's aloofness, he preferred her quiet to her absence. When she wasn't there, he could hear everything: the cat whining down the hall, the drunks peeing against the side of the wall in the alley and Mr. Abernathy yelling at his wife.

"Stand up, Mark, let's put some ice on your bump."

Looking back as she walked toward the refrigerator, her thin, checkered coat hanging loosely about her shoulders, she asked, "Mark, what do you want to be when you grow up?"

"Humm?" She wasn't usually this talkative, and he was annoyed that she wanted to talk about jobs when his head hurt so badly.

"Answer me, Marky."

"I don't know. A carpenter or electrician, something like Dad."

"You're not like him, Mark."

She really was determined to irritate him today. "I am, too."

"Don't be upset, baby. It's just that your dad is big, and burly, made for hard work. He's smart enough, but he's not a thinker, not like you."

"But Mom—"

"Shuu…now promise me you'll get an education and make something of yourself."

"All right, but why are we talkin' about this now?" He winced as he put the towel-wrapped ice cubes up to his head.

"I need some assurance."

"What?"

"I've decided to let you live with your dad." Ice cubes tumbled to the floor while his arms wrapped around her waist with amazing alacrity. Her arms circled him in return. Mark knew she was crying but he only felt joy.

Chapter Three
A Gift for Mama

Shelly had only begun to dig the hole for the roses before leaving for school this morning, and she was having a hard time concentrating in class. She squinted her eyes. A jumble of yellow against green scribble-scrabble met her gaze. It didn't mean a thing to her. On her best day she had to use all of her mental ability to focus on math, and today, instead of dividing, she wanted to be multiplying the amount of time she had to find and plant roses for her grandmother.

"Shelly, Shelly Madison. Are you paying attention?"

"Yes, Ma'am?"

"And the answer would be?" Mrs. Flech said, dragging her yardstick down the board, causing the children to squirm from the hideous screeching.

"I'm sorry, Mrs. Flech. I'm worried about the roses."

"The roses?" Mrs. Flech quipped from the front of the classroom, her back to the blackboard with her arms crossed and her foot tapping. Her black-rimmed glasses teetered on her slender nose as she homed in on Shelly. Shelly glanced cautiously from side to side and then pulled open her wooden desk and started flipping through pencils, paste and a ruler. All of the other students in their neatly filed rows turned in her direction. Twenty-five pairs of fifth-grade eyes scanned her every move.

Shelly was thinking of short blades of graceful grass marred only by the small clump of dirt that she had time to dig this morning. When she saw Andy McCay passing by, she left the spade upright in the gaping hole. Andy was a sure sign she would be late if she didn't get going.

"Yes, Ma'am, for Mama Rose. They weren't there this morning, and Mrs. Cromwell promised." Shelly got up from her desk and proceeded up the long aisle, forcing her eyes off the polished green floor and onto her teacher's frowning face.

Emerson was a kindergarten-through-eighth-grade school. There were two classes per grade level and twenty-six to thirty students per class. It was the neighborhood school in walking distance of most of the houses and the few apartments where the children lived who attended there.

Shelly had walked alone this morning. She and her friend Mark had made up since that strange day at the park when they were swinging together. They didn't talk about it. The second week that Mark stayed at Mr. Schultz's on weekdays and came to Emerson, they simply started walking to school together as if nothing bad had happened. Karen from across the street had walked with them this week. She waited for them to pass her house, and when they did, she appeared from her doorway and ran to catch them. They didn't really like Karen. When she giggled her big rabbit teeth jutted out, and she giggled all the time. And she put on airs, always fingering her hair and dusting off imaginary dirt from her clothes. She smelled of overripe fruit. Mark said it was like fresh strawberries, but it made Shelly's nose itch. Mark didn't come out this morning and when Shelly walked past Karen's house, she didn't come out either. Shelly could have sworn, however, that she saw the bodice of Karen's bright red dress through the glass pane of her front door.

"I hope you haven't been passing notes," Mrs. Flech said, advancing on Shelly and holding out her broad pudgy-fingered hand. Shelly placed the scrap of paper in her palm and looked nervously around. The blackboard to her right was covered with Jimmy Swan's printing. On it he had written "I will not chew gum in class," one hundred times in heavy chalk letters that very morning. As Shelly stood there running worried hands up and down her yellow and blue plaid skirt trying to smooth out the wrinkles, she waited for Mrs. Flech's response. Pam—the only other colored girl in the class—looked on sympathetically.

Mrs. Flech squinted her narrow gray eyes and read out loud:

> *"Dear Shelly,*
>
> *Mrs. King told Mr. Merrick, who lives next door to Mr. and Mrs. French that you wanted to plant roses for Mama Rose's birthday. Mrs. French, the plant lady, is my mother's best friend. My mom says don't worry. You'll get the roses tomorrow.*
> *Good Luck,*
> *Tommy C."*

When Mrs. Flech was done reading, the class sat up tall as if holding its collective breath.

"And what does this mean to you, Shelly?"

"See, right here, Mrs. Flech." Shelly attempted to point to the part about the roses. Mrs. Flech pulled her hand away, crumpled the torn strip of notebook paper and tossed it in her already stuffed wastebasket.

"Shelly," she spewed with disdain, "I'm not going to punish you. It appears someone has already taken care of that. This is a cruel joke. Tommy Cromwell is always making promises that he can't possibly keep. No one would give expensive rose bushes to a child to plant. Now go sit down." Several of the boys and girls snickered as Shelly dragged her feet back to her desk. Her pretty plaid skirt was now terribly wrinkled from her squeezing it in tight heaps on both thighs as Mrs. Flech rendered her sneering reading of the note.

Shelly walked back to her seat as one might in a funeral procession. Sitting with a heavy thud, the metal legs on her chair gave a loud screech. For a while she rested her chin on her palms, using her elbows as an anchoring support atop her desk. Her eyes started to sting. Tears streamed down her arms, causing them to itch as they formed telltale pools on her desk. After a few seconds of trying to appear brave, she surrendered to despair and laid her head atop her thin arms. She wept aloud. No one disturbed her.

The final bell at Emerson was normally a welcome trumpet, signaling release from Old Lady Flech's torture chamber, but today it was squawking disappointment, the herald of doom, an unavoidable pronouncement to face the dashed dream.

If only she and Mama Rose had never gone to Mrs. King's house, she would have never gotten the dumb idea of planting the roses. But Mrs. King did need the help. Who knows what would have happened if they hadn't gone there when Mama Rose found out she hadn't been coming to the grocery store as usual.

It all started when Mama Rose asked Mr. Miles if he knew why Mrs. King was not making her daily walks to the store for fresh produce. He said that he had also been concerned and had stopped by Mrs. King's house one day after work. Mrs. King said she had pneumonia but wasn't that bad and didn't need any help. When Mama found out that Mr. Miles's visit had been an entire week ago, she left the store and went right to Mrs. King's. She found the proud but weak little lady in need of groceries. A few dishes were out of place and dust was thick. Not much else was wrong, except that it was obvious that Mrs. King could not take care of herself.

Mama Rose had gone over there almost daily after that, bringing Shelly with her when possible. Shelly overheard Mama Rose say that the King house was a pristine cottage. All Shelly knew was that it was really small and really tidy. There were round and oval tables in all of the nooks and crannies. The pretty glass statues were untouchable. You could look at them and tell. She ached to pick one up and see for herself if they were all as fragile as they looked, but she'd feel sick if she broke another one. Mrs. King said they could keep the first one their little secret.

When Mrs. King realized that Mama Rose was going to help her whether she liked it or not, she quietly whispered to Mama Rose that she could not pay her for her services. Mama Rose did not take offense. She smiled and said God would pay her.

On one of these visits, Mama Rose was telling Mrs. King how much she liked her rose garden and that next year she'd like to plant one, God willing. Shelly waited until Mama Rose went into the kitchen to prepare Mrs. King's meal. She told Mrs. King she had been saving to get something special for Mama Rose's birthday in May. Shelly could still remember Mrs. King's weak smile as she sat in her wooden rocker clutching her soft woolen blanket up to her neck. Shelly took a delicate blue throw pillow from the sofa, gently held Mrs. King's small gray head up and placed the pillow behind her neck. Mrs. King looked crooked but grateful. Shelly then reached into her rough corduroy jumper pocket. She dislodged used tissue paper, lint and a Bazooka gum wrapper before pulling out her shiny dimes and quarters: a month's worth of candy money savings.

Mrs. King squeezed her fragile hand around Shelly's and told her how much one rose bush cost. Shelly's stomach flipped. "Don't worry," she said with a gentle nod and another smile, "have faith." Shelly knew it would be impossible for her to save enough in time for Mama's birthday, so she did what Mrs. King told her. She prayed and forgot about it until yesterday when her prayer was answered. But she had been a bad granddaughter. She should have done more. How could she forget about it until it was too late? Mama Rose deserved a good present for her birthday and now she wouldn't get anything.

"It's time to go. Didn't you hear the bell?" Pam said, tapping her lightly on the shoulder. Shelly roused herself and through bleary eyes looked up at Pam's dark chocolate face. Her short black hair was coming loose from the rubber bands. Shelly wanted to laugh but couldn't summon the strength. She got up slowly. Pam handed Shelly her jacket. Shelly put it on and used her long sleeves to wipe the soggy feeling from her cheeks. She had cried so much that her eyes felt swollen tight and they stung like someone had thrown black pepper into them. Even now her chest heaved quickly in and out, causing her breath to catch in her throat. Pam wrapped her arm around Shelly's waist and Shelly wrapped hers around Pam's neck. As they exited the room, Pam told Shelly to wait in the hall while she ran back into the classroom to retrieve her satchel.

Gloom stretched before Shelly as she and Pam made their way down the center hall and out of the building. She couldn't ever remember feeling so helpless. This must be the "'pression" that the old folks talked about. Outside, the sky was bright with sunlit warmth and excitement, yet her insides felt all dry and worn. Maybe she could find some fabric squares and make a little quilt pillow for Mama. She deserved something. Two blocks from her house she waved goodbye to Pam, who hugged her and pressed the note from Tommy into Shelly's hands. Pam was a good friend, Shelly decided. She was harsh sometimes but honey-sweet at others. Shelly stood there for several minutes watching Pam's slight frame fade into the distance, before she dropped the note on the ground and headed for home.

The last stretch was the hardest. Everyone she saw was smiling. When she passed the Anderson house, Mr. Anderson waved and yelled a big full-toothed hello. Mrs. Cate, a small, calm woman, shouted, "It's a great day, Shelly girl. Don't you think?" It was so unusual for her to make a sound above a peep that Shelly spun in a complete circle only to find Mrs. Cate's back turned as she went back to diligently cleaning her shop window. What had come over her! Shelly passed her cute re-sale shop with the gaudy glass jewelry hanging in the window almost every day. Shelly loved to go inside there. Something about Mrs. Cate's baubles was intriguing; the blue quarter-sized diamonds were her favorite. Every time Shelly went in, she would try on clothes and jewelry while imagining all sorts of adventure. It seemed the entire neighborhood was glad about something today, so Shelly managed a faint smile as she passed her favorite store. She didn't want to spread her sadness. Mama Rose said the "'pression" was catchy, so Shelly decided to keep it to herself.

About a block from her house, she thought she saw a man walking away from her front yard with tools in his hands. He was big like Mr. Schultz.

Perhaps she should quicken her pace. Roses or not, she had to do something for Mama Rose and time was of the essence. Before she knew it, she was standing in front of her own house. Six bundles of sticks lay neatly stacked on the grass as if someone had stopped their car, laid them there, and drove quickly away. She would come out later and move them before Mama got home from work.

As she moved toward her stairs, she saw it. The place where she had only begun to dig was now a neat rectangle patch up against the foot of her porch. It was perfect for planting roses. Who would have done such a thing? The tools she had left out in her hurry to go to school were now laid neatly between her house and the Schultz's. She didn't know what to think. The space was dug for the roses and there were the odd bunches of sticks. On second thought, she'd better clean them up before she forgot. Shelly went over to remove the first bundle. It looked like it had dirt and string attached to the bottom. There was a note attached:

> To Shelly,
>   For Miss Rose, one of the best people we know. They don't look like much now, but give them some growing time; eventually they'll have brilliant blooms.
> Mr. and Mrs. French

Shelly ran up her stairs, pulled the string around her neck up and over her blouse collar. She retrieved her house key and opened her door. Just over the threshold she dropped to her knees, "Thank you, Jesus, and excuse me, I have work to do." She rushed passed the floor lamp and up the stairs to her room. First she wiggled out of her jacket; next her crystal white blouse flew off. She nearly ripped the button off her skirt before forcing the metal zipper down. Her slip and saddle shoes followed in quick succession. She grabbed her gym suit from the bed and pulled it up over her legs and onto her body. Then she quickly fastened the snaps. With one gym shoe on and the other in her hand, she rushed out the door. Grabbing a spade from the pathway between her house and Mr. Schultz's she headed for the rectangular patch to dig a hole for the first rose plant. With one foot on the top of the spade, she pushed hard, as she had seen many of the ladies do when they were planting something. Even with the dirt already tilled, the ground had a mind of its own. This was going to be a lot harder than she thought.

After several minutes of trying to get the right leverage with the spade that was taller than she was, Shelly decided to try the hand spade. Crawling around in the grass and soil was dirtying her hands and gym-suit. She smiled when she thought of what Miss Nelson would say if she could see her. Miss Nelson believed that young ladies should be pressed and clean. She would faint if she could see her now getting grass and ground-in dirt all over her sky-blue outfit. Shelly giggled. First Miss Nelson would gasp, her pert pink lips forming a perfect "O". Then she'd collapse in a graceful heap, her perfectly pinned bun still holding her vibrant red hair in place. All the girls in gym class would howl, and she, grubby and tattered, would get an unscheduled trip to the principal's office. Shelly wasn't worried though. This was a perfect chance for her to use the washer. She loved pulling clothes through the rolling wringer while turning the crank. Mama Rose would get a double blessing, a rose garden plus a load of laundry freshly done.

The flutter of blackbird wings drew Shelly's glance. Her neighbor-hood was so nice. Quaint, clean houses lined the block. Each distinct in its own way—brick, stone, or wood—they were all well built and well kept. And the people were good, too. Shelly didn't always think so. At first they made her feel different, but now they accepted her and Mama Rose. Most people liked them. Shelly perked up her nose. Ahh, the spicy scent of apples and cinnamon; Mrs. Ross was making pies. Children were playing everywhere. That brought a frown to her face. That silly "sometimey" Karen had promised to help her, but just like this morning, she was nowhere to be found. The "ditzy" girl was probably off someplace playing dolls.

Shelly reeled toward the sound of tires screeching behind her. She spied the white and red rubber of Mark's sneakers as he bounded from a car. Jumping to her feet, she yelled as though he was a million miles away, "Where were you this morning? Did you come to school today? You didn't transfer back to your old school, did you?"

"Wait a minute. Hold on!" Mark raised both hands excitedly. "I spent a last day with my mom."

Shelly crinkled her nose, a concerned expression playing over her face, "Is she dying?"

Mark bent over laughing, "Shelly, you are the funniest person I know."

Shelly didn't think anything about "last days" was funny. "What," she said, placing her hands on her hips, "what was your last day with your mother?"

"I'm afraid you're not going to like it."

Shelly got suddenly serious and placed her hand on Mark's shoulder, as she had seen Mama Rose do when someone had something important but scary to say, "You can tell me."

"But it's a big secret and I'm not sure you can keep a secret. Can you, little girl?"

Shelly turned her back and crossed her arms while sticking her lower lip out.

"Okay, I'm sorry." Still she didn't move.

"Babydoll," he said with a smile in his voice. "Princess Babydoll," he sang teasingly while dancing around her, poking out his tongue and wiggling his fingers at his ears. When there was still no visible reaction, he resorted to tickling. "Stop," she yelled, "I have work to do!"

Shelly turned her head to watch the lady Mark arrived with walking slowly up the stairs. The sun's light was becoming intense, but she thought she could see the lady smiling at them. Shelly smiled back.

"That was your mother, right?" She was squinting as she watched the lady disappear into Mr. Schultz's house. Getting a good look at her was hard. She didn't seem to want anyone to know her.

"One and the same. Shelly, what are you trying to do?"

"I'm not trying to do anything." Shelly waltzed over to where she'd put a rose bush in a deep hole. "I'm planting roses for Mama Rose. You know, roses for Rose. It's her birthday; I want to surprise her."

"I have a surprise."

"What is it? Tell me."

"Okay, I'm coming to live here."

"All the time? That's the secret?"

"Yep."

"I knew it. I just knew it. You're my best friend," she said, batting her eyes like she had seen Marlene Dietrich and Bette Davis do.

"I know," Mark replied teasingly with his hands outstretched as if he might tickle her again.

"Now help me dig, Marky," she snickered.

A neat patch was dug right up against the house behind the manicured grass, which met the sidewalk. One bush was nearly planted. There were five left to plant. Mark took off his lightweight windbreaker and got down on his hands and knees. "Wow!" Amazement filled his voice. "Did you dig that plot all by yourself?"

"No, I dug one little bit before school. I thought you might help, but you weren't here."

"Who did it then?"

Shelly raised a brow, looked toward Mark's father's house and then quickly shook her head, "I don't know. Hurry up," she added, cupping her hand frantically in a "come here" motion. Together they dragged one plant after another from the sidewalk to the soil patch. Mark would use the spade to dig for a while then hand it off to Shelly. Nimble fingers, brown and white hardly distinguishable one from the other, so well did they flow together, worked the dirt up against the base of the plants. Mark's swarthy hand held each bush in place while Shelly sat back on her hips to give it one last look before they tightened the dirt and made the placement final. After two trips, the two found themselves covered in soil.

"That's your gym suit, isn't it? Miss Nelson isn't going to be too happy about you getting it all dirty like that. I bet it'll never be blue again. It's black with dirt."

"Just like you," Shelly returned.

"What?"

"Mark, you're almost as black as me now."

"And how is that possible, Miss Shelly?" he asked, taking a clod of dirt and smearing it down the side of her cheek.

"Don't!" Shelly squawked, quickly standing to kick dirt at Mark. He gave chase, knocking her down in the grass on the opposite side of the walk. They rolled one on top of the other, smiling and laughing for several minutes.

"Oh no," Shelly gasped noticing Mark's wristwatch. "What time is it?"

Mark pulled his arm to his face, "Almost 4:30."

"Mark, I have to finish the roses. Mama Rose will be home soon."

Together they worked and played for almost an hour. The day was hot, about ninety degrees. Sweat poured from each of them. Suddenly Shelly sniffed, "What's that?"

"Ugh, Shelly, I was trying to be nice and not mention anything. But, did you remember your deodorant today?"

Shelly gave him a shove, and he shoved back. Tumbling, Shelly reached to catch herself, "Ouch!"

"What happened?"

"My hand."

Mark pounced forward, grabbing her bleeding hand, "Augh, Shelly, I'm sorry. I'd never hurt you."

"It's not bad," she moaned, her face twisting, stifling the urge to cry.

Mark scrambled to Shelly's side; his long rolled and cuffed Levis scraping the walkway as he did. He pulled his handkerchief from his pant pocket and wiped the dirt from her hand so that he could see the source of the bleeding better. He spotted the large thorn prick toward the top of Shelly's index finger. Mark tenderly raised Shelly's finger to his lips, first to blow on it, then to suck away the blood.

His brown hair was sweaty and wet and his eyes looked sorry. Shelly put her hand to his cheek and said, "Don't cry, Mark." He smiled and pulled her head onto his shoulder. She closed her eyes. They sat like that for what seemed a long time.

*I*rene leaned her shoulder against the wall next to the window in Jake's kitchen. Holding the yellow curtain back slightly, she peered out. She was as graceful as a swan and far more beautiful. Waves of pure raven hair cascaded about her shoulders. An easy smile crossed her face. Jake leaned back on his dining room table, crossed his arms and watched her. She had lost weight and a bit of her hearty coloring. Still, her intensity intrigued him. Still, her quiet elegance drew him.

"Irene, your smile is so beautiful, I missed it more than..."

Irene turned abruptly, her stern face plastered back in place. "What?" she snapped.

Jake was taken aback by the abrupt transformation and decided to change the subject. Walking toward her he questioned, "Something interesting going on out there?"

"No, not exactly," she said, pulling the curtains tightly together, cutting off their view of the lovely houses, green grass, swaying branches and other things. "Jacob, what were you working on when I came in?"

Now uneasy, Jake moved his drawing around on the table, "Things, things I've been doing in my spare time, designs for woodwork projects. You know, like Mark's cradle. Do you remember his cradle?"

"Yes."

Her voice softened. Could she really be interested in his pastime? "I sometimes still make things. I've even sold a few."

Irene's eyes darted toward the kitchen window, then back to the table where his drawings were, "Did you know that in Washington, D. C. the Supreme Court ruled that restaurants can no longer refuse service to Negroes. Why just the other day, Marky and I..."

"You don't still call him that, do you?" He said, crossing the yellow linoleum floor toward the kitchen window. Irene moved into his pathway. He sidestepped her and pulled the curtain back. "What the..." he ground out.

Quickly unlatching the painted wooden window and pulling it up, he yelled, "Mark, get in here!"

"Jacob," Irene said, stretching her arm toward him.

"What?" he rounded on her, unaware of the effect his action was having.

She bowed her head, turned and moved toward the door. Jake reached out and grabbed her hand, still soft. She reacted as if she had been scalded. So this is how it was with them. For one moment, when they were standing at the table together, it felt like it used to, easy. He was her security. She said he made all the world seem obsolete: as long as she had him she could make it. And Irene, Irene was his purpose. Before her everything was tasteless, odorless. When she left, he really wondered if he could go on. She was leaving now, thinking the very worst of him and with good cause. He was powerless to stop her.

He watched in silence as she raced to the foyer and out the door. Mark approached her. She rushed by him, pulled her car door open, turned the key, pumped the gas, nodded toward Mark and sped off like a bank robber. Jake slumped back onto the edge of his heavy oak dining table. How had he managed to do it again? Why did he continually alienate the one person, other than Mark, that he really wanted in his life?

When Mark entered the house, he found his father sitting on the edge of the dining room table. The lower half of his face was cupped in his right hand, which was supported by his left arm, crossing his body.

"You okay, Pop?" Mark took a few careful steps in his father's direction.

"Go upstairs, boy." Mark tensed and stood still.

"But Shelly and I were—" he turned slightly, extending his arm to gesture toward the outside.

"I saw what you and Shelly were. Now go upstairs." Mark threw his jacket down to the floor as hard as he could and stomped up the stairs. The vibration from Mark's slamming bedroom door shook the downstairs floor.

Looking out of his bedroom window, Mark could see Shelly still on her knees. Her fingers worked deftly; he figured she was trying to make up for the time he'd cost her playing and…well, she probably didn't mind the rest. He'd never be sorry for it no matter how mad his dad was.

She looked up at his window and smiled. His heart skipped a beat. He suddenly felt shy and pulled away from the window. Why couldn't his stupid dad leave him and Shelly alone? He pondered the question now, sitting just out of Shelly's sight. Who was Jacob Schultz anyway? When he and Mark were alone, Jake was loving and kind. But just mentioning Negroes made Jake mad enough to spit. He seemed to like Mama Rose, a little, despite her color, but he absolutely hated Shelly. And what was going on between him and his mother? She seemed scared of Jake, yet she let him, her treasured son, visit; and now he'd even be living with the man.

His mom was so timid, weak. How could they have ever been a couple? Jake said she was different once. Though she was always shy around strangers, there was a spark of something else, a simmering fire he had said. Mark wished he had known her then. He laughed. He and Shelly would make a better couple than Jake and Irene, any day, even if she was colored. Whoa, what was he thinkin'? Nobody would accept them as a couple. He really wouldn't want to try it either. Some things were just not possible. Mark walked over to his bed, lay back on his soft chenille bedspread with his hands behind his head and pondered the meaning of his life.

Like parched trees lit by tongues of flame, the years and summers pass. The last summer of unfettered friendship races into the morass. Behind us lay impossible dreams. Before us lie mysteries yet to be seen. What I can't hold in my hand, I let go. The time has come. The time has gone.

As Shelly headed for the playground after school, she remembered the poem Mark had given her to read a couple of days ago. He had gotten an "E" for excellent on it in English. She could see why he was proud of it, but why did he show it to her? He hardly ever gave her school stuff and the look on his face, it was so strange, twisted like. If he didn't want her to have it, why did he give it to her? She read it fast the first time, gave him a smile and said, "Yeah, it's good." That didn't seem to satisfy him. She promised to read it again when she had time to think about it. His face unwrinkled a little then and he squeezed her hand and walked away. Could getting ready for high school be making him this weird? What was he so worried about anyway? Nothing was going to change but his age.

"Your turn. Shelly, quit diggin' your potatoes, girl."

Shelly pressed the wrinkles out of her pleated skirt with the palms of her hands and refolded the cuffs of her bobby socks. She admired her long legs, which were starting to take on a more shapely form since she had turned twelve. Swaying back and forth to the beat of the song, she turned her attention to the ropes and said, "All right, I comin'."

Jumping double-dutch rope on the playground was one of Shelly's favorite things to do after school. The only children outside, besides her friends, were kids from Mr. Carter's class who stayed late for punishment. Now they hung from the monkey bars. The boys' arms dangled toward the ground while the girls clutched their skirts, keeping their underpants from showing any longer than they had to. They looked so funny it made her want to laugh.

Everything felt wonderful today. Mama Rose was letting her do her own hair now. She had taken the metal straightening comb and laid it on the stove burner, careful not to turn the gas flame up too high. When she thought it was warm enough, she removed the hot comb from the burner and placed it on a wad of toilet paper. If the paper turned a little brown, not black, and the hair didn't smell too much like tar or irritate her nostrils, then the comb wasn't too hot. She had done it just right this morning. Evenly she pulled the comb through one plot of hair at a time, subduing the natural ripples of her hair into long flattened strands. It now hung two inches beyond her shoulders and bounced gingerly when she went up and down in the jump ropes. Two black girls, one new to the neighborhood, and Karen, a white girl from across the street, played with her.

Whoosh, she was in the ropes. Up and down she jumped. She whirled and turned, kicked and split. At times suspended in mid-air, at others riding the waves of the wind. Pam and Karen sang, "25-30-35-40-45-50." The score was getting higher and higher.

Radiant: this was a radiant day, Shelly thought. Clouds like handfuls of popcorn dotted the blue, May sky. She wished she could touch one; see if it felt crunchy, the way it looked. All day, everything had gone her way. And now she was winning big, couldn't remember the last time she outscored Kim, turn after turn after turn. Yep, this was about as much fun as a girl could have.

Shelly did another spin in the ropes. Kim, one of her friends, was biting her bottom lip and tilting her head. She noticed her wink at Pam and Karen before changing the jump rope song, "I like coffee, I like tea, I like a white boy and he likes me…"

Shelly turned again. This time she was face to face with Mark and Luke, who were passing by.

The song Kim was singing so embarrassed her that she missed a beat, stepped on one rope and got popped in the face with the other. Her hand flew to her right cheek. The pulsing sting was vibrantly fierce. Despite her best efforts, she let out a wail and went to her knees. Plastic coating was hardly enough to protect the jumper from the massive bee-like sting that happened when the player got swiped by the wire that was embedded in their clothesline jump ropes. Shelly could feel her cheek growing larger under her palm.

Mark started toward her. Luke grabbed his arm. Mark and Luke had been friends for their whole eighth-grade year. For Shelly, this school year had zoomed by. Mark would be going to high school in the fall. It was like a million miles away. Was he going to be like a kind of grown-up now?

"Hey, man, you better leave that colored girl alone. Some of the kids are saying…" Mark snatched away as Luke continued his speech.

"Don't go saying you weren't warned," Luke yelled after him.

Mark reached out to her. Shelly let him pull her up.

"Ooh, girl, you see that? That white boy's in loooove."

"Kiss, kiss," Karen said, puckering her lips at Mark and Shelly.

"Come on, Shelly, I'll walk you home."

Side by side they walked in silence down Main, toward their homes. Businesses lined the street. The new supermarket with its red and yellow-lighted sign and huge banners had all but put Mr. Miles's small grocery out of business. He said he would be closing within the year. The new Shell gas station and a liquor lounge also took up a large part of the block. Through all these changes, one thing had remained the same. Mark had been her best friend for over four years. Admitting this was hard, but Mark was changing, too. At fourteen, he had gotten taller and lost his baby fat. His real muscles were starting to come in. Shelly thought he'd probably be a strong man. But it wasn't just his body that was different. He didn't like the old games as much. Shelly missed the winter nights just before dark, lying in the snow on their backs making snow angels. She could still feel the icy chill of the flakes around her bare ears. Her hat was constantly coming off, and Mark was constantly pulling it back down to make sure she didn't catch cold. Gone were the days of packing snow into tight cubes to build their igloo houses.

In the summer they pretended to be a family and used the crawl space under Mark's back porch as their playhouse. She remembered laughing when Karen came along asking to be the mother. Before she came, they were brother and sister. It was weird to think about somebody being the mother and the father. Mark probably wouldn't mind playing Mom and Dad now. He sometimes looked at her in that goofy way just before running his hands through his curly hair. It was kind of like that day on the swing: a little pleasant and a lot uncomfortable. Shelly wished things could be like they used to be. Why'd he have to go and change on her?

It was a sweltering afternoon. Sweat slid down Mark's face. Shelly pulled her thin cotton blouse away from her wet skin. Mark wiped the side of his face with his wide hand, as he looked at her out of the corner of his eye.

"You don't always have to be rescuing me, Mark." She reached over and laid her hand on his arm. "Why do you keep doing it?"

Mark shrugged.

"You know what Karen told me? They call you a 'nigger-lover' and some of the colored kids call me 'Oreo.'"

Mark arched a brow and bored intently into her eyes.

"You know, black on the outside and white on the inside," she explained.

Mark lifted her hand and laced his fingers through hers. As her legs went to jelly and began to wobble, he doubled over laughing.

It's not funny, Mark," she said, attempting to whack him on the arm. He sidestepped her reach.

"I'm sorry, Shelly; it is funny. Look we're friends, nothing more, nothing less, okay?"

"Okay, I guess. But I can take care of myself." Fiery heat rose to her cheeks.

"Shelly?" His eyelids were half sheltering his bright eyes.

"What?"

"You ever been kissed?"

Jake was home from work early, and it was a good thing. He was going to have it out once and for all with Mark about his colored girl. Sitting on his green leather recliner, he tried to relax. He couldn't. Agitated, he walked over to his wide living room windows and with one knee propped on the window seat, he watched Mark and Shelly strolling together, all toasty and warm. Try as he might, he had not been able to make a dent in that friendship. When he forbid Mark to play with Shelly, he'd find them under the long beams that supported the back porch or behind the grand oak trading secrets or playing marbles. When he sent Mark off with Tom or Travis to play kickball or jacks, Mark would abandon them early or skip it all together in favor of being with Shelly. They seemed to spend the least amount of time together when he left it alone, but, for Mark and Shelly, a small amount of time together was once a day.

Too bad she had to be Negro. Jake had seen her thoughtful acts towards people, and she was a polite little thing, always saying, "please," and "thank you." Rose had to be proud of her. She was following right in her footsteps. None of that mattered, however; black and white didn't mix and that was the plain and short of it. The more he thought about it, the angrier he got.

Mark waved a silent goodbye to Shelly and headed toward his porch. Jake let the heavy beige brocade curtain fall back into place.

"Hey, Pop, what you up to?" Mark asked, pushing the door closed behind him.

"Come in here, Mark, we need to talk," Jake called, teetering on the edge of the stuffed tweed chair that faced the entryway. By now, Mark would usually be fidgeting, anticipating what Jake was going to say. Jake thought he was unusually calm.

"Mark," he said with preamble, as Mark walked nonchalantly toward him. "I didn't make the world like it is." He motioned toward the beige and green tweed couch. Mark sat down.

"And I sure can't change it, don't even want to." Jake waited for the normal preemptive protest from Mark. It didn't come. "White people and coloreds got no business together. If God had wanted that, he would have put us together in the first place."

To this Mark raised a brow, pulled the ottoman up and propped his feet on it.

"Wait, Pop, let me save you some time." He reclined back on the soft couch, putting his arms behind his head for support. "I'm not going to be so close to Shelly anymore."

Jake was dumbfounded.

"I've decided that I'm only hurting Shelly and myself." His voice became more serious as he sat forward, placing his hand under his chin for emphasis, "I'm sorry to say it but our society is just not tolerant of the mixing of races. Shelly and I have been good friends, but where can we take this friendship? There's a lot of unrest in the United States, and it's best if we don't add to it. I think it's best for both of us if we stop depending on each other now." With that he reclined again, a look of satisfaction crossing his lips.

Jake knew he should leave well enough alone, but when it came to the subject of race mixing, he got excited. "I'm not saying you can't have relations with women of the darker races when you get older, if that turns your crank. But that's private. It's okay if it's not a public thing."

Mark pulled himself to the edge of the couch. "So you're saying it's okay if me and Shelly...?"

"No, not Shelly. It can't be her — but any other Negro woman..."

Mark's face was so contorted, Jake, at first, had a hard time identifying the emotion that it registered. Disgust was about as close as he could figure. Even by his own estimation, Jake was not a genius but even he knew when he had gone too far. Mark didn't say anything else. He eased slowly up from the couch, gave Jake one last scowl and walked carefully up the stairs. Jake thought he looked as though he was struggling to contain his emotions. He recognized the symptoms.

*M*ark's breathing had become erratic. His eyes raced from side-to-side, searching his room for something to break. Fastening his glance on the opaque lamp sitting on top of his chest of drawers, he grabbed it and squeezed. He was surprised it didn't break right away so he threw it, wrenching the cord from its socket as he did. It shattered in the corner where one wall merged to become the next. Repugnance was too calm a word to describe what Mark was feeling toward his dad. He could still see that calm face, those quiet blue eyes and unmarred mouth saying those vile things. Every time he thought his father had gone as far as he could go on the race issue, he amazed Mark by going farther.

This had to be the most raunchy thing his dad had ever suggested, and he hadn't used one swear word to say it. Unable to find anything else to break, Mark marched over to the already shattered lamp and stomped it to bits.

He could hardly remember coming up the stairs, only the sensation of the firm oak railing under his palm remained. Slamming his door seemed his only revenge at first. The thunderous vibration had caused his framed poster of Marlon Brando to fall to the floor. Now what? He tossed himself onto his rumpled bed. The soft mattress absorbed him. The stale white walls closed in on him. His only salvation, the window seat, where he had kneeled almost daily, peering out, hoping for a glimpse of Shelly, would be comfortless now. He wouldn't be looking for her anymore.

He had made a very mature decision today, one that would save him and Shelly years and years of trouble. Had he really? Or had he taken the coward's way out? No, he was being brave. It was best.

Blast his father and his racist ideas. Mark's stomach churned, his eyes blazed and his fists swelled. Thank God he was upstairs and his father was down.

Chapter Four
1958

City buses held a kind of fascination. Just what kind of people would sit next to you? Where were they going, and what were they about to do? These are the questions that went through Shelly's mind as she extended her leg to step onto the high rubber-coated stairs while watching the metal and glass doors divide. The lime-green conveyance was crowded this time of day. Besides the men with their jackets hanging over their arms and the women in tall heels and A-line skirts, there were lots and lots of kids. Well, not kids exactly, more like young adults. Were they all going to Franklin High?

The bus lurched to a stop and several more young people climbed the awkward steps of the bus and dropped their coins into the metal money receptacle. Silver buffaloes and copper Indians clanged joyously, making their way to the bottom. Shelly couldn't help imagining what she could do with all of those coins.

The adults didn't even attempt to conceal their annoyed smirks as more and more students crowded on. Newcomers clutched the metal supporting rails, trying to steady themselves now that all of the dark green vinyl seats were taken. The tall man seated next to her shuffled his feet to the side. The spit shine on his black wing-tip shoes looked worth protecting.

Shelly had already seen more colored kids on this bus ride than she ever did in her neighborhood, except when she went to church on Sundays. It was like a rainbow since colored kids came in so many shades. There were those you had to look at twice to know if they were Negro or white. There were those so dark the old folks called them blue-black; and there was every shade in between: butter-cream, caramel, tan, and mocha. Mama Rose said one of the most fascinating things about havin' a baby when you're Negro is that you always get a surprise when the baby comes out. Shelly loved the variety. If Franklin High was anything like this bus ride, it was going to be one big adventure.

When the bus stopped about a quarter-block from the school, a wave of students gushed from the open doors. Shelly thought it was amazing that no one got toppled and trampled. Once out, the girls opened their pocketbooks, pulled out mirrored compacts and checked their appearance. Shelly's eyes widened as the girl next to her twisted her silver tube and the bright red tip emerged. She applied a thick coating to her lips while her friend held the mirror so that she could see. Umh, umh, umph, what would her former gym teacher, Miss Nelson, say? Girls acting like women.

From out of the crowd Pam and Kim appeared. Pam wore a blue jumper dress with white bobby socks. Her short black hair was curled and combed back off her face. Her perky nose and almond-shaped eyes complemented her dark complexion perfectly. Shelly thought she looked very pretty today. Kim wore a yellow cardigan and a forest-green skirt. You could just see the lime-green rounded collar of her cotton shirt peek over her sweater collar. It was obvious that everyone had put a great deal of thought into the outfits they picked for the first day of high school.

The first thing Shelly noticed about Franklin High School was the enormous old wooden doors. They had to be nine feet high and four feet wide. The four large supporting pillars resembled something out of the Roman Coliseum. She was sure ferocious lions would rush out at any moment and devour the timid freshmen who stood at the bottom of the slab stairs and gazed fearfully upward, unable to make their feet move. Other students: apparently gladiators, rushed rudely by. They, of course, had never been afraid of a new experience.

When Shelly entered the doors, the school swallowed her up. She was engulfed in a sea of white faces, and what had seemed like a large number of brown ones became so dispersed among the crowd that Franklin was beginning to seem a little more like Emerson.

"Hurry up," Kim was saying as she grabbed Shelly's elbow and pulled her through the tall and taller people.

"What are you lookin' for?" Kim asked as she stopped and bore down on Shelly with that all-knowing expression. Kim was a light-skinned girl. "Yellow," is how some Negroes referred to her complexion. Her thin brown hair framed her plump round face and her cherry-round nose, which stayed in Shelly's business. "You look queasy, girl." Kim stopped and placed a curled index finger on her lip. "I wonder why? Oh, I know. It's because Mark's here, isn't it?"

"No."

Kim poked her lower lip out and bobbed her head in an "if-you-say-so" gesture.

"Now, Kim, you know Mark and I barely speak any more. I think he has 'highschool-itis.' You know: if he associates with a grade-schooler or even a freshman, it wouldn't be cool."

"Are you sure he doesn't have 'white-itis?' You know, if you're friends with Negroes, whites won't like it."

"Mark's not like that."

"All white people are like that," Kim expounded, while wiggling and wobbling her entire torso.

*A*flurry of white flashed before Mark as he kicked the covers off of his bed, anxious to get started with his day. First days of new school years were electric, and this day was fully charged. Mark couldn't wait to see what would happen. So why was there a tiny nagging in the corner of his mind? Whatever it was it could wait until later. He had a kingdom to conquer.

Mark bathed, brushed his teeth, combed his curls into place, and threw on the outfit that he had laid out the night before. He flew down the stairs, stopping just long enough to snatch his jacket from the closet and grab a piece of toast from his father's breakfast plate. Jake turned in protest, his mouth too full to do anything but grunt. Mark smiled, waved, and was out the door in one fluid motion. He was one of the first kids to arrive on campus. He perched next to one of the large circular beams, pulled out his pocketknife, and pretended to be occupied cleaning his nails.

Pretty, he thought as Vanessa waltzed by, cutting him one of her cutest smiles. He winked, suddenly aware that he was uncomfortably warm. It had to be in the high seventies. Too warm for letter jackets, but all the jocks wore them on the first day. It was their signature outfit, letting all the new kids know who they were. The first bell rang and kids seemed to appear from nowhere to rush the huge entry doors. When Mark entered the building he nodded at Jimmy Johnson, an impressive Negro boy, who was standing at his locker with Tyrone and a bunch of other Negro students. Jimmy had started Franklin at the end of the last school year. He was a good ball player with an easy personality, well liked and potential competition if he had been white. Too bad everybody was so into making judgments based on color but Mark thought, what could he do about it?

Mark walked down the wide hallway. The ceiling lights reflected off the floor, which was quickly overrun with padding feet. It was fun to watch the girls adjusting their hair and popping gum. Viola and Clara had made an art form out of pulling the gooey globs in and out of their mouths and twirling it around their fingers. Lucky gum. Josh and Luke were mesmerized. They didn't flinch until they saw him approach.

"Hey, Mark," Josh called out. At the sound of his name several heads turned and a large group of kids made their way to where he was standing.

"Good to see you, man," Josh said, giving Mark a hearty handshake. Vanessa and a few other girls joined the crowd. Mark was used to being the focus of attention. Being a jock and captain of the forensics team had its perks. And he was good-looking, at least that's what all of the girls said once his face had cleared up half way through freshman year. His coaches liked his intensity and his teachers admired his intellect. And since he had learned to use his "intimidating manner" rather than be ruled by it, he had just the edge he needed to keep the guys in check. It seemed nobody wanted to see what would happen if he really got angry. He could understand what his mother was talking about now. He had potential, possibilities, and he was going to milk them for all they were worth.

"Look at him down there, smelling himself. So arrogant, I bet he thinks his stuff don't stink." Smelling himself? Shelly could feel her friend's anger as Pam pushed through kids milling in front of their lockers, making their way to the water fountain.

"Who?" Shelly questioned, careful not to sound overly curious.

"Mark, of course." Pam unlatched the flap of her satchel and took out her science book. Agitated, she flipped it open and thumbed through looking for her class schedule. "Oh, people like him and Karen make me so mad." Her shoulders were tight and her fists clenched at her sides. All of this indignation must have been on Shelly's behalf since Pam and Mark had spent only a small amount of time together.

Roused by loud voices, Shelly turned just in time to see Mark cruising down the hall surrounded by a group of kids who seemed thrilled to be orbit to his world. They were close enough to touch the white of his jacket and finger the purple eagle monogrammed on his chest, yet no one did. Shelly looked down to make sure that her cotton anklets had not retreated into her shoes. As she looked back up, their eyes met. His were big brown candy drops, surrounded by sooty lashes, just like she remembered. She sucked in a huge gulp of air and waited, and waited some more. Seconds passed, more seconds, still nothing. Turning abruptly, she dropped her head and began fumbling for her locker key.

"He snubbed you good, girl." Shelly could feel Pam's sneer as she finally located her key in the rounded pocket of her skirt. "Told you," Pam continued. Shelly pretended not to hear. Her hands trembled and her stomach ached.

*W*ith Luke and Nick talking about how hard the football practice schedule was going to be and Vanessa asking him if he thought her yellow wool sweater was too sheer, Mark would have missed Shelly altogether if he hadn't looked up to give Vanessa an answer. When he saw Shelly, his mind become muddled and his mouth wouldn't open. What would he say anyway, "Hi, Shelly, wasn't it clever of me to avoid speaking so much as two words together to you for over two years?" It didn't matter; even if he had wanted to speak, somehow he was frozen when his eyes met hers. His voice caught in his throat.

"Mark, isn't that Stacey?"

It's Shelly, Idiot.

"…or whatever-her-name-is down the hall?" Luke asked.

"Yeah, so?"

Shelly looked stiff—artificially unmoving. Had she heard the coolness in his voice when he responded to Luke? Suddenly, like she had heard his thoughts, she moved away from her locker and walked nonchalantly in his direction. Ahh, this was the Shelly he knew; it was most likely her turn to ignore him.

"Wait, Shelly! Why are you in such a big rush?" The high-pitched squeal came from behind Shelly. Mark could only make out a flash of red and the top of a blond head approaching. With her attention now focused on the girl who was calling her, Shelly was heading straight for a gang of kids standing in the middle of the hall. Didn't that girl ever watch where she was going? Mark averted his eyes. Shelly banged right into the group of kids. Like a mighty flood, her books tumbled from her arms and scattered everywhere. The blond, with the squawk for a voice who had been trying to get Shelly's attention, simply walked away and started talking to someone else in the group. Shelly bent down and listlessly gathered folders, note pads and texts.

Instinctively, Mark headed in her direction.

"Here, let me help you with those." Shelly, now on her knees, turned.

"Name's Jimmy Johnson. What's yours?" Mark froze in his tracks. He felt…what? Incensed, angry? He knew Shelly was cute. Did he think other guys wouldn't notice? Jimmy picked up each book, deliberately touching Shelly's hand every time he handed her a new one. Her skirt inched up as she knelt in front of him. Her bare knees brushed his pant legs and he leered at her. *Snap out of it, Mark*, he told himself more than once. What was it to him anyway? He made a quick detour to the fountain. He couldn't taste the water, and the slippery wet porcelain sink felt as though it wavered beneath his grip.

"You new here?" Jimmy asked with serpentine subtlety.

"Yes, I'm a freshman."

What was she thinking, batting her eyes at him like that? Did she want him to get the wrong impression?

"You couldn't be."

"I am," she said, smiling way too big for Mark's taste. Mark paused, straining to hear their exchange, as a girl passed between them stumbling on what must have been her mother's high-heeled shoes.

"It's just that you look so, so mature." Jimmy was saying this with his nose inches from Shelly's.

Mark snorted, thinking that to him Shelly still looked like her skinny little self.

"Here you go," Jimmy surrendered the last book giving her hand one last caress.

Shameless. Mark was about to go over and tell Shelly she'd better be careful of upperclassmen when someone accosted him from behind.

"There you are, Mark Schultz. I told Shelly we'd probably see you today. We hardly ever see you around the house anymore." A soft voice was whispering behind his left ear and the smell of fresh strawberries streamed across his shoulder.

Run, Mark, she's coming! Shelly's words flooded his mind, *She's too white. Her face doesn't fit her teeth. Her fuzzy hair's a perfect match for her fuzzy brain. She's a mousy irritating little thing.*

"Mark, you aren't paying a bit of attention to me." The soft and now familiar squawk continued. Mark turned around slowly.

"Whoa, Karen!" Mark stumbled backward reaching his hand toward the locker in order to steady himself. He hadn't paid much attention to Karen over the years, and boy, had she changed. Her face had filled out and her teeth went in. This must have been their intended position. Her pretty blue eyes complemented her now well-managed blond hair, and that cleavage, set off just right against the bright red of her dress, didn't seem right on a fifteen-year-old girl.

"Wow, Karen, you've…"

"Changed. That's what everybody says. You like?" She asked, stroking her waist and hips with long red painted nails.

Mark didn't think he should answer that. What she did next was impossible to ignore. She squeezed up right next to him as close as she could get. Her plump breasts pressed into his chest, very pleasant. "I'm trying out for cheerleader, Marky."

"Don't call me that." That pleasant sensation: all gone.

"But, I've heard Shelly…"

Stone-faced, through gritted teeth, he said very simply and quietly, "Don't call me that." Karen couldn't always be called bright, but she got it.

"I'm striking it from my vocabulary today," she said, nudging closer to Mark.

*F*ascinating *Franklin! What else could possibly happen to make these first few weeks of school any more interesting,* Shelly thought as she sat flanked by Pam and Kim on the bleachers watching the practice game: invitation only, no less. Wispy clouds, interspersed with thick heavy ones, blocked out the sun. A quick rush of wind made her pull her black cardigan tight around her neck. The wood they sat on was rugged and scratchy; still, when she looked around at the scant number of spectators, she knew she was among the privileged. Everyone there was a personal friend of one of the football players. They would get to go to an after-party to have snacks with the team when the practice was over. Pam, Kim and some girls she didn't even know were saying that Jimmy Johnson had a crush on her. "Whatever," she said every single time they proclaimed it. It didn't seem possible, why? She hadn't done a thing to encourage him. At her best, she got ridiculously nervous and awkward when he was around. What could he possibly find attractive about that?

Still, he was the one who had invited her and her friends to this practice game. All this week Shelly had walked with Mama Rose to help her drop off her peach cobblers and other goodies to friends and acquaintances. It was wonderful to see the looks of gratification on the faces of the happy recipients, but Shelly was appreciative that the week-long saga was coming to an end. The long walk was starting to wear her out. When she arrived early this morning for school, the hallway was empty except for Jimmy leaning near her locker. Was he waiting for her or was it a coincidence that he was standing there? She lowered her eyes and walked toward him.

"Hey, Shelly, I've been waiting for you."

"Oh."

His hand went to his chin, rubbing the area that plainly predicted the hint of a soon-to-arrive beard. Why was he nervous? He had to know what everyone thought of him. He was liked and respected; didn't he know that?

"Why were you waiting for me?" Her voice was weak and crackling.

"Will you come to my practice game after school?"

Her head had dropped; she shuffled her feet, scratching her right ankle with the toe of her left shoe. She stuttered, "Uhh, huh."

"Bring your friends if you like." He reached into the pockets of his navy-colored pants. His legs were long as were his fingers, Shelly noticed as he pulled out three tickets.

"How did you know I'd need three tickets?"

With his head tilted and a shy smile, he said, "I notice things. It's at 3:05. I expect to see you there; okay?" He glanced back as he was leaving, giving her a stunning smile. She didn't understand what was happening but you could never have too many friends, so she went.

Kim kept elbowing her, saying, "Can you believe it, Shelly; can you believe it? I think we're the only freshman here." Pam sat with her dark-brown legs crossed and her elbows resting on the bleachers behind them, dissatisfaction and tedium competing for dominance on her face.

"Well, will you look at that?" she was finally heard to say. Karen, front and center, came bounding out with the cheer squad. "What was that you were saying about us being the only freshmen?" Pam leaned in and gave Kim a hard look.

"Oh, her," Kim replied casually, "she's not natural. That girl can and will do anything when it comes to getting a boy." They turned in unison to get Shelly's reaction, which it almost killed her not to give.

It was true. Karen's mature figure and constant machinations put her into every circle that Mark could be found in. When the jocks walked down the hall, Karen was the leader of the group that stayed on their heels. Becoming a cheerleader was another step in her plan to be everywhere Mark was. And it was painfully obvious to Shelly that Karen had no other aspiration for her high school matriculation.

Shelly might as well get used to these flagrant moves by Karen, as fate had been cruel to her. Franklin's policy was to place the freshman lockers near the seniors so that the younger students could learn about the school from the older ones. And as it happened, her locker was quite near Mark's, allowing her to be privy to many a conversation she'd rather not have knowledge of.

Enjoy the game, she told herself as she watched the players attired in full football regalia—helmets, layered padding, flimsy purple jerseys

and clicking shoes—break into two teams and pummel themselves until the coach called "time."

September had gone by like a blaze burning through tissue. All of the uncertainty of adolescence was crashing down on Shelly. She was developing into a woman, which brought her both pleasure and discomfort. Boys looked at her more, though she couldn't imagine why, and Jimmy never missed a chance to compliment her on her opinions or tastes or the way she treated people. It was okay that he didn't think she was pretty since she really didn't want him to think of her in that way. People were pairing up though. Kim was talking a lot about a boy named Stanley, whom Shelly had yet to meet. And the juniors were all abuzz about their dance at the end of October.

Speaking of things on fire…Shelly's brain was fried. Algebra had been grueling. Kim had been too busy to help her, and Jimmy canceled her tutorial yesterday; an unscheduled practice came up. She was forced to do pages twenty-four through thirty on her own. When she tried to explain her answers, many of which were correct, she just couldn't put the steps into words. Mr. Cantrell stopped just short of accusing her of cheating. Could this day get any worse? She headed purposefully toward her locker, going through her brown leather purse as she walked. Surely she had put her tin of aspirin in her bag this morning.

Blam! Miss Phillips' door made a thundering clack as it flung open. Shelly was spun in a complete circle by the passing whirlwind whose name was Karen. "Hey, Mark!" she shouted in that all-too-familiar squeal. Karen intercepted her prey on his way to his locker. Funny, Shelly hadn't even noticed that he was ahead of her.

"Mark, are we going to the junior dance?"

This ambush was obviously preemptive. The tickets hadn't been on sale a full hour. Karen must have been worried he'd take one of those other girls who was always hanging on his neck: so predictable, no pride. Next, Karen stopped him in his tracks and wrapped her pearly white arms around his waist. He let her; in fact, he pulled her up tighter. Scoundrel!

It was about a week and a half into school when Karen found out that Shelly could no longer be of help in her pursuit of Mark. Mark didn't even look in her direction when he passed her locker, which was a daily occurrence, so Karen dropped her like a bad penny. She didn't even bother to try and torment Shelly with her flirtations anymore. Karen had him sewn up, at least as far as Shelly was concerned, and Karen knew it. Mark leaned down and whispered something in Karen's ear. For Shelly, the urge to punch someone was becoming palpable.

Shelly squeezed her eyes shut, trying hard to dispel the scene she was witnessing. They fluttered wildly open at the sound of pounding feet heading in her direction.

"Hey, Shelly." A panting Jimmy now stood by her side. She was pretending to re-arrange the things in her locker.

"Hi, Jimmy." She tried but was unable to accent her voice with a smile.

"You don't look so good," Jimmy said with such gentleness that Shelly felt misty. "Maybe I can cheer you up. Have you heard about the junior dance?" His short wavy hair framed his face so nicely.

"Hasn't everyone?" she said, trying to sound upbeat.

"Would you like to go with me?" His head was tilted, his eyelids partially closed, a foreboding shyness tainting his apparent confidence.

Karen was hugging Mark around the neck in response to the comment he'd made kissing-close to her ear. When she stood on her tiptoes and turned his face toward hers to brush a kiss over his lower lip, Mark suddenly froze. Shelly wondered why. Anyway, it spoiled Karen's kiss.

"I have to go to my locker," Mark stated abruptly, getting himself closer to where she and Jimmy were standing. Shelly couldn't imagine he actually cared what was happening between her and Jimmy. Still if he was jealous…she was being ridiculous. Mark couldn't care less about her and Jimmy.

"Jimmy, you must have somebody else you can take." She looked at the floor, wondering if the glare reflected how stupid she felt. "Somebody you know better than me?" Her voice clanged in a high pitch. It sounded phony and strained, even to her own ear.

"Yeah, that's true," he said, suddenly dropping his head and tapping his toe.

"Then why me?" Shelly tried forcing herself to look up. She couldn't.

"Because you're kind, gentle, smart..."

"How do you know all that?" Her cheeks were inching up. Jimmy was making her feel better. She noticed his hand moving to cup her chin. It was rough, like maybe someone who had to work hard.

"I just do. Guess you could say I'm a good judge of character."

A glimpse in Mark's direction said he was looking their way. Karen moved in to grab Mark around the waist. That move emboldened Shelly.

"I'd love to go to the dance with you," Shelly answered, syrupy sweet, and without thinking more about what she was doing, she stood on her tiptoes and gave Jimmy a hug around his neck. Jimmy's smile was stunning. His wool pullover itched her forearms. What was she doing? She realized how inappropriate she was acting and jerked her arms down from his neck.

Mark yanked open his locker and leaned in. Shelly imagined him fighting the urge to scream.

But this had been her problem, hadn't it? She had spent way too much time focused on the boy across the hall instead of the one standing before her. *Be grateful*, she thought as she took in Jimmy's brilliant amber eyes framed so handsomely by pure black sculptured brows. She let herself see his smooth, richly-dark skin, his square shoulders and erect posture. Perfect. Mark didn't have a thing on him. No wonder Karen looked at Jimmy in that way of hers. He even had a hint of a mustache, making him appear older than some of the other boys.

You know what, Shelly thought, *Mark has a life and I have a life and they are not the same anymore. Maybe if we had both been colored or both white, things would have been different; they're not. If Jimmy wants this little ol' fresh-man to be his girl, I'm going for it.*

Shelly had the feeling all along that Jimmy was a great boy; now she was going to start acting like it. Pam and Kim said he was too handsome for words, dreamy. Shelly hadn't seen it, so she made the mistake of asking Pam if she thought he was as cute as Mark. Pam screwed her face so tight and peered so deeply into Shelly's eyes a real feeling of dread came over her, "You have the nerve to ask me that. Most girls in this school would kill to be with Jimmy." Shelly thought Pam had misspoken and she was about to correct her. She was anticipated, "Yes, even the white girls, though they'd never admit it. Shelly, you baffle me. You've got the best boy in this school 'ga-ga' over you and all you can think about is that Mark Schultz. What's he got anyway? I don't get it."

Shelly thought about it. Yes, Mark was attractive. But that wasn't what she thought about when she thought about him. It was his laugh and his mean look. They told the most about him. What made him happy and what made him sad. She missed him doubling over, holding his hand over his mouth trying to stifle that deep timbre when she had made a strange gesture or said something mean about someone, God forgive her. He was so sad. She could see right though his bravado and thin smile.

"You're thinking about him right now," Pam had squawked. "You're hopeless, Shelly. You'd better realize what a good guy Jimmy is before he loses interest in you. Maybe I should do you both a favor and tell Jimmy you're still hung up on that Mark."

"I'm not," she remembered answering, "It's just that he doesn't seem himself."

"You'd better be talking about Jimmy," Pam said, pointing a coffee-brown finger at Shelly's nose.

The bell rang. Shelly felt for that moment she was saved.

Well, that was all over now. Good guys didn't come around every day. She was a smart girl. It was high time she started acting like one. Jimmy stood smiling, his hands perched on her shoulders, apparently pleased with what he was seeing.

Several weeks of the school year were already behind her and Shelly was beginning to realize that being timid wasn't going to get her anywhere at Franklin. And she was determined to get somewhere, not just for herself but for the entire school. Mark had said she only had two speeds. Either she was calm and passive or she was a roaring lion. She wasn't sure about his analysis, but she had no doubt as to which mode she was operating in at the moment.

For the fourth straight day, Shelly sat alone at that hard Formica table. Her only companions: dry green beans, soggy French fries and a tasteless brown hamburger patty. The only thing that ever made this food worth attempting was having company while you ate it. Shelly was determined, though. In no way did she think she was brilliant, but she believed in her ability to accomplish what she needed and often what she wanted. She helped Mama Rose keep up the house and she accompanied her on many goodwill missions.

She kept her grades up, maintained a social life and now she was going to do something about this separate-but-unequal high school of hers. Managing to make a few friends outside her circle of colored kids gave her confidence. She knew it wouldn't be easy. Some of the colored kids called her "Oreo," barely out of her range of hearing, and some of the white kids looked at her like she didn't know her place, like she was over-reaching her status. Still, if somebody didn't do something, things would always be just the way they were. And if Shelly knew anything at all, she knew she didn't want things to stay this way. So she sat at the long lunch bench with only her large hand-painted sign for company.

A few curious people wandered by: Mr. Cox, the art instructor, and Miss Philips, the biology teacher. Some paused to give a curious stare, others looked amused. One boy actually snarled. Her friends were conveniently absent; they probably didn't share her enthusiasm for her latest project. And then he stopped, "Shelly, why do you waste your time on this stuff? Nobody's going to come over and sit at your..." he paused to pick up her sign, "your 'All-Together-Race-Relations Table.'" Shelly scrunched up her nose and furrowed her brow. She stood while slamming her fist on the table. Her metal tray caused a shrill clang, which drew attention to their conversation.

"I'm not surprised to hear you say that, Mike. It's much easier to go along with the crowd, isn't it? Say three or four big strong boys chasing one frightened little girl. Now that takes courage. Let's see. I must have been seven, no, eight. You and your buddies were how old?"

By now a crowd had gathered. Mike's face colored as he looked down at the sign, now slightly crumpled in his hand.

"That was a long time ago, Shelly," he gritted out. "Nobody wants..." The crowd had grown to ten or twelve. Mike slid the sign toward her, his pale hand trembling. With his shoulders slumped, he looked defeated. From the other side of the lunchroom over clanging trays, sloshing soup and slurping straws, Mark strained to make out as much of the conversation as he could.

It had become easier for Mark to stay out of Shelly's fights. She had proven she was quite capable of taking care of herself. And he almost felt sorry for Mike. He had confided to Mark long ago that he was sorry for what he and his friends had done to Shelly. Mark was starting to think that Mike had a kind of crush on her. While he might be truly reformed of his racism, he was still a genuine klutz with little or no finesse. And Mark didn't feel the least bit inclined to help him in his quest for a better relationship with Shelly, if in fact that was what he was after.

Oh no, not him again. Jimmy emerged from behind the group of kids who had just started to disperse. Walking with his proud strut, he sauntered around behind Shelly and put his hand on her shoulder. Her whole body jerked, ready for a fight. *This is gonna be good,* Mark thought. Mark sat up tall and leaned toward the two. But when Shelly saw that it was Jimmy, she smiled. Jimmy sat down next to her, *too close*. His lips touched the tip of her ear as he whispered something. It caused an immediate re-action. She threw her arms around his shoulders and hugged him long and hard. His lips curled into a triumphant smirk and Shelly, suddenly shy, withdrew her embrace. Just then about six colored football players, Ralph, Fred, John and some others came bobbing along: they had their own way of walking, a cocky long stride. They headed right for the "All-Together-Race-Relations Table."

For about ten minutes nothing new happened. They were sitting, gob-bling chunks of burger, chugging juice and talking among themselves, when Tommy Bradley, interest apparently piqued, walked over and said a few words to one of the football players. He then walked clear across the lunchroom to his own table. Mark covered his mouth with his fist in an attempt to stifle a giggle. Tommy Bradley, while extremely intelligent, was the poster child for squares. His constant squinting through pop-bottle-bottom glasses and limp handshake made him an easy object of ridicule. He could only hurt Shelly's cause.

The girls and guys who were sitting at Tommy's original table went into an immediate huddle as Tommy gathered his books and lunch bag. He gave the group a weak smile as he ran his finger around the neck of his starched shirt collar. He said a few words before heading back to Shelly's table. The squares were now engaged in some serious decision-making based on the looks of them. A thin blond pointed at Shelly's table and took some notes. Another girl shook her head, made a sweep-ing gesture with her hand and nodded vigorously. There was more talk, a bit of eating and silence, before they all moved en masse to Shelly's "race-relations" table. Tommy and Shelly looked up at the same time and gave pleased looks to the approaching group.

"So what?" Mark grunted aloud, causing Karen to question what he had said. "I said, most of those kids are 'out-of-it' anyway. Who cares what they do?" Karen cocked her head to one side and squinted. Mark knew she didn't have a clue as to what he was saying. So what else was new? Mark stirred his green beans around on the plate and chugged his chocolate milk. He couldn't figure out why it made him uncomfortable to see white kids at that table with Shelly. They were squares, for god's sake.

Mark watched the group discussion. He could tell when they quibbled. Tommy's pale lips pursed and Shelly gave her signature nose crinkle. For the most part, the football players seemed satisfied with what was being said; only one, Jeffery, offered any dissent. Eventually one of Tommy's friends passed his notebook down to Shelly. She smiled. They must have hit on just the right strategy as they all nodded their heads in agreement. The colored guys shook on it and the square kids wrote something on the note pad, probably a pact. They had a tendency to overdo. Shelly stood: eyes sparkling, shoulders flung back, and head held as if she was wearing a crown. Her pressed hair hung gently over her shoulders. Mark preferred it natural. He liked the way the wavy black curls mixed and mingled with the subtle sandy streaks. The soft pink sweater she wore hugged her modest curves and her long skirt made her look very much like a lady. Yeah, she was feeling pretty good. She had made progress today. Tomorrow she'd make more. That's just the way it was with Shelly. So why couldn't he be happy for her?

She walked out the large double doors, her entourage in tow. He and Karen followed not far behind. The smell of sizzling burgers and soggy fries escaped with them into the crowded hall.

Karen turned to give Mark a devilishly sly look and planted herself right next to Shelly. She then proceeded to tap her on the shoulder. When Shelly didn't immediately acknowledge her, she pecked harder. "Shelly, what'd you think you were doing in there?" The hall was stunningly silent. Suddenly he and Karen were under the great hot spotlight of peer scrutiny.

Shelly spun on her heel in response to Karen's pointed question, "Karen, you must be one of the most phony people I've ever known." Advancing on her, she continued, "You're what Mama Rose calls a 'user.' Colored people were good enough for you to associate with until you could do better. Or in my case, until you could get what you thought I had." Here,

Shelly looked directly into Mark's eyes. She continued, "Well, now you got it. I hope it makes you happy. So be happy and stay off my case and outta my face."

Mark felt like Shelly was scolding him personally, though she hadn't said a word to him. That was about to change.

"And you, Mr. Popularity, I used to think you were about something, you know, more than a pretty face. You used to care about people and the things going on around you. And now look at you, wastin' your gifts. You'll be lucky if God doesn't take 'em away. Forensics; you'd think that for once you'd use your persuasive ability for more than winning trophies."

Mark could still read Shelly. She knew she should stop, but it was as if one of those demons Mama Rose was always talking about had gotten hold of her. She puffed her jaws full of air and wailed, "I bet your dad's proud of you now!" To punctuate her sentence, she rolled her eyes in disgust. Mark thought about responding, but she wasn't finished. "Have you ever seen one of these?" She fumbled through her satchel. The *Chicago Protector* newspaper nearly whacked his face as she unfurled it in front of him. She held it there like a royal proclamation. He wanted to say: as a matter of fact, I have seen the *Chicago Protector*. It champions the causes of Negroes, especially here in Chicago. She continued, "Have you ever read it?" He hadn't.

Mark stood there. Shelly hadn't spoken to him directly in years. And now she was blasting him in front of everybody. He could feel heat rising to his face. Man, he wanted to wipe that smirk off her face. He wanted to punch something, maybe her. He wanted to scream, swear or spit. It felt as though anger would burst from his every pore. Steamy hot tears welled in his eyes. God, when was the last time he had cried? He couldn't remember. If a tear actually fell, he really would have to kill somebody. He never thought he could hate anyone, but right now he was pretty sure he hated Shelly. *Shut up. Sit down.* He yelled it in his head. *Ughh. How much longer could she go on?*

The next day Shelly sat there at that same stupid table with that same stupid sign. Jimmy sat there with the colored football players and the square white kids were back. Every now and then Mark sensed Shelly's glare. He knew she was looking over at his table where the popular white kids, jocks, cheerleaders and their groupies sat. He knew she was silently willing just one of them to come over. That would affect the whole school. It would legitimize her efforts.

He wanted to know what was happening; but he was determined not to even look at Shelly after what she did to him yesterday. Maybe he'd just sneak a peek. Why wouldn't Karen sit down? She kept flitting around like she was made of glass. Didn't she realize she was blocking his view?

No, it couldn't be. Mike, hair slicked back, crisp shirt and pressed jeans, had gotten up from where they were sitting and was slowly sauntering across the glossy cafeteria floor. He pushed through several kids, standing, chewing fast and saying nothing. He was heading straight for Shelly. *Was he going to start up yesterday's argument again?*

"Sit down, Karen, I want to see this," Mark demanded, using his hand to motion her to the left.

Mark leaned into the tabletop, propping his chin on his hand while focusing all of his attention on the conversation happening across the room. Shelly crinkled up her nose in that familiar way, "Listen, Mike," she started in a near shout while rising from her seat, "if you think…"

"Hold up, Shelly," Mike started, his freckles brightened, "can I sit with you guys?" He lowered his big red head and waited for an answer.

Karen looked first at Mike then quickly at Mark. Her expression: pure astonishment. She was so preoccupied with the scene across from her that she nearly missed the edge of the bench as she plopped down next to Mark. Mark was astonished, too. He knew Mike liked Shelly more than he let on, but was he willing to give up the gang for her? They'd never accept him now; that wasn't all bad.

"What is it about that girl?" Karen stated flatly.

Shelly had something special, all right. It was quiet and deep. She was real, touchable and lovable. And she was passionate. Her sense of justice drew like-minded people and people who wanted to be better than they were. And she was commanding. Sure, she raised her voice every now and then, but she didn't really need to. There was power in just being Shelly. Mama Rose had raised a girl who wouldn't settle. Mark couldn't help but wonder if she was in over her head this time, but he certainly admired her spunk. When Mark asked her once why she had run from Mike and his friends all those years ago, she stated simply: "I might be brave but I'm no fool." He smiled when he remembered her pounding her hands on her skinny little hips while stomping her foot and making her declaration.

Mark and Karen watched for a while, waiting for Mike to reveal his true motive. He never did. He simply sat at the "All-Together-Race-Relations Table" and lent his presence to the cause. Mark stood. Karen scooted quickly to fill the available space. Appreciative, she looked up and batted her fluffy brown lashes. This usually got Mark all hot and bothered.

"Mark, Mark! Where are you going?" Karen questioned as he started to walk away.

He didn't answer. Mike was a football player, but he wasn't popular. It would take someone cooler to sell the "All-Together-Race-Relations Table" to the rest of the students at Franklin High.

Shelly's mouth dropped open at the same time as Karen's when Mark took a place at the end of her table. She didn't say anything to Mark as he sat down, but she was proud of him. He could feel it and it was the best feeling he had had in years. He didn't say much, but when he sat there, others followed. Soon the table was full. Mark leaned in and looked slyly at Shelly. She inched up the corner of her mouth in response. "Good" was the only word that came to Mark's mind.

*R*omance radiated from the dimmed red light bulbs, which were elegantly positioned throughout the room, while purple and pink streamers leaped and laced their way across the ceiling. It was all Shelly could do to keep her feet planted on the ground, but then why should she? High heels and patent leather stomped as waists wriggled and ponytails bobbed. The night of the junior dance had arrived, and she couldn't be more pleased. Surveying the room, she was overjoyed to know that she had been part of the planning committee. Only a freshman who was actually attending the dance could even be considered for the privilege. A quick scan revealed that there were precious few freshmen in attendance. Josh Haskel and Jimmy were spinning the tunes. If laughter and continuous dancing were any sign, then her idea to have two disc jockeys was another winner. Josh had an extensive collection of records and Jimmy knew all the best dance songs. Everyone was grooving to the smooth tunes of the Platters and swooning to Elvis.

This was the most amazing thing Shelly had ever been a part of. And all she had to do was to join the fray. So why was she hesitating? Why couldn't she simply be happy? It was because there was something else, something not so pleasant lingering, a longing, a kind of dull ache. The threads of her thoughts began to unravel.

Most of the colored kids were on the right side of the gym while most of the white kids stood and danced on the left. Sure a few brave kids meandered from one side to the other, but she had hoped for so much more. Still the "ATRR" table was having an effect. There was probably more mixing because of it. And for a so-called square, Tommy Bradley wielded a lot of authority. He was the one who had gotten her on the planning committee. His speech, supporting her membership, had emboldened some and embarrassed others. The end result was that she was included on the team. His final comment was that she inspired him. Shelly couldn't have been more honored.

So here they all were, the cool colored kids, which was her group, since she and Jimmy were a couple, the white jocks and their groupies and everyone in between. They were all partying and having a wonderful time, even if it was mostly on two separate sides of the room. Coloreds danced with coloreds and whites with whites. Still in time: perhaps.

Shelly was beginning to understand what had happened to Mark. He was living in what he thought was the "real world." Who could blame him? Though she couldn't see how his daily life was changing for the better. But when he sat at that table, so did the hip white kids. And even if he wasn't doing much talking, at least not to her, the others kids were talking to each other. And people where getting to know each other. That was progress and she and Mark had made it happen. Just like the old days.

The old days. Were they really gone forever? It made her heartsick thinkin' of him. He wasn't being his true self. Or was he? What was wrong with her? Tonight wasn't for or about Mark. It was for her, and for Jimmy, and for partying like there was no tomorrow. She looked over to her deejay boyfriend, who glowed from the luminescent lights as he swayed to the beat and smiled his brightest. She gave him a sassy wink.

Karen wore a pale-blue taffeta dress. It brought out the color of her eyes. The wrap-over neckline highlighted and drew attention to her bust line. The sheer netting in a contrasting deeper blue barely concealed her deep cleavage. Mark was definitely into her. So why couldn't he keep his eyes off of Shelly? She seemed to be having so much fun. She was wearing a pink shell and a blue pleated skirt. It was kind of "school-girlish." Mark figured he knew who had helped her pick it out. The skirt was on the short side, though, making Shelly's behind more prominent. Mark was having a hard time keeping his thoughts from wandering. And just when he was beginning to wonder where Jimmy's thoughts were, Jimmy left his disc jockey post and headed for the object of their attention, after putting on the slowest, most sensual song they had played all night.

"Let's dance, Binky," Karen's insistence on using pet names was a constant source of irritation for Mark.

"Just a minute," he stooped and pretended to adjust his laces. He wanted to be free to see what Jimmy was up to. From his lowered vantage point he could see just how tight Jimmy was holding Shelly. He wondered why Shelly would let him do that.

His next thought was of Karen on his back, literally. She had walked around behind him and pressed her body to his rear. He was still mad about Shelly, but it could wait until another day.

$\mathcal{M}$any competing thoughts vied for Mark's attention as he and Karen walked home from the dance. He felt weary and excited at the same time. Karen was looking really sexy. She was pressed up against his side, her soft arm wrapped firmly around his waist. Everything inside him screamed for release. He nuzzled his chin in her hair. The aroma was fresh and airy. She leaned into the crook of his arm and laid her head on his chest. The night air whirled around, low-hanging tree branches fluttered in response. Mark should have been thoroughly exhilarated. He wasn't.

"Binky?"

"Yeah?"

"Did you have a good time at the dance?"

"Yeah, couldn't you tell?" Mark twirled a wisp of Karen's golden hair around his finger.

"Sometimes I could. But sometimes you seemed…far away."

"Listen, Karen, we've had these talks before. It's just that I have stuff on my mind, okay?" He silenced her with a kiss. At first it was a light brush of their lips. It quickly deepened. Mark's hands moved slowly up Karen's arms, then roved over her back and down her hips. Sparks of fire coursed through his body.

A rasping Karen whispered, "Follow me, Mark." She grabbed his hand and pulled him around to the back of her house. He followed, his breath catching in waves of anticipation. Once behind the brown brick façade that sheltered them from curious eyes, Karen pulled his white shirt up and over the waist of his pants. Her supple fingers crawled up the bare skin of his back, sending a searing surge up his spine. It was a feeling he was becoming accustomed to. Karen was his steady but she was not his only. She seemed to be aware that there were others but she never questioned him and he certainly didn't volunteer the information.

Mark reached into Karen's hair and wound his fingers through it, pulling her head back so that her moist lips could meet his. Her reaction nearly brought him to his knees. With shaky legs, he stepped back. "Karen," he gasped, releasing her, "I have to go."

"Wait, Mark." She clutched his rumpled shirttail as he lifted his coat from the ground, "My parents are probably asleep. I can go in and open this window. You can stay over. No one will know." When Mark tugged his shirt away, she flung herself into his chest, winding her arms around his neck. The aroma of her perfume had become heavy with desire. "Please stay."

"I can't," Mark forced himself to say while seizing her wrists and placing them down by her sides.

"What's wrong, Mark?" Exasperation filled her voice, "Sometimes I wonder…"

"See you Monday, Karen."

Rubbing the back of his neck, he turned and walked toward his house. Slowly watching his own feet step one foot in front of the other, he questioned himself again. Why, why had he ended another incendiary date with Karen short of the finish line? What was wrong with him anyway? He stopped in front of the Plotski house, ran his fingers through his hair and looked up into the night sky. It was perfectly clear, pitch-black accented with glistening speckles of pinpoint light. If only everything could be as simple as a starlit night. He thought the whole thing over and told himself, over and over again: I don't want complications.

Mark found consolation in the fact that in his state of deep concentration he had managed to come within one house of his own, barely noticing the time it took to get there. He'd drift swiftly into a deep sleep, saying goodnight to another perfectly exasperating day. He sighed out loud when he saw Mama Rose coming down her steps.

"Not tonight, Mama." Somehow she was always there when he needed to talk, but tonight he just wanted to sleep.

"You sure look wore out, boy," she said, boring into his eyes with her intense piercing gaze, while ignoring his directive.

"Mama Rose, why is it that even when you know something is not good for you, you still want it?"

She smirked, "Well, now that's a good question. You want something that doesn't belong to you?" She didn't give him time to respond. "Something that's illegal? Maybe it's immoral?"

"No, ma'am, it's none of those."

"Then the question you ought to be asking, boy, is why?"

"I don't understand what you mean."

"You ought to be asking," she spoke slowly and deliberately as if talking to an idiot, "why-you-can't-have-it?"

Mark pondered that for a while before asking, "Mama Rose, why are you out here so late?"

She smiled, "Now that's one 'why' you shouldn't have to ask."

With that she turned, shook her salt-and-pepper head and walked back up her stairs mumbling, "And you used to be such a smart boy."

Freshman year, a time of thrilling beginnings and heartsick endings, had come and gone. It was a clanging gong, a resounding nil: over, over, over, done. Sophomore year found Shelly hurling toward making a decision about Jimmy Johnson. This Monday had already been quite an ordeal. All day long people had been calling her Jimmy's girl and she guessed it was true, but when she searched her feelings, she wasn't so sure. He had nearly kissed her twice, once by his locker and once as they were leaving the building. She turned her face just in time. He caught her on the cheek. Her stomach still flipped when she thought about his downcast lids and dejected expression as she avoided meeting his lips.

She liked him, she did. He was dashing, romantic and smart, all the things that any girl would want. Harry Belafonte and Sidney Poitier put together had nothing on him. Even Mama Rose said he was a fine boy, and she was hard to impress. And Shelly had to admit it, she got a rush just being around him. But being around him, well, it was complicated. Sometimes he'd tilt his head to the side and curve his slender lips in a way that made her feel like he was hungry, and when he touched her, it was as if his hands were expecting something. They were on her waist and ever so slowly they'd go lower. She'd pull them up. They'd be holding hands when he would suddenly pull her close for a sumptuously agitating hug.

At times she felt like giving him whatever he wanted and other times she felt like running and screaming. Mama Rose's voice would echo from someplace far and quiet but all too clear, "Shelly, your mama was a good girl. It was trying to give what she didn't have that ruined her. She loved your dad something fierce, so much so that she let herself get tricked into sex. She was too young to make a choice like that. She got pregnant the first time. Kenny married her, all right, but he wasn't satisfied. She was too shy and inexperienced. Her innocence and unwillingness to try new things frustrated him; soon he left her for a more seasoned woman. The relationship soured her. Commitin' came hard after.

"Now, girl, I don't want this for you and neither does God. I ain't gonna spare you. Havin' sex 'afore marriage is a great sin. It's not that God don't want you to pleasure your body. It's just all the complications that come along: babies, VDs and the rest. Keep your panties on. If a boy really likes you, he'll like you still." Shelly had tried to explain this to one or two boys but "their understandin' wasn't quick," as Mama Rose would say.

When she told Jimmy her mother had wanted to abort her and that the only reason she was alive today was because Mama Rose had been willing to take her any time her mother couldn't handle being a parent, he said he understood and that he could wait. Shelly honestly didn't know what he was waiting for. She didn't know when she would ever be ready.

The squeal of brakes lurching to a stop effectively ended her musings over Jimmy. She got on the bus. From her window she could see Karen and Mark running. Would they make it? She thought about telling the driver to wait; that was until she heard that annoying, "Binky, are they going to stop?"

"Binky." Shelly wondered out loud how the White Knight liked his new nickname.

*B*inky. Man, that name grated on him. Some of Karen's charm was starting to wear thin. He'd asked her not to call him "Marky." He didn't even like it when Shelly did that. And he asked her not to call him "HH," Her Hunk; so he figured he'd just have to live with "Binky" for a while longer, that was until this school year was over and he left for college. Then he'd forget about everybody and everything that didn't get him exactly where he wanted to go.

Still there was a name he used to like, the "White Knight." Mark's thoughts gathered on the wind and flew to a frosty sunlit morning in the park. The snow was a foot deep in some places and generous flakes continued to fall. Their hidden place was under a cluster of grand oaks, near the willows by the frozen pond behind the shelter. It was a place of vibrant dreams, long winnowing talks, deep confessions and secrets of the heart. He was talking about his grandfather, of whom he knew little, except that his father dreaded the man and that effectively made him a dragon.

"Sir Night, I wouldst request you."

"Babydoll, what would you have me do?" Shelly crinkled up her nose. That meant she was angry.

"Princess Babydoll," he corrected himself, "what would you have me do?"

"Slay yonder dragon." She pointed. All he saw was white mounds of glistening fluffy snow.

"Here, put your magic glasses on." Before he could figure out what she meant, she smeared wet slush over his eyes, and before he could get angry, she pointed in the direction of the mound, "Do you see it now?"

He did, he really did. With a running start he trudged valiantly toward the snow beast. With a mighty thrash of his stick sword the dragon's head flew off. A strong blow from Shelly's sword sent his arms crashing to the slick and crunchy surface. With his hand, Mark made a final plunge into the snow dragon's chest and pulled out his heart. Most girls would have been grossed out by that part. Shelly never was.

"Are your hands cold, Sir White Knight?" she asked with a real look of sadness in her eyes. He wore one mitten caked with cracking ice. Shelly wore the other.

"Yes," he admitted. She took off his mushy wet glove and threw it to the ground. Before he could ask any questions, hers was off, too. She then took both his hands, clapped them together and held them inside hers. Mark felt as though they were saying some kind of sacred prayer. Next she blew her tender breath on them and instead of icy cold, swirling warmth engulfed them.

Mark thought again about the snow dragon being his grandfather; maybe, or perhaps it was all the things that go bump in the night, the things that frighten small children everywhere, keeping them from their peaceful sleep. He never felt afraid when...

"Mark, Mark, 'million-miles-away-Mark.'" Karen snapped her fingers, "The bus is here. Where do you go when you do that?" She sneered through gritted teeth.

"A place I never want to go again." Mark flashed her his persuasive smile.

"Then why...?" she started to say, but the air in her head took up its usual space, rendering her incapable of important thought.

"Just one kiss, Shelly, and I'll let you go inside." Jimmy's gaze was glued to her mouth. His arm, which was propped on the house's wooden frame, collapsed at the elbow, causing his lips to be a breath away from hers. The yellow-orange sun dipped behind a far-off house. A lost breeze caused her to shiver. The leaves from the tree-of-heaven danced tenderly. Their rustling chanting mystical songs, romance flitting, elusive but ripe.

"You won't let me do anything, James Johnson," she erupted while slapping his hand away from the wall. "I do exactly what I want, and you know it."

"Do you want to kiss me?" His proud shoulders drooped, causing his blue sweater to sag. His eyes rolled skyward. He had been more patient with her than any other boy she had known. She thought for a moment and said, "I'm curious."

He looked as though he was waiting for an explanation. When she didn't offer one, he asked her what she was curious about.

"Well, I was…" he leaned in as she spoke. He was really going to kiss her now, "Wait, I feel like someone's watching."

"If you don't want to kiss me, Shelly, just say so." He threw his hands up in exasperation, "There are plenty of other…" His eyes blazed as he turned to stalk away. His patience was clearly at an end.

"That's not it," she said grabbing his wrist. "Let's go around to the other side of the house." Shelly could have sworn she heard a hard sigh.

Mark had gone undercover the last couple of days, a sharp contrast to his regular summer behavior, which had been one big party. He was always leaving with some girl or guy. When Mark was getting his things together before leaving earlier that morning, Jake took out his newspaper and sat on the porch, determined not to move until absolutely necessary. Mark passed him where he sat. The boy was fidgety, actin' nervous like he had something to hide. It set Jake to thinking about his last visit to ol' Stan's barbershop. It made him sick to think about the things they were saying. Who would have thought that his son could be the topic of that discussion? It stopped as soon as he rounded the red-and-white pole. Men could be as gossipy as women, but few were stupid enough to risk offending him outright. All he ever cared about was Mark and his mother, Irene. Maybe college would straighten his son out. Jake sincerely hoped so.

Sundays were peaceful except when Mama Rose's church was putting on one of their bazaars. Old biddies had been in and out all the blasted day, their hats flopping this way and that as they carried loads down the stairs, carefully placing them in their laundry carts and whatever else would make the trek to their church. When Rose came out struggling with cakes, roasted chickens and those god-awful smelling collard greens, Mark offered to drive her and the other crones to the church. He was gone for most of the day; at about 6:00 he returned. Jake looked at the clock. 9:00 P.M.; it was still early really but he felt weary. He was also curious to see what Mark was finding to do in his room all of this time. He made his way upstairs. Standing outside of Mark's room, Jake eased the door open with his foot.

"What you doin' at that window, boy?" He belted without thinking.

"Er, nothing, Pop." Mark bumped his head jerking it back into the window. His expression was that of a child with his hand in the till of the corner candy store.

"If I didn't know better, I'd think you were spying on that—"

"I wasn't. I was…"

"—colored girl," Jake finished, "I'll give it to her and her grandma, they seem to have some brains and that Mama Rose is a real hard worker. But no son of mine is going to get mixed up with a colored girl. Anyway, I thought you were all over that?"

Jake didn't wait for a reply. He simply huffed off. He had tried to change. He certainly would never forget what Rose had done for him and Mark so many years ago. But mixing the races could only lead to pain, and he didn't want that for his boy. He left Mark standing next to his window, chest heaving, back against the wall.

Shelly came downstairs early, her hair in pink foam rollers and still wearing her baggy aqua pajamas. Mama Rose gave her an askance glance. Sitting at the silver-edged dinette table she drummed out a simple beat, her eyes darting from the window to the door.

"Mama Rose, is it true that Mark's leaving for college today?" She was trying to appear casual as she buttered the same piece of toast for the third time.

"Guess so, girl. Don't you talk to the boy anymore?"

"No, not much; it's like he hates me. Whenever I come around he acts all stiff. Sometimes he gets that horrid mean look on his face." She laughed, "You know, like the one he used to scare those boys who were chasing me when we kids."

"Yes, I know. I think that boy has lots of thoughts about you. I doubt any of them have anything to do with hate." Mama set a cup of weak tea in front of Shelly.

"Oh, Mama, I know you know lots of things, but I can count the words Mark's said to me over the last couple of years. As a matter of fact, I doubt he talks to anyone." Shelly raised the sweet milky substance to her mouth, "Ouch!"

"Yes, it's hot. Poor little Miss Know-it-all, well, I know it would surprise you to know that he's talked to me a time or two." Mama Rose moved to open the refrigerator. She pulled a metal tray of ice out of the freezer. Cubes of ice popped out as she retracted the lever. Wrapping a single cube in a clean dishcloth, she handed it to Shelly to cool her scorched mouth.

"When, Mama? I've hardly seen him say more than hello to you." She took a bite of the over-buttered toast and felt her swollen lips turn up. She decided to use the cold pack Mama made. It immediately soothed her.

"And I guess if you didn't see it, it ain't so." A honk, outside, interrupted their discussion.

Shelly rushed to the screen door. Standing out of sight she saw a young man about Mark's age sitting in a citrus-colored Mercury. It was a long sleek convertible with a metal-encased spare attached to the rear. The red lights on either side of the trunk resembled feline eyes and the grill around the license: gritted red teeth. It had to be expensive. Who did Mark know with that kind of money?

"See ya, Pop!" Shelly heard Mark yelling to his father as he ran down the steps of his porch. He heaved a hefty green duffel bag and an over-stuffed suitcase into the tight backseat. Long muscular legs vaulted the passenger door. A momentary glimpse back. Was he looking for her? She felt it, a shift in the cosmos. Life was never going to be the same. A hard lump rose up in her throat.

Chapter Five
It's Cold Outside

Snow and sleet, sleet and snow, the weatherman on WGN had predicted it, and although it had been slow in coming, the chill and the moisture were in the atmosphere. Rose knew because the arthritis in her left knee tended to twinge before the snow started falling. And the way this wind was kickin' up, it was sure to be a doozy.

"Jacob, Jacob, open the door! Jacob, I know you're in there. Fine, then, I'll just sit here until you do!"

Harsh pounding followed the banshee yell.

"What's going on? Mama, do you hear that pounding?"

Rose hurried from her room, pulling the belt tight on her floral housedress as Shelly's question rang behind her.

"Sure do, girl. Don't get up; Mama'll take care of it."

"But, Mama, what if…?"

"Listen, child, you know I can take care of this. Now go on back to sleep."

Rose crept down the stairs. Shelly slept lighter these days. Opening her closet door, she took out her heavy jacket and headed for the porch. Like a slap, the hard chill hit her face. She stepped gingerly. Since a deceptively thin cover of slick snow was already in place, she snapped on her fur-lined boots. The shouting had come from the direction of Jake's house and Rose was pretty sure she knew whose voice it was, but when she looked there, she didn't see anyone. She crept closer. Ah, there she was, a petite figure, huddled in at the foot of his door.

"Is someone up there?" She called already knowing the answer. The small figure moved a bit. "Hello there, you okay?"

"Huh?" A woman's trembling voice responded. "Uhh, yes," she said, getting to her feet and pushing the quickly coming snow from her hair and face.

"Irene?"

"Do I know you?"

" I'm Mama Rose, child."

"Oh, Shelly's grandmother. Do you know where my son is?" Her voice quavered, unable to veil her obvious shiver.

"Irene, your son went off to college over two months ago. Didn't you know your boy was gone?"

"No, ma'am. I'll be leaving now." Irene moved slowly, her feet slipping as she did. She held onto the stone post to steady herself.

"No, Sweetie, I don't believe you will."

By now Mama Rose was within reach of Irene. She clutched her frigid hand and led her down the set of stairs that left Jake's house and up the stairs that led to hers. To Mama Rose, Irene looked as though she hadn't eaten in days. And the way she was shivering, Mama Rose guessed that she was chilled to the bone and probably had not been in a warm place for several days.

Rose opened the door to her place. Irene let out a soft sigh when the heat rushed out to greet her. "What are we doing here?" she questioned.

"Sit down," Rose replied, pulling Irene's thin coat from her shoulders. "No, there." Rose directed Irene away from the hard dinette chair and toward the cushiony soft love seat.

"Everything all right?" Shelly yelled from her room.

"Perfectly," Rose called, peeking up to make sure that Shelly wasn't coming. When she turned her attention back to the love seat, Irene, poor thing, was sound asleep.

*I*rene awoke with a start. What, when? Her brain was so muddled. Where had she ended up this time? Oh yeah, Miss Rose's house. Her nose was running, her hand instinctively reached for her coat pocket. She wasn't wearing it and she was in bed. A bed: cottony as a bulbous floating cloud. She pulled the sumptuously thick covers up around her knees and under her chin. She sniffed again and reached for one of the handkerchiefs obviously laid out for her on the table by her bed.

Sitting, rocking, hugging her knees to her chest; she felt wretched. Life had only been kind to her once; it was when she met Jacob and married him. Slowly she had been learning to trust. She could remember their first date as if it was yesterday. She insisted on meeting him at the restaurant: Namio's. She always liked Italian food and in her daydreams of Mother and Father, she imagined herself Italian. Her dark features and wavy hair could easily be Italian, and if she wasn't there was no harm in pretending. Everyone needed to be part of something.

Mr. Namio was kind to her. He allowed her to work at his place once or twice a week when the neighborhood grocer, where she had worked, laid off their newest cashiers.

She rode from her tiny apartment to the restaurant on the bus. Who would she sit next to this evening? Who would she have to engage in conversation so as not to appear snobbish? But she mustn't be too friendly if she sat next to a man, or she'd risk her conversation partner coming on to her. Tonight Irene set next to a kindly drunk who leaned a little too near when relaying the events of his day. The fragrance of whiskey still stung her nostrils. She hoped none of his scent had attached to her. Fortunately the ride was short and the walk to Namio's was less than a quarter block. Unfortunately, it had started to sprinkle.

Her pace quickened as the light rain turned into a pelting storm. The wind rippled against her, causing the rain to defeat her umbrella. Her black felt hat was starting to sag. She wanted more than anything to make a good impression on Jacob. She didn't know why he affected her the way he did. The people that she trusted were few, two to be exact: Mr. Namio, based on experience, and Jacob, based on a gut feeling. He made her stronger. All her life she had had to fight men with wrong intentions, jealous wives, and foster siblings vying for the sparse specks of love divvied cautiously among them. In Jacob she saw the hope for something solid, something of her own. Just when she thought the fight had gone out of her, he came along. He made her think there was something more worth fighting for.

When she opened Namio's large glass door, Jacob was sitting in a romantic nook. The red-and-white checked tablecloth was accented as usual by a glass vase containing a single plastic rose. There was also a pink votive burning on a flower-print china saucer. No other table had that adornment. Jacob appeared to be giving himself a final examination, smoothing the pressed crease of his pants and adjusting his lapel. She couldn't imagine why. He always looked perfect to her. When he looked up, his expression was so intense she was sure he disapproved of what he saw. Maybe the rain had spoiled her hair; she had tried so hard to keep the strongest waves from her face.

He quickly stood to his feet and rushed to greet her. Helping her off with her coat, he stared. She couldn't bear it any longer.

"What's wrong, Jacob? Is there something wrong with the way I look?"

The stare changed to a genuine look of shock. "Irene, I've never seen anything more beautiful than you are right now."

There it was, all at once, that feeling she had longed for: a place to belong. She didn't know what the future would hold for her, but she knew she would be with Jacob.

It was all a lie. And now she felt as if she was standing on an icy precipice, one foot dangling and the other sliding quickly, the line between reality and insanity becoming quickly blurred. She lived for Jacob, she lived for Mark, and now there was no one.

"Irene, Irene; you all right up there, chil'?" Rose was at the door.

Irene wanted to answer, but it was as if the words were swollen in her mouth, lingering too thick to come out. No, she wasn't all right. She had never been. The closest she had ever come was when she lived right next door with her own little family. Jacob had taken that away from her just as easily as he had given it.

Mama Rose opened the door, "Ahh, honey, what ya doing sitting here in the dark with all your clothes on? I told you to come up here, put on one of my gowns and get some rest. You look exhausted."

"Miss Rose. I'll just stay for a bit, if I can. I really need to go."

"Where?"

"Home."

"Listen, baby, I've seen enough people and enough stuff to know you ain't got a home."

"Miss Rose, I need to be going."

"All right, you can go."

"Right now?" Irene stopped rocking and sat up straight.

"Why not? Seems like you're in an awful hurry."

Irene bounded from the bed, "I'll just get my shoes and bag." Light-headed, she slumped toward the dresser. Mama Rose caught her and guided her gently toward the bed.

"Shelly is going to a friend's for the weekend. You don't need to be in a hurry. Lie down for a few minutes. I'll get her off and then we can talk about when you're leaving."

Irene didn't argue. Hunger had obviously made her weak, and she really wasn't looking forward to going home, if it could be called that. She would rest for a few more minutes. Irene pulled the double-stuffed pastel-pink quilt from the foot of the bed over the other thick blanket. This might be her last comfortable sleep. Why not take full advantage of it. When all of the covers were snug around her, she laid her head back on the two pillows she had stacked. She sank into the warmth that surrounded her, shifted positions several times, then allowed her heavy eyelids to close.

Dreams: dreams of Jacob's muscular arms around her, her sweet-faced baby grinning up as she held him securely, clean linen, fresh baked bread and tender kisses whisked her to another life. Like a delicate ballerina, she swirled in wisps of pretty pink mist. Over and over she twirled, she danced, she swayed. She could feel her smile get bigger and bigger. Joy was taking her away. The pink mist had a most alluring aroma. Her nose began to twitch. The scent beckoned her. She inhaled so hard that she startled herself and was soon awake.

For a minute, nothing in her grimy apartment looked the same. Vague recollections invaded her serenity: pounding on Jacob's door, walking up stairs, but where? Miss Rose's house: goodness and kindness. How long had she been sleeping? Searching the room, she saw the round-faced alarm clock sitting on the mantle, 11:30. Oh no, she had come at 8:00 A.M. and slept for, for almost four hours? A knock at the door roused her. "Yes, Ma'am, come in."

Mama Rose, carrying a tray piled high with biscuits, bacon, dark heavy syrup and some white stuff in a bowl that looked slightly like a thicker-grained cream of wheat, nudged the door open with her foot. She entered.

"Miss Rose, that smells wonderful."

"And it's all for you with just one condition."

"Ma'am?"

"Mama, call me Mama; everyone does."

The irresistible smell of bacon called to her, and she agreed without so much as a word about Mama Rose not being her mother. In fact, at this moment, she felt as though she was. No other woman in her life had ever gone out of her way for Irene.

"Slow down, you act as if you haven't eaten in days."

"Two," Irene shot back.

"Does Jake know?"

"Miss Rose—"

"Mama."

"Mama Rose, Jacob doesn't care about what happens to me."

Mama Rose shook her head, "You'll stay here today."

"I don't want to be a burden."

"Don't worry, honey. You won't be. There's plenty around here you can do. An old woman, like me, always needs something."

Irene looked at her breakfast, tasted the white stuff: *delicious*, she thought. Mama Rose called them grits. As she scanned the immaculate room, she had a hard time believing this woman needed anybody or anything. But she agreed to stay and even to come back if she ever felt alone or like she needed to talk. All of a sudden she felt light, a feeling that she was hardly acquainted with anymore. At first she didn't know what to name it. The feeling skipped and skidded around her consciousness. Suddenly she grasped it: hope. There was something to look forward to. Like a lost friend, hope had returned.

*I*rene liked coming around when Shelly wasn't home; that way she could command all of Mama Rose's attention. She had only run into Shelly once, having become adept at timing her visits just right. In the beginning she felt like a thirst-deprived woman dying for something new to quench her parched spirit. Mama Rose was the provider of the needed nectar. Later she felt like she was actually of use to Mama Rose. With Shelly away more and more, she had become Mama Rose's right hand, dispensing good will and aid right along side of her. If it were a time when Jacob was likely to be home, she'd meet Mama Rose at her destination.

She didn't want to run into him either. Mama Rose talked about Jacob. She would say things about him that surprised Irene: like how he'd ask Mark to recite his speeches over and over again, never tiring of them; and how every now and then he'd kiss Mark on the cheek when a hug just wouldn't do. She had protested, asking Mama Rose not to tell her these stories, but Rose always did just as she pleased. And although she was truthful to a fault and frank beyond need, she never said a bad word about Jacob and hardly anyone else.

Irene thought that living next to Jacob would be intolerable for anyone, especially a colored person. She knew from firsthand experience how he felt about them. How could that hateful man also be the loving man of Rose's stories? He was a true paradox.

Saturdays were particularly good visiting days. Shelly stayed away with her friends or she met with one of her action groups. All-Together-Race-Relations, a club she created in high school, had extended its efforts into the community. The young people in that club were determined to make their neighbors aware of the daily struggles of the people living right there with them. If people could see the bigger picture, everyone would live a lot better. According to Mama Rose's stories, some of the white families complained about Shelly's efforts. They worried that their kids were becoming a bunch of demonstrators. Mama Rose knew many of the people personally and felt that none of them was any threat to Shelly or her group. The colored families and those of other races applauded Shelly. Mama Rose said that some of the whites secretly admired her as well.

Tall and steady James Johnson had picked Shelly up early today. He was a well-mannered boy, handsome and sure. Irene had watched them on more than one occasion from the corner. They'd stand close, next to the house, talking and waiting for friends. James's bearing gave an air of pride; fortunately it didn't tend toward arrogance. He was obviously smitten with Shelly, but did she feel the same about him? It was hard to tell. She seemed guarded for a woman in love.

A blast of heat escaped from the oven door as Irene removed her pork chop casserole. As soon as the bubbling dish cooled, she and Mama Rose would have their dinner. They had volunteered all day at the church nursery while the workingwomen enjoyed a day away. Irene pulled back the curtain over the sink and took a quick look.

Jacob had had a busy day. She knew because she had watched him come and go several times. At 7:00 that evening he left dressed in a sports jacket, gray slacks and a white turtleneck. He had developed an almost imperceptible bulge around his waist and a small streak of gray on his right temple. In her opinion he had become more handsome with age. It was too bad he didn't have a better temper.

"What's wrong with you today, Irene? You planning on getting a jump on the dishes?"

"No."

"Irene…"

"Humm…"

"Coppers and cakes, birds and bills."

"Yes, I agree." Irene nodded her head absent-mindedly.

"Yes, right. Jake home yet?"

Irene jerked her head around. A nervous twitch was playing at her lip. Now exposed, she pulled the curtain back a bit more and stated quietly, "He dates a lot, doesn't he?"

"Some. Do you mind taking that casserole out of the sink as we continue this conversation? I really don't think I made the gravy that thick."

Irene's hands flew to her face. She felt cool and sweaty. "Did I really put it in the sink?"

"You did."

"Who's this lady?" Irene asked, curiosity consuming her.

Rose came closer to the window and peered out. "That's Lydia, his Wednesday girl. She must have earned an extra day."

"Extra day." Irene mumbled, " I can almost smell the cheap perfume." The window wasn't open but some things were obvious. The woman wore a bright white dress splattered with a gaudy red carnation print. She looked like a dime store plastic bouquet.

"Did you say, Wednesday girl?" Irene continued.

"Yes, your husband doesn't like to get too attached to one. He worked a system out, different girls on different days."

Irene peeked again, "She's so tall and blond."

Irene turned quickly letting the curtain drop.

"See something you don't like?" Irene didn't answer. Rose continued, "Happens lots to people who just look at life. You know you really have to live it to appreciate it…Irene?"

Irene's back was again to Mama Rose: stiff. Her hands were still, paralyzed, one on each curtain. She spoke not a word, but her silence screamed.

Chapter Six
Wood and Stone

Shelly never liked concrete stairs or porches. Warm and welcoming wood was what she preferred. Mama Rose told her stories of being raised by peaceful pastures near leaning fruit trees and meandering bayous. Every day she left her door she was greeted with fragrances too tantalizing to describe: all manner of scents blending and intertwining with the next, only winters were exempt. "It was glorious, truly glorious," Mama Rose would often tell Shelly. It was obvious to Shelly that Mama Rose was trying to recreate the essence of her childhood home in their current one. Planters filled with velvety white flowers lined the wood railings; potted zinnias and azaleas stood in every available space. Ivies wound their way up posts and Shelly's first attempt at crocheting lay prettily over the back of the glider. At first Shelly thought it was tacky and not good enough. But Mama Rose placed it with such love that it seemed, well, lovely. She had a way of making everything beautiful.

This concrete porch of Mr. Schultz's house was so unlike her own. How could these houses stand side by side? As she marched up the broad steps, she thought about the occupant of the house, and it fit, stone. Maybe she was being unfair. He had softened toward Mama Rose, some, and he owed her.

Shelly wondered: to this day, Jacob Schultz could only manage an almost inaudible "hello" and an occasional nod in her direction when they passed on the street. But she was no longer a threat to him. Mark was long gone. Maybe Jake would at least listen to what she had to say before throwing her out. And even he would repay a debt, wouldn't he?

She rang the bell rather than open the heavy screen door and pound on the inside one. No one came. She rang it two more times: long.

"Keep your shirt on," a voice boomed from inside, "Shelly?" he said, pulling the door open, "Miss Rose sick or something?"

"No, Mr. Schultz, can I please come in?" Jake looked terribly uncomfortable. Shelly told herself it could be for a number of reasons, not the least of which was the early hour and his state of undress: he was wearing a thin robe. Apparently he had grabbed the first thing he could get his hands on.

"It'll just take a few minutes." Shelly had heard the news late last night and she barely made herself wait until Mama Rose left for work to come over.

"Tell me what's going on, Shelly." His voice actually sounded concerned. Light from the sun's rays reflected off the golden tablecloth, illuminating his face and softening his expression.

"Mr. Flannery is going to evict Mama Rose and me. I mean he's not going to renew our lease. Mrs. Flannery heard that Mama Rose was planning to ask her husband if she could buy our house when our lease is up. When she told Mr. Flannery, he came to see us. He said he has relatives moving in from out of state and they'll be taking over the place when our lease is done. Mr. Schultz, I know that you two are friends. Maybe you could speak to him today. You know how hard my grandmother works and what a good person she is. She really doesn't deserve this. Mr. Flannery has always known that she wanted to eventually buy the place."

To Jake's look of surprise, she continued, "She has been saving all of her extra money from her cooking and cleaning jobs up town."

"That's commendable, Shelly. I know white people who don't work as hard and have no idea of actually owning their homes."

Shelly decided to let that comment pass. Looking directly at Jake's face she continued, "She came here to make a better life for us. She said she couldn't save my mother, but she was determined to save me. Mr. Schultz, I don't care about myself; but Mama Rose, this is her dream. Our old neighborhood was dirty and rat-infested…"

Jake laid his hand on her shoulder. She jumped.

"I can't make him sell his house if he doesn't want to."

"Mama Rose won't say anything, but she's heartsick. Can't you try?"

He hesitated, "I'll talk to Flannery, Shelly. I can't promise anything. He's a hard man. I have a few repairs to make around the house. I'll go this evening."

She managed a weak smile, a thank you, and got up to leave.

*W*asn't this just what Jake had hoped for: to never have to worry about Mark and Shelly again, their connection permanently severed? People would miss Rose though. The community changed for the better when she arrived. Mama Rose never stood on ceremony. She spoke to everyone, knew everyone's problems. When Mr. Smith lost his job, Mama Rose lent his family money. When Kate Lucas's baby was born, Mama Rose stayed by her side until her mother could come. People were always making excuses to pass by her house and participate in one of her talks. She had a way of seeing past the words and getting to what was really in their hearts. One time she'd have you bent over laughing and the next time you'd want to strangle her. "Too close for comfort," Rose would say with a wink. She helped people to see things in new and different ways. He was ashamed to admit it, but he knew this from personal experience. Years ago when she helped Mark, she told him that all he needed to do was to remember that God's children came in all colors. If he went to Flannery, his debt would be paid. Yes, he'd do it and be done.

Jake knew that Joe and Margaret Flannery were from the old school: "Keep a nigger in his place," is what they would say. They owned four houses including their own. All of them were run-down and ill-kept. He knew because he had worked on them when Flannery felt a repair couldn't be avoided. Jake was sure the property value of Rose's house had doubled since she moved in. Tons of work went into it, too much in his opinion. Before she moved in, her house was by far the most run-down of Flannery's properties.

Sometimes he'd watch Mama Rose try to repair a doorframe or adjust the wooden slats on her porch. When she was at work he'd take his tools over and straighten out the mess she had made of it. He'd see other neighbors doing for her, too. It wasn't charity, more like mutual aid. These were the people that Mama Rose had helped in some way.

Her porch was like an outside living room. He thought there were too many flowers, too many oranges, pinks and bright purples, and it was too gaudy for his taste. Still it was these touches that made Rose's place special. She deserved her chance. He'd try to help her get it.

Okay, Shelly had to admit it; Jake had mellowed toward her grandmother. She suspected he was the one who put up the delicate picket fence around the rose garden that she and Mark had planted so many years ago. Now she was certain of it. Maybe he wasn't such a hateful human after all, just a man who was worried about his son.

It wasn't that Shelly didn't trust Jake Schultz. She just wanted the assurance of knowing he hadn't abandoned his mission. As soon as it could properly be called evening she took a broom, a book, knitting needles and yarn out to the porch. She busied herself there, waiting for Jake to leave, which he soon did.

Feeling calmer, she sat down to knit. The black wool would make a nice scarf for James. Up one row, down the next, she wasn't really much good at it. The needles felt even more awkward in her hands today than usual. They were soon laid to rest. Jane Austen's *Pride and Prejudice* was her favorite novel. Tonight she couldn't get off the first page. When she realized that she had read it three times without actually reading it at all, she spied Jake's massive form headed back toward their homes. It was too quick. Joe Flannery would not have been persuaded in such a short time. Jake hadn't been successful. His heart wasn't in it. Listening to his excuses would have to wait for another day. She picked up her busy-work and headed for her room.

Jake could see Shelly pretending to read. He knew she was really waiting for him. He wasn't looking forward to the confrontation. In all the years Shelly and Mama Rose had been living next door to him they had never really asked him for one thing. And to tell the truth, he owed Mama Rose. Going to Flannery was beyond stupid, but would he have been able to face Rose again if he hadn't? The encounter still stung.

A sense of folly came over him as he approached the run-down two-story house. The previously white shutters were now a putrid gray-green. Dust and dirt lay an inch thick on the welcome mat and a foul stench wafted from the windows, Margaret's cooking or cleaning. She had been a fair-looking woman when she was younger. Time, it seemed, was much too cruel to some. He knocked hard on the door. The doorbell hung from its plate by two wires. The door flew open and a loud booming voice screeched a familiar greeting:

"Jake, honey, what brings you here?" Margaret's wide potato face wore a hideous grin, made worse by her intense red lipstick. She grabbed him by his hand and dragged him inside. Joe rose from his recliner slowly. He was a tall wiry man, always smoking something, cigarettes or a pipe. Jake thought he'd start out light.

"I see tobacco's still your best girl."

"I'm his best girl," Margaret said, closing the space between herself and Jake. She pressed her over-ripe and withering bosom up against his chest.

"Girl's got a crush on you, Jake, always has. It's been a long time since we've seen your sorry puss around here. To what do we owe the pleasure?"

"About Miss Rose…"

"You heard. That nigger had the nerve to think she was going to own my property," Margaret bellowed.

"Yeah, well, her granddaughter came to see me this morning…" Jake tried to remain calm.

" Uppity little…"

"I said I'd come and speak to you."

"Speak to us about what?" Joe questioned, advancing on him, "No, don't tell me; you've turned nigger lover."

He was sure that Joe was reflecting on their first meeting. He had come to him asking why he had rented to Negros and now he was asking why Joe wouldn't allow them to buy.

Joe and Margaret took turns spewing obscenities and racial slurs. They accused him of being weak and easily influenced. They told him that ownership made niggers equal to white folks in the eyes of the law. They'd never consider such a thing. Suddenly he was nine years old again and in his parents' living room. The smell of mothballs and ammonia assailed his nostrils. He wasn't a man who was easily intimidated, but at that moment he would have preferred to be any other place. His uneasiness shook him to the core. Max and Maxine loomed above him. He had to get out of there.

Nothing was accomplished. It was a fool's errand. He vaguely remembered telling them that Mama Rose was different, that everyone in the neighborhood liked her. At hearing this, Margaret tangled her face so that her top lip touched the tip of her nose; she balled her hands into gripping fists and hurled herself in his direction. He really didn't remember how he got out of there, but he had. Now he was walking toward home and toward disappointment.

Fortunately for him, Shelly hadn't waited for an explanation. Fine, he didn't have anything good to tell her. At the end of the month he'd help them load the moving trucks. Shouldn't he be happy?

ake rolled over in his bed. His mouth was cottony. He yawned a tremendous yawn and reluctantly planted his feet on the rug. "Moving day." He shook his head, trying to wrap his mind around the thought. His cavernous room had been a place to play and have grand adventures when it had belonged to Uncle Thomas and he had been a visitor. When he inherited the house, he imagined sharing it with the perfect woman, Irene. When Mark became a curious wanderer, this room had become his place of solitude and escape. And today, the day that Rose and Shelly were moving away, it was just one more reminder of how small and lonely his life had become. These were the thoughts Jake would have had if he allowed himself to think such things, which, everyone knew, he didn't. Besides, everyone knew he was harsh and unfeeling. Why should he do anything to contradict their perceptions of him now?

He pulled a flannel shirt from the closet, put on a pair of work pants and was at Rose's before the sun was ready to greet him. Rose would be up, too. She didn't like the sun to catch her not taking advantage of its brightness, as she was so fond of saying. They had often run into each other in the wee hours on their way to some destination or another and he had, unavoidably, been victim of her advice on many of these top-of-the-day rendezvous. Jake sucked in a gulp of air on his way up the stairs.

The porch was barren. Rose had moved all of her planters, dismantled the glider and gotten rid of the bench. No flowers, no plants, no crochet projects and no reminders that her porch had been the heart and soul of the neighborhood. Her door was ajar. He'd go in and get started. A large gilded mirror lay a few feet from the entry; he leaned to move it. "Be gentle with that, Jake. My mother bought it at an antique shop in New York." He silently mouthed the words she had just said to him. New York? No wonder Rose put on such airs. It seemed there was no end to the places she'd been and the things she'd seen.

Jake was floored at the number of valuables Mama Rose possessed. Her stuff caused you to scratch your head though. There was an absurd mix of quality and junk, a menagerie of the useful and useless. But to be honest, even the junk took on the look of luxury in her place. It was all arranged with care and thoroughly clean. He could appreciate that, being a man who liked a neat house. Still he wondered at her reasoning. She had placed a cheap blue vase with artificial flowers right next to a genuine Swedish crystal candy dish. Why would she have artificial flowers when she grew so many real ones? And where did she get the money for the things she had? The painting that sat above her couch looked to be the same caliber as the ones in his childhood home, and he knew how much his parents paid for them. They had a habit of price-dropping whenever people called.

Mama Rose had told some cock-and-bull story about her family coming up from the South during the war and doing factory work. That part wasn't hard to believe. Work was easy enough to come by and coloreds generally got paid as much as whites, the need for manpower being as great as it was back then. But what was hard to believe is that they'd save all that money rather than running out to spend it on something frivolous like fur coats, knowing full well they had no place to wear them. Then there was the part he absolutely refused to believe. Mama Rose said that she had lived in the basement of an apartment building with about five other colored families in makeshift shacks, one separated from another by only plywood or in some cases cardboard. The white man who owned the building asked as much rent from the basement tenants as he asked of the white tenants living above. Rubbish. Was she trying to get sympathy or something?

All day long and into the night coloreds, whites, Jews and everybody in between went up and down the stairs loading Rose's belongings into cars and trucks. At the end of the day, Mrs. Cole had asked him why he wasn't driving. With a gruffness that didn't become even him, he told her that he had been up before dawn moving things before any of them had arrived. He was tired and thought he'd let somebody else have some of the fun. The truth was that he didn't want to know where Rose lived so he wouldn't have to lie to Mark if the subject ever came up.

There was that one last load and for better or worse, he'd be officially done with Rose and Shelly Madison. Speaking of…she was now calling his name.

"Mr. Schultz, would you mind coming over here?" He pretended not to hear her and picked up a huge box and hefted it into the backseat of Nancy Cole's pea-green sedan. He had gotten a glimpse of Shelly's expression. Poor girl. He couldn't remember when he had seen such a pained and dejected face.

"Mr. Schultz, please." It wasn't to be avoided; he had to go over. She was sitting in James Sr.'s truck with his son Jimmy. James had found himself the envy of the neighborhood. His new truck had the largest flatbed available; it was highly polished to a midnight glisten and spotlessly clean. James Johnson Sr. was a proud old Negro man; word was his son was even prouder. Jake had overheard numerous stories when he found time to sit on his porch and read the *Times*. On Sundays when the church wasn't having anything in the afternoon, Rose and her hen party would talk about Widower Johnson. The word was James Sr.'s brother, Kenneth, was into policy playing, running numbers: a betting and gambling operation. His was one of the most well-established businesses on the South Side. He always paid off with a smile and never cheated the betters or his employees. A Robin Hood-type, Kenneth Johnson put large amounts of money into the community to benefit the poor and struggling in the area. It was he who had loaned James the money to start his moving and car repair businesses. They even had employees that young Jimmy, rumored to be a smart boy, supervised. And he just about ran their moving company.

Jake remembered how appalled he had been to learn that young Jimmy charged two rates: one for coloreds and a higher one for whites which, Jake had to admit, was still lower than most white companies charged them. When Jake had asked Jimmy why he did it, he said he charged only what the market would allow. He said that there was such a thing as "white rights," something that you got just from being white in the U.S.; he was just trying to even things out a bit. Here he stopped, looked Jake right in the eye, put his hand on Jake's shoulder and added with a sneer, "Don't worry, Mr. Schultz, when you're ready, I'll move you for free." Jake wanted to like the boy who would end up with Rose's granddaughter, so he chose not to make anything of that comment.

He made his way over to the passenger side of the truck. He could tell Shelly was struggling to keep herself calm.

"How can I help you, Shelly?" He rested his hand on the door window seal. She reached out and grabbed his hand. Holding it in hers, she stroked the back of it gently. Jimmy frowned. For some reason, Jake didn't mind.

"Mr. Schultz," she started, "I want you to know that I realize you did your best for me and Mama." Jimmy grunted.

Still trying to like him, still trying to like him, Jake repeated in his mind.

"But things just didn't work out." She turned her head and ran her free hand over her mouth while turning slightly away. Jimmy blew an aggravated breath, looked straight ahead and clutched the steering wheel with both hands.

"I want you to know that through all the good and the bad..." her eyes were soft and tender. Jake felt his gut go tight. "You and ... that you were a good neighbor and that this was the best place anyone could ever live." With her head fully turned away, she dropped his hand.

He stood for a minute, not knowing how to respond. As he pursed his lips to say goodbye, that uppity Jimmy threw the car in gear and floored the gas. Jake stood for a long while staring after them. His breath was short and becoming labored. Physically he was strong as a horse, always had been and always would be, of that he was sure. Yet he felt awful. A crushing blackness descended on him. He shook himself. This was nothing but his imagination. Still, he would miss... Could he actually be this demented? Everyone had gotten along just fine before Rose came— seems so long ago—and everyone would get along just fine now that she was gone. For an instant, no longer than it took to swat a lazy fly on a 100-degree day, Jake felt his heart ache. He was tired. He lumbered to his room and slept straight through the night and far into the next day.

For weeks his fears of confronting Mark had been allayed. Mark was visiting home less and less and he had stayed away a particularly long stretch this time. He rarely called and certainly never wrote. Walking around his empty house and looking listlessly out the window had become Jake's major pastime. No one new had rented Mama's house, which was hard to believe with the housing shortage. Joe and Margaret were having to eat that lie about relatives wanting the place. Ugh, their kin living right next door; now there was a scary thought. They were such poor business people. They probably hadn't bothered to advertise. And word of mouth through the neighborhood would be slow in getting around. No one wanted to take Rose's house away from her. It was illogical, but then when people were emotional, there was just no telling how they would act. Jake had prided himself on being strong but there was such a void in him these days that he was actually tempted to drink. If it didn't make him such a moron, he believed he would have succumbed long ago, anything to lessen the nagging feeling of melancholy that pervaded his days and nights. There was just no bright spot. He sure missed Mark. If he didn't come home soon, Jake would break down and call him.

Moonless and overcast, the entire Midwest was in a state of despair. That was as far as Mark was concerned. He was so unhappy and the gloom that hung about him, he could just about touch it. Was there any reason to feel this way? How could anyone bear it? Was there any cure for it? He looked out of his dormitory window and such a pang of homesickness hit him that his stomach lurched. His roommate, Charlie, certainly didn't help. He moped most of the time, and what a slob. Mark cleaned, he messed. How could a grown man miss the glass entirely when pouring a drink and walk away as if nothing happened? And do you think the slob could confine his clutter to his side of the room? No, that would have been too easy. When there were piles of homework, trash and food in his own bed, he'd just hop into Mark's. Mark had tried begging, threatening and blackmailing. If there was a secret to getting Charlie motivated, he certainly hadn't found it. Charlie was out tonight. He'd actually found someone who would put up with him, a nice girl, really, with long brown hair and an intelligent wit. Mark had seen her first and invited her up for lunch. She took one look at sorry Charlie and took to him. She preferred him—go figure. Gazing out the window and seeing one brick dorm after another, Mark realized he had to get out of his room. He had never imagined he could be so self-pitiful. A trip home was definitely called for. Missing class wasn't his style, but as with all things some change was good.

The drive was long and tedious. The country roads meandered up one hill and down the next. Hours of dire dark lay behind and even more lay ahead. Daffy deer darted to the edge of the road and smiled—smiled— he was going daft. If he didn't get home soon he'd become a statistic, running into one of those ten-foot high bunnies he kept seeing.

Rumpled, bleary-eyed and half-crazed, Mark arrived home at about 2:00 A.M. He got a sudden twinge when he realized that nobody but Charlie would miss him back at school. And Charlie's only regret would be that he didn't have anybody to find his assignments, which were more than likely hidden under multiple books, plates with bits of food still on them and sundry other generally disgusting stuff. The only people he associated with were students, professors and employers. He didn't have any real friends. He didn't see any reason to form attachments. College was just a vehicle to get from where he was to where he wanted to be. Why pick up passengers along the way, was how he saw it. Visits home were seldom, but they grounded him. A hearty hug from his dad, an occasional sighting of an old friend, one of Mama Rose's impromptu talks, a sneak glance at Shelly and he was good for a few more months. His focus was on what was ahead, not what was behind. He didn't need much to keep him going.

Finally his home was in sight. He was too tired to exorcise the demons that had plagued him all the way to the house, a feeling of foreboding, impending doom. He really had to lay off the horror novels for a while. He exited his small car and trudged wearily toward his door. Quicksand would have been easier to manage than trying to work his fatigued legs. The screen door weighed a ton under his unsteady grasp.

He turned the key in the lock and was immediately greeted by an eerie glow. He was temporarily mesmerized by miniature black-and-white particles intermingling, converging, so congruent and continuous you could hardly tell where one ended and the other began—static. Jake had left the television on. He lay across from it slumped on their soft tweed sofa, his mouth gaping and his eyelids slightly parted. When had he taken to doing this? His dad was a man in control of his surroundings. He didn't like to wake at odd times or to be uncomfortable when he slept, yet there he was.

"Pop, wake up, Pop." Mark gave his dad a vigorous shake.

"Huh, what? Oh, son, I knew you'd come." Jake's large fingers rounded Mark's shirtsleeve. Tugging hard he gave himself a heft up.

Mark's brow knit and he ran his free hand through his hair. Now standing, Jake was no longer asleep but he certainly wasn't awake.

"Pop, you okay?"

"Oh sure, Mark. You must think I've gone crazy."

"Well, the thought had crossed my mind. What's going on around here? Since when did you start falling asleep downstairs in front of the set?"

"Since…Mammm…"

"What, Pop? You're mumbling."

"Nothing, boy. Here, let me look at you." Jake pushed Mark back an arm's length, firmly grasping his shoulders. He looked him up and down, "I'm surprised, that's all. It's good to see you." He pulled Mark firmly into his chest and wrapped his muscular arms around him for an encompassing hug.

When Jake held on extra long, Mark pulled back, tilted his head and looked directly into his father's eyes. Something was going on. He was weary from the drive and decided to let it go until morning.

"Pop," he said in a last attempt to fully rouse Jake.

"What time is it, son?" Jake was starting to steady himself.

"2:00 A.M."

"Oh man, you must be tired. Let's go to bed. You can tell me all about school tomorrow. I'm really glad you're here, son."

Mark opened the door to his room. It was as he'd left it, albeit a bit nippy. He went over to the closet to get extra blankets. This was odd; one of Jake's ties was strewn sloppily on the window seat. Maybe he had a date come over and had sat on the window seat to watch her leave. He felt his mouth curl into a smile. He really was suffering from sleep deprivation. His dad was anything but sentimental. He definitely had not been sitting in that seat looking wistfully after some woman. Still it was obvious that he had been there. Maybe his tie was draped over his shoulder after a long day, and he happened to hear a noise outside on the way to his room and came to investigate.

It wasn't anything big, but these little things said something had changed. His father was meticulous about keeping things clean and in order. For a minute Mark puzzled about what was going on with his dad. It was probably nothing. He had been so wired from the caffeine it took to get him here that his mind was probably conjuring up things to think about. At any rate, whatever it was or wasn't, it could wait until morning. His brain was beginning to feel thick and clumsy; forming coherent thought was becoming more and more difficult.

*D*iscordant strands drifted in and out of his consciousness. "Come out, come out, wherever you are." He stretched his arm in her direction. She was there. She wasn't there. Just beyond the length of his grasp she lingered. She was begging his touch. She was rejecting him.

"Come on, this isn't funny. Come out." A distinct ache and a feeling of longing accompanied him as he succumbed to a deep sleep.

Mark woke famished. He literally ran down the stairs and to the cupboards to grab the corn flakes while using his free hand to grab the jar of milk from the counter where his dad had left it. As he kicked his leg over the back of the chair to sit at the table, he caught a glimpse out the window on the side of the house that faced Mama Rose's porch. In the space of a second, his mind's eye noticed that something was different.

He focused more closely on the porch. Mark had a feeling he wasn't going to like the answer to the question he was about to ask, "So what did Mama Rose do with all her stuff, the bench and planters?"

"She took 'em with her, I guess."

Watching separate flakes of yellow floating scattered on a sea of white, he continued, "With her?"

His voice became strained as the milk and cereal stuck, clumped in his throat.

"Where'd she go?" he muttered.

"How should I know?" Jake spat out, slamming his palm loudly on the table.

Mark felt as if all of the air had suddenly been sucked out of the room. He couldn't swallow and everything looked blurry, "I'll be back, Pop. Just remembered something," gripping the table with both hands, he slowly pushed his chair back, got up, and walked quickly up the stairs.

"What's the matter, son?"

Jake asked the question to which no response was needed.

Mark went to his room. Nothing was changed. Neat chenille still covered his bed. Posters of his favorite cars still hung from the walls, along with Elvis. The blue stuffed cushion still occupied the window seat; his knees would have given out years ago without that cushion. Everything was the same, yet nothing was the same.

That feeling of comfort: gone. The predictability that everyone claimed to hate but secretly craved was stripped from him. He hardly ever talked to Mama Rose anymore, but when he needed it, really needed it, she would talk to him. And even when he didn't talk to her, he could stand outside her house and look up at her porch. The wooden bench handed down from Grandma Fanny told about a time when Mama Rose was a child in Louisiana sitting by the dark and mysterious bayou. She said the flowing water would soothe her weary spirit when the ignorance of adults became too much to bear. Then there was the glider covered with Shelly's handmade throw. It was multicolored and the stitching was uneven. At first she was ashamed of it, but Mama Rose called it beautiful so many times that Shelly said it was an abomination to call it anything else. Abomination, now there was a word. Who said abomination any more?

Mark envisioned flowers: brilliant red, blushing purple, faint yellow and pink—gone. And the smells, he knew he was home long before he reached it because the perfume of Rose's flowers called to him. The roses! Mark rushed to the window. Covered but still there. Thank God.

A deep pain rose from the pit of his stomach and raced through his chest as he collapsed into the chair near the window. Something like nothing he had ever experienced gripped him. He couldn't make himself explore it. When he tried, the pain was so piercing he felt as though he would die. Home, his feeling of home was gone; the longing was so abysmal it was as though an invisible shield protected him from delving too deeply. He wanted to flee the emotions he was experiencing, but the same shield that protected him closed him in. It was inescapable; it was everywhere.

Seized by an idea, Mark became energized. He rushed to the door; pulling it open, he started to call his dad. He would ask his father to employ the same detectives he had used to locate him and his mother all those years ago. They could find Mama Rose and Shelly. The absurdity of the request hit him like ice water on the face of an imbecile. There would be no detectives and no help. The darkness overtook him. He didn't emerge from his room until the next day, packed and ready to return to school.

Downstairs Jake waited for a son who would not be coming today and perhaps not ever. Had he done the right thing? He looked around the room. He had always been so proud of his accomplishments. Managing his own home at seventeen, working his own construction and fix-it business, and raising his son, alone. Mark was his biggest accomplishment. He was loving, kind and intelligent. He would be respected: an educated man, somebody. He might not know it now, but someday he'd have everything. Nothing and no one was going to get in the way of this. He had done the right thing by not telling Mark about their leaving, so why did he feel like such a jerk?

The house was too empty. Mark had been gone a year and Jake thought he'd never get used to it. High school hadn't been like this at all. Mark stayed out late with his friends and sometimes went on trips with the football team, forensics, or some other activity he was involved in. But he always came home. Since that fateful visit when Mark discovered that Mama Rose and Shelly had moved, he made constant excuses not to come home. Jake missed him terribly.

Then there was Rose. When she had first moved away, people would come by looking for her. From time to time, they'd ask him about the old crow. So much fuss over a Negro. Why in the world were people so worked up? So they didn't have their mid-evening talks, offers to sample Southern cooking or delicate hand-crocheted scarves. Why she insisted he take one of those ragged-looking things was still a mystery to him. He'd get around to tossing it one day. Even Irene didn't bother to visit now that Mark was gone. Life was losing its luster. If he wasn't still young and looking toward something better, he might have thrown in the towel like so many others living through these turbulent times. But he did hope for something, though he wasn't sure what.

College whizzed by for Mark. He graduated with honors and went on to study advertising. Something about using his gift, as Mama Rose put it, made advertising a natural choice. She said he needed— *GET OUT OF MY HEAD, MAMA ROSE!* No matter how many years it had been, some saying of hers was always on the edge of his thoughts. Anyway, she was right, he had a natural gift for persuasion and an even more apparent gift for perceiving people's needs. This made advertising a good fit. Give the people what they want and make sure they know they want it.

At times Mark had been tempted to feel guilty about never being the right age or having some circumstance that allowed him to opt out of military service, but this particular war in Vietnam seemed so ill-fated. Frankly, he was glad to be spending 1968 this side of the war, a civilian, out of the trenches and away from the controversy. He was sincerely grateful to those who were there. The irony of it all: young troops promoting democracy, the very thing that allowed him to be here while they were there. Who could make sense of it all? Anyway, here is where he was, and his success still surprised him.

Working for just a short while with a firm, he was on the verge of going solo. And he would have, had he not met Mason Dobbs, a portly but brilliant man, who offered him an almost guaranteed partnership in the space of a year. All Mark had to do was to prove his mettle. It was the challenge that most attracted him, but he also reasoned, becoming partner at an established firm would set him as a major player in the business he meant to make his own.

Chapter Seven
The Career

*B*randon and Dobbs was one of the up-and-coming advertising agencies in the Chicagoland area. It had over fifty employees: three advertising executives including Mark Schultz, the new guy who had spent a very brief stint in marketing before his hasty promotion. He had already handled several accounts, and this physical move was only making the promotion official. Today the entire office was ablaze with speculation: How good was he really? The buzz was that he was a real "looker." Was he really being positioned for partner—wouldn't that ruffle a few well-established feathers?

Mason Dobbs, Chief Executive Officer of the company, told Lois, his secretary, to clear out Eric Brandon's office. Brandon, who graced the company with his presence only occasionally, was the money of the company. He didn't hold any official title but did insist that his name appear on the stationery, the business records and the front of the building. Advertising had been his father's business and dream. When the old man died, Eric Brandon II didn't have the heart to abandon the company; instead he quickly took on a "partner," Mason Dobbs, and left the day-to-day operations to him. Brandon made courtesy appearances, insisted on having an office and weighed in on what he considered the most important decisions. It was his rarely used office that Dobbs was clearing.

He moved Mr. Brandon's nameplate to a room a few doors down, which lacked amenities and had become a sort of storage space.

Dobbs personally oversaw the move, which included a couple of files, a telephone and a personal water cooler. On his way out of the office door, he looked at Lois, shook his head and tipped his lip at the corner. "An empty office for an absent partner." He then gripped his pants by the belt and hoisted them up. He adjusted his wire-rimmed glasses and walked away laughing to himself. Not ten minutes later he hustled back to Lois's desk. "Miss Niffe, please don't mention that unfortunate comment I made earlier to any one; very unprofessional, very unprofessional."

"No, sir, I've already forgotten it." Too bad the man never joked, didn't even seem to have a sense of humor. His attempt at making a wisecrack was funny in and of itself. She had told three people before he was safely out of earshot. Oops.

This moving of offices was also too juicy to keep a lid on. Why would Mr. Dobbs be clearing Brandon's office? Would he be taking it himself? No, he was much too modest for such an ostentatious setup. She'd take a little run down to the general secretarial area. Everybody knew what horrible gossips they were. Someone was bound to know something.

Lois nearly toppled herself as she pushed her chair back from her desk. She did a bit of a wheelie before using the heel of her pump as a brake to regain her balance. She jumped from the chair and did a most undignified sprint toward the ladies already huddled in deep conversation.

"Have you seen the new guy they brought across from marketing?" Diane was asking the ladies of the secretarial pool as she sat tentatively on the edge of Gail's desk.

"Oh my god, I think I'm gonna pee my pants. He is absolutely gorgeous."

"I hear Mr. Dobbs is grooming him for partner."

"That explains it." Lois rushed toward the assembly, bumping Diane as she slid to a stop. She managed to grab her hand before Diane hit the floor.

"Explains what?" Diane growled, as she allowed herself to be helped back to her feet.

"The office—"

Nina cut Lois off. "I hear he might be, you know…" She threw out her wrist and fanned an over-ripe girl kind of flourish, "A 'pretty boy.' It could refer to his face or it could refer to something else."

"No, you don't think Schultz is queer?" Lois's hand flew to her mouth.

"I can't say for sure."

"But he's so masculine, so strong-looking. I'd love to be wrapped in his oh-so-muscular arms." Diane licked her lips and hugged herself while whirling her hips.

"Amanda had that pleasure, but the relationship didn't last long. She said they were intimate but it didn't go anywhere." To their puzzled looks, Nina said, "You know, sex."

"You all know I'm an absolute man-lover, right?" She waited for their confirmation, "But if I were a man, I'd get with Amanda…" Diane started.

"Shuu, who's that with Mr. Dobbs, getting off the elevator?"

"It's him!" Diane stood up tall and adjusted her blazer.

Mr. Dobbs was the working partner. It was no secret that although he appeared obtuse, Dobbs was brilliant and overworked. He was looking for a real partner, someone to lighten his load. Brandon, the moneyman, would have to okay a new partner and he would be inclined to choose either Amanda Cole or Cameron O'Neil. Dobbs didn't particularly like or trust either. However, he knew they were both capable, if not remarkable in talent. He had almost given in and deferred to his partner's judgment when he met the impressive Mark Schultz.

Dobbs was a stark contrast to Mark Schultz. He was about five-foot two, pale and pot-bellied. A cordial manner and a quick smile were the only complements he ever wore with his usual long-sleeved white shirts, black tie—slack at the neck—and black pants. He threw on a less-than-pressed jacket, which he kept in his closet, for events that he deemed more formal.

And Mark, Mark was the embodiment of "tall, dark and handsome." He was six three, broad-shouldered and long-legged. His hair was midnight brown with flecks of gold shimmer and his eyes, an intense brown, the depth of which seemed endless. A dimple at his left cheek gave his face a hint of whimsy while his strong jaw disallowed any attribution of femininity that might be associated with his striking features. He was pleasing and appeared kind, but there was something guarded about him and a hint of fierceness lurked below his surface. His clothes, while impeccable in fit and style, could barely improve the man who wore them.

The women stood in awe, at first unable to speak when Mr. Dobbs made the introductions.

Irene pulled her wool collar up around her neck. Her teeth chattered, but she was determined to complete her trek. Her sometimes on-again-off-again car was off again, broken down for what seemed to be the hundredth time. She didn't mind walking. She was used to it, and it had been a long time since she had felt any real fear—caution, but not fear. Tonight she was angry. The pink underbelly of the looming clouds, with gleaming streaks of leftover light shining through, seemed a mocking contrast to the neighborhood below where Mama Rose was now forced to reside. This neighborhood was dingy, dirty and disgusting.

Irene had long ago resigned herself to living in this type of environment. When she gave Mark to Jacob, her quality of life deteriorated quickly. She just didn't seem to care anymore. And without her son she didn't have to try as hard to find decent accommodations. Often she settled for any place she could stay warm at night. These days even that wasn't a guarantee. Irene stopped on the corner. She fumbled through her ripped pocket hoping that her 75-cent, silver-plated lighter had not fallen out of her coat. "There you are," she mumbled. She turned her body toward the building and lit a cigarette. She puffed it quick and hard, trying to get it done so that the smell would subside before she reached Mama Rose's. This living situation was making her sick. A woman of Rose's stature should not have to endure this. She smiled when she thought about what Rose would say: Endure, honey, I adore whatever God grants me. I'm alive and well, anything beyond that is gravy. Such a fine woman, she deserved so much better.

These long walks gave Irene time to think. She had learned that people were frail and loaded with insecurities. No one was constant but God and he forgives any who wish it. There was no one too bad for redemption. Hope reigned. So, even this dingy drug-infested community was filled with those who would repent and come to live better lives. Still, the daily sight of heroin addicts huddled together in the doorway of an abandoned building, not a half-block away from Rose's and the vacant lot next door, cluttered with an inexhaustible source of garbage and broken glass, constantly marred her efforts to make her little yard look nice. Irene knew it was Rose's dignity that made her continue to try. A few of the other residents had taken note. Some of the people in the nearby buildings had started to try to do something in their yards and on their porches, even though many lived in buildings where the landlords should have cared for such things.

By now Shelly would be gone and Mama Rose would be alone. Like at the first house before Rose and Shelly moved, Irene had basically memorized Shelly's schedule and managed to stay away when she was home. She figured Shelly knew something about her, but she didn't ask Mama Rose what she shared, and, frankly, she was happy for the anonymity. Shelly was a busy woman, working at her sales job, participating in her clubs and lately she had become seriously involved with James Johnson, a high school sweetheart. Irene had seen him several times from a distance. He was handsome enough, and Rose only had good things to say about him. It seemed foolish to think about it now, but Mark and Shelly had seemed so compatible as children. Jake was probably right about that one however. What kind of life could a white man and a colored woman have in these times? Still, a mother's fondest wish was to see her child happy, and Mark had never been the same since he and Shelly stopped being close.

If it wasn't going to be Mark, Irene figured James Johnson was as good a man as any. Poor Mark, would he ever find his soul mate? One more block and she'd be at Rose's doorstep. It wasn't right for Rose to be alone so much. She needed company.

"Mama, Mama!" Irene knocked hard. Rose was slow getting to the door.

"Are you okay in there?" she was saying as Mama Rose opened the door.

"Yes, I'm okay. What about you?"

"I was worried about you, Mama."

"Irene, why are you always worrin'? God takes care of me, honey. And what he don't do personally, the Smith boys across the street will." Rose was pointing to a big Negro man in his doorway wearing an awful scowl.

"You know people over there? How? That building was empty only a month ago."

"I talks to 'em. It's as simple as that. You want to know people. You show yourself friendly, that's all. Now give me your coat and sit down for a while."

"Don't you ever feel lonely or worried?"

"I guess everybody feels that way sometimes. But I don't waste time dwellin' on it. I gets my Word and I pray. I've prayed so many times in the past for God to make me strong. He done gone and answered that prayer."

"Are you sure you're okay, Mama? What took you so long to answer the door?"

"I was talkin' to an old friend of Shelly's. She's got some trouble."

"So you really are okay?"

"Look, baby, I done told you. I'm strong. God made me this way so I can help others."

"Do you think you could help me?"

"I've been waiting for you to ask, simply been waiting for you to ask."

Irene and Mama Rose talked while they dusted the shelves and the furniture. Irene admired the vases on the table, the silver polished trays and the fine tapestry Mama Rose had unfolded. "Where did you get this stuff, Mama?"

"Oh, different places. Some was given to me by my mother, handed down from generation to generation, some I scouted for myself. I know quality from junk."

Irene squinted at an odd piece, giving it a thorough examination.

"That would be junk. Little Annie sold it to me for three times what it's worth."

"You're a blessed woman, Rose."

They bundled up and walked the two blocks to the hardware store where Mama Rose was to get a part for her wringer washer. Irene felt humbled by the number of people who went out of their way to greet Mama Rose. She didn't think that Rose had much money, but she stopped to give a few dollars to some of the people standing on the street. "Mama, why did you give money to that man and not the other one who asked you?"

"Well, honey, Frankie is a good boy, a little slow though. I've watched him. He'll do whatever he can to earn his way. He's swept alleyways, toted trash, cleaned up the meat slaughter area of the meat company over north and just about anything else he could get his hands on. If he's asking for money, he's run on a bad spell and he's discouraged. This little bit of cash might be just the thing to encourage him to try again tomorrow."

"And what about the other one?"

"Daniel, I'm afraid to say, is lazy and the Bible says if you don't work, you don't eat. He's intelligent but conniving. I have no doubt he's hungry, probably spent his last on that fast woman I saw him with earlier. A couple of days on an empty stomach is likely to help him far more than a handout. I try to give people what I think they need and not simply what they want."

"What do I need, Mama?" Irene slowed and pulled a hat from her pocket. Her ears were starting to prickle from the cold.

"That's easy."

Irene waited, and waited, and waited. "Well, Mama, what do I need?"

"Patience."

Irene laughed, something she didn't do nearly enough.

"You also need grace, to love and to be loved, and you need to forgive."

Irene suddenly became pensive, "But I don't know how."

"Who."

"What?"

"You don't know who."

"Mama Rose, I don't think I'll ever understand your riddles."

"Irene, you need to know Jesus the Christ. When you know Him, I mean really know Him, everything else will come."

"Introduce me, Mama."

Brandon and Dobbs had been vying for a number of new clients and rumor had it whoever landed the Kincaid account would make partner. It was unorthodox, but it had Brandon written all over it. And to be frank, Mark knew they had been pitting him against O'Neil and Cole. They were good but he was better; he was confident of it. Nevertheless, in order to maintain his edge, he had to stay on top of every project. While Dobbs was obviously in his corner, surprise projects like the one he was given today were obviously designed by Brandon to test his mettle. Well, he had performed these tests in the past and he could do it again. What Brandon thought of as a challenge, Mark saw as an adventure with a predictable end. It wasn't pride; it was confidence in the abilities he knew he had.

Mark was fortunate enough to rent in a cozy suburb not far from work. His recent acquaintance, Robert Jones, had made him aware of an opening in his building when a long-time tenant had to be relocated to a nursing home by his family following a prolonged illness. Mark swooped in under the radar before the landlord had a chance to place an ad in the paper. It was a well-maintained older brick building with updated amenities. The rent was reasonable, and best of all, it was right upstairs from Bob, with whom he often collaborated, and had become a friend of sorts. Today the coworker/collaborator part of the arrangement was paying off in spades. Bob was doing some research for Mark. He could pick it up, go to his apartment, work on it and be in bed by 10:00. Mark strolled up the long walkway, opened the door and entered the vestibule. He walked up three hall stairs and made his way to Bob and Donna Jones's door. A hard knock brought Bob running.

"Come in, Mark. I just finished the projections you need for the presentation tomorrow. Should have figured you wouldn't even rest your coat before coming to get them. I know what a workaholic you are. People are starting to talk." Bob stood for a moment, apparently waiting for a response to his banter.

Mark scanned the room looking for the folders and note pads that should have been in Bob's hand. Didn't this man get it? The meeting was first thing in the morning and he only had the rest of the evening to prepare for it. He was known for his preparedness and for his ability to meet the tightest deadlines, but his miracles didn't just happen. They did require some work. He needed the updated Blake information and he needed it now.

"Don't you have any social life?"

Mark cut a quick smile and extended his open hand.

"Okay, man. I can take a hint, even the not-so-subtle ones."

Bob was the closest thing Mark had to a friend these days. He was a hard worker and could easily excel if he were more driven. But that was probably the reason they got along: no need to compete. Bob seemed content with his life. And it was obvious he had what he wanted most in the world, Donna. Mark could almost envy him, almost.

Yep, Bob was happily married to one of the sweetest women Mark had ever met. Donna was genuinely giving and open. Mark sniffed the air. He followed a sinfully aromatic fragrance to the dining table situated not five feet from him. Added to Donna's other qualities was the ability to whip up the most delicious meals. His mother was rumored to have that ability. Mark had vague memories of a meal or two. He wondered if her meals looked as delectable as the one laid out on Donna's table.

"Three settings?" he wondered out loud.

"Oh yeah, Donna has a friend over, a really nice girl she met in college." Mark was sorry he'd asked; he really didn't care.

"Getting them," Bob said when Mark raised his other hand and shook the two toward heaven in desperation. "Wait here."

Bob left the living room and went into his study. Mark looked at his watch and walked into the kitchen to get a glass of water. Hearing stirrings in the living room, he walked back out.

"Hey, man, enough's enou…"

"Mark!"

"Shelly!" They stood staring at each other as if they had both seen ghosts.

A few minutes later Bob and Donna came strolling out of the study with sheepish looks on their faces. "Oh, Mark, man, I'm sorry to have kept you waiting, I see you've met Shel—"

"Yes, we've met," Mark replied.

"Have you?" Donna jumped in.

"Yes," Shelly added, a quiver in her voice. "We were neighbors when we were children. I'd see Mark, from time to time, when he stayed with his father." Mark was vaguely aware of Donna and Bob staring at him; he didn't care.

"Here is the research you were so anxious to get." Bob grabbed Mark's arm and started to escort him to the door. Mark twisted at the waist, but his feet remained planted. So did his gaze; it never left Shelly.

Donna seized the moment. "We've got lots of food here, Mark, would you like to…"

"Donna, he's got work to do. You know our Mark. All work and…" It was clear that Bob was having fun at his expense.

Again, Mark didn't care, "I'd love to, Donna, thanks for asking."

Melding, shattering? He couldn't tell which. He was supposed to be preparing the Blake report, yet there he sat eating food he couldn't taste while watching an apparition who couldn't be real. It was the same one that came to him in unguarded moments: that time between sleep and wake where your conscious relinquished and your unconscious relished.

"Mark, Mark."

You know how they say before you die, your life flashes before your eyes? Mark's was flashing before his: puffy white snowballs in midflight, scorching hot sun beating down on weary faces, rescues, hidden places, stolen hugs, almost kisses, emotions consuming and muddled, a baby, a girl, a woman too exquisite to be real.

"Mark!"

"Huh, what?" He actually shook his head trying to clear his thoughts.

"The food."

"I'm sorry, Donna. You were saying?"

Donna and Bob turned to each other, fascination and amazement playing on their faces. "I said the food must be good. Your plate is empty and you haven't said a word."

*H*ow could God be so cruel? Years. It had taken years to get Mark's ghost to quit walking up and down in her soul. She wasn't going to that place ever again. Mark left ten years ago without so much as a "See ya, take it easy." Maybe the old times hadn't meant anything to him. Did they really mean that much to her? Yes, they had. They were friends, the deepest kind. Even the years of not speaking had not really changed that. Only the departure: the cold leaving had made her doubt. He's no good, and no good will come of this unfortunate reunion. She couldn't look at him; she wouldn't.

Shelly looked to the right, then to the left. Donna and Bob looked perplexed. She wanted to say something to make things better for them, but she couldn't seem to get her brain to cooperate. She felt all twisted inside, crazy almost. She was actually afraid to talk. She didn't know what might come out.

"Well, that was pleasant," Bob stated, to which the silent party nodded in unison.

"Okay." He got up, retrieved his contribution to Mark's presentation, pressed it under his friend's arm and led the zombified man to the door.

"Shelly," Mark called across the room, "have lunch with me tomorrow."

Shelly's neck snapped up and her evil tongue betrayed her, "Yes, I will."

"Good, I'll pick you up here at 12:30."

To that, Shelly gave a subtle nod, and Mark was hustled out the door by a broadly grinning Bob.

The dishes were cleared and washed, and curiosity was killing Donna. Finally a chink in the elusive, all-business, Mr. Schultz's armor. In the many months that she and Bob had known Mark, he had remained a mystery. He lived upstairs from them. Occasionally he'd stop by to talk with Bob, usually about business. And even more occasionally he'd play tennis at their club. He never stayed with a woman for very long, and as attractive as he was they usually broke it off. However, this never seemed to bother him. There were even some rumblings about him being homosexual, but Donna couldn't bring herself to believe this. There was just something too masculine about him.

Mark ate slowly, painfully slowly, and although he tried being natural, he kept staring at Shelly. It was so obvious; Shelly had to have noticed, though she seemed to be working overtime not to. Then the surprise lunch invitation; no one could ignore that. What was going on? As soon as Mark left, Donna cornered Shelly.

"So, Shelly, what do you know about our inscrutable Mr. Schultz?" Shelly stood by the balcony window, her fingers splayed against the glass, peering wistfully into the distant dark.

"Well, to start with, the last time I saw him he broke my heart." A quiet smile teased her lower lip.

Donna's curiosity was really piqued now. "Oh yeah, tell me more." She quickly closed the distance between herself and Shelly.

Shelly's neck snapped up, "I was just joking. I was sixteen and I had a childhood crush on him, I think. He went to college without saying goodbye, that's all. I don't know why I really expected him to. We hadn't had much to say to each other the two years before he left."

"I think he regrets that now." Donna couldn't help the mischief brewing in her imagination.

"What would make you say a thing like that?"

"Well, to start with, this is the first time that Mark has ever sat down to an unscheduled dinner with us. The man just doesn't know how to do spontaneity."

"So he was hungry. What does that mean?"

"He came here for papers for a presentation tomorrow that he was just told about today. If you knew Mark, you wouldn't have to ask another question on the subject."

Shelly glanced at her redheaded friend in her neat apartment of tasteful red, gray and white, trying to make sense of what she was saying. Did Donna think that Mark's lunch invitation extended beyond a polite smile, a common courtesy offered to a former neighbor and childhood friend? She wouldn't allow herself to make anything of it. Too much energy had already been spent on forgetting the man.

Irene felt like a chain-smoker. A single pack normally lasted her for months, yet this one was gone in a week. She wondered why she had taken up this filthy habit in the first place. She was often forced to bum cigarettes off strangers. It was too extravagant a pastime for a woman who at times couldn't afford food. And why hadn't Mama Rose said anything to her. Irene knew the woman absolutely detested the smell of smoke. Why had she kept silent? That was only one of the questions she had for Rose. It had been two weeks since she asked to be introduced to Jesus and Mama Rose hadn't even tried to convince her to become a believer. She had seen her work tirelessly to convince others. Was she wrong? Were there people too far gone to be saved? Did Mama Rose think she was one of them? And what about Shelly? Where was she? Had she eloped with James and Mama Rose simply neglected to tell her?

Irene's pace was quick. Her steps ate up the concrete between her apartment and Rose's small house. She was absolutely fuming. It wasn't like Rose to be so guarded. They had to be better friends than this after all this time. Irene was actually miffed with Rose. It worried her. What if Rose was angry with her, too. This could be the end of their friendship.

"Rose." Irene knocked on the door. There was no answer.

"Rose," she said louder, as she added a ring of the doorbell.

"Rose, Rose!" she shouted, agitation filling her voice.

"Is the place on fire?" A calm and familiar voice spoke from behind her.

"Rose." Irene spun on her heel, losing her balance and teetering onto the thin metal railing on the porch.

"That's my name, don't wear it out." Rose quickly made her way up the stairs to steady her friend. "What's wrong with you, chil'? If I didn't know better I'd think you've been drinkin'."

"I haven't, but I want some answers from you."

"My, but we're feisty today. It looks good on you." Rose placed her gloved hand on Irene's cheek before turning to open her door. "Hold this." She gave Irene the paper sack that held her groceries. "I was hoping you'd come today."

"I didn't think you wanted to see me anymore." Irene sat down hard, dejected and sullen.

"Is that why you left Jake?"

"Jacob? This is about you, Mama Rose."

"Oh, I'm Mama again, am I?"

Irene rolled her eyes, "Mama Rose. I thought we were friends."

"We are."

"Then why aren't you concerned about my soul? Why haven't you spent the time on me that you do on some of your other projects?"

"Project? Is that what you think you are to me? Sweet baby, you are like my own sweet daughter. I couldn't love you any better if you were. Now get up off your behind and help me get these groceries put away. You are what we, down south, used to call a" hard case." I couldn't just introduce you to the Lord. I had to let you feel the need. It'll mean forgiveness."

Rose was talking in riddles again.

"But I don't have anybody to forgive. I live and let live. I understand the things you said about Frankie, Daniel, Mrs. Portman, even the Flannerys." By now Irene was removing her coat and sitting comfortably with her head arched up in Rose's direction. This house was cramped compared to the house on Maple Street and even some of the other places Rose had lived after there, but it worked okay for two people.

"Does Jake know you smoke?" Mama Rose walked into the kitchen, turned the knob on the faucet and washed her hands with a bit of laundry detergent.

"Jacob again! What does…" struggling to control her tone, "What does he have to do with anything?"

"I don't know. Why is it that the mere mention of that boy's name makes you crazy? You didn't smoke when you were married, did you?"

"No."

"So why did you start?"

"He hated it."

"Is that why you didn't smoke or why you started up now?"

"My smoking doesn't have a thing to do with Jacob. I was just saying that he never liked cigarette smoke, that's all."

"And he hurt you really badly, didn't he?"

"Listen, Mama, if you don't want to introduce me to Jesus, just say so. There are plenty of churches just waiting to save a sinner like me."

"No one's forcing you to be here, Irene."

"But I thought you wanted me to know Jesus."

"Yes, that's what you said you wanted."

"It is. Can we get to the point, though?"

"I think we just did."

Chapter Eight
Cameron

*C*ameron O'Neil was the man everyone expected to get the job that Mark was undoubtedly being groomed for. He was everything that corporate America wanted: ruthless, cunning and syrupy sweet when it served his purposes. Before Mark came on board, he was also the reigning stud at Brandon and Dobbs. His height, very blond hair and blaze-green eyes made him the favorite with the women.

Cameron, though set back by Mark's arrival, was by no means resigned to Mark getting the promotion he assumed would be his. He believed the rumors about Mark being homosexual but had not found a way to exploit it, yet. There had to be a way to get at Mark. With a little patience and some self-made luck he was sure to find it.

Slow days at the company were rare, but they happened. It seemed these days since Brandon and Dobbs was pondering its choice of partners, the "solo" projects were coming fast and furious. These were projects in which Cameron, Amanda or Mark took the lead and the primary responsibility. It was Mark's day to shine or not. For Cameron, a slow business day left extra time to plot.

Walking toward the secretarial pool, Cameron slowed to note his appearance in the glass partition: virile, keen eyes, suave apparel and to all this was added an outstanding intellect with a dash of cunning. Yes, he was the man to beat. It didn't matter if Dobbs had temporarily deluded himself into thinking otherwise. He passed the door of Amanda Cole, the woman who would be king, and gave her doorknob a gentle twist. Humm, she had it locked, a small precaution she used to keep him from getting a heads-up on her latest project. Oh well, he could always look in on Schultz, the main object of his curiosity.

The "ching" of the elevator drew his attention. *Jones's wife*, he thought, *now there's a woman who could certainly do more to improve her appearance.* Another young lady stood to her side. Cameron stopped in mid-stride. An unassuming beauty, he could tell from her posture and presentation even though her back was to him. And without even a word he knew there was something unique about her, an authority. No woman could ever tame him, but he might be willing to let her try.

Could it be? She's colored, a fact that was temporarily obscured by her long sleeves and skirt, and she was stunning. This day was turning out to be highly entertaining. She was five-foot "fivish" with long legs, a nice small waist and a plump little bottom. Her breasts were smaller than his usual preference, but he could almost feel his fingers weaving their way through her luxuriant wavy hair. It begged to be stroked. This would be a first, dating a colored woman. Yes, he'd consider making an exception for her. He'd be discreet, of course.

*T*he building was much bigger than it looked from the outside. And this suite of offices and cubicles seemed to go on forever. Glass partitions sectioned off the large secretarial pool, which rested in the center of office-lined walls. Judging by the number of doors, the smaller offices ran down each hall with much larger offices at each of the four corners of the building. Everything was official and sterile. The glare of the lighting was almost distracting. Shelly supposed aloud that it was very unlikely anybody nodded off in this place.

"So where's Mark's office?" she asked Donna. Out of nowhere, a tall, well-dressed man sprang to her side. Before Donna could reply, he was giving directions.

"It's down the hall and to the right. Who's inquiring?"

Though taken aback by the question, Shelly responded politely, "A friend."

"I'd assumed as much."

"What did you say?"

"Nothing. I'll be happy to escort you ladies to your destination." Without waiting for a reply, he started walking them down the hall. Shelly could not help but notice how attractive he was: blond, full hair and the most beautiful tropical green eyes. Turning to Donna for her opinion, she was given a quick look of disapproval. Donna grabbed Shelly by her arm and marched her two paces ahead of the handsome stranger. Shelly looked back over her shoulder and shrugged, attempting to give some explanation for her friend's rude behavior.

The hall where Mark's office was located had maroon-colored carpeting. Everything in this part of the building was elegantly apportioned and more formal than the initial space would lead you to anticipate. Mark was just opening his door as Donna prepared to knock.

"Shelly, Donna?" His perfect teeth and dimpled cheek brought back pleasant memories. Abruptly his expression changed. Their escort had caught up to them and was now standing at Shelly's side.

"What are you doing here?"

Donna jumped in, "Shelly and I were in the neighborhood, and I thought it would be nice to show her where you and Bob work."

"I'm busy right now. I'll see you in a couple of hours, Shelly." With that he dismissed all three and was on his way. Shelly didn't know how to feel, but her disappointment was palpable. Donna looked embarrassed.

"Well, it seems Schultz is in over his head today. Can I show you ladies around?" Before Donna could open her mouth, Shelly, with a hint of defiance, said yes.

Shelly could tell Donna wasn't happy with her decision, but she needed a vent for her anger, "Donna, I know you have errands; please go on without me. I can find my way home."

Donna pulled her arm, moving her away from bright eyes, "Shelly, what are you doing?" She whispered, "That's Cameron O'Neil. He's, he's notorious."

Cameron pushed the knot of his tie up and snorted.

"I can take care of myself, Donna."

"I know you can. It's just that—"

Shelly cut her off, "I'll be fine."

"Okay," Donna sighed, "just don't be late for your lunch date with Mark." With that, Donna tilted her nose upward and rolled her eyes as she turned and headed off in the opposite direction.

Shelly was beginning to wonder if she had made a wise decision. Her escort did everything at a frenetic pace. He walked fast and talked fast. He seemed to her like a man who was trying to get from zero to one hundred without stepping on the tens along the way. And he was determined to have her experience everything that Melmare suburb's downtown had to offer. First they stopped in a quaint little perfumery. "Smell this," a unique black vial was lifted to her nose by finely sculpted fingers. "Is it not the most divine fragrance you've ever been given the pleasure of inhaling?"

"It is." She found herself saying, temporarily taken by the spirit of the scent. She wondered why Mark had acted so strangely.

Cameron's eyes narrowed on hers, "And two doors down is Madame Michele's Chocolate Square. You must allow me to treat you." Before she could lift another fragrance to sample or think anymore about Mark, Cameron had locked her arm in his and was heading for the door.

"Mr. O'Neil," she started.

"Cameron, my dear. You really must call me Cameron."

"Cameron, are you sure it isn't twelve o'clock yet? I have a lunch engagement."

"We have plenty of time. Besides, can you imagine a more glorious day for a walk, and this area is so pretty this time of year. If Schultz is too busy, I'd be happy to stand in for him until he can make himself available."

They visited two more boutiques. Cameron explained to her that the smartest women were choosing their fashions there. And he apologized profusely when they spotted a clock and she proclaimed, "Oh no, it's 12:30!"

Cameron tweaked the corner of his mouth, placed a hand on her shoulder, and stated simply, "Let me drive you home."

"You've really been kind, Cameron, but I shouldn't be a bother. Maybe Mark hasn't left yet. I could get a ride with him."

"You don't know your friend very well, do you? He is extremely punctual, and for that matter, so am I."

Shelly's brow wrinkled at that bit of information, considering how he had just helped her to be late for her lunch with Mark. She decided to let it pass.

"I can catch a cab."

"No, my dear, you most certainly cannot." At that he grabbed her arm and locked it in his. To her imploring expression he added, "I'll brook no refusal. I'm thinking of you and Mark."

She, too, was thinking, thinking of a hard-faced scary boy who, like an avenging angel, had come from nowhere to ward off her evil pursuers. He, too, had offered her his arm. Had it all been an illusion?

The afternoon was cooler than the morning, and noticing Shelly's shiver, Cameron took off his coat and draped it over her shoulders. She was too cold to refuse. They walked even more briskly to his car than they had walked earlier, if that were possible. Cameron drove a sterling silver Jaguar. At Shelly's stunned look he explained: I live the way I intend to, not the way my circumstances presently dictate. There is a method to my madness. His smile was so sly and seductive that she shuddered, jumped in the car, and turned her attention out the window.

The ride home dragged on and on. Cameron talked about his climb to success, his drive and determination to be the best he could be. He also asked lots of questions about Mark. She answered a few, but thought better of getting too personal; besides what did she really know about Mark anyway? Forty-five long minutes later and she was again at Mark, Donna and Bob's building. She distinctly remembered the ride to Brandon and Dobbs being only thirty minutes. Still she was thankful to finally be there.

Cameron came around to open her door. "Let me walk you up."

"No." Shelly turned and held her hand against his chest.

"I insi—"

"Not this time," she interrupted.

He gave a gallant bow and watched her from behind. Sensing his stare, Shelly turned slightly. A shiver went up her spine. She envisioned the distinct image of a fox watching a hen.

Leaning slightly against the doorframe of the Joneses' apartment, Mark stood with his arms across his chest and his legs crossed at the ankle. In addition to his expensive gray suit, he knew he was wearing what Shelly had affectionately called his "evil look." Suddenly he slumped against the hard lacquered door. *What's taking her so long? "Whites got one set of time and coloreds got another," is what Pop would say. And the next day Mama Rose would say, "Boy, how many colored folks your dad know?"*

Maybe she's decided not to come. His stomach lurched at the thought. "I must be getting hungry," he reasoned. *God, I acted stupid at the office. Maybe she's mad. I'll apologize as soon as she gets here, if she gets here.*

Shelly hurried up the walkway and opened the heavy entry door. It was such a quaint building her friends lived in, just two stories high. The door had a half-circle cut-glass window above it and the vestibule was a throwback from better times, a time when craftsmen took pleasure in their work. The floor was a beautiful tiled black-and-white checker. And a finely polished brass lamp ornamented with alabaster hung from the ceiling. It was a nice place for her to figure out her life, to take a selah.

Gosh, she was over an hour late. What must Mark think? She'd apologize as soon as she saw him.

*T*he downy texture of the carpet should have muffled her steps. Still, he could hear her coming or maybe sense it. He straightened to his full height. She was walking fast and smiling. Smiling?

"You're late, Shelly, don't you peo…"

It had been a while, but not so long that Mark couldn't remember how Shelly reacted to his near-racist comments. She hated when he sounded like his dad.

Her chest heaved as if she were struggling for breath, "Why you puffed up—"

Mark buckled over laughing, "Shelly, you never could swear," wiping back near-tears from his eyes. "I'm sorry, Shelly, really I am. It's all my fault. If I hadn't been such a jerk at the office, you probably would have been more anxious to get here."

Plunging her hand angrily into her purse, she pulled out her key and twisted it in the lock. It didn't open. "Let me help."

"No." Mark reached for the keys anyway. They did a little tug of war. He ended up with the keys. She looked up to express her disapproval. Mark's breath caught in his throat.

"Do that again, Shelly."

"What?" she snapped, crinkling her nose.

"That," he exclaimed. "God, I've missed that," he leaned down and softly touched his lips to her nose. She gasped. He did, too. He quickly turned the key in the lock and changed the subject.

Looking agitated and uncomfortable, Shelly asked, " So where are we going for lunch?"

Mark looked at his watch, "Our reservation was for 1:00."

"I'm sorry, Mark. Cameron said—"

Mark felt his face twist and contort, "Don't even tell me you spent all that time with O'Neil."

"Okay, I won't tell you."

Mark grabbed her shoulders hard. "Mark, you're hurting me."

"I'm so sorry," he grabbed her tighter. Pulling her into his chest, he held her there.

What is wrong with me? Mark was beginning to feel like he was losing his mind, like he was a child struggling to get a hold of his emotions. Where was all this coming from? "Maybe this wasn't such a good idea, Shelly."

"What?" Shelly roused herself, "What's not a good idea?" She shook her head trying to make sense out of what he was saying, "You mean the restaurant? We've got plenty of stuff right here to eat. Let's make lunch."

"No, I have to go." The door slammed behind him.

Shelly stood there looking at the door. Mark left, didn't say goodbye, didn't look back. Standing frozen in the middle of the living room, fists clenched, head throbbing, all she wanted to do was scream. A slew of obscenities spewed from her lips. She turned her back and headed for the guest room, "How's that for swearing, Mark Schultz?"

"Mama Rose wouldn't like it." She whirled around so quickly she had to grab a chair to keep from stumbling.

"Mark, if you think…" she started in a near shout, pointing her finger as she advanced. Her yelling was quieted by a searing kiss. She was floating, she was aching, she was soothed, and she was tormented. She was in love and had been since the day mean Marky had smiled at her so many years ago.

At 8:00, Mark pulled himself from her arms and tried to leave. It wasn't until 10:15 P.M. when they heard the key in the lock that he actually got up from the couch. When Shelly tried to pull her arms from him, he tightened them around his waist, forcing her tightly up against his back. He ran his fingers the length of her limbs giving her a shiver that made her want to swoon. "What will Donna and Bob think?" she whispered.

"Let them think whatever they want, I don't care." He pressed his lips firmly to hers for another intoxicating kiss. Her hand instinctively went to his temple where she caressed and twirled the short curls of his hair. The moisture of his firm lips lingered on her mouth and she was suddenly overjoyed that the Joneses were home. As her heart thundered wildly in her breast, she realized she wasn't going to be able to take much more of this.

She opened her eyes in time to see Bob pecking on Mark's shoulder.

"Hey buddy don't you have a presentation at the 8:00 A.M. briefing on the new account?"

"Huh, oh yeah. Meet me for lunch tomorrow at the office, Shelly. Pick me up at 12:00. That way I know you'll be on time." Shelly grabbed a pillow to toss at him. Looking into his smoldering eyes changed her mind. She hugged the pillow instead, trying desperately to hold on to what they had just shared. He gave her a look that suggested he understood and said in his sexiest voice, "Until tomorrow, my Shelly amour."

Bob interjected at this juncture, "Mark, aren't you forgetting about—"

"Nothing," Mark replied. Shelly thought Bob looked concerned, but then realized they had gotten along perfectly fine before she came along, so she let it be.

*T*he glow of Mark's table light greeted him when he entered his apartment. The place looked different, smelled different, felt different. Tonight he felt like doing something he rarely took the time to do. He walked out onto the balcony and breathed the air. He looked out at the corner deli. Its blue neon light still lit the night. A few people walked in and out. Most other lights were already darkened. Shelly filled his senses. His skin tingled. He was alive again. He walked back through the large glass doors and to his desk. After a long night of poring over his data, he felt ready. Now weary, he lumbered into his room and fell fully dressed into his plush bed. Shelly's scent was in his clothes. It encircled him. He pulled his covers close and imagined he was not alone, and without any effort at all, he drifted into a peaceful sleep. For the second morning in a row he awoke without the clock. If he kept seeing Shelly, he wouldn't need an alarm at all.

*"H*ard night, old man?" Cameron greeted him as soon as the elevator door opened. "How was lunch with Shelly?" Mark felt anger rising, but he felt more like his old self today. Cameron had never been able to rile him before.

"Fine, we're old friends."

"So I've heard."

Was that jealousy in Cameron's voice? Couldn't be. Why not test it anyway.

"She's coming here today to pick me up for lunch."

"Hmmph, should be interesting."

Now what was that supposed to mean? Mark left Cameron by the elevators. O'Neils hands were tucked in his pants pockets, and he was smiling like a Cheshire cat. Mark walked briskly down the hall to the main conference room. With about ten minutes remaining before everyone arrived, he reviewed his notes. The first half of the presentation went off without a hitch. And then Dobbs called for the figures. "Mark, may we see the numbers now?"

Mark was momentarily transfixed. He honestly didn't know where the graphs were. He picked up one or two folders looking for the duplicate copies of the predicted net and gross sales over the next two years, as well as the number of new clients Mr. Abbott would reach, when he noticed the tripod. That's right, they'd decided to enlarge all the figures and graphs to five times the normal size in order to accommodate Greg Abbott's failing eyesight. Mark walked confidently over to the corner, hoping upon hope that the Abbott charts were, in fact, attached to the tripod face down. He flipped the charts over, reattached them and brought them over to the group. That's what Bob had been trying to tell him last night: he still needed to pick up the charts from the art department. Bob must have had them set up just before the meeting. Good old Bob, he'd thank him profusely for covering his butt, right after his date with Shelly.

At the end of his presentation, Mark noticed that Cameron's head was slightly bowed. He was stroking his tie, an annoying gesture, and he had that wry smile again. Had Cameron picked up on his uneasiness when he couldn't locate the graphs? O'Neil was sharp, but he wasn't that perceptive. Besides, hadn't he recovered before anyone had a clue?

"Great presentation, boy. This agency is just what Abbott and Sons is looking for. Keep up the good work," Greg Abbott said with a hearty handshake and a pat on his back. However, just outside the door, Dobbs was waiting.

Dobbs had invested more in Mark than he cared to admit. They had met quite by chance riding the "el" train. If the night was dark, the subway was darker still. A few of the lights in the underground cavern were out. It made the sparks of the train skidding to a stop that much more vibrant. Too bad he couldn't say the same for himself. He was exhausted. He had gone to see Dom Rosco, a man he hoped would be a new client, in an obscure part of town about as far as the city limits reached. Mr. Rosco had a great product and was interested in increasing his revenue base. However, he had no concept of how the advertising business worked but had all kinds of opinions about how his campaign should be run. Dobbs rubbed the bridge of his nose in an attempt to smooth away the wrinkles and the immense tension lodged there. The metal doors opened and he squeezed into an over-stuffed car. Bodies were melded together and it was his unfortunate lot to be housed next to a man whose girth took up the space of two or more people. His hair was black and oily, and he had the distinct smell of stale dishwater. The stench was so strong that he found himself moving unconsciously toward the opposite end of the "el" car.

Surprisingly, there appeared to be an empty seat. By the time he made his way to where it was located, the lights were flickering. He took a chance and sat. It was obvious he was on somebody's stuff, but this was preposterous. Who would dare take up a seat with their things in an "el" this crowded? He stood to his feet and grunted. The lights flicked brightly, giving him just time enough to get a look at the man sitting by the stuff. He was well dressed and of an impressive size. He did not move his things. Dobbs stood a few minutes more. All of a sudden the lights came on, and he did what he seldom did in a situation outside of the office. He decided to engage in an interpersonal conflict.

"Excuse me, sir, but if no one else is sitting here, I've had an extremely long day and I'd like to sit here myself. Do you mind?"

The young man looked up at him, cocked a brow and grudgingly moved his papers and books from the seat next to his. The lights, which had been flickering, came on and stayed on. Dobbs found it impossible to ignore what he saw.

"*The Hidden Persuaders?*" He questioned, looking at the dated report in the young man's hands.

Mark shrugged but Dobbs persisted.

"You follow Packard's work? Do you believe there is any validity to his assertions and of those who have followed?"

"What?"

That he was clearly annoyed was apparent. "Do you believe that people act on unconscious motivation and that those motives can be manipulated?"

"Listen, mister, you seem to be an okay fella, so I've got time to answer one question. In my line of work you would be a fool to ignore anything that might play a role in persuading people."

"I see. In that case I would like to ask you to indulge me one last question, and I promise not to trouble you further." He decided to take a chance. He believed the payoff would be worth it. "Say you have a client who sells work shoes. They have great support, they're very comfortable, attractive even, for a work shoe, and only a bit more costly than the standard competition."

"Rosco's."

"You know the business? Is your company negotiating with him?"

"If you mean has he approached us? The answer is: no. If you're asking have we approached him? The answer is: not smart enough. His business could be big with the right advertising. I'm thinking of going solo, taking him on myself."

Dobbs made the clever young man an offer on the spot. And Mark came to work for him six months later. In the meantime he had discovered that Mark Schultz was a rising star at Smith, Jones and John. Even though it was a well-established firm in the Chicago area, Mark felt that the owners lacked vision and they certainly were not "hungry," as he put it. He welcomed the opportunity to work for a company he could help to "put on the map" and be a notable part of their success.

Mark's inauguration to Brandon and Dobbs came with Rosco's shoe account all sewn up. Dom Rosco loved the idea of his work shoes being associated with luxurious living. The television spot Mark's team produced showed men working in a factory. It was the end of the day. Everyone was tired and sweaty, everyone, that is, except the man wearing Rosco Luxury Workers. He was cool and calm. In fact he felt so good that he imagined himself at home in front of a crisp blaze, his feet up and a cool drink in his hand. The inscription that ran across the bottom of the set read: *Millions want what you have. Rosco's: your feet have never had it so good.* When the commercial aired, sales went up twenty-five percent.

The next campaign was: *These shoes will work for you. Isn't it time someone did?* In this commercial the worker imagined a maid doing his share of the work while he watched, feet comfortably propped up. Another jump in sales followed its airing. Mark had a knack for reading the client, the market and the times. And he was innovative.

Instead of competing with this talented young man, Dobbs thought he'd woo him with the promise of partnership. For Dobbs, it would be a marriage made in heaven. Now if he could only make good on the promise. Much depended on his existing partner, Eric Brandon. Brandon was his not-so-silent partner. Eric put up all the funding and did none of the work. But he had opinions. He liked both Amanda Cole and Cameron O'Neil. They did have their talents. Amanda was creative and could read the market. And Cameron was shrewd, too shrewd for Dobbs's taste. If Cameron smelled blood he'd go for the kill faster than any shark. Dobbs couldn't help but wonder when such a talent would turn into a detriment.

Still, he needed a working partner, and before Mark Schultz came along, he thought he'd have to settle. He was sure of Mark, but Brandon, who was the moneyman, needed proof. Mark would have to consistently pull in more revenue than Cameron or Amanda. So far he was holding his own. If he could pull off the Kincaid account, he'd all but sew up the partnership. And finally Dobbs could comfortably relieve his load and feel that his company was on its way to living up to his expectations.

Dobbs sat on the corner of his desk peering down at the promising young man sitting before him. His dress was as impeccable as ever, his likable cockiness still intact, but unless he missed his guess, Mark's edge had lessened in severity. An almost imperceptible degree, he would admit, but to a person like himself, who studied human nature, it was enough to cost him his bid against Cameron and Amanda if he wasn't careful.

"You looked a little shaky there for a minute, boy. In all the time I've watched you, I've never seen you flinch. I've called in a lot of favors to get you considered for partner. Don't fail me."

"I won't, Mr. Dobbs; don't worry."

"And, son, whatever the problem is, get rid of it."

As Mark exited Dobbs's office, he noticed Cameron O'Neil standing in the shadows, a familiar glint lighting his eyes.

So it had been a narrow escape after all. Mark had to give it to Dobbs; the man didn't miss much. Well, it was over now. Abbott had been properly dazzled and regardless of his minor goof, unless he missed his guess, Brandon and Dobbs would be receiving a call this afternoon that they had gotten the Abbott account. He cleared the rest of his schedule. And, God help him, he couldn't concentrate to do another thing. He sat with his feet propped up on his desk simply waiting for the clock to strike twelve. He was smiling so big his dimple hurt; he wanted to bypass lunch and just get to the holding part.

He heard footsteps advancing quickly toward his door. Shelly must have been as anxious as he was. He swung around from behind his well-organized mahogany desk toward the forest-green drapes; gold embroidery gave them a regal look. Mr. Dobbs had so much faith in him that he already occupied executive space, the excuse being there were no other offices available.

Just as the footsteps ceased, Mark pulled open the door; she almost fell in.

"Shel…"

"No, it's Amanda." Cameron stood behind Amanda Cole. He looked thrilled to make the announcement of her arrival.

Note to self, Mark thought: *remember to knock that goofy smirk off Cameron's face as soon as convenient.*

"Ching," the elevator made that all-too-familiar chime.

"Hello, Mark, aren't you glad to see me?" Amanda flung her arms around his neck pressing her D-cups hard into his chest. He reached behind his head to loosen her grip.

"What's come over you? We're at work, you know." He looked over her head at Cameron who was still standing at his door watching the show.

"Do you mind?" Mark threw out.

"No, I don't mind, what about you, Shelly?" Mark watched Cameron watching Shelly advance toward his door. The look of pain on her face made his chest hurt.

He was dumbfounded, just standing there. Amanda continued her nudging and groping. Mr. Dobbs rounded the corner and was heading straight for the melee.

"You know," Cameron started drolly, "I never believe workplace gossip. When Meg told me that you two were dating, I just coul…" Mark's glare cut off his soliloquy.

Amanda purred in Mark's ear, her hands swirled hungrily around his neck, "So who is she?"

Mr. Dobbs caught Mark's eye.

"Well, Mark?" Amanda continued, her grip getting firmer by the second.

"Just a friend!" Mark said in a near shout.

He could see the tears pooling in Shelly's eyes. He was helpless to intervene. She stalked off toward the elevators. Mama Rose hadn't raised a weakling or a fool. He had to do something or whatever they were doing would be over before it started.

Amanda suddenly let go of him. Mark didn't know what game Amanda was playing, but he had a feeling that Cameron was in on it. He couldn't focus on that now. He had to go after Shelly. His shoulder bumped Cameron's polished veneer as he hurried by him, but Mr. Dobbs cut him off in mid-stride. "What goes on here, Schultz?"

"Er, nothing, Mr. Dobbs," Mark tried to sidestep him. Shelly was getting away. Dobbs stepped in his path again.

"Come with me, Mark."

"Not now, sir—"

"Now, Schultz," he demanded, leading the way to his office. Cameron headed toward the elevator. Mark could barely listen, thinking about those two faces: Shelly's—his heart ached—and Cameron's.

$\mathcal{C}$ameron lingered just long enough to hear the exchange between Mark and Dobbs. When he was satisfied that Mark had been compromised, he turned his attention to Shelly. Walking swiftly, he made his way to the elevator. He stood there stomping his foot; the fool elevator was particularly slow today. The bell-like sound chimed. Finally. Distracted, he almost bumped into a young woman exiting the elevator. Brushing quickly past her, he observed her profile. *Oriental*, he thought, *and attractive*. The melting pot had hit Brandon and Dobbs in a most impressive way. If he had had more time, he certainly would have investigated more closely, much more closely.

Outside the main floor, Cameron spotted Shelly. She was in the process of going into the crosswalk where a car was quickly approaching. "Hey, lady, you'd better watch your step." He tugged her arm with gentle urgency, pulling her out of harm's way. A teary-eyed Shelly spoke to him.

"Oh, Cameron, I wasn't paying attention."

"I know you weren't. I could see how upset you were over that scene at Mark's office. He didn't tell you about Amanda, did he?" Cameron didn't wait for her response, "Yes, well, they've been dating for sometime. Rumor has it that it's serious." The tears that Shelly was obviously fighting to hold back now ran freely down her cheeks; she sniffled.

On the verge of feeling guilty, Cameron noticed Shelly doing something odd with her face. *Why is she wrinkling her nose in such an awkward manner? The affectation distorts an otherwise perfect profile.*

"What's wrong?" Shelly said looking up at his eyes.

"Nothing," he said, unable to resist the urge to smooth out her brow with his finger.

"Oh, that," she responded, "It's a habit. Other people have commented on it."

"Come over here. Let's sit down." The wooden bench must have been cool on the back of Shelly's legs. She rubbed the goose flesh starting to surface. Cameron's attention was drawn to her long brown calves.

"Here, take my coat," she tried to wrap it around her shoulders. He pulled it down over her legs, figuring if he was going to play savior it probably wouldn't be a good idea for him to grab her thigh.

*T*he usually supple butter-like leather of Dobbs's cream-colored chair seemed hard and unyielding today. It felt as if the chair would eject its occupant at any moment. Mark smiled, thinking how grateful he'd be for just such an occurrence.

"And finally, young man, I'd like to say…" Did he say "finally?" Mark roused himself, sat up straight and stopped drumming on his thigh. Now free, he sprang to his feet, gave Mr. Dobbs a sheepish nod and left the office.

I'm free. What to do? Set Amanda straight; go find Shelly? Definitely go find Shelly. Mark walked quickly to the elevator. He was resolved to do… what? He didn't know but it had to start with Shelly. Mark watched the numbers tick away on the elevator. "Arrrg!" he let out an audible roar and headed down the stairs. Once in the stairwell, Mark remembered why everyone chose the elevator. The dim area was muggy, giving an immediate damp feeling from head to toe. It seemed no one had taken any thought of upgrading the condition of this part of the building. Mark took the steps two at a time and was surprised to note that not taking time out for regular exercise had taken a toll on him.

Once outside, Mark found himself winded and out of breath. He leaned forward, both hands planted on his knees. Panting, he hoped

Shelly had had as much luck catching a cab as most people did this time of day. As soon as he caught his breath, the wind was knocked right out of him again. Cameron! Mark marched over to where he was sitting with Shelly. On his way over he could see Cameron stroking Shelly's face with his fingertip while giving him a backwards glance. Was he trying to bait him? It was working.

Mark bore down on Cameron with a determination that would have shaken him to his core had he continued to look.

"Mark, Shelly doesn't want you here."

Mark latched onto Cameron's arm with intensity so fierce he thought he might shatter his shoulder. "Don't touch her," Mark's teeth ached from gritting.

"Sheee doesn't want you here." Cameron winced and wrung himself free of Mark's grip. The silk shirt he was wearing allowed him to slither loose.

Shelly looked up and gave Mark a look somewhere between disappointment and despair. "Did he hurt you?" she said placing a graceful hand on Cameron's shoulder.

Cameron placed his hand over hers and squeezed, "No, I'm fine really."

Mark's insides exploded. Couldn't she see him bleeding? Didn't she care how torn up all this was making him? He willed himself to back away from the bench. Leaving became of the utmost import. If he didn't move he wouldn't be responsible for his behavior or Cameron's life. This was insane. An immediate change in vicinity was required, now.

Chapter Nine
Moving On

Donna and Bob's apartment, though spacious, was starting to close in on Shelly. If she had just kept her focus on why she had originally come here, to decide about James and to help her friend Donna through a difficult time, everything would be fine. Instead she was sitting in Donna's guest room hiding tear-soaked tissues beneath the cushion of her favorite burgundy and blue stuffed chair.

"Shelly, how much longer are you going to mope around here?" Donna had no idea how accurate her question was as she yelled it from the living room.

Shelly looked around the quaint guest room, which would be the baby's room in about seven and a half months. She wanted the best for her friend who, it seemed to her, had always wanted to be a wife and mother. She left college early to become Bob's wife and now she was expecting.

Donna wrote to her as soon as she found out she was pregnant:

> Shelly,
>
> I am pregnant again. Bob was so distraught after we lost the first two babies, I don't know how I'm going to tell him. I know he would try to be upbeat but he'd worry. I need your strength. Can you please come to me as soon as possible? You never take vacations. I know; I've checked with Mama Rose. Plan on staying for a while.

Mama Rose told me you could. She said you needed more to do than to keep sitting around worrying about things you can't change. I know you had to have taken the assassinations to heart. Mr. King and Bobby Kennedy were your heroes, weren't they? I'm so sorry I didn't write to console you. But as usual it's me who needs your help.

Shelly, say you'll come. If you had been around here after the first miscarriages, you would know how much I need you. You've never met Bob but he is the most vibrant and joyful person. After the babies, he was sullen and weary all the time. If you were here, I could tell him when the time is right. I know we haven't spent much time together since school, and I am asking a lot, but I've never really asked you for anything big, and I really need you now. I promise we'll have fun just like the old days, and you'll love Bob. He's never entertained any of my family, and he said he would treat you as if you are my long lost sister.

Write me soon telling me when, not if, you'll arrive.

All my love, your dear friend,

Donna

Before the doctor even confirmed Donna's pregnancy, Shelly's letter arrived. Mama Rose was in the kitchen warming teacakes and sipping weak coffee. There were two cups poured. Shelly was sure one was for her though she didn't know how Mama Rose knew she'd be home early. She picked up the extra cup and slurped, careful not to burn her lips with the steaming liquid. "This is so sweet. Did you pour the whole tin of sugar in it?"

"No, I didn't. My guest did." Mama Rose turned and gave her a delicate nod.

"Your guest? Does he or she have a name?"

"Yes, he or she does have a name." Mama said, sipping her own coffee from a sheer crystal cup. "Listen, baby, the mailman just passed. Go out and get the mail and take a fifteen-minute walk. Can you do that for Mama?"

"Yes, Ma'am," Shelly remembered saying as she squeezed her grand-mother's nose and walked out of the house. Curious, she never did find out who that discreet visitor was. Mama Rose was entitled to her privacy, however. Every now and then she insisted on it.

Shelly and Donna had not been close after college, only writing a few times, but they formed an immediate bond. The kind that was constant regardless of contact. The kind you knew you could depend on.

Shelly sat on a park bench with her letter. Wispy clouds like long eye lashes graced the sky. She pulled her yellow cardigan closed over her blouse. A cool front was headed her way, and so was James.

"Mama Rose told me I might find you here." He had been working at his father's office and was wearing a brown business suit, with a thin caramel-colored tie. James was such a hard worker. He had gone to a community college after high school and virtually ran his father's moving and car repair businesses. The professors at his school had told him he could be anything he wanted and many questioned why, with a mind like his, he could settle for learning just enough to take over for Mr. Johnson. His very simple and direct answer was: my father needs me.

"What are you reading, Shelly?" he said as he approached. A tall shadow behind him bespoke the manner of the man before her.

"It's a letter from an old college friend. She wants me to come and see her." He read over her shoulder before coming around to the front of the wooden bench and sitting next to her. He stretched his arm around her shoulder, then decided to fasten the top button of her sweater. She must have looked shocked because he continued, "Shelly, how many times have I asked you to marry me?"

"Many, but, Jimmy…"

"Please, Shelly, I prefer James."

"James, I haven't really taken your proposals seriously."

"No, you haven't, not like your crusades, or your job, or your work trying to help fix this race-broken city. So…am I a joke to you?" His words were like hot pepper seasoned with a smile.

"No, James. But it's so…"

"So what, sudden? Shelly, I've wanted you since high school. The reason it took me so long to ask is that you've always kept your distance."

"Have I changed?" She was searching his eyes for answers she had not been able to find herself.

"Not really," James was holding her chin in his hand, "but I have. I know what I want. You are a good and loving woman, besides that you are smart and bold while at the same time delicate. We hold the same beliefs, and we both want better for our people. I believe you know I'm not desperate. I've simply been holding out for you because I think I'm in love with you. You don't have to love me now. It could grow, but I want you to seriously consider my proposal."

"I'm not sure."

"Shelly, I have a suggestion. Go to your friend. She needs you. You know what I want. When you come back, have an answer for me. This world's a hard place, but it's easier when you don't have to go through it alone." He tilted her chin back to better see her eyes, "Fair?"

Confusion whirled around inside her brain as she watched James walk away. She wanted to chase him down, to yell at the top of her lungs: yes, I'll be your wife. What woman in her right mind wouldn't? But her legs disobeyed her command to move and the connection between her brain and her tongue was apparently severed. No matter how she willed herself off the bench, there she remained.

James looked over his shoulder; his white-toothed smile gave the appearance of confidence. She knew he was anything but. James had been a wonderful boy and he had grown into a more wonderful man. He was respected, revered, even envied but never pitied, until today. Shelly knew she had strung him along for too long. She would go to Donna's and she'd come back to James with an answer.

Donna pushed her sweeper vac over the wide expanse of her hard wood floor, lingering by Shelly's bedroom. She could hear her sniffling, attempting to avoid bawling outright. She had never thought Mark devious or dishonest. Those traits belong to men like Cameron O'Neil. Yet according to Shelly, Cameron had been the one to reveal Mark's love affair with Amanda Cole. Donna shook her head. Shelly, though often reserved, was never one for resignation. Donna had met Shelly at Clarkston Junior College in a particularly difficult statistics class. There weren't many colored people on campus and of those, very few were women. They sat next to each other in class. Donna noticed that Shelly's assignment was blank like hers. Every class after that they commiserated over their inability to understand the subject matter. After one really grueling study session, Donna had gone to see Professor Marshman. He spent over an hour making sure she had a good understanding of the problems, but when she tried to explain the concepts to Shelly she couldn't, so she suggested that Shelly also visit the professor. She waited outside the office, working on English while Shelly talked to their teacher:

Shelly walked into the class and pulled the door up behind her. "Professor Marshman, I'm Shelly Madison. I'm in your 304 Statistics class."

"Yes." His answer was so sharp that Donna got up from her desk and decided to spy from the small pane of glass in the window. It was easy to hear since the door wasn't completely shut.

"Well, sir, I'm having some difficulty with this concept." Shelly began, again.

"Let me see." He grabbed the notepad, pointed to her problem and said, "Here's your mistake."

"I know, sir, I was hoping…"

"Have you read the material?"

"Yes, sir."

"Attended the lectures?"

"Yes, my problem is— "

"Your problem is…," he stopped himself and said, "Go review it again."

Shelly took her notepad and started to walk away. Suddenly something came over her. She turned. "No, sir."

"Excuse me?" His eyes widened as he slammed his notes down and peered over his glasses.

"No, sir, I don't believe I will read it again. You work here, right?"

He looked startled. "And I pay tuition." She laid her notepad down on his desk, "My problem is this, right here. Explain, please."

And he did.

Donna admired her from that moment on. The only woman she'd seen with that kind of power was her mother, whom unfortunately, she did not admire. Her mother was ruthless and self-centered. Until Shelly, Donna didn't know power could be kind. And now Shelly was sitting defeated in her room because of Mark Schultz. Donna's blood boiled.

Shelly stood and lifted the side of the heavy cushion of her chair. She retrieved the mound of wet tissue stuffed there and put it in the wastebasket, taking time to cover her secret with crumpled newspaper so Donna wouldn't notice. Her world was upside down. Donna still wasn't ready to tell Bob about the baby. Jimmy—correction, James—needed and wanted an answer to his proposal. She certainly couldn't go near that now. Mark had opened and stripped her heart, and what was up with Mama Rose? That was the only stability she had ever known. Her grandmother was more mother to her than most people's would ever be. Yet she had practically shoved her out the door on the day she had left to come here. What was going on with her? Maybe she just needed her space. They had lived together for more years than most adults cared to. Who knows? Some things were sure, her career was on hold, and she had money. Now was as good a time as any to take stock of her life. And Donna's request that she come and stay with her until she felt she could tell Bob about the baby had come at a perfect time. She didn't think she was much help to Donna though, feeling so confused and hapless. If it weren't for this whole Mark thing, she would be just fine. She needed to get back to her old self, to go about her own life, without Mark.

Donna had gone through a great deal of trouble, redoing the room in Shelly's favorite colors: sky-blue with plum accent pieces. Overstuffed chairs accentuated with petite flowers were placed close together so that Donna could sneak in and share popcorn with Shelly over movies like they had done in college. Yes, Donna was right. She had spent too much time moping. She felt like she was hiding out and she had never been one to hide. She was here to make some life decisions, and decision number one was moving on. Shelly washed her face in the coldest water she could stand, pulled her hair into a tight ponytail and opened the bedroom door.

"Donna," she hesitated, "has Mark called?"

"No," Donna said softly, "and he's been avoiding Bob and me." She quickly added, "None of this is like him. He confronts things head on. I think something…" here she leaned to cup Shelly's cheek with her long fingers, "…or someone has messed with his head."

Shelly didn't want to follow this line of reasoning. She hedged before asking, "What about Cameron?"

"What about him, Shelly?" Donna snapped, "I don't care if Cameron did make us aware of Mark's relationship with Amanda. The man's a snake. You don't want to answer his calls."

"So he has called."

"Yes, he has. But Shelly, I'm warning you."

"I need a diversion, you said so yourself; I should get out of this apartment, out of this room."

Donna didn't argue.

"Besides, Donna, you admitted that you don't have any real knowledge of Cameron. So Bob thinks he's calculating. How many people in advertising fit that description? And I'm not looking for a relationship, just something to occupy my time."

wo days later the phone rang. Shelly answered as Donna was coming from the kitchen eating her second thick ham sandwich in two hours. She wiped a mayonnaise smudge from her cheek with a large cotton napkin.

"Yes, Cameron, I am available tonight." Shelly smiled, feeling more like her old self.

"Are you sure, Shelly? It's just that he's so, so slippery," Donna said, not being careful of her volume.

Shelly frowned at her friend. "Wasn't it you who said I need a diversion?—Oh, no, not you, Cameron. I'll…"

Donna shrugged defeat and plopped down on the sofa.

"I'll be ready at 7:00. Pick me up here." Shelly hung up, pushed her shoulders back and headed for the bath and a shower. An hour later she emerged from her room.

"Wow!" Bob announced, quickly looking up from his coffee where he and Donna were sitting near the balcony. "So you and Mark are back on track, lucky man."

"I'm not going out with Mark. I have a date with Cameron."

Bob opened his mouth to protest when the sip of coffee he had just swallowed went down the wrong way. He hacked, sputtered and gasped for what seemed like five minutes, at the end of which he ignored Donna's stay-out-of-it glare. In response to her unspoken request, he said, "I will not. Mark is my friend and Shelly is about to make a complete fool of herself."

"You mean like I did at the office a week ago, standing at Mark's door with him practically yelling, 'We're just friends?' Oh, and did I forget to mention that woman fondling him in plain view of everyone? How could I do worse that that?" Shelly responded.

Bob looked, to Shelly, as if he was about to make further protests when the bell rang. He followed her to the door. She took the chain off and opened it wide. Cameron walked in.

"Put your tongue back in your mouth, Cameron." Cameron did not address Bob.

"Sorry, it is not like me to make such an uncouth entrance, Donna. Though I am sure you can understand my preoccupation." And to Shelly, while offering his arm, "Miss Madison, shall we depart?"

*T*hey were barely out the door when Bob accosted the wall-mounted phone.

"What are you doing, Bob?"

"She was gorgeous, Donna. Did you see the way her hair was arranged atop her head and the way those spiral curly things floated sensually about her cheeks? And how did she get into that peach dress? It was hugging her hips so tightly I though it would burst—"

"Honey, if you didn't love me so much I think I'd be jealous."

"She's a beautiful girl, and I'm worried about her with Cameron, but you know where my heart lies even if you have been a little stingy with lovemaking lately." Donna looked somber, so he turned his attention back to the situation at hand and so did Donna.

"I'm calling Mark."

"You're not."

"I most certainly am. Do you expect me to sit back and do nothing when my best bud is losing a fight he doesn't even know he's in?"

"He's a fool if he doesn't."

Bob waited impatiently for Mark to answer the phone, "Mark, Bob here."

"Yeah, what's going on?"

"Mark, Shelly's going out with Cameron."

"What? When?"

"Now, they left our apartment not two minutes ago."

Even over the phone Bob could feel Mark second-guessing himself, "It's none of my business what Shelly does. She's a free agent."

"I just thought you should know."

"Yeah, okay, thanks."

*M*ark stalked to the drawer next to his bed, opened it and pulled out his keepsake box. He had only smoked one cigarette in his entire life and only half of that. He thought smoking was a disgusting habit; something weak people did to either fit in or to pacify themselves. Still, Skip told him he should hold onto it in case he ever needed it to relieve stress. He had kept it all these years to remind himself of his high school days and as a testament to his strength.

"*W*ell, Miss Madison, I can honestly say that I cannot remember when I have had a more relaxing and enjoyable evening. There is something refreshing about being with someone so uncomplicated; you are a most unique woman. Do we have to end so early? Might I come in for a few moments?"

O'Neil should get an Oscar for this performance. He actually sounds sincere.

"Cameron, I've really enjoyed your company but…"

To this he put a finger to her lips and said, "One minute, for a cup of coffee; it's a long drive home."

Mark could make out most of what Cameron was saying when he was facing his direction. His hiding place was at the end of the hall around the corner that led to the stairwell, not far from where they were. He felt like a teenager spying on his unfaithful girlfriend, and he wasn't the least bit calmer. *This is too ridiculous*, he thought, as he turned to go back up the stairs. At that moment he heard Shelly's door open and close. Looking back quickly he thought: *she did it; she actually let him in. Somebody's got to tell her what a fool she's being.* Not a minute later he was pounding on the Joneses' door.

"Mark?!" Shelly was clearly shocked, judging by the look on her face, "You look terrible." Covering her mouth, she coughed quietly. Mark wondered if the lingering smell of smoke was affecting her.

"It's late. What do you want?"

Mark stood there barefoot, hair disheveled, shirt unbuttoned at the neck. He hadn't planned on being seen.

"Mark, old man, what brings you to us so late at night?" Cameron's smile glistened as he eyed Shelly's neck like a vampire about to take a bite. And his hand, it was resting on Shelly's hip!

"Shelly, what's going on out there?" Donna called from somewhere in the apartment.

Shelly turned to respond. Cameron flashed Mark a "wait-till-you-see-what-I'm-going-to-do-next" smile. Before he could display all thirty-two, the guttural sound of anguish emanated from his lips.

Shelly turned back to see a thick red ooze seeping between Cameron's fingers as he closed his hand over his mouth. His sputtering gave Mark guilty satisfaction.

"What happened?" Shelly demanded. Mark shrugged his shoulders. She slammed the door in his face.

*E*scorting Cameron to the table, she guided him to the nearest chair. She carefully nursed his split lip and bleeding gums. She applied ice, gently touching a wrapped packet to his swollen mouth. Looking down on Cameron, Shelly could plainly see the shrewd man that her friends complained about, and, just beneath the surface, she could see the cockiness that Cameron almost basked in. But she could also see vulnerability and right now it was his most endearing feature.

The cleavage that gently swelled above the V-cut of Shelly's perfect peach dress would have normally claimed his undivided attention, but her smooth lips and engaging eyes made him think of deeper things. In the honesty of her eyes, he could see his means to bring Mark down. But just beyond that, not obscured and not deceptive, he could also see her sincerity, her sweetness, and openness, and at this precise moment the desire to be warmed by Shelly's virtue outweighed the desire to defeat "what's-his-name," even if he had bloodied his mouth.

Mark stood for a long time outside Shelly's door, simmering. What could Bob and Donna be thinking to let Shelly get mixed up with Cameron? Who was he kidding? It was his fault as much as anybody's that she was embroiled with that viper. Still, she was a woman now and his days of protecting her had long passed. He'd better take care of his own life and leave Shelly to take care of hers. The walk dragged on for several steps as he padded back down the long hall, rounded the wall that led to the stairwell and slowly took the stairs back up to his apartment. When he reached his door, fatigue overtook him. His shoulders slumped like those of an old man as he collapsed onto his sofa and looked around. Everything was in order, as usual. A housekeeper came in every other week, but she never had much to do. Mark cleaned up after himself. His house was functional, if not inviting. There was nothing there that didn't serve a purpose. A glass dining table with two black metal chairs sat off center of his large room. A desk with a typewriter, telephone, calendar, notepads, and pens stood next to a small file cabinet. The leather couch where he sat overlooked the entire scene.

Just beyond this was a sliding glass door that led to the balcony. He rarely went there, never had the time. Sitting on his couch rubbing the heels of his hands against his dusty dry eyes, he was suddenly overcome with defeat. It was as if he was mixed and mashed into a turmoil that twisted and distorted who he really was. Only this battle had been going on for so long it had become a part of him. Who would he be if he let go of this invisible fiend turned friend? He didn't understand it really. Whenever he thought he was getting close it eluded him, again.

The only thing he really understood right now was that he didn't want to feel this way anymore.

After a fitful night's sleep on his couch he awoke. Blinding rays burst through his unshielded floor-to-ceiling sliding windows, causing him to squint. He had neglected to pull the drapes or make his way to his bedroom, but he was better today, and he was determined to get back to his orderly life and to let Shelly get on with whatever kind of life she wanted.

Days turned into weeks. Mark had managed to keep his promise. He wasn't interfering in Shelly's life. And he had no intention of letting her interfere with his. He avoided Donna and Bob as much as possible, and the few times he ran into Shelly she was with Cameron. They grated on his nerves more than he cared to admit. The worst part about it was that Cameron seemed different, less conniving. He actually appeared to enjoy Shelly's company. He was genuinely attentive to her. And to his disappointment, Shelly looked to all the world as if she wanted to be with Cameron. So what? He had more important things to think about, but for the life of him he couldn't figure out what they could possibly be. Shelly and Cameron were spending a great deal of time together. Mark was getting used to it. There was no forced affection between them. This was the only reason he had allowed their relationship to continue.

Chapter Ten
The Decision

*A*manda felt as if the clock was ticking out of control. Mark was no longer distracted and now worked with the passion of a starved man in pursuit of the last steak in the butcher's window. Was there no way to slow this man down? Amanda Cole, one of Mark's chief rivals for partner, made her way down the long hall that separated her modest office from his. She reached his door. It was ajar, so she didn't bother to knock. The luxury of this office with its strong mahogany desk and meeting table should be hers. She had worked years trying to get to this point.

"Mark, do you have the Kincaid report?"

"Is there some reason you are yelling, Amanda? I was just looking over the company's current market share and sales demographics."

She sat down in one of the excessively comfortable conference chairs to review the figures. "Just preoccupied, I guess. Impressive." Out of the corner of her eye, Amanda spied Cameron walking Shelly toward the elevators. She immediately came up with a plan. Excusing herself for a moment she went to discuss the matter with Cameron.

Walking as fast as her A-line, forest-green skirt would allow, she caught up to him and Shelly. "Cameron...Cameron, may I speak with you for a moment?" she rasped, a bit out of breath.

"What can I do for you, Amanda?" He stopped, shoved his hands in his pockets, and looked extremely annoyed. Shelly smiled and continued toward the elevators.

"Is that any way to talk to an old friend and a potential career rival?"

"Now, Amanda, you know we are anything but friends, and the longer Mark sits in that office, the more likely he is to occupy it indefinitely. So you see, my dear, you and I are neither friends nor rivals. If you'll excuse me." He moved to go around her.

"But, Cameron, I've got a plan. It includes your little friend, Shelly."

"Leave her out of this."

"Do I detect?…No, not the renowned Mr. O'Neil. Now, here's what I was thinking."

The "B" in the "Kay's Burger" sign flickered dimly, while the rest of the sign was boldly lit even though it was mid-day. Yellow and blue neon made it visible for blocks. Shelly turned toward Cameron giving him her now-familiar crinkled nose gesture. He ignored it. Then she asked, "Is this where we're eating?"

"Yes, they have an excellent French dip. I thought it would be nice to do something different today." A queasy feeling tripped his stomach.

"Well, it really is a change from the restaurants you usually like, but I'm game."

A farrago of thoughts plagued Cameron's mind. Hesitantly he ventured, "Perhaps you're right, my dear; we can come back on another occasion."

"Nonsense, I'm no spoiled brat; besides, I haven't eaten a good burger in months."

The restaurant was crowded, mostly men in suits. A few women, also doing business over lunch, dotted the landscape. Business lunches with bright lights; Cameron felt like he could see the wheels turning in Shelly's mind as she tried to figure out what he was really up to. They began to wend their way through burgundy tablecloths until they ran into a bank of booths against the wall at the very back of the restaurant.

"Mark!" Shelly sputtered.

They noticed him at the same time. He sat huddled with Amanda and Kincaid. A few last pitches to the man who seemed impossible to please. Mark didn't look up. Cameron began to hope they could leave without being noticed. He was wrong.

Amanda laid a stack of papers on the edge of the table; Mark looked over to see the stack and spied her. "Shelly."

Cameron grabbed Shelly under her arm and made to turn and leave.

"O'Neil, to what do we owe this honor?" Kincaid, their prospective new client, shot out, "I didn't expect to be able to meet with you until later today."

Cameron could feel Shelly's gaze. It was boring into the side of his cheek. He couldn't look at her. He wouldn't.

His rivalry with Mark was still an issue. But there was something real about what was happening between him and Shelly. She was lovely. Initially, only her physical beauty attracted him; later she was a tool to bring Mark down, now he just liked her company. Life was more pleasant when she was around, children less annoying. Huh? Who was he fooling? He couldn't wait to enact Amanda's plan, and now here he was. The moment of truth was upon him. How badly did he want this? Why couldn't Amanda keep her cunning to herself for once?

"It's good to see you, sir."

"The feeling is mutual," Kincaid waited. "Are you going to introduce us to your companion?"

"This is…" Cameron stopped, suddenly not sure how he wanted this situation to play out. He also didn't know how to interpret Kincaid's interest. Was he pleased to see him bold enough to date a colored woman or was he luring him in to get him to admit his foible? He didn't know and he was desperate to know.

"This is Shelly Madison, sir."

Everyone was quiet…waiting.

"Cameron, I've never known you to be coy, and you've never known me to be indirect. Is Miss Shelly Madison your girlfriend, business associate, cousin?"

Cameron opened his mouth; he was mute. He was either unwilling or unable to answer. Kincaid was an eccentric. He was shopping for an agency, and he made a habit of getting to know the staff before committing. Yet he was very private about his own life. This plan of Amanda's was ill-conceived and definitely backfiring. Schultz was the one who was supposed to be put on the spot and—

"She's my fiancée, sir. Cameron was kind enough to bring her here to meet me. He must have gotten the time confused."

Confused? Aghast would be a better word. Amanda had the unmistakable look of glee. Kincaid bowed his head. What was he thinking? One thing was certain, Amanda's plan was working: Mark had made a declaration that would paint him as a man who would intermarry. Not the end of the world, but certainly not wise in a business where appearance was everything and in times where race was nothing if not controversial. Yes, the scheme was going according to plan, so why did Cameron feel as if things were spinning wildly out of control and like he wanted to empty the contents of his stomach right there in the presence of the entire account executive staff?

When Shelly finally found her voice, she planted her feet, put her hands on her hips and declared, through gritted teeth, "I am not his fiancée." With that said, she turned and started through the gaggle of tables. Hardly a head turned as she marched toward the exit. Cameron thought to reach for her, to grab her arm. He wanted to follow her, he really did.

Mark's chair skidded back; he stood. "You'll excuse me, sir, Amanda, Cameron." It was sealed then, Mark had followed Shelly. He had not.

*O*utside the restaurant, Mark looked through crowds of suited men and women meandering in front of a bakery and a movie theater, the sumptuous scents of flaky pastry and fresh popped corn arresting them in their tracks. Down the block he scanned the area in front of a beauty salon, a novelty store and furniture shop. There was no sign of her. Shelly had to be running to have made such good time.

He walked swiftly, searching and calling, "Shelly...Shelly...Shelly!" Where could she have gone so fast? "Shelly!" He yelled louder. Several people leaned or turned to assure themselves that the raving loon was of no threat to them. He passed a few curious little shops that he had never noticed before. On his left was a dimly-lit window with a dusty green antique settee on display. Bone china teacups dangled on strands of thin threads attached to the ceiling. It was odd and out of place, just the sort of shop Shelly would—

"What?" she answered, as she and Mark nearly collided.

"What were you doing in there?"

"Why are you shouting at me?" she yelled in reply.

A simmering heat was rising to Mark's face; getting angry wasn't going to help a thing. "Mark, I know what you were doing back there: saving me, again. I thought we both agreed I could take care of myself." With a mix of emotions playing over her face, she blurted, "And besides, Mark, I can't marry you. I'm already engaged."

This was outrageous even for Shelly. "I hope you're not serious. Cameron's not the man you think he is. I've only allowed this little thing between you two because..."

"Allowed? Okay, Mark, why have you allowed it?"

"Because I wasn't ready..."

"You know what, Mark, it doesn't matter. I came here to make a decision. Cameron is not my fiancé, James is. I'm going home to make it official."

Through a nasty, unexplainably bitter haze and overwhelming light-headedness, resolve came. "You're not going to do that."

"Mark, I honestly believe you are losing your mind. I have never seen you so weird or unsure. When you liked me, you really liked me. And when you abandoned...I mean, when you didn't want to be around me anymore, you left. I could always respect your ..."

"Resolve."

"Yes."

"Then you're going to love me now," he proclaimed. He rounded her and stood wide-legged with his arms folded across his chest in an attempt to slow her stride. She kept walking, so he walked backward as she advanced. The wind whipping at his trench coat made hard flapping noises. The sound competed with his speech.

"What are you doing, Mark?"

"Talking to you; I need your full attention. Can you stand still for a moment?" She didn't; he continued, "Okay, no problem. I can walk backwards, used to do it all the time when I was a kid." To her look of disbelief, "Really I did."

"Mark, I really don't know you anymore. I'm going home to marry James. He's more…"

"More what, Shelly? More predictable, more sure, more Negro?"

"Prejudice is your problem, not mine."

Mark wanted to blow. But that wouldn't get him what he wanted. "Shelly, you ever walk backwards, like I'm doing now?" Her signature nose crinkle was coming on. "Just listen. I'm going somewhere with this. When I lived with my mother I played a game. I'd walk backward when I left her apartment. I'd take careful note of everything I saw, drunks staggering down the street, stray cats and dogs, trash and broken glass on the walk. I'd purposely take in all the smells: moldy stores, rotting food; and I'd say to myself, one day I'm leaving all of this behind, never coming back, never looking back." Shelly's pace slowed. "I never felt that way when I went to live with Pop."

"Like you needed to walk backwards, you mean?"

"Yes. I thought it was my father, his loving care, his tidy home. Do you know when I discovered it was more than just him?" To Shelly's blank stare, "It was when I came home and found that Mama Rose had moved."

"Everyone loves my grandmother, but are you trying to tell me that her moving somehow affected your whole life?"

"Yes…no…Shelly, I'm trying to tell you that ever since you moved away I've been living my life as if I were walking backwards. I couldn't have you or wouldn't allow myself the possibility of being with you, so I just started walking backwards, living as if nothing mattered, living like I was trying to forget everything and everyone I left behind. I've only just now realized it. You're marrying me, Shelly." She stopped walking. Mark hoisted her off the ground, turned around and started walking forward.

*M*ark carried Shelly to Harris Company Bank, a block and a half from where they started, and she let him. He didn't put her down until he reached the revolving door; they walked into the same small compartment and wound their way into the entry. Mark bypassed the counter set up with withdrawal slips and went straight to the teller window. All the while never letting go of Shelly's hand. He worried that a momentary lapse would break the spell and allow her to escape. He wouldn't allow himself to stop and think. That had been his problem all along: too analytical. He simply wanted to stop fighting, to give in to the need.

Once at the teller window he made his withdrawal request. The teller, Nancy Eberheart, appeared to be uncomfortable but handed him the slip to sign, which he did as quickly as possible. She looked past him to Shelly and grimaced. Then she asked if he was sure of the amount. The look he returned to her made an immediate impact. She said, "Of course you are," and quickly counted the money out, nervously adjusting her sleeves and looking, to all the world, like she wished he would leave as soon as possible. He didn't. He asked for her phone instead.

"Please don't call the manager, Mr. Schultz; I didn't mean to offend you." He could only speculate as to what her concern was and he didn't have any time to ponder it. Besides, his attention was being drawn to a vague plea in his ear, "Mark, my hand." To this request he released his death grip on Shelly. She used her other hand to massage the one he had been holding. With both his hands free now, he dialed the airport. "Yes, as soon as possible, two tickets to Vegas. I'll be paying with cash when I arrive." Shelly pecked him on the shoulder and opened her mouth to pro-test. He kissed it shut. She was so stunned and apparently embarrassed by the public display of affection and the awed looks from passers-by that she soon decided to go along with whatever, without further complaint.

Shelly had never been in an airport, let alone ridden in a plane. When the whirlwind of events that preceeded the flight were done, she stood at the glass window looking out onto the tarmac. The airplane was tremendous. How in the world did these huge monstrosities ever become lighter than air? Her stomach felt like a million butterflies had already taken flight: heavy blind butterflies on a mission to destroy the thin strand of resolve she had managed to muster. It was a lucky thing she hadn't eaten that juicy hamburger she had planned. She was sure she would have lost it by now and spoiled this rather unorthodox wedding Mark had planned. Her nervousness was palpable. But when Mark asked her how she felt, she insisted she was fine, just fine. Once on the plane, she insisted on sitting by the window. She said she wanted to experience all there was about her first flight. Truthfully she felt that if she could see outside, she'd feel more in control. She was wrong.

"Mark, how fast are we going?" She was clutching his hand. She couldn't help it.

"I don't know," he said, prying her nails out of his wrist. "Are you worried?"

"No!"

"O..k..a..y." He dragged out, "Stewardess, can we get a drink here?"

"Shelly, Shelly." She finally heard Mark calling. "This is for you. It'll calm your nerves."

"But Mark, I don't…" She thought better of it. Perhaps it would calm her nerves. She took the drink from his hand and swallowed fast.

"Wow, hope I'm not marrying a lush."

That was the last thing Shelly remembered until she was standing, half-dazed, gazing into Mark's dancing brown eyes. If his face would just be still, everything was bobbing. Tremendous pink blossoms and garish yellow ribbons hovered tenuously above them. They threatened to crash onto their heads as a funny thinnish mouse wearing a gold lamé jacket and clown glasses waited for her to repeat after him. She expected his flashing silver bow tie to squirt water if she said the wrong thing. She remembered, first, Mark's worried look and then his look of relief as the mouse pronounced them Princess and White Knight. It was just like when they were kids, only different. Mark kissed her softly on the lips. She reached up to touch them, trying to reassure herself that this had not been a dream, but before she could raise her hand Mark grabbed it and pulled her behind him. Her feet tingled and throbbed so badly in her tight sling-back shoes that she wanted to scream. The urge was about to overtake her when the mouse and his assistant the bunny—her nose was bright red and she kept giggling—shouted, "Thank you for patronizing Minnie's Little Chapel of Love. A toast for your departure!"

Sitting in the taxi next to Mark with a bit of moisture drizzling down her cheek, she couldn't figure out if her head or feet hurt worse.

"How do you feel, Babydoll?"

She was beginning to be able to distinguish Mark's face from the array of colored lights that sparkled and gleamed as they zoomed down the road. "Say it again."

"How do you feel?"

"Nooo."

"Babydoll?"

"Aren't you forgetting something?"

"No, I don't think I am." She pinched his thigh.

"Ouch. Princess Babydoll, how do you feel?"

"My head is throbbing." She pressed her fingers to her temples.

"Well, you should know better than to drink like that."

"Like what…"

"All those drinks: so fast."

"Mark, I don't drink. You were the one that said I should have something."

"I just wanted you to calm down."

"Mark, are we actually married?"

"Should I be insulted? I'm only the love of your life. You told me so over and over and over again."

"Oh, Mark, did I? This is so embarrassing. Are you sure we should have done this?"

A cold chill came into Mark's voice, "You have doubts?"

Shelly could tell by the white-knuckled grip he had on the cab seat that no matter what she really thought, if she wanted to get home in one piece, her answer had better be, "No."

"You know what I figured out?" He didn't wait for a reply, "I really like Jimmy James Johnson."

"'Jimmy James?'" she heard herself question.

"Yes, he was the one who suggested that you take some time to consider his proposal, some time apart. Bob told me."

"Yes, but…"

Her mind was becoming more and more muddled. They had champagne when they arrived at the chapel, and the chapel lady gave them more to celebrate their union. Lazily his last words drifted into her mind and lingered there, "I owe that man my life." Shelly thought that was a really sweet thing to say.

Shelly vaguely recalled brightly glowing purple and red flashing lights, a throng of people squeezing up against her, the "cur-ching" of slot machines and the smell of cheap booze. The wedding in Vegas was a bleary but whimsical affair. The plane ride from Vegas was a colossal fog. Even if she had been alert, she still would have been too overwhelmed to talk or think. She could only feel and her feelings had led her here. She hoped this was where she was supposed to be.

*H*ad he done the right thing virtually forcing Shelly into marrying him? He was pretty sure he wanted her. Hadn't he always? Who was he fooling? This was the most important thing in his entire life. Shelly was his entire life. He had never wanted anything more than this

woman and this moment. Well, that wasn't exactly true. What he wanted at this precise moment was just beyond the threshold of his apartment. The wooden door and a confession was all that separated him from his destiny.

Shelly entered the apartment with wide eyes. A quiver coated her words as she spoke, "We're here." She scanned the room. "Looks functional. But I like it," she was quick to add.

"Are you nervous?"

"No," she blurted just quickly enough for Mark to know she was.

"Would you like something to drink?"

"Absolutely not!" she belted, sitting forcefully on his leather couch.

"Wait. We forgot something." Mark clasped Shelly's hand in his and walked her back out the door.

"Mark, I'm tired."

Once outside, Mark picked Shelly up.

"Sweetheart," she whispered breathlessly against his cheek.

Mark stopped and looked into her eyes, "Now you say it again."

"Sweetheart?"

"Yes," he said, carrying her over the threshold, past his large glass dining table and straight to his room. He kicked the large door open and set her carefully on the edge of his well-made bed. He'd never really noticed it before but his room was fairly barren. Everything was monochrome: black lacquer, gray covers, and white curtains. Shelly was the only life and vibrancy in the room. He longed to touch her. He moved to sit by her, throwing his trench coat off to the side.

Blowing his breath softly against her creamy cheek, he kissed her. Her back straightened and her spine stiffened. Wearing yellow, she looked as ridged as a frozen lemon Popsicle. Mark thought she was nervous so he decided to go slowly. Drawing her into his arms he felt her breathing come quicker. Her chest heaved against his side. This did not help his composure. Becoming wild with excitement and anticipation, he decided to put some distance between them. He let his body go limp and slid down the side of the bed to sit at her feet. Folding his arms he rested them on the gentle skirt pleats of Shelly's lap and laid his head there. For a moment he was at peace; that is until his hand started to wander and his fingers began gliding effortlessly up and down Shelly's calf. He removed her black sling shoes and carefully rubbed and massaged her feet. Looking up, he expected to see a wife at ease. Instead—even with the lights dim—he could make out an expressive mixture of worry and confusion.

Pushing up to his knees he wrapped his arms around her small waist, letting them rest on the swell of her bottom. A move which was meant to bring her comfort seemed only to alienate her further.

"Shelly, baby, what is the matter?"

"I… I…I'm not sure." She leaned her delicate frame away from him, nervously clutching and pinching the thick bedspread. She seemed so fragile in this big stark room.

Mark desperately wanted to attend to her words. Instead he found himself peering into her beautiful eyes. He stroked her wavy black hair and twirled strands around his fingers, watching the ebb and flow of the curls as he did. He didn't want to see it, but the look of torment on her face was plastered firm.

"Honey," he whispered while pulling her down to the floor and into his lap. "Please tell me what's bothering you." He ran his hand down her arm. She went rigid again and offered no verbal response.

In desperation Mark grabbed her face, gently rubbing her cheeks with his thumbs, "Babydoll, tell Marky what the problem is."

Shelly wrapped her arms tightly around his neck. The rapture of her exotic wild wind fragrance and the moisture of her dewy lips against his ear was almost his undoing. He struggled for control.

"What is it, Sweetheart, please tell me," he whispered at the base of her neck.

"I've been lying to you."

Her body pressed against his still shirted chest.

"What is it?" he said breathlessly.

"I'm not…" her voice trailed off.

"A virgin?" Mark supplied, completing the sentence for her.

"No…"

"It's okay, Shelly. I didn't expect—"

"No, Mark, I'm not experienced. I've never done this before."

Mark's arms went limp. His head fell back onto the foot of his bed as he looked up at the ceiling, which now looked a hundred miles away. The covers of his bed lay in a heap around Shelly and him. The comfortably warm air in his room turned ice cold. He felt exposed. This was either going to be harder or easier than he expected.

"Shelly," his voice was soft, almost inaudible, "me neither."

"What, Mark?" she rasped, tears running full force down her pretty brown cheeks. "What are you saying?"

"Shelly, I'm a virgin. I've never said that out loud. Sounds strange, doesn't it? Anyway, I've never done this before either."

Shelly leaned in and gripped his hands as if to comfort him, "Mark," she said with a hint of a smile in her voice, "you are so sweet; you don't have to say that to make me feel at ease. I know you've gone slowly for me. I'll be okay, just give me a little time."

"It's true," he said, locking his fingers between hers while intermittently kissing and caressing her palms. "I have gone slowly for you. I want you so much I'm aching." He was on his knees again, pulling her into his body with as much force as he could. "But it's also true that I've never done this before." Mark felt her disbelief as she tried again to pull away. He tightened his grip around her body. "Listen, baby," he said while licking her earlobe; she went soft and sultry in his arms. "I've done just about everything you can imagine with a woman." He thought, from her body molding to his, that at least the truth of his experience was becoming apparent to her; now to convince her of the other part. "But I've never actually had sex with anyone." He allowed her to pull away just long enough to search his eyes and his soul.

She must have found what she was looking for because his next sensation was of Shelly unbuttoning and removing his shirt. Then came the tender touch of her palms on his bare back. The teasing pressure of her satiny fingers working their way up his back and deftly lifting and pulling his tee-shirt over his head caused him to tremble. He inhaled, filling his lungs with the sublime sweet scent of her. He squeezed his eyes shut, ran his hand over her lips, playing at her tongue while using his other hand to trace her perky nose and eye lashes. Next he felt his hands move of their own volition, pushing their way into Shelly's hair, applying pressure to her temples as they wound their way in and out of her glorious mane.

The intensity of Shelly's grip said that she would go anywhere with him now. But he wanted more. He wanted her wild with urgency. He wanted her to feel what he was feeling, a fierce passion, and a raging inferno. Thoroughly entwined, they struggled to get closer to one another. Mark forced Shelly to his chest, while continually caressing and kissing her cheeks, chin, neck, ears and mouth. After several painfully blissful minutes Mark abandoned his quest to make Shelly feel anything. He surrendered to his own need and covered her body with his.

Totally engulfed by each other, Mark and Shelly shut out the world, tasting, touching, caressing and meshing every part: body and spirit, the two became one soul.

Shelly awoke with a start. Was there someone in her bed? She opened her eyes slowly scanning the room. With great effort, she sat up on her elbows. "My God, I'm married." Memories of her name being breathed over and over against her ear gave her a sudden chill. A smile lit her face as she carefully pulled the covers away. Mark's massive leg was draped across her body. She marveled at the mastery of God's workmanship as she noted the perfect mingling of her deep brown against his milky white. She couldn't help but think how absurd it was to believe that skin color should separate kindred spirits. She had met her destiny years ago and his name was Mark Schultz. There were few things in life she was sure of, but of this she had no doubt. With great difficulty she turned her slight body under her husband's impressive weight. She'd run quietly to the restroom and be back before Mark noticed her absence. A dull ache caused her to move more slowly than she anticipated.

"Shelly, Shelly!" Mark bolted upright in his bed. Darkness thick and black descended upon him. Despair lingered at the threshold of his consciousness. It seemed so real this time, that sweet dream that had dissolved over and over again into a hellish nightmare when he awoke to realize that his princess had once again eluded his capture. This time he could taste her, the ecstasy so real, the release more real. Mark turned to clear his head and saw the light under the bathroom door. It wasn't a dream. Shelly was here with him in his room and they were really married. He laughed to himself, realizing that this little woman had so upset his life that he nearly went into a panic at her leaving their bed. Their bed—he liked the sound of that. *She's coming.* Mark lay back down and feigned sleep. He wasn't ready for Shelly to know the power she had over him. He hoped she wouldn't notice the smile on his face.

Shelly crept quietly in, her apparent intention to get back in the bed without disturbing him. Instead she knelt in prayer.

"Father God... oh no," she gasped. Mark could feel tugging on the bed covers. She was apparently attempting to cover herself as she knelt. He bit his lip to keep from laughing aloud.

"I'm sorry, Lord. You made me. I know I don't have to be shy in front of you. Anyway, I know I don't pray like I should, and sometimes I don't act as I should. But I love you. You've always watched out for me, and to-day you've given me a gift too wonderful for words." She buried her face in the blanket, trying to muffle her cries. "God," she continued, "thank you for my husband. I've always loved him and if it's true what Mama Rose said, I guess he was always mine. Mama Rose said you'd give me the one person who was truly mine and I would know it for sure. Well, I know it. I can't really put into words what I feel. Thank you seems so inadequate, but it's the best I can do. Please accept it. I love you, Lord. Thanks for keeping me. Oh, and one more thing. It really doesn't matter if Mark was a virgin or not. I love him anyway. Please forgive him if he's told a little lie to make me feel better."

"I wouldn't lie to you, Shelly." Mark scrunched and leaned so that his nose was touching hers. "What?" he questioned. "My inexperience didn't show?"

"How would I know?" Shelly quipped, pulling back and socking him in the shoulder.

"That's true. You're just as ignorant as I am."

He grabbed her fist in mid-air, averting her attempt at a second strike. "And guess what?" he said pulling her onto the bed and into himself. "I'm not going to prove it to you now."

"What?" her lips mouthed against his chest.

"That I was a virgin before tonight."

Even in the dark, Mark knew that Shelly was aware of his intention.

The morning came too quickly. The sun shone brightly through the window. Mark shielded his eyes and Shelly crinkled her nose. Mark never got enough of that affectation. He pulled her into his arms and kissed her soundly. The desire to make love to his wife was upon him again. Sharp knocks at the door disturbed their solitude and his intended course of action.

Mark swung his legs over the side of the bed and yanked his robe from the closet. Shelly turned to watch, supporting her head on her hand and elbow. He was splendid: tall, sinewy and taut. Her breath caught in her throat and her body winced involuntarily. She lay back down and tried to get control of her breathing.

Mark left the bedroom walking softly. Reaching the entryway, he took the chain off the door.

"Donna? Cameron?" What would bring them to his door together?

"Mark, I need to talk to you. Do you have any idea where Shelly is?" Donna was clearly agitated.

"Yes, she's…"

"Shelly!"

Both Cameron's and Donna's mouths dropped open. Shelly emerged from the bedroom barelegged and wearing Mark's trench coat. She took one look at Cameron and dropped back into the room. Donna ran quickly after her. Mark smiled at Cameron's aghast stare.

As Donna followed Shelly into Mark's bedroom, she reflected upon the men she had left standing at the door. It was apparent to Donna that Mark was gloating without uttering a single word. It was equally apparent that Cameron's expression of anguish was real. It pained her to think that she would actually have to kill Mark if he had hurt Shelly in any way. Mark's bedroom was exactly as Donna imagined: quality and function. There was a bed, very wrinkled and tossed at the moment—poor Shelly—a nightstand, an oversized chest of drawers with an extra-large gilded mirror over it—he wasn't too vain—and a couple of lamps, no excess.

Shelly had retreated to the private bath. Donna called to her. She wanted more than anything to ask what all of this meant, but she needed to get to the important stuff first. "Shelly, Irene called me."

"Irene? You don't mean Mark's mother?"

"Yes, Mark's mother."

Shelly emerged from the bathroom with a sheepish look on her face, "But how? Why? Does she even know you?"

"It's Mama Rose, Shelly. Irene called to say that she's not doing well."

"Whoa, Mark," Cameron uttered, "I didn't know…" He interrupted himself realizing that the flow of his comment could possibly lead to another bloody lip. He decided to use a little tact. "What's going on with you and Shelly?"

"My wife and I are just getting back from our honeymoon."

"Repeat that please. I don't think I heard you correctly… "

"I said Shelly and I were married yesterday."

Cameron felt his face contort. An instant irritation lodged in his jaw. It hurt. It hurt all over. "Well, I guess that explains it," he continued. He could hear his voice echoing back into his head; it sounded hollow and shaky. "Dobbs just about had a coronary trying to contact you. Kincaid is anxious to see the specs for his proposed ad tomorrow."

"Okay, give me a few minutes. How did you get house-call duty?" Mark asked as he went to get a suit from the hall closet.

"I volunteered; got curious about what could keep the conscientious Mr. Schultz from checking in. Guess I got my answer. God, she must be…"

Mark was in the guest bathroom brushing his teeth as Cameron finished his sentence. He realized he should be grateful that Mark had not heard his last words.

"Shelly, Shelly, I have to go to the office. It's going to be a long one. I'll probably be gone long into the night; don't wait up. I'll see you tomorrow morning. Shelly, can you hear me?" Mark didn't want to interrupt what he knew was a delicate conversation between Shelly and Donna, and he really did need to get going. Thinking he had heard a faint response, he dressed quickly and was soon out the door with Cameron.

Cameron, who had been standing so that he had the advantage of hearing bits and pieces of Donna and Shelly's conversation while listening to Mark, didn't bother to update the latter. He wasn't sure, but he thought somehow it would work to his advantage.

"Mark," Shelly called as she emerged from the bedroom bath putting on one shoe and then the other, "Irene called." She came into the living room area and was surprised to find him missing. Well, she'd call him later. She needed to get to Mama Rose now.

"Donna, I'm leaving."

"Where's Mark?"

"I think he went in to work with Cameron."

"Did he know about Mama Rose?"

"I don't think he did," she answered, her voice in a whisper, "I've got to go now."

"Let me drive you."

"No, Donna—"

"Shelly, I insist; you're not yourself. Bob will be just fine until I get back."

"All right, but I'm leaving now."

Shelly and Donna ran downstairs to Donna's apartment. Donna told a groggy Bob about her plans, said she wouldn't be gone long and that she'd see him this evening. Shelly changed into pants and comfortable shoes and Donna grabbed a coat. They were packed and on the road in thirty minutes' time.

Once in the car, Donna started, "Shelly, I know you have Mama Rose on your mind and I understand that you are an adult, and I was pulling for Mark, I really was, but do you think—"

"Donna, we're married."

"You're what? Oh, Shelly, how wonderful," her enthusiasm trailed off as she added, "If only Mama Rose wasn't ill and you didn't have to leave now to deal with this." "Alone," Shelly knew Donna wanted to add.

*M*ark got home really late. He was exhausted but wanted nothing more than to pick up where he left off with his wife, even though he had promised not to disturb her until morning. He turned the key in the lock and practically tumbled into his silent apartment. "Shelly? Shelly!" he called loudly. He went into the bedroom and was a bit shocked to see the bed as they had left it. He didn't know what kind of housekeeper he expected Shelly to be, though he hadn't imagined her a slob. Well, no matter; he was neat enough for two.

The bathroom door was open. She wasn't there. "Where is she?" he wondered aloud. He turned, went out the door, slamming it behind him. He hurried down the stairs so fast he hardly remembered the trip.

"Who's there?" Bob said rubbing the sleep from his eyes, "Oh, Mark, I was expecting you," he said as he opened the door.

"Where's Shelly?"

"That didn't last long."

"What?" Mark said distractedly.

"Shelly's influence," to his curious stare, "you know, making you more laid back."

"Do you know where she is, Bob?"

"Yeah, Donna said you might not know. Irene called."

"My mother?" The look of total astonishment on his face must have worried Bob.

"Yes, your mother," Bob said as if talking to a half-crazed man.

"What did she want?"

"She said Mama Rose was sick."

"Oh no, so Shelly went home?"

"Well, yes, what are you going to do? The Kincaid presentation is tomorrow."

"I know; Cameron can handle it."

"You're going to let that slime do the presentation? You might as well give him your promotion while you're at it."

"Shelly needs me, Bob. You'd do the same."

"I would, but I'm not the incredible Mark Schultz."

Mark bowed his head: what to do next? "Give me the address, Bob."

"I don't have it. Don't you know where your mother lives?"

Mark grunted loudly, turned, and left Bob there with his questions. He didn't have time to explain that since he was a child his mother had been like a phantom, in and out of his life like a ghost. He had no idea she even knew Mama Rose, let alone that she was a close friend of hers, if in fact she was. He was going home. His dad was his only hope of knowing where Shelly and Mama Rose were.

*T*he drive home took about an hour and a half. Mark's anxiety made it seem a heck of a lot longer. He made the trip without noticing a single landmark. So many thoughts plagued him. What if his dad had no idea where Shelly and Mama Rose had moved? Mark shook his head to vanquish the thought as he took the steps two at a time. "Pop knows; I know he does," Mark heard himself say aloud as he removed the spare key from behind a loose stone. Everything was the same, neat and overstuffed.

"Mark, boy, come here; give your old man a hug. I didn't expect to see you...I don't know when I expected to see you." Jake lumbered down the stairs, rubbing his eyes. "It's like you forgot your own address."

"Pop, I don't live here." Mark struggled to keep the agitation out of his voice, "Anyway, Pop, I'm looking for Mama Rose. Do you have any idea where she lives now?"

"No, I told you that years ago when they first moved away. I thought you had forgotten about that old woman and her girl— "

"Be careful, Dad, Shelly's my wife now and if..."

Jake sat down so hard Mark thought the wooden chair would give way under his weight. He looked like a huge bear that had just felt the sting of several bullets from a hunter's rifle. He was paralyzed and didn't speak for what seemed like several minutes. When he did find his voice, he stuttered, "Wheenn? Howw?"

"None of that matters right now, Pop. Mama Rose is ill and I've got to find her."

Jake collected himself, got up from the table, and started up the stairs. "Pop, where are you going?" Mark felt dangerously close to losing control in a way he had never done before. Fortunately, he didn't have to wait long; his father was already on his way back downstairs.

"These are for you." Jake dropped a handful of letters on the coffee table by the couch where Mark was standing.

"Letters, Pop?" Mark lifted one and pointed to the return address, "Is this Mama Rose? These letters are over nine years old." Now it was Mark's turn to drop like a rock, which he did with a hard plop on the stuffed chair. He looked up at his father. Mark felt his face twisting into an unearthly scowl. It couldn't possibly communicate the venom he felt.

"Yes, that's right, Mama Rose wrote to you after she moved. I couldn't figure out what an old black woman could want with my son except to match-make him to her granddaughter. I thought it was for your own good, Mark." He looked away and down. "Maybe she still lives at that address."

Mark nodded and thumbed through the other letters. He found it curious that Rose had never used her full name. She had always been Mama Rose to him; he shook his head. No wonder he hadn't found her when he tried all those years ago. Jake was pulling the telephone and the directory over to where Mark was sitting. Mark found Rose's full name in the directory. The address was different from the one on his letters so he called the listed number; no answer. He groaned fiercely, picked up the pile of letters and put them into his coat pocket, which he hadn't bothered to remove. He stood and headed for the door.

"I'm going with you, boy."

"Why?" Mark spat.

"Let's just say I owe it to Mama Rose."

ark and Jake walked outside into an unseasonably warm November night. They headed for Mark's Mustang convertible.

"Son, that little red car's too cramped and we'll need room for Shelly. My car's bigger."

Without a word, Mark turned and headed for Jake's steel-gray Buick Special station wagon. When they were both seated, Jake turned on the radio and adjusted the volume to low. For the first few minutes neither one spoke.

"Mark?" Jake blurted.

"What is it, Pop?" Frustration made him run his hands through his hair.

"You said you and Shelly are married?"

"Yeah, Pop, and if you're going to start—"

"You have some special arrangement then?"

"What is that supposed to mean!?" Mark stated in a near shout.

"Don't curse me, boy."

Mark snickered. His dad could be one of the most vulgar men alive, especially when he was in the midst of one of his tirades, but let him dare to raise his voice and you'd think the world was coming to an end. His father was full of contradictions.

"I'm asking if she's the kind of girl who can do without... you know, maybe she doesn't want babies."

Mark never thought he was slow, but perhaps fatigue was taking its toll. It took him several minutes to unravel the strands of what his father was insinuating. "You think I'm queer?"

He knew his face was registering both amusement and disgust.

"You don't need to worry about me, boy. I accepted it a long time ago. I love you no matter what."

Mark had always known that his father, with all of his prejudices, flaws and stubbornness, loved him. But this latest confession raised him a peg or two in Mark's book. Though no one had ever asked to his face, he knew his dad was not the only person to think this. He was curious.

"What makes you think so?"

Jake looked as if it pained him to lay it out. But Mark knew he wasn't the type to beat around the bush.

Jake's hands gripped the steering wheel more tightly. "You know, I've never been one for gossip. In fact, to me, a man who gossips is no better than a woman." Mark let that pass. "Sometimes at the barber shop, some of the guys would let slip that they considered you a safe date." Jake paused, Mark thought, to let that sink in. "Remember Sam Couch?"

Mark nodded.

"His daughter, Marjorie, told him that he'd never have to worry about her getting pregnant while she was dating you. Sam said he had a hard time believing that about you, you being so big and athletic. But when other guys said their daughters gave the same report, he started to believe it. I knew what Sam was getting at. He was bold but he wasn't stupid. He wanted to see what I had to say without getting me angry enough to smash his face. I think he was surprised when I didn't react. Talk like that confirmed what I already believed."

Here, Mark couldn't help giving his father something more to think about, "Sam was right."

Jake heaved a tremendous sigh, as if to brace himself for the rest of the story. "He didn't need to worry about Marjorie getting pregnant, but I don't think any of those fathers would have considered their daughters safe if they'd known what I was doing with them."

Jake brightened, "Oh yeah, like what?"

"Like everything you can imagine short of intercourse."

Jake looked proud. Mark felt like he had sunk to a new low.

"You stopped every single time. Why?"

"Because," he hesitated, "it wasn't right."

Jake's face registered an expression somewhere between humor and curiosity.

"And is it right with Shelly?"

"You got that straight," Mark grinned.

Jake didn't get the joke. "You passed up every single white girl in the big city and couldn't keep your hands off—," he stopped himself. "How long?"

At first Mark didn't understand his question, then he did, "Since we got married."

"You're telling me that you've been a virgin all of this time. You're twenty-eight years old," he paused to catch his breath. "You and Shelly just got married, right, and you've only just had your first taste? That's impossible."

Mark gave a "suit yourself" shrug. Forty minutes passed in collective silence. Jake needed to know more.

"Why did you feel you had to be married?"

Mark had only recently figured out all of the reasons himself. He wanted to help his dad understand, and he wanted to say some of the stuff out loud to get it clear in his own mind.

He told his dad about sneaking over to Mama Rose's house to talk about things. She seemed to know about life and stuff more important than the here and now. Mark realized at that moment that he was rushing to Mama Rose as much for his own sake as for Shelly's.

"I know this is going to sound strange to you, Pop, but it was Mama Rose who first talked to me about relationships between men and women. When Shelly and I were still kids, we were in a swing together; I got er... aroused. I was confused. Mama Rose asked me what I was thinking so seriously about when I passed her house. She was always doing that."

"I know," Jake mumbled. "She's there when something needs to be sorted out, whether you like it or not."

"Not you, Pop?"

"Why not me? Why should I be spared? Was there anyone in our neighborhood ten years ago who didn't have to suffer through her prodding?"

"Well, anyway," Mark continued after giving his father a side glance, "she started telling me how things between boys and girls changed as they got older. One thing led to the next and she was showing me in the Bible."

"The what?" Jake interrupted.

"The Bible." Mark continued, "It says that sexual intimacy is meant for love and marriage between a man and woman that God puts together. My mind flashed to Shelly on the swing, her crinkled nose when I yelled at her to get off me. I felt pain and happiness all at once. It was getting late so I left. I didn't think about that conversation or that day much after that, but I think you'll agree it had a lasting effect on me."

"Are you trying to say that one conversation with Mama Rose kept you a virgin all those years?"

Mark glanced out the window. The surroundings were starting to change: dilapidated and decrepit came to mind. "Did you know I went to church with her sometimes?"

"To that little Negro Baptist church she was always bragging about?"

"Yep, sometimes on Sundays when you were at work and Shelly was off somewhere. I'd 'accidentally on purpose' drive the way Mama Rose was walking and give her a ride."

"That can't be true. One of those colored people would have bragged about seeing my boy in an all-Black church. You know, just to get back at me."

"Why would they want to do that?" Mark teased. "I never went in. I parked on the side of the building. The speakers were loud and I could hear all the songs, 'I wanna be ready when Jesus comes,' and the preaching, 'For this cause shall a man leave his mother and father and cleave only to his wife.' Mama Rose started to 'accidentally on purpose' bring two Bibles. She'd leave one in the car with the pages for that day's sermon marked. I read along. I'd even bring it home sometimes. I think it was all that. You might even be partially to blame."

Jake raised an inquisitive brow.

"Remember you said Mom was different; that she wouldn't let you touch her at all until you were married?"

"Yeah, so?"

"Maybe Mom had some kind of religion."

"You're stretching it, son. I don't like saying this, but I think your mama was ill-used some kind of way as a child. She'd say things like, 'nobody's touching me again who doesn't have a right to.' And I know for sure one of her foster parents tried something with her."

Mark was sorry to hear that, but he'd asked for it. His father was nothing if not frank. Talking about his mom reminded him.

"Mom's with Mama Rose."

Jake looked, to Mark, as if he thought Mark was intentionally trying to aggravate him.

"Can you speak plainly, son? What are you talking about now?"

"Irene, you know, your wife, she's with Mama Rose."

Jake, who seemed to have been holding his breath for the last sentence, heaved a huge sigh. "Good."

"I didn't expect that response."

"I haven't seen your mother in so long. I've been worried sick. I'm relieved, that's all. Glad she's all right, you know?"

"You could have fooled me. I didn't think you cared about her at all. You never did anything for her. You let her live like a pig."

"Hold on there, boy," Jake planted a heavy and not-too-friendly hand onto Mark's shoulder, a clear warning. "You don't have a clue as to what you're saying. I lo...care for Irene. She's stubborn, would never let me do a thing for her. I know I should have done more but when I tried she threatened to run. I couldn't lose you both. When she let me have you, I felt I had done the best I could. At least I could be your dad even if I couldn't be her husband."

"You mean you wanted to?"

"Wanted to what?" Jake snapped, suddenly distracted.

"To be her husband."

"I did."

"But you don't want to anymore. I mean, so much time has passed."

"Yeah, right." Jake said, as he deliberately stared straight ahead.

Jake didn't seem at all convincing to Mark.

Left to his own thoughts, Mark's mind raced. What was wrong with Mama Rose? Why had she moved to this neighborhood? Why was his mother relaying messages for her? Were they close? Putrid fumes drew him back to reality. His familiarity with the smells grated his nerves. At the stop sign, a makeshift dump lay right outside the window. Trash mingled with urine: suddenly he was twelve years old again, walking backwards, wanting more than anything to get what was his and to get away from the apartment where he lived with his mother.

*W*ould anything surprise Jake ever again in his life? The shock he figured Mark expected him to express was suddenly upon him. He wasn't even aware that Irene knew Mama Rose. The last time he had seen Irene was a few weeks before Mark left for college. She'd been wasting away. Her mind seemed to be as fragile as her body. He could remember it vividly.

He came home late. One of his dates had gone south and he wanted nothing more than a good night's sleep to forget about it. Irene was pacing on his porch. Impatience was written in her every step. This wouldn't be pleasant. It didn't matter; he was always glad to see her.

"Irene, you been here long?"

"Long enough," she said, taking a last puff off a cigarette and grinding the butt with her toe. He wanted to ask her when she started that disgusting habit, but he really didn't want to waste time antagonizing her. As it turned out, she was already agitated, as was evidenced in her attitude when she yelped, "Where is Mark?"

Ignoring her question, Jake turned his key in the lock hoping for a few minutes with her.

"Irene, Mark should be here any minute. Can I offer you something to eat?" he finished as she followed him in out of the cold.

"No," she said, plopping down at his dining room table. He could see by the way she dropped her head that she wished she hadn't been so hasty in her refusal, as her eyes darted longingly at the smothered pork chops and green beans on the counter.

He wanted so badly to make her comfortable. He couldn't resist offering to help one more time. "Irene, where are you staying?"

"That is not your concern, Jacob."

"I realize that, Irene. It's…well, you are the mother of our child and I feel obligated."

"You don't have any obligation to me. I am not your responsibility. I'm getting along fine. Where is Mark?" Irene was fidgeting nervously in her seat. She jumped up and went to the door. Swinging it open widely, she looked up and down the street. "Just tell him I came by."

"Irene, you really should stay. He's going—"

"I have to go, Jacob. Just tell him I came by, okay?"

"Sure, Irene, I will. Are you sure there's nothing I can do for you?"

"Nothing."

That was over ten years ago and still he thought of her. It was about time to give up. He knew it; so why couldn't he?

Jake looked at Mark out of the corner of his eye as they approached the address they had gotten out of the directory. Hopefully Rose still lived here. He figured the neighborhood would be bad, but he thought this had to be one of the worst in the city. Vacant lots littered with debris were common sights, and burnt-out, boarded-up buildings were plentiful. He suddenly felt ashamed. Mama Rose was too good a woman to have to endure such a place. Maybe there was more he could have done to spare her this.

"Are we almost there, Pop?" Mark said, impatiently drumming his fingers on the dashboard.

"A couple more houses up, on the right." Jake pointed.

Mark looked at Jake, his mouth open. Jake's mouth was open as well. A perfectly manicured smallish house stood like a jewel in the midst of filth. Mama Rose even had two miniature pines on either side of the cement stairs. On the sky-blue door hung a large hand-painted sign that read, "Welcome." Its print looked vaguely familiar to Jake, the tilt of the letters and the delicate strokes. Everything about her was delicate, or it used to be.

Walking up to the porch, Mark knocked on the door; no answer. At the same time Jake noticed a note carefully wedged into the doorjamb. It was Irene's handwriting, the same as on the welcome sign:

> Shelly,
>   I've taken Mama Rose to St. Paul's Hospital. She's not doing well. Come as soon as you can, 720 West Ranston.
> Irene Schultz

On the other side was a note to Mark:

> Hi, Sweetheart,

> *Somehow I just knew you'd find us. I realized too late that you didn't have this address and when I called, you had already left. We are going to St. Paul's Hospital to see Mama Rose.*
> *Love Always,*
> *Shelly*

Jake could see the relief on Mark's face as he read the letter. He knew where Shelly was but… "Let's go, Pop, I need to find out how Mama Rose is."

Mark bounded down the stairs, Jake close on his heels.

"I'm driving, Pop."

"Okay, Mark. Just don't get us killed."

St. Paul's was a community hospital: a solitary brick structure, only four stories high. Mark was thankful; perhaps they wouldn't have all of the restrictions that some of the larger hospitals did. Mark walked briskly up to the revolving door, his father directly behind him. He approached the reception desk.

"Yes, sir, may I help you?" An elderly woman with blue-gray hair offered a weary smile.

"We're here to see Rose—"

"Yes, Mama Rose, why not? We have a special area prepared for her on the second floor. Take those elevators down the hall and to the left."

Mark turned a confused face to his father, who was already making his way to the elevators and jerking his head in summons. The lights in the rickety elevator flickered once or twice and the car bumped to a stop. One foot was out the door before the solid metal obstructions were fully parted. Mark stalked down the hall. Jake grabbed his shoulder, "Do you know where you're headed, boy?"

Mark turned toward his father; he did not.

"Over here," Jake suggested, pulling him toward a well-lit bank of desks where three nurses stood and sat.

"I suppose you know how late it is?" the wiry nurse said, pushing a yellow pencil behind her ear as she looked up at her visitors, her frown plastered firmly in place. "Who are you here to see? Wait, don't tell me... Rose."

"Yes, can you please take us to her room? Is she doing okay?"

"I guess you're aware that even a place like this has some rules. This is family-only visiting hours. Might I inquire as to your relationship to the patient?"

His brain, already on overload, went into panic mode. Like a raging bull, he was preparing to trample the firm-stanced matador of a nurse and storm the offending doors. Just as his weary brain was about to attempt communication, his father chimed in, "Grandson."

Nurse Smithers jutted her neck out and rubbed her head, "He is the patient's grandson?"

She looked from Mark to Jake then back again, "And you must be her son?"

"Yes, Ma'am, that would be correct."

"I've heard everything. Come on, it's too early in the morning to argue. You might as well join the rest of your 'relatives'."

Jake and Mark looked at each other momentarily and followed the nurse to a cramped waiting room crowded with people.

"Your family," the nurse said with a flourish and left them standing there to figure out her meaning.

Browns, yellows, tans and whites in various states of agitation all assembled in that small room, all claiming to be Mama Rose's family. Mark noticed Shelly in the corner gently rubbing Donna's hand, telling her that she could go home and assuring her that she would be all right with Irene. As if sensing his presence, Shelly's face tilted in his direction. Seeing Mark, she leapt to her feet. Mark rushed to her side. Within moments they were holding each other tightly, stroking faces and wiping tears.

Jake stayed in the background. He was finally able to acknowledge the love he had tried so hard not to see. Suddenly he couldn't remember why he had fought it so hard. It was there, in Mark's eyes, in Shelly's. He knew because…Irene. It couldn't be. It was. Even kneeling with her back to him he could tell. She had filled out and there was something else. As Irene held the hands of a little child's in hers, the child who had been crying began to smile. She leaned to kiss Irene on the cheek. Irene gave her a tight hug and rose to her feet. She turned slowly. Stunned, Jake felt himself falter. The look of confidence he saw on Irene's face was like nothing he'd ever seen in her before. And the smile on her face did not abate when she looked at him. He turned, not wanting her to recognize him, not wanting to spoil her mood.

To hold her smile and not have her face go sour in his presence, was a small gift, but one he wanted to savor. Curious, Jake again surveyed the crowd. She really was here, but who was she? It wasn't the reserved but able Laura Irene Mills whom he had courted and married, and it wasn't the Irene Schultz he had last known, the woman who seemed alternately bitter or afraid of her own shadow. This was someone totally new. Was that possible? Could people change completely? He didn't think he ever could.

"Hello, Jacob, what are you doing here?" Jake shook his head. It had to be Irene; she was the only one besides his parents to call him Jacob.

Out of the corner of his eye she stood. He could now see a bit of the old Irene as she averted her glance when he looked at her, as if she could read his thoughts. He felt her give herself a mental shake. She stood up straight and met his eyes. It was his turn to be nervous.

"I…I came with Mark."

"Our son is here? Where?" Excitement struck her like lightning. Jealousy wrapped itself around Jake like a heavy cloak. It weighed him down. He could only point.

"Mark!" she belted. Mark turned.

"Mom?" Jake could see the disbelief working across Mark's features. "Is that you?" It had to have been years since he'd last seen her.

"Yes, Marky, it's me."

"You look…"

"Better?"

"No, good!"

"Thank you," she approached him with some trepidation.

"You're here with Shelly?"

"Yes, Mom…"

"You're together, then?" She looked radiant. Genuine pleasure heightened her beauty.

"Yes, Mom, we're married."

"Oh, Mark, how wonderful. Mama Rose'll be so glad to hear it," suddenly more somber, "when she wakes up."

"Will she wake up?" Mrs. Miller, a lady from Jake's block, asked from the edge of the crowd.

Shelly's knees buckled with the question. Jake could see Mark pulling her to his side. He shook his head. It all seemed so silly now. All the wasted years. Could anything good come out of this lost time?

Irene turned with assurance, "Mrs. Miller, Mama Rose is going to be just fine. We've all just got to believe." With that a certain inspiration came over her.

"Everybody up," she commanded. "Join hands. We're going to pray for Mama Rose. The Bible says…" Jacob felt as if he had been transported to some alternate universe. Who was this vibrant woman commanding the masses? "…where two or more are gathered, Jesus is in the midst." She stopped and took a quick count. "There are at least twelve of us here. We are going to rock the heavens." Jake didn't move. He wouldn't if he could have. Praying was something he seldom did. And public prayer, well, that was out of the question.

A resounding, "You too, Jacob!" jolted him from his thoughts.

"What?"

"I said, you too. This room is gonna be so full of prayer, God'll have to hear us." All heads lifted; every eye was fastened on him.

Jake shook his head, "No."

He just couldn't. What kind of hypocrite would he be, praying after all these years?

Irene glanced his way for a moment. He felt awful, but he just couldn't. They prayed hard and long. Their prayer was interrupted twice, once by a nurse who came to tell them to keep it down and once to tell them there was no change. Most of the people prayed silently, some out loud. Jake imagined this was a Baptist tradition. Irene, who wasn't praying loudly, but certainly wasn't silent, seemed to be praying in a foreign language. Why would she be doing that?

Another hospital worker came in. She looked as though she was very moved by their desperation and sincerity, "Miss Rose looked to be coming out of her coma for a minute, but slipped back in. Y'all keep praying," she said as she rushed from the room.

Jake felt like a complete heel now. When was the last time he had prayed? Oh, yeah, sitting on his son's bed wondering where Mark was the night that she had saved him, Mama Rose.

"Jacob, the Lord desires your fellowship."

His head snapped up. It was Irene again—her voice, yet not her…he couldn't find a way to describe it. The circle was broken. She held her hand out to him. It was the very hand that had struck him to his core when she pulled it away as if he were the most loathsome creature alive. It was the hand that had held his through storms both real and imagined. It was the hand that had rocked their son and been denied to him countless times. This hand was being extended to him now. He was afraid to accept it for fear it was a phantom, but he was also afraid to reject it. After all he had never expected to have this chance. Jake closed his eyes. The next awareness he had was his hand in Irene's.

Irene's voice became frantic. The pitch of the entire crowd became fevered. He wanted so badly to open his eyes and see if the sights matched the sounds resounding in his ears. The exhilaration that surged within him was frightening. Like a jolt, Blam! The door came crashing open.

"She's awake! Come quick!" A hunched-over Negro woman motioned for them to follow as she raced toward the opposite end of the hall.

The crowd rushed the door. A nurse, new to Jake, suddenly appeared, "You can't all come. Just next of kin." All but Jake held their ground.

"Ma'am, you decide," the nurse said, bestowing a most respectful nod to Irene. Could it be that Irene with her very black hair and sun-kissed skin had convinced this staff that she was, in fact, Rose's daughter. If someone told Jake that the moon had rolled up next to his car tonight, he'd believe it. This was truly a night of possibilities.

Irene gave a nod to Mark and Shelly, who immediately started behind her.

"Irene, can I come?" His voice sounded helpless but instead of thinking about how he must look groveling to be part of this group, he focused on his desire to be with those closest to him. She said yes without looking back. The glaring light shone on their odd group as they made their way to Miss Rose's room. Jake felt exposed right down to his core.

Outside the room, through the window, they could see Mama Rose struggle to take off her oxygen mask. "Let my children in," she said weakly. Mark, Shelly and Irene entered. Jake thought to go in would be to intrude on their moment. All of them shared a bond with Rose. They were her family. He watched through the window. Mark, Shelly and Irene flanked Rose's bed, Mark on her left, Shelly on her right. Irene stood directly behind Shelly with her hands resting on Shelly's shoulders. She seemed to Jake as though she had known her forever. As Jake looked on the scene, a pang of loneliness came over him. This was too much. He turned to go back to the waiting area. He had taken about four steps when a nurse tapped him on the shoulder.

"She's asking for you, Mr. Schultz."

"No, Ma'am, you mean the other Mr. Schultz. He's already in there."

"I'm sure you're wrong, Mr. Schultz. Miss Rose might be a lot of things, but senile is not among them." Jake was equally sure that this nurse was wrong, but what did he have to lose. He turned and walked in.

"Come over here, son." Rose was saying as he entered the door. He nudged Mark with his elbow. Mark didn't move. "You gonna make an old women yell?"

All eyes turned toward Jake. He stood stock-still.

"You talkin' to me, Miss… er Mama Rose?"

"Yes, indeed I am."

Slowly Jake moved toward the bed and instinctively to Irene's side.

"Ah," Mama Rose said, opening her eyes completely. "I see you've come home. I have what I've always wanted now: to know that my children have love in their lives. I can rest in peace. She closed her eyes and took in a deep sigh. Her breath appeared to cease.

"Mama!" they yelped in unison.

"But not today." Her smile was impish as she raised herself onto her elbows and peered into each face. "Today I'm going home with my family."

The meaning of the words made no sense intellectually. But Jake could feel them in his heart. The feeling of home, as she put it, was overwhelming. His eyes roved from left to right trying to see if anyone could read him. He knew Rose could but he could still hold out hope concerning the others.

The next hour was a flurry of activity. Doctors checked and re-checked Mama Rose. It was obvious the woman had had a stroke. What wasn't obvious was how her miraculous recovery had come about. She was demanding to go home and the doctors were refusing, saying she needed to stay at least a day for observation. Mama Rose actually threatened to go back into the coma if they didn't let her go.

When the other "family members" in the waiting room heard the news, the cheering and hallelujahs were so loud the administrators said that if Rose would sign an agreement releasing the hospital from all liability, they'd let her go. She signed and they left.

Two brothers from the church volunteered to take Donna home. One would drive her car and the other would trail to bring the driver back. The enthusiasm was contagious. Donna said she didn't want to leave but this episode had gotten her thinking about her own family. It was time Bob knew about her pregnancy. She felt better about it; and if things started to go wrong, she'd ask Irene and Mama Rose to pray. Shelly gave her a big hug and Mark looked as if Shelly owed him an explanation.

The family headed for Mama Rose's house. Jake offered his house to Mark and Shelly, but Shelly could not be persuaded to stay anyplace but with Mama Rose. And it was obvious Mark wasn't leaving his wife's side.

Wife: how Jake had missed his. It seemed he would be the only one not going to Mama Rose's. At least he'd have their company while driving them there.

The drive home had that same "yucky" feeling. It just wasn't right that Mama Rose and Irene were living in that neighborhood. He was sure that Mark could take care of them, but perhaps he had better stick around, just to make sure everybody got settled. "Mama Rose, I was thinking…"

"We'd love to have you stay awhile, Jake. It's been too long, all of us together."

"We've never all been together."

"Don't you think it's about time?"

Mama Rose's mind-reading and cryptic messages had sometimes unnerved him; today he was grateful he didn't have to use extra words to make his meaning clear. When they opened the door to the house, he paused. A feeling of nostalgia so great rushed him that he felt dazed. The kitchen: its décor took him immediately back to his first date with Irene. The red-and-white checkered tablecloth, the off-white curtains, the metal chairs with white padded seats…he remembered it as if it had happened yesterday.

Irene showed up wearing a deep plum dress. The neckline was cautiously revealing and the hemline allowed a fair amount of her calf to show. He remembered wanting to see more. She was polite but reserved. It had taken him months and cost him hundreds in extra trips to the grocery where she worked to convince her to go on a date with him. He was trustworthy. He reassured her time and time again that he would be a perfect gentleman.

They hit it off in an unconventional kind of way. She didn't want to be touched but said she felt at ease talking to him. Over a number of dinners and tons of Namio lunch specials, her history unfolded one detail at a time.

At the tender age of four, Irene was dropped off at the downtown police station by Kate, her rotund auburn-haired mother with the pretty face. She was given a generous hug and a kiss on the cheek as parting gifts. When Irene clutched her mother's skirt and buried her small face in its folds, her mother pried her little fingers from their grip, smiled and said, "I'll be back." Irene knew she wouldn't. From that time on, she was shifted from one foster placement to the next. One moment she lived in grandeur: a house with a maid, three stories and chandeliers. The next moment she shared a dingy efficiency with a kind-hearted woman and her four other foster children. When she moved into Judge "No-name's" home, she thought she finally had a place to call her own. He was kind and generous to her. She took care of their younger children and helped with the cooking. Mrs. "No-name" treated her coolly, but Irene thought with time she'd win her over. After a few months of gifts and compliments, the judge's attentions became uncomfortable.

If Jake could kill the man, he'd do it today. Irene never said who he was and seemed agitated whenever she spoke of him. One night while she was sleeping soundly in her pristine bed with the mint-colored lace canopy, surrounded by delicately striped wallpaper, the vile creature came into her room. She knew because she awoke to what she thought was a nightmare. The judge, in only a thin robe, lay on top of her. Without giving it a second thought, Irene reached for the paring knife she kept by her bed for slicing apples, her favorite nighttime snack. She raised her arm high and plunged down with all of her might. Fortunately for the judge, she hit his most fleshy part, his butt. She managed to laugh when she talked about how he shrieked as he ran from her room stark naked except for the thin robe dangling from his backside. The royal-blue appendage was held firmly in place by the paring knife still wedged there.

Irene quickly gathered up what she could put into her overused overnight bag, including many of the expensive gifts the judge had given her. She stopped only long enough to see who was standing upstairs snickering over the banister. Mrs. "No-name" winked at her and waved goodbye. It was their first and last pleasantly shared moment. Irene was sixteen at the time and had lived on her own or with whomever she felt she could trust until she married him.

Why in the world would she decorate Mama Rose's kitchen like Namio's Diner?

Mama Rose seemed exceptionally well for a woman who had barely eluded death. Mark insisted on helping her up to her room, and she insisted that Mark and Shelly take the bedroom across from hers. She further insisted that they go to that room right away to get some rest. Mark wasn't sure what the hurry was, but he wasn't unhappy about having Shelly all to himself again. Shelly asked Mama if she was really okay and if she needed anything. To that Mama replied that Irene took good care of her and would see to things. Mark could see Shelly fighting off the feeling of being replaced. She'd feel better when she had some rest.

Downstairs, Irene was wondering if the stroke had somehow affected Mama Rose's memory. There was no downstairs bedroom, and although she had slept on the couch many times in the past, she couldn't very well do that with Jacob in the house. And besides, weren't they all there to have a reunion of sorts? Mark had barely spoken to her. And now with a quick kiss to her cheek, he was off to bed.

Jacob obviously sensed that she was preoccupied; his voice intruded on her thoughts. "Irene, it's been a long day for you. Why don't you come over and have a seat?"

Irene pulled slowly away from peering up after Mama Rose and walked slowly toward the kitchen table, still glancing over her shoulder. When she reached the kitchen, Jacob was there, holding the chair for her. She sat down. A wave of embarrassment hit. She had decorated the kitchen like Namio's dining area. Jacob had to realize it. She never expected him to see this room. That night in Namio's had given her such a feeling of hope. It wasn't until she had put the final touches on the room that she realized what she had done. Once done, she liked it too much to change it.

"Jacob, I don't know if it's a good idea for us to be…"

"Irene, I know why you left."

"What? What are you talking about, Jacob?"

"I know why you left and took Mark."

"Jacob, I hardly think that matters…"

"I'm sorry, Irene. I never could handle alcohol. It's just that being anywhere near my parents makes me crazy. The minute I walked into that house, things I had tried desperately to forget came flooding back to me. I almost passed out when you went into my father's study."

"You knew about that room?" Irene jumped to her feet. Her face wound into a jumble of disgust.

"Wait," he said, gently grasping her hand. "I was only a boy the last time I was in there. Irene, I must have been traumatized or something. I didn't remember half the stuff I'd been through until I was grown. The grotesque clippings of hangings and the framed manifestos of white supremacy made me sick. Everything in there glorified the sufferings of people who weren't pure white or were Jews. They hung like trophies all over that room. My parents are sick, Irene, and they made me sick."

"Jacob, you were always loving and kind to me. That is, until that night when you accused me of…" Irene breathed in sharply and cocked her hand on her hips. Her voice trailed off; she had made up her mind years ago that she was done being hurt by Jacob Schultz.

"I remember that too, Irene. I accused you of being unfaithful and that it might have been with a Negro."

"That was not the word you used, Jacob! You are no different from your parents."

"I want to be."

"What? What do you want to be?"

He slid his chair closer to hers. She did not pull away. His look of contrition and pain held her fast. He continued, "Irene, I'm all alone. When you left, I convinced myself that if I got Mark back I'd be okay, and I was for a while. Then he started to grow up. It's true, I didn't like Shelly or Mama Rose. It was partly because they are Negros; but they had some kind of hold on Mark, and I was afraid they'd take him from me."

"Jacob, Mark loves Shelly. I think he always has."

"And no one should come between a man and the woman he's meant to be with." He tried searching her eyes. She turned her head away.

"Jacob, it has been a long day."

"I know," pushing back in the chair abruptly. "I'll get my jacket."

Jake literally dragged his feet as he walked toward the front door. His hand hung heavy on the knob. Speaking in a low voice he said, "I love you, Irene."

Also very quiet, "That's easy to say, Jacob."

"But not so easy to do, right?" he said, turning quickly. "Not like letting your young wife stay away years with your son."

"Letting?"

"Yes, letting, Irene. I knew where you and Mark were long before I sent the authorities. I kept hoping you'd come back. I thought you understood how much I loved you both. And how about going months without touching you when we started dating? Do you know how I ached to be with you? Letting you decide every little touch, every single kiss. No, that wasn't a man in love. Why I loved you more—"

"Don't you mean pitied?"

"You'd like to believe that, wouldn't you, Irene? That way you could justify breaking my heart!"

Jake snatched the door open and bounded down the stairs. He reached the handle of his car door and remembered how fragile Irene was. He started back up the stairs. As he leaned to push the door, Irene pulled it open.

"We're not done talking," she was yelling as he fell in. "Jacob, how can you say you love me when you…"

Jake gathered Irene into his arms and held her as tightly as he could. He might never touch her again, but he'd have this to remember for the rest of his life. It would do. Irene wiggled a bit. Jake tightened his grip. He didn't want her to see the tears building in his eyes. He whispered into her ear, "I can't change the past, Irene, but if you give me one more chance, I'll never let you down."

"You will."

Jake squeezed harder and then let go. He'd tried and failed. Sometimes you just don't get another chance. At least he'd have Mark and he was confident he'd be able to accept Shelly now. He'd have them.

"I'm sorry I bothered you again. You're obviously not so fragile anymore."

"No, I'm not. And you would eventually let me down. It's impossible to be everything a person needs. But, Jacob, that's not what I'm looking for."

"And neither am I, right?"

"Don't put words in my mouth, Jacob. I'm saying that only God never fails."

"Oh yeah, I almost forgot you're a godly person now and he's all you need."

"Yes, that's true." Irene put her hand under her chin and stared at him.

"Irene, I'm sorry I'm keeping you from Mama Rose. It's just that I was hoping…"

"Hoping what, Jacob?"

"Foolish things, Rennie." As he reached to stroke her cheek, she reached for his hand and carefully pulled it down. She moved away from him, sat on the couch and patted the cushion next to her.

Rose worked with renewed vigor, with eagle's wings. Her old joints, which had begun to stiffen, were fluid and energized. Fixing breakfast was just the beginning. Her first question of the day was: what to cook? Aha! Biscuit bread: it was a dense cross between a flapjack and shortbread. It was doughy, but not the kind that made your mouth fill up like cotton. There was a crispness to it that everyone liked, even Jake. Where was the Alaga? She searched the pantry, behind the salt, catsup and cereal boxes. Ah, there it was. Biscuit bread just wasn't the same if it didn't have that rich thick Alaga. It was the only syrup that had enough gumption to stick with her bread.

Umph, umph, umph. She wondered if Jake and Irene knew that their bodies had woven and intertwined during their sleep. The subconscious had a way of taking us to where we really wanted to go. Speaking of places one wanted or didn't want to go, the doctors wanted her to come in today. In fact, they had made it a condition for allowing her to sign herself out. They said they wanted to keep tabs on her recovery, to make sure she didn't have a setback. Dr. Frensco had been talking to the nurses within Rose's hearing, "I don't hold out much hope for her coming out of the coma soon, and when she does, there's sure to be brain damage." Rose smiled. Some folks thought it was too late for the brain damage part. Mrs. Crane had, at one time, said she was crazy as a June bug in the snow. She said, "Rose doesn't have the sense she was born with, going out in ice or desert scorch to help any low-life she runs into." People didn't have a clue as to what they were saying. Didn't they know that that was the reason God saved her? Her work here wasn't done.

Yes, she'd go to the doctor and baffle them as usual. God's handiwork couldn't be explained. She wouldn't be leaving until God said so. When that time came, she'd be glad to go.

The next question: whose offer to accept, James's or Jake's. Both men had offered to drive her to the doctor later today. Jake wanted to be as close to Irene as he could get. She didn't feel he needed any extra help with that. Jimmy or James Johnson, whatever he was calling himself now, was a different story. Shelly hadn't meant to be callous, but she had been. Rose would soften the ground with him before Shelly had to try to explain herself.

*I*t was absolute bliss lying next to Shelly, but the real world was beckoning. Mark needed to go to work, that is, if he still had a job. "Babydoll, Babydoll, wake up." He rocked her shoulder softly. The sensual smile on Shelly's face made getting out of bed seem absolutely painful, "I've got to get back to work."

"I know. Do you have to go now?"

"Yes, sweetheart, we could live on love, but I do like to eat now and then." With his hand on her cheek, he gritted out, "You can stay here if you need to."

"I think I should." She looked sick.

Mark went downstairs to call his dad on the phone; he needed a ride back to his car. Shelly went to Mama Rose's room to check on her.

"Mark, Mama Rose isn't in her room!"

Mark shushed loudly and lifted his hand to summon her to come down from the upstairs. Her footsteps were loud and quick as she bounded down. She bumped into him when she reached the bottom. She seemed disoriented. Mark could tell just when her mind cleared. Her jaw immediately dropped as she saw Irene and Jake sitting asleep on Mama Rose's high-back love seat. Their bodies were twisted and contorted but their serene faces told quite another story. As Mark and Shelly were getting used to that sight, they spied Mama Rose in the kitchen, looking quite chipper and already in the process of cooking breakfast.

"I expect you young people will be getting back to your own place. Irene and I have things under control here, and I'm sure Jake will be around if we need him."

As the smell of Mama Rose's eggs and bacon wafted through the living room, Irene wriggled and awoke. Finding the room full of people, she jumped wide-eyed to her feet. Jake mumbled something, looked around and stood up next to Irene. He was apparently too close, as she moved to allow space between them. Mark gave Shelly a sideways glance. She looked at her feet. Mark thought she was trying not to let Jake see the pity in her eyes. It was plain to see that his father wanted to be with his mother like he wanted to live. Mark wished there was something he could do.

Smoothing her dress, Irene started, "Er, Jacob and I were catching up and we…"

Mark felt as if he'd never seen this Irene before yesterday. She looked new. And her personality was transformed. She moved and spoke with confidence. All of her timidity and "ghostliness" was gone. Drawn to her beauty, he approached her and gave her a tremendous hug, "Mom," was all he could think to say.

"Save some for your old man," was the first thing Jake said, and upon saying it, he approached Mark and gave him a hearty hug. "Congratulations, son, Shelly."

Jake turned toward Shelly and extended his arm. Shelly walked gracefully over to accept her ceremonial hug. Jake wrapped his broad arms around her shoulders and gave her a great squeeze. Mark met his father's eyes for a brief moment. There was heartfelt longing in that hug. Could it be that he actually accepted their marriage? No, that was too much to imagine.

Everyone in the room was silent and in disbelief except Mama Rose who said, "Breakfast is served."

*M*ark and Shelly left right away, Shelly telling Mark she could show him how to get back to the old place by bus or they could hail a cab at the corner. Rose found it telling that Shelly walked right by her beloved biscuit bread, a family treasure. Shelly loved it more than any other food. Rose had set a plate out for her. The cake was dripping with thick Alaga syrup and a glob of Oleo. Mark and Shelly, holding each other's hands, didn't give a second look at the table. They made their way out the door and walked away unfazed by the sight or aroma of her masterpiece. Under other circumstances, Rose might have been offended, but she was too occupied studying the sight before her: Irene and Jake.

Jake, being a man of no small appetite, sat with his fork poised in mid-air. If she didn't know better she would have sworn that her biscuit bread was doughy. Jake chewed methodically on his one bite. He never took another. He didn't say a word, and Irene talked as if she'd never ever have another chance. The pity was she wasn't saying anything. She wasn't talking about what she and Jake had talked about last night. She wasn't talking about what happened in the hospital while Rose was in the coma. She wasn't talking about Mark and Shelly. She was prattling on about the weather and a book she found in the library, and she was talking so fast that Rose's head started to hurt. Was this girl going to give her another stroke?

"Irene, dear, what are you going on about?"

The sound of Rose's voice roused Jake, who appeared to be mesmerized by Irene's every word. He was looking straight at her mouth through the entire diatribe.

"Er, Irene, Mama Rose, thanks so much for this wonderful breakfast."

Rose thought she showed great restraint in not pointing out to Jake that he hadn't eaten anything, unless he counted the one bite he just swallowed. It only took him half an hour to get it down.

Jake removed his napkin from his lap and laid his fork on the plate. Irene's head snapped in his direction, her mouth gaping open, suddenly speechless.

"I should be going," Jake concluded.

Irene jumped to her feet. Jake's lips turned up on one side; an uncertain smile threatened to erupt.

"Mama Rose, what time did the doctor schedule your appointment? I'd like to drive you."

"Thanks, Jake, but I believe I'll have James Johnson do that."

"All right then, but please, if there is anything at all that I can do for you, don't hesitate to call. I'll come back to check on you later today."

"Our phone works, honey. We can call if—"

"It's no problem, Mama; I insist." He pushed his chair out, retrieved his coat from the rack and left.

"Well, I think that was more for your benefit than for mine. What say you, girly?"

Irene never moved from where she had initially stood staring. Mama Rose was beginning to wonder if mental illness could be passed from husband to wife and back again.

*I*rene was finally able to pick up her rubber legs and move toward the narrow utility closet, which was crammed in the corner of their small green kitchenette. Her hands wobbled as she pulled the broom out and moved listlessly about the floor. Like a ghost whining in the distance, Mama Rose's voice was saying something.

"Looked to me like you and Jake…"

"Humm?" Irene heard herself respond.

"I said," Mama Rose continued, putting her hands on her waist as she came into view, "it looked to me like you and Jake were mighty cozy. Why, when I came down here this morning, you and Jake were about as snug as two bugs in a rug."

"Ah, Mama, I feel so strange. I'm not sure what happened with me and Jacob earlier."

"Good or bad?"

"Huh?"

"Sit down, dear, let's figure this thing out." Rose led her to the small sofa where she and Jacob had sat and slept during the wee hours of the morning. Rose pulled up one of the metal chairs from the dinette table and talked to her very slowly and deliberately.

"The 'strange' you feel, is it good or bad? Do you feel that you got something out of your time together? That maybe you and Jake understand things, each other, better?"

"Yes, I guess that's how it is."

"And…" When Irene didn't speak quickly enough, Mama Rose's thinly veiled impatience became apparent. "Irene, if you don't want to talk about it I won't pry. But, if you do want to talk you had better start now. I got a doctor's appointment in about six hours."

"Mama, it was wonderful and frightening all at the same time. Jacob told me things about his childhood, like how he used to be terrified by his mom and dad and how that was where he got his racist notions. For the first time he seemed sorry about that. When he opened up about being afraid, I wanted to soothe him, to tell him I understood. I couldn't, all I could do was tell him that I felt fear too: when I was growing up and when we were no longer together. He asked me about the smoking. I guess that really turned him off."

"Do you know why you don't smoke anymore?"

"Because you said you wouldn't have it in your presence."

"And that's the only reason?"

"No."

"Then why?"

"I don't need it anymore to keep people away from me."

"And did you tell Jake that?"

"No."

"Why not? That would have told him a lot, like maybe you're willing to try trusting again, to give people a chance."

"I can't say for sure, but he might have gotten that impression. Except there is so much, Mama, things you don't know: unforgivable shocking things."

"Unforgivable. I doubt that."

"Mama, Jacob apologized for that horrible night. He said he didn't even remember it happening until years later. He said he didn't even know that he accused me of," she felt her voice go quiet, "being unfaith-ful."

"And you can't forgive that?"

"Well I...could you? Mama, wait till you hear this. It makes me sick to say it: he accused me of being unfaithful with a Negro. He accused Mark of being black."

"It makes you sick to say it. Why?"

"Because of his racist attitude. It's embarrassing. How can I love a man like that?"

"Do you love him?"

"Did I say I did?!"

"As a matter of fact, you did. The question is: Do you mean it?" A wash of weariness came over Irene with the force of a slap. She was glad Mama Rose had an escort for her doctor's appointment. As for her, she was heading upstairs for a very long nap.

Jake bolted through his front door and paced the floor several times before removing his coat and tossing it no place in particular. After about ten minutes he found himself standing idly in the middle of his living room. His legs collapsed and he allowed his body to sink into the soft cushions of his couch. His head fell back and he stretched his arms out to his sides. The past twelve hours had been the most exhilarating and exhausting he remembered experiencing. His son was married, and to Shelly, for God's sake. His estranged wife lived with Shelly's grandmother. Apparently she had been living there for months, a surprise to him, Mark and Shelly. Mama Rose had and recovered from a stroke. And Irene, once lost to him forever, had spent hours just inches away from his grasp. Several times during the night he had felt her body wonderfully close to him. They had to have touched. He even thought they embraced once. He didn't open his eyes for fear the entire evening had been a dream. He hadn't imagined it. He and Irene had sat a hair's width away from each other on Rose's tiny sofa and looked into the mystery that had been their past.

Fear followed him from the Schultz home when he left there and it had been his constant companion ever since. It seemed funny now that he could see it after all this time. Max and Maxine never loved or even liked him, and when Uncle Thomas died, he was alone. Irene had been his salvation, and he was hers; but it was too much. He wasn't everything she needed, and it became painfully clear the night he got drunk. He became the beast of his nightmares. He ravished Irene with all of the insecurities that had been so liberally heaped upon him. Was he testing her, trying to see if she would be able to accept and love him no matter what? He still couldn't figure it all out, but he didn't need to; she said she forgave him.

Jake was unable to contain the flood of emotion that was upon him. "She forgives me. She forgives me." The words washed over him: waves and waves of comfort and relief. Jake could still see her face as she said it. She wasn't stern like a minister offering sacrament in a formal service, but soft like a woman who had looked into her own soul and seen her own frailty. She even said she had done some things wrong. He huffed at that but continued to listen. "Jake," she said, "I could have done more. I depended on you, took from you but what did I give? I was your wife, your partner. I could have soothed your pain. If I had been whole, I would have been able to see your needs."

"You were perfect," he protested.

"I wasn't, but with Jesus to guide me, I feel complete, like I'm as perfect as I need to be because of him. Do you understand?"

"Irene, do you think there could ever be a chance…"

"Jacob," she said covering his hand with hers, "let's take this a little at a time." She leaned toward him and abruptly pulled back. Was she going to kiss him? He was losing his mind. He had to be. But he was so drawn to her at that moment, she felt it too. It was real. It was.

James Johnson was a patient man. He could wait a long time for something if it was worth it, but his patience had just about run to its conclusion. He rapped on Mama Rose's door with all the finesse of an enraged ogre. It was a chilly afternoon so he pulled the wool collar of his coat up around his ears. He knew that as soon as Mama Rose saw his eyes, she'd know that the churning on his face went clear down to the bowels of his innards. How could she? What in the world would possess Shelly to march out of that hospital holding Mark Schultz's arm? Didn't she have any respect for him at all? They were practically engaged. Of all the women he'd ever known—and he had known some quality women—Shelly was the last woman in the world he would have expected this kind of behavior from. She was sweet and gentle. Age had only improved her, made her more thoughtful and kind. This was monstrous, like something he'd expect from the thoughtless or ruthless type. He knew that Shelly and Mark had been childhood friends, but unless he was experiencing some state of delusion when he saw them leave the hospital, they were much more than that now. This was like a waking nightmare. She smothered her head in the crook of Schultz's arm and wrapped hers around his waist. How many times had he coached her to do just that to him? With Schultz it seemed so natural and unrehearsed. What did Mark have that he didn't? Shelly, apparently. He knocked again, harder this time. Mama Rose would give him some answers. He felt his hands start to ache as she called through the door.

"Hold on there. I'll be out in a minute."

Rose opened the door. She looked so cute. Her small five-foot tall body was adorned in a heavy winter coat and a double-thick crochet cap. Her face registered a temporary grimace in response to a harsh wind. A bright-toothed smile and eyes that already registered sympathy quickly replaced her frown. James knew he wasn't going to like a thing she had to say.

"Mama, you never cease to amaze. You look as good as new."

"You don't look so good," she said in her all-knowing, I'll-get-right-to-the-point kind of way.

"Jimmy James, I've got somethin' to tell you, boy. It's not going to be easy but I've never known a stronger man. Shelly and that boy you saw her with at the hospital are married."

"Well, that didn't hurt much, just felt like somebody sucker-punched me in the chest while holding a ten-pound weight."

"I know, baby," Rose said, lightly stroking his hand.

"When did this happen, Mama? I don't understand. Shelly and I were going to be married."

"No, dear heart, you weren't. I have to confess there was a time that I thought you and Shelly might end up together; but it just wasn't meant to be. Shelly and that boy have loved each other since they was children."

"But, Mama, she never mentioned him except in passing in all the years that we were dating."

"James, the poor girl didn't know it herself. I suppose he didn't either, though I expect it was easy for anybody who had ever been around the two of them to see. I bet you even saw it."

He thought back to high school. Did Shelly go out of her way to ignore the boy that the whole school was abuzz about? Sure she had. Even girls who didn't like him or who would never consider a relationship outside their race paid some attention to him. But Shelly tried extra hard not to notice him. Yeah, it was all coming back now. On occasion, she had actually walked the other way when Mark was coming down the hallway.

"You're right as usual. I should have wondered why Shelly, who never walked away from any fight, practically ran from Schultz. She's gentle now, but in high school, she seemed to have something to prove." Mama Rose nodded her head knowingly.

"That was about him, too, wasn't it?"

"Some of it. Without really thinking about it, Shelly was trying to change the world. She wanted to make it easier for people like her and Mark, who cared for each other, but couldn't show it."

"If I had only known. How could I have been so stupid?"

"Don't blame yourself. How could you know something she was trying so hard not to show? If Shelly's heart hadn't been taken, she would have married you in a snap. I half-believed she would. But when God has something for you..."

"Don't tell me you think God had something to do with this?"

"Don't you? You got a better way of explaining how these two found each other after ten years?"

"That's a relief."

"What?"

"That she wasn't seeing him all along, cheating on me, deceiving me."

Rose looked dismayed.

"Okay, I know what you're going to say. You didn't raise her like that."

"That's for sure, but you have a right to be upset. And I have a right to get to the hospital before they cancel my appointment," she said frowning up at him.

"I'm sorry, Mama. I'm responsible for detaining a woman who just rose from the dead. You must have some good deeds you need to be about."

"I most certainly do. My first one is to explain to you the story of a little girl who loved a little boy and a little boy who loved her back. Then I'm going to tell you all about a boy who changed his name from Jimmy to James and became a man. You won't believe the future that God has in mind for him."

Chapter Eleven
Dinner Party

When Mark arrived at his father's house, he called Mr. Dobbs, who only said, "Take the rest of the week off. We'll see you Monday." It was Friday. About an hour after arriving at his own apartment a messenger showed up. Mark signed for the note, which turned out to be an invitation to a white-tie dinner at Chuck Kincaid's, their prospective new client's house, Saturday night: To Mr. Marcus J. Schultz, of Brandon and Dobbs, and guest. All very cryptic, Mark thought.

Mark, a man known for his practicality, told his new wife to freshen up, they had something to do. When she was ready, he announced, "We're going shopping!"

Shopping had never been the kind of adventure it was today. Their first stop was Mark's favorite tailor for a new suit; why not? This was his first real date with Shelly and perhaps his last Brandon and Dobb's outing. They should do it right. Merman's was a quaint shop off the main strip. They were known for their efficiency and high-end clientele. A hint of frosty mint hit them as they opened the sculpted glass door. Mark meandered to the rear of the subdued-sage carpeted flooring. He picked a suit off the rack. A female tailor came to serve him.

"Will your assistant be picking the suit up tomorrow, Mr. Schultz?" She peered over at Shelly, who was busy looking at ties, so he quickly corrected the tailor.

"Mrs. Schultz will not be picking the suit up. Please send it to our apartment in the morning." Mark didn't attribute her comment to the fact that Shelly was colored. But before he left the shop he was seriously considering a new clothier.

Their next stop was Lord and Taylor's, Mark's favorite department store, upscale and quality. He had never spent any real time in the women's department, but watching Shelly go in and out of the dressing room trying on clothes for his approval was actually invigorating. One thing he hadn't counted on was the people watching them. He was used to women taking special note of him, but this was different. People were interested in knowing what his relationship to Shelly was. Some even had a look of disdain. Was Shelly always under scrutiny when she was in mostly white company?

"Mark, look at this," Shelly said excitedly as she approached him.

"Now where have I seen that color before?" he said, feigning ignorance.

"It's exactly the same color as the midnight blue of your…" She stopped, giving him a gentle punch to the shoulder when she realized he was teasing her. "I'll try it on. Don't move."

Shelly sauntered out of the dressing room. She smoothed her delicate fingers down the sides of the dress and did a sensual pivot, while gracefully raising her arms above her head, then down to her sides. The silky dark blue dress conformed perfectly to her figure. He couldn't resist holding her. A tall thin woman with Grecian features leered at them and actually gasped. Shelly was undisturbed. Mark was beginning to understand what he was in for. Would he be able to deal with this daily without losing control? Was he up to the challenge?

They visited several more departments under varying degrees of scrutiny. Soon there was only them in the store, only them in the world. Like children, they collected their packages and headed for home. Shelly cooked a new-wife kind of dinner, simple but tasty. Dessert was all Mark really wanted.

Saturday evening came quickly. Mark had to admit he was a bit nervous. What was this dinner all about? It was formal and he was required, rather than requested, to bring a companion, curious. Kincaid was rumored to be eccentric, a bit quirky. This certainly was in line with quirky. Mark hadn't been in the office since leaving for Mama Rose's house. Dobbs wouldn't talk to him. And Kincaid, not yet a confirmed client and certainly not a friend, was holding a party that he was invited to. Who else from the firm was invited? He wondered.

"Hello, Wife," Mark said as Shelly emerged from dressing, "You look devastating."

"Devastating?"

"Yes, I'll be devastated if we don't get this party over with so I can get you home again and to myself."

"You really are a new husband, aren't you?"

"I am. What's wrong? And don't say, 'nothing.' You have that look."

"It's my jewelry."

"What about it?"

"Nothing really, it's just…not perfect. I wanted to be perfect tonight."

"You're looking at the wrong person, baby. You're always perfect to me."

Mark put Shelly's wrap around her smooth shoulders, allowing his hand to glide the length of her arm, and they proceeded to the stairwell.

Mark was barely able to make out the address from the street. It was hidden among clusters of exotic pines and other fanciful-looking greenery he had never seen before. He and Shelly drove about a quarter mile and stopped at the unattended gatehouse. A series of medieval iron spires quietly parted as they approached. From there they traveled a looping chalky road that went on and on. Finally a crystalline house with a lavish white frosting exterior came into view. Shelly turned to Mark for his opinion. His eyes were as wide as hers. They parked under an expansive archway.

"Shelly, snap out of it."

"Mark, have you ever in your life?"

"No, and honestly I've seen a lot. But, honey, I have to tell you I'll be glad to get this over with, whatever it is."

Shelly wanted to be sympathetic to Mark's predicament: not knowing if this was some elaborate way for Dobbs and Brandon to can him. But she was excited beyond anything she could imagine. It was her first date with Mark, a dream date. He was never more handsome, dressed in a midnight blue tuxedo. He had wanted traditional black, but yielded to her less conventional tastes. She said it would set him apart: make him stand out. If only he wasn't so anxious. She was sure vulnerability was a new look for him. As she stepped back to take another adoring look at her handsome hubby, a wiry man appeared at their side, introduced himself and drove their car away. No sooner than he had done so, another man opened the gold ornamented doors to the mansion and ushered them into the foyer.

Shelly blinked several times. "Opulent" rolled over and over again in her brain. It was the word she used when no other word would suffice to describe extravagant beauty. When her eyes were able to focus, she scanned upward. An extraordinary lamp hung from the ceiling. Tiny shards of green jewels circled its base. The lamp radiated a shadowy emerald glow. In the distance, white posts stood on either side of the staircase, which towered to the upper levels. An assortment of deep richly-colored pillows lay at the foot of each pillar: odd but attractive.

"What do you make of all this?" Mark whispered as the crisply uniformed servant removed Shelly's wrap.

"It's exquisite."

Mark nodded his agreement.

"And there is something else..." Shelly continued, but before they could take anything else in, they were escorted to a large dining room, which Shelly assumed was one of many judging by the size of the house. Presumptuous purples, deep reds and extravagant blues hung in silks and velvets from the walls and created halos above the dining table. And what a unique dining room table. Something about the style was familiar to Shelly. *Hibachi, that's it*, Shelly thought. *Yes this was like an enlarged Hibachi.* The glass topped table sat on a single rectangular pedestal. Inside the glass showcase top were silver boxes of various shapes with carved designs, and the lip of the table the same wood as the pedestal extended beyond the glass, definitely Hibachi. She came closer allowing her hand to rest on the edge. This wood had a high luster and the grain: it was Zelkova wood. As Shelly took in more subtle detail, it dawned on her: Oriental, yes, Japanese. She had studied Oriental décor before leaving her retail job.

Engraved bronze place cards were arranged on the dining table bearing only the first names of the guests. Eric Brandon, one of Mark's bosses, was to sit at the foot of the table nearest the entryway. Amanda's card was to his immediate left, a card for someone named Akiko was next to her, Schultz's guest was to sit to her left—Shelly smiled, that would be her— thankfully to her left was Mark. Mr. Kincaid's card was to Mark's left and at the head of the table. At least he was that conventional. To Mr. Kincaid's direct left there was no place card. Next to the apparently empty seat would be Mr. Dobbs. To his left would be someone named Anita, and to her left Cameron. And that apparently completed their dinner party. Nine people, two of whom were totally unknown to the rest: Akiko and Anita.

The man who had led them to the dining room did not leave their side until they were seated. If Shelly had known he was waiting for them, she would have sat quicker. "We are the first here, honey."

Mark looked at her and gave a knowing smile. If this was not such a formal affair, she would have punched him right then and there.

Eric Brandon, the elusive partner of Mason Dobbs was the next to arrive. The tall, thin, impeccably dressed man was virtually unknown to his executive staff. They had all met him and he signed their paychecks, but contact was rare, and contact that wasn't directly business was unheard-of. He sat uneasily at the foot of the table after greeting Mark and being introduced to Shelly. But not before saying: "So this is the young lady who would change the world."

Amanda and Cameron arrived at the same time. They made to sit next to Shelly, who was happy to point out the very obvious place cards, which put Amanda a seat away from her and Cameron across the table. Dobbs hurried in as if late, nodded to everyone and looked worried. He wasn't late. Shelly felt sorry for the poor disheveled man and hoped for his sake that Mark was still in line for partner. Amanda or Cameron might lighten his load, but Shelly couldn't imagine either one of them offering anyone any real sense of ease or comfort, and poor Mr. Dobbs needed that if he needed anything at all. All the known players were there.

Shelly patted Mark's hand and whispered, "Enjoy the game."

Mark smiled and gave her a "come hither" look. Was he going to kiss her in front of all these people? His lips were upon hers before she could fully form her opinion on the matter. For a few brief seconds she ascended the lovely room she was seated in and experienced a small part of heaven. When she opened her eyes, a mysterious man was standing in the doorway opposite the one they had come in. She recognized him from the hamburger restaurant: Chuck Kincaid. He appeared to have been staring directly at her and Mark with a very serious expression. Shelly didn't know what to make of any of this. He was petting a short-haired gray cat whose eyes glowed fluorescent green in the dim lighting. The cat suddenly jumped from his arms and returned through the door that Mr. Kincaid occupied. A servant came immediately, offering him a bowl of water to wash his hands, which he did. He then took a small cloth from the servant's arm and took his time drying his long fingers as he surveyed the rest of the room. His dress was unusual. His Nehru collared evening jacket was very long, flaring slightly at the waist. Its color was very deep though not black. When he was ready his expression became cordial, and he greeted his guests. Hors d'oeuvres were served even though the remaining two guests were yet to arrive. After the enjoyable delicacy, which Shelly was loathe to admit she had no idea if it was animal or vegetable, a small woman appeared at her side. Amanda informed the woman that she was finished with her dish, and that she, the small stranger, could take her plate away. Kincaid's hand made an abrupt movement, which caused his dish to clang. Shelly noticed his lip twitch. He didn't look at all pleased. Shelly followed his gaze back to the small lady at her side. Her eyes moved up toward the woman's face; she wore a pleasant expression, unassuming. Her garment was a kimono, dark: the same unusual color as Kincaid's suit of clothing. The obi tied around her body had the same regal feel of the house décor. This woman was no servant. Shelly motioned toward the nameplate at her right. The lady nodded, yes, and sat quietly next to her. Mark and the men who noticed her arrival rose slightly and sat back down. She was so quiet Shelly didn't really think Amanda had given her a second thought.

Shortly after the woman's arrival, a stunning young Oriental woman appeared in the main entryway. She nodded slightly before moving toward the older lady sitting next to Shelly, gracefully handing her a small wooden box with gold inlaid carving. She then walked over to sit between Cameron and Mason Dobbs. Her dress was a sleek-fitting brilliant plum. Everyone noticed her entrance. All the men stood except Kincaid. Shelly was about ready to kick Mark, when he seemed to remember he was married and turned to give her a reassuring kiss on the cheek.

Cameron ogled the poor woman shamelessly. Shelly felt bad for him. They all sat.

"Haven't I seen you somewhere before?" Cameron asked his attractive neighbor, before she had a chance to fully situate herself.

"Not that I am aware, sir, perhaps…"

"Are you a fashion model?"

Shelly turned her attention to Akiko and immediately liked her. She reminded her of Mama Rose and her jewelry: exquisite.

"Akiko. May I call you Akiko?"

"Why yes, dear." She had kind eyes.

"May I look at your necklace? It is exactly the kind of thing I was looking for to wear tonight!"

"You like?"

"It's splendid, enchanting."

"Yes, it's very nice," Amanda cut in, taking a moment to give the necklace a cursory glance, "but I think a man of Mark's stature should be able to afford something more…" Amanda twirled her hands near her face as if savoring the exquisiteness of her words; she finished with a splash, "extravagant."

Shelly noticed annoyance crease the corner of Akiko's lip and felt in total agreement. Other than that subtle facial expression, no comment was made on what Amanda said.

"I have others," Akiko continued. She opened her box. Deep green velvet compartments revealed their wares.

"May I?" Shelly asked holding out her hand. Akiko placed beautiful turquoise and topaz in Shelly's palms, amethyst, sapphire, and rubies around her neck, and clusters of garnets on her wrists. Amanda, looking very bored, had already turned her attention to Eric Brandon, who was only mildly interested in conversing with her.

Mark marveled at Shelly. She was such a genuine person, generous and forthright. She was completely without contrivance. Having no knowledge whatsoever as to whom Akiko might be, she treated her with delicate courtesy, like one might treat royalty. Mark also noted Kincaid. He didn't really engage in conversation with anyone but he watched everyone. What was his game?

Dobbs sat nervously, fidgeting with his tie and looking wearily at Mark from time to time. Poor Dobbs, he simply was not aware of his brilliance. He didn't have to come up with the best ads or read the market perfectly; he knew how to surround himself with people who could. And that in and of itself was an invaluable talent. Mark hoped Eric Brandon was aware of what he had. If Dobbs were to quit, their firm would go up in flames. Only a man like Dobbs could manage so many egos and near-egos: Mark included himself here. If only the man wasn't such a worrier.

"Attention, everyone, I'm sure you are wondering why I've asked you here. Mr. Schultz, I liked your ads very much."

Amanda and Cameron glared at Mark.

"Thank you, sir, but Amanda and Cameron—"

"But they lack something."

"Mr. Kincaid, Mark was, unfortunately, unavailable to pitch his own ideas…" Amanda piped up.

"I'm afraid I have to concur. I gave the presentation, but the work was done by Ama…er mostly by Mark Schultz," Cameron filled in.

Shelly looked like she was about to boil over, but she must have figured if Mark could keep his cool, she could keep hers, too.

"The ads need something more."

"I agree, sir…" Mark started.

"Yes, sir…" Shelly chimed in. All eyes were on her. Mark wanted to tell her to stay out of it but thought better of it. "Your line of jewelry is beautiful but it could use some pieces like these in Akiko's box. Jewelry that fits many tastes, styles and income levels."

"No, dear. My hus…"

"Yes, Shelly. What do you know about the advertising business? I'm sure you've never seen Kincaid Jewels. And do you have any idea what was even in Mark's campaign?"

Mark had seen this before. Amanda's remarks were meant to render Shelly speechless. Poor Amanda, she was in for a surprise.

Mark watched Shelly. He could see her silently willing him to be quiet. "I can take care of myself," her eyes were saying.

"Actually, Amanda, I was studying to be a buyer for Sinoms department stores. Jewelry would have been just one of my specialties. Kincaid Jewels are top of the line, but the company lacks mass appeal. All the jewelry is marketed to women with a great deal of money."

Cameron looked at Kincaid's face. Perhaps he thought the train was leaving without him. He jumped in. "That's as it should be, Shelly. Mr. Kincaid's product is for a more refined taste, a woman of means."

"Cameron," Dobbs announced, from his otherwise silent end of the table.

"Thank you, Dobbs. As I was about to say, I believe you have a point, Mrs. Schultz. I asked my wife, Akiko, to include her jewelry in my line."

"Wife!" Amanda mouthed to Cameron across the table. Cameron, instinctively, moved away from Anita.

"She has continually refused, thinking her creations unworthy of note. Perhaps your wife's knowledgeable and genuine assessment of her work will convince her otherwise. I've had renowned jewelers assess them. They agree with you, Mrs. Schultz. In fact, I asked Mrs. Kincaid and my daughter to this meeting, hoping one of you sharp people would encourage my wife to enter the business."

"I like Mrs. Schultz's idea," Akiko said quietly.

"What idea? She's not even…"

"Amanda!" Brandon scolded. He wasn't the brightest advertising man, but he could smell money and the opportunity to make it.

Shelly looked perplexed. Mark intervened, "Something like: Designed with you in mind."

"Yes, that one," Akiko confirmed.

"Yes, that one," Kincaid agreed.

"Gibson, dinner please." Dinner was served. While eating, Shelly and Mark worked on variations of the ad with suggestions from Anita, Kincaid's lovely daughter. All agreed on: 1) When love is apparent, 2) When caring takes shape, you'll find her wearing Akiko, 3) It just looks expensive, 4) And you thought jewelry was just for her, and finally, 5) Beauty at any price.

Everyone but Cameron and Amanda enjoyed the exotic and sumptuous meal laid before them. They ate crow. For the first time since the evening started, Kincaid, now smiling, sat back and looked content. Dobbs ate heartily, conferring a knowing look toward Brandon. Brandon ate quickly, sparing a few words for Cameron and Amanda to let them know that their jobs were secure. They would continue in their current capacities. He informed Mark that the firm would continue to have only two partners: Mason Dobbs and Marcus Schultz. It would be renamed: Dobbs, Schultz, and Brandon, retaining his father's legacy. Financial backing and controlling interest would be his contribution. The day-to-day would be left to those men and women more capable than he. Brandon further suggested that Dobbs and Schultz might consider employing Mrs. Schultz in some capacity. She seemed to have a knack and a sensitivity lacking in the "dog-eat-dog" business of advertising.

Chapter Twelve
Proposals

For the last few weeks, Shelly had been acting strangely. Her confidence seemed to waver and she was nervous and fidgety. She had moved into Mark's apartment adding little touches like vases of lightly scented flowers and doilies. New floral drapery with swags graced the front window and a delicate tea set adorned his kitchen counter. Small things, he knew, that helped her bring some of her childhood home into theirs. She said she was going to feminize their bedroom, which gave Mark the shudders. He could only hope she wouldn't go too far.

Just when he thought she was getting used to being his wife, she insisted on going back to work. Everyone, including Cameron and Amanda, agreed that Akiko's jewelry warranted its own name and place in the market. Shelly was doing some consulting with the newly established business and had invested some of her own money in it as a not-so-silent partner. The mood swings and brooding were so unlike her. Heck, who was he fooling; he didn't know what she was like, hadn't been around her regularly since they were children. Yet for the first few weeks she was just as he remembered her, flip, funny and flirty. But something had changed.

Yesterday an elderly neighbor had been particularly rude to Shelly. They were just leaving the apartment for a walk to Marco's Deli on the corner when he reminded Shelly of one of the many times that Mama Rose had dressed down his father.

Mark was sitting in the window seat of their Maple Street home. He was about sixteen at the time. Jake was coming up the stairs to their house as Rose was going down the stairs of hers. Jake announced in a bellicose voice, "Rose, what is that putrid smell coming from your kitchen?" He sniffed the air for emphasis, "Do you people actually eat that stuff or do you use it for fertilizer?"

Mark and Jake had seen Rose hauling in bunches of greens and thought for sure she had been picking them all day and by now had a tremendous pot boiling on the stove.

"Why, Mr. Schultz," as she called him when she was particularly perturbed, "I haven't cooked a thing today. Angela Smith is to blame. She brought her dish over this afternoon. Said it was your favorite. I was simply warming it. I know you don't always have time to cook, but I'll be sure to tell her that you found the odor unsettling and won't be able to enjoy it. You will be seeing her later tonight, won't you? It is Thursday."

Jake did have a date with Angela that evening. Mark knew as soon as he saw the stunned look on his father's face, just as he knew Mama Rose had bested Jake again. After Jake got over his initial shock, he burst out laughing, slapping his large palms on his knees. He turned and walked away after looking over his shoulder and telling Mama Rose she was one for the books. Only Mark had seen his confused expression as he rubbed the back of his neck and continued up the stairs.

At the conclusion of Mark's story about Jake, Shelly, who had been walking casually by his side, threw her arms around his neck and gave him a very uncharacteristic public kiss right on the lips telling him how much he sometimes reminded her of his father. Mark was in the midst of trying to figure out if he had just been complimented or insulted, when the prickly old woman sighed loudly and told Shelly that even a wife wouldn't be so brazen on the street, let alone the hired help. Shelly froze in his arms. He tightened his grip on her waist. Instead of an explosion, she nodded to the woman and moved about a foot away from him. At the time he viewed it as her way of making light of the situation. Perhaps these everyday affronts were getting to her. Her birthday was in a week. He'd take her to his favorite restaurant and they'd come home and make reckless love. He was feeling better already.

$\mathcal{T}$he allure of Chez Marcea had always been the effect it had on the ladies Mark had brought there. But today the whimsical blue pastel lights were having an effect on him. He felt like he had never really seen them before tonight. The frosty luminance behind Shelly cast a magical glow around her, making her even prettier, if that was possible. Normally, Shelly would love a place like this but tonight her weak smile said more than her words.

"What?" Mark questioned, his voice riding the wind, floating from the terrace and never piercing his wife's troubled heart. He idly forked another mouthful of veal, unable to taste his treasured scaloppini sauce. Exquisite bone china and glimmering silver lay atop a fine white linen tablecloth, begging him and Shelly to partake of their wares. His beautiful new bride sat bolt upright saying something was missing; in addition to her shimmering pink gown, she wore a most pained grimace.

Mark, who was for the first time in his life feeling as close to complete as possible, was now perplexed. "What do you mean, honey?" he asked.

The words dropped to the table: flat, dull. He was desperate to keep any hint of panic out of his voice. Shelly shook her head, not lifting her eyes from the veal on her own plate.

"Aren't you happy?"

"Yes, but…"

Yes but, yes but! How could this be happening after all they had been through? Had he missed something? Had the daily offenses offered by those who didn't understand them been too much? He hadn't seen it coming; thought their love had been enough.

"Mark, Mark?" Shelly was snapping her finger by his nose.

Roused, he answered, "Shelly, sweetie, what's wrong? You seem so miserable."

"It's just that…"

"Tell me what it is." Previously uninterested heads turned in their direction. His voice must have been louder than he thought. Startled, Shelly surveyed their audience. Her initial expression was disturbed before turning amused.

"You always make me laugh," she said while reaching across the petite table to stroke his cheek.

Still uneasy, Mark grabbed her hand, "Tell me what's wrong, Shelly. Is it us?"

"Well yes, but…"

"Shelly, you knew this wouldn't be easy. But you said you could handle it. My pop is coming around and I'm willing to take on the world…"

Shelly knit her brow and gently leaned her head to one side, "What are you talking about, Marky?"

"Come here," he demanded, lifting her hand and pulling her carefully around to his side of the table and seating her on his lap. "Tell me what's wrong, baby. I'll make it right."

"You can't."

His stomach churned. Was he actually going to be sick? Patience, he kept telling himself. "Shelly, what is it!"

Shelly leaned into his chest, wrapped her arms around his neck, and wept.

The aromas of fresh garlic, ripe tomatoes, and leafy basil wafted from the dining area to Jake's bathroom. The peppery scent tickled his nostrils. He washed with a fury, hardly able to contain his excitement. Irene was allowing him to court her and now she was in his kitchen cooking dinner. He smiled thinking about it. They had reached a milestone; he was sure of it. Their first kiss in almost thirty years had happened two months ago. What tomorrow? The world! In a few minutes they would be having an intimate dinner. Maybe this would be the night. Even with her new-found religion there was nothing to hold them back. They had never been divorced. He washed quicker and changed to a form-fitting sweater.

"Twenty or fifty, I'm still a handsome stud," he thought, admiring his reflection in the mirror above the sink. A splash of aftershave and a wink at the dashing figure staring back at him and he was down the stairs with a speed he didn't know he still had. "Irene, I'm starved; is dinner rea… Irene, why are there five place settings?"

She was bent at the waist, looking into the hot stove. He watched her gloved hand carefully extract an apple pie. Cinnamon, nutmeg and apples: ummm.

"Rennie, I thought it was just you and me."

"I'm sorry if you're disappointed." She placed a lattice-crusted pie on the counter. Rich fruity syrup oozed over the edge of the pie tin, "but I've invited the rest of the family."

"Oh." He sat with a thud and fumbled aimlessly with his napkin.

Irene smiled when the doorbell rang, "Can you get that, Jacob?"

"Yeah, sure."

A stinging wind burned his skin as he pulled the door open. Shelly came in first, dusting heavy flakes from her collar. Mark was on her heels, Rose's arm entwined in his. He unwrapped a heavy wool scarf from his neck, dumping mounds of slushy white to the floor.

"Sorry, Pop," he said, attempting to sweep out the fallen flakes with his foot.

"Hey, Mom and Dad," Shelly said. Jake had told her to call him that some months ago. The look on her face told him it still felt funny.

"Mama Rose," Irene sang, before Rose could get her greeting out.

"I told you he wouldn't like it," Mama Rose said, pulling off her boots with the aid of the sofa arm.

"What'd you say, Mama?" Jake questioned.

"Oh, nothing," Irene interjected.

"We're doing this my way," she said to Mama Rose.

"Okay, everybody, sit down. I think you'll enjoy the meal. These are Namio specials: *Insalata alla Napoletana, Pollo alla Romana* and for the less adventurous, lasagna and asparagus. I got all authentic ingredients from Mr. Namio himself, including Jacob's favorite, apple pie."

"It was my favorite, wasn't it?" he brightened a bit, "I almost forgot."

"Wow, Mom, you can cook!" Mark's wide eyes and near drooling expressed his amazement.

Irene smiled, "Yes, Marky, but I stopped a long time ago," she said while setting large platters of food in the center of the table. Radiant fragrance surrounded them. "God has given all my gifts back and then some. Bless the food, Jacob." She took her seat next to him, "I'm hungry. Aren't you?"

Jake said the only blessing he knew, "God is good. God is great. Let us thank him for our food. Amen." Out of the corner of his eye he could see Shelly and Mark cut each other a glance. They were on the verge of snickering. Who could blame 'em? He could.

Mark was eating so fast it was a wonder his silver didn't spark, and Shelly, though taking bird-sized bites, had gone through one plate and was asking for the vegetable tray again.

"Pass the lasagna, Pop. How's your day shaping up?" He winked at Shelly. She elbowed him in the side. Rose sat rigid and uncharacteristically silent. It was as if everyone there knew something that he didn't.

"We're going to be famous, Pop," Mark continued. "Name's going up on the new sign outside the office tomorrow. It's incredible. Dobbs has given me the lion's share of the responsibility for the major accounts…" Soon Jake could only see Mark's lips moving: the words no longer made any sense; neither did this dinner. Was Irene trying to avoid being alone with him? She had asked him if he was disappointed. Yeah that was probably a good jumping off point, but disappointment didn't begin to describe it. He wanted to turn to Irene and yell, "Quit playing games with me, sweetheart. I can't take it."

Now Shelly was showing everyone a drawing that she and Mark had made of their new wedding rings. Mark, she said, had promised to have Madame Akiko Kincaid create them as soon as he could afford the purchase. Which she realized wouldn't be for some time. Being suddenly elevated to partner didn't mean their lifestyle would change overnight.

Next Shelly gushed her now famous slogan, "Designed with you in mind." She recounted how she had come up with the winning ad at the Kincaid dinner party. Seems Chuck Kincaid was testing the Brandon and Dobbs staff. This was all very interesting, Jake thought, but what he really wanted was to get this dinner over so that he could be alone with Irene.

Mama Rose, who had previously been silent, piped up. "Church was wonderful today. The Spirit really poured out. Sister Sylas, God bless her soul, couldn't keep her seat. Reverend Marvin was expoundin' on free will. God, in all his wisdom, never forces us to do anything. Not even to choose him. Every time Pastor hit on a good point, Celia Sylas was up wavin' her hands and yelling out praises. It was a joy to see."

"Joy to see," Jake mumbled.

But Rose wasn't finished. She had become animated; all eyes were glued to her now. "In about a year, children, the church is going to Africa. The good news has got to be spread far and wide before our Lord returns and I, for one, can hardly wait."

"Hardly wait," Jake heard himself mumble again before tuning out completely.

"Jacob, Jacob." Irene was calling.

"What's wrong, son? Cat got your tongue?" Mama Rose added.

"Hum, oh nothing. What were you talking about?"

"Mama's thinking of moving again," Irene said, bounding from her seat.

"What? Where will you live?"

"Shuu," Irene said, her rich dark hair coming down from its bun. Boundless waves were framing her beautiful golden face. Before Jake could fully take in the vision before him, she sat on his lap, hard.

Jake could feel the heat rising to his cheeks. "Irene? Don't get me wrong… I like what you're doin' but do you think—"

Putting her finger to his lips, Irene turned, reached her arm across the table and snapped her finger, "The box, Shelly."

An exchange of a small box from Shelly's hand to Irene's took place. Irene knelt in front of Jake. He was positive that his face was aflame now. "Irene, what…" He was reaching wildly in an attempt to get her up off the floor before her next statement caused him to go limp.

"Will you marry me, Jacob Schultz?" Irene popped the lid off the black velvety box. It had concealed an intricately designed gold band with a small emerald at its center.

"I love you…"

Jake snatched her up before she could complete her statement, hugging her cushiony body to his.

"That's our cue, children." Mama Rose said, rising to her feet and grabbing her coat from the hook.

"We haven't had our dessert," Mark said with a smile that strained his dimple.

Jake could only glare at him. Mark took his joke, his wife and his coat and went out the door without looking back.

*M*onths had passed since his mother's January proposal to his father and still they weren't married. Mark hadn't a clue as to what they were waiting for. They should be standing in this church, not him.

He looked around; Mount Prospect was very pleasant inside. How many times had he sat outside listening to soulful renditions of "Wade in the Water" and "Take it to Jesus." He was so curious; he'd almost gone in several times when he drove Mama Rose all those years ago. Now here he was standing in the narrow aisle between the finely grained wooden pews.

"Hello, young man." A booming voice emerged from Mark's right, "I'm Pastor Marvin and you must be Mark."

Mark couldn't help his next statement, "Yes, sir. You knew because I'm white." Pastor Marvin, a big man with a generous smile, looked puzzled for a moment and then decided to correct him.

"No, son, I knew because of your wife's brilliant description, big guy, strong jaw, short dark curly hair, swarthy complexion, dimple."

"She didn't spare you the dimple?"

"No, not even that. She gave us every detail. Except perhaps your unusual sense of humor."

Mark understood as more people came in the building. He counted about twelve white men. Okay, he wasn't the only one there.

"Listen, son, since Mama Rose joined our little church we've become very diversified. She's a one-woman United Nations, she is, every day fulfilling God's mission of compelling them to come from the highways and the byways." His grin was so enormous, enthusiasm bursting with every remark. And the appreciation Pastor Marvin felt when talking about Mama Rose was obvious. Who could blame him? Mark knew Mama Rose's convictions from firsthand experience. He was most appreciative of the effect it had had on his and Shelly's life.

Speaking of Shelly, why hadn't the silly woman just told him she wanted him to come to church? Did she think he'd be angry with her? The way she was acting he could have sworn she was about to announce that she was leaving him or something. Thinking about that gave him a queasy feeling. Where was she anyway? Hadn't she set the meeting time for 6:00 P.M.? Ah, she was coming, rushing; some things never changed.

"Hi, sweetie."

"Hi, baby." She was radiant. Her long sleek burgundy skirt made her appear anything but churchlike to him.

"Sit down, Mark." Shelly said, pressing lightly on his shoulder in an attempt to coerce him.

"So there's more to this than just getting me here for a Bible study."

"Yes," she said, a bit too somber for his taste.

"I don't want to ever be without you."

His look of concern must have been grave as he reached for the arm of the pew and sat down. Shelly reached over to smooth the wrinkles from his forehead, while kneeling in front of him and stroking his arm.

"Shelly, please tell me what you're talking about. Are you sick?"

"No, dear. I'm going to heaven." She stopped as if that was supposed to mean something to him. It didn't.

$\mathcal{T}$he Wednesday after they had attended their first Bible study, Mark had gotten home from work early. He was looking forward to a quiet night alone with his baby. He changed to his red, stay-at-home-and-slum shorts and his old jersey. His stomach grumbled; didn't they have some vanilla ice cream? Now, there was an idea. He walked over to the refrigerator and opened the freezer door. The paper pint carton was wedged between what looked to be a roast and something indistinguishable. He pried it out. With a teaspoon in hand, he marched over to the couch, kicked his legs up on the glass coffee table and waited for the white stuff to melt. When he was able to squeeze the paper carton with little effort, he plunged in. Holding the spoon a few inches above his mouth with his head tilted back, he waited patiently for the cool sticky sweet to melt from the spoon and onto his tongue.

"What are you doing, honey?" Shelly burst from their bedroom speaking rapidly while buttoning the cuffs of her pink chiffon blouse. "Wednesday, Bible study. You remember." She was wearing her "you-know-what-I-mean" look.

"Listen, Shelly, I haven't got a thing in the world against religion. You know that, but if you think I'm about to start going to Bible studies, night services and all that stuff every week, you've got another thing coming."

"But, Mark, I thought you understood. I don't want to go to heaven without you."

"Then don't." He could feel the cocky upturn of his lip.

"Marky, that's not funny."

"Don't call me that."

"What?"

"I said, don't call me that. And don't give me that look."

"What look?"

Worry crossed Shelly's face. God help him, he couldn't stop.

"I'm tired of the manipulation. Every single time you don't get your way you get that sorrowful look."

"Sorrowful look! I care about you, that's all. You know me, Mark. I've always tried to do what's right, to look out for people, to take on people and things that were wrong."

Mark felt his resolve giving way.

"But there was always another problem, always something else that was wrong. Things too big for me to fix." Tears started to stream from her beautiful eyes. "I understand, now, that alone I'm so limited, but with Christ I have all power. There's another thing, I've been good because I was afraid."

"Afraid?"

"Yes, I didn't want to go to hell."

"Oh, you think that's a real place now?"

"Don't you?"

"No, yes…How the hell should I know?"

"Mark!"

In a flash he was consumed by a torrid wave as vile as anything he had ever experienced. He ranted about being badgered and controlled and roared he needed space. Shelly started backing toward the door. "Mark," she kept saying, horror streaking her brow. He couldn't stop ranting. She was backing away, her feet consuming huge areas of floor.

"Go, if you want. I don't care!" He vaguely remembered her stooping to scoop up her brown leather purse and pulling the door behind her. He was left alone in the living room with his thoughts and his god: Pride.

Steamy sweat poured from his body. Weary and wrung out, Mark padded barefoot to his room. It was 1:00 A.M. and he didn't have a clue as to where his wife was. So what? She deserved it, trying to save his soul. Who asked her? Mark walked over to his bed and pulled the stuffed quilt back. Shelly's familial touches were everywhere now. Family patchwork quilts lay rolled on the foot of his bed. A pale-blue glass lamp, probably from the bauble shop, sat on his nightstand. It provided only enough light for reading or making "peek-a-boo" love, as Shelly called it. A large shaggy rug lay on the hardwood floor underneath his bed to keep his feet from being cold when he got up. She was a thoughtful wife.

Enough thinking. He jumped into the bed and pulled the covers up tight. Sleeping had been impossible. He rolled over onto Shelly's side of the bed, stroking the covers, searching for her warmth. Emptiness filled his grasp. Twisting and turning he fell into a restless daze. Shelly was there. The waves of her hair tickled his chest. The dew of her breath reassured him of her presence. He reached to tighten his grip on her body. His arms encircled mist and smoke. Mark awoke with a start. He lay rigid staring at the ceiling. Every problem had a solution. He had always been able to figure his way out of any circumstance and this was no different. The answer wasn't coming. He drifted in and out of agitation and fitfulness; it hardly resembled sleep.

6:00 A.M. Mark jerked the covers back, threw his legs over the side of the bed and bowed his throbbing head while sitting a few moments to contemplate his predicament. He looked around his room. Mission accomplished; she had indeed feminized the place. Her scent encompassed him. His whole body ached.

Mark resolved that this was never going to happen again. One night without Shelly was all he ever cared to experience. He knew exactly what he was going to do: fake it.

Shelly was easy work. She was so happy to get her sweetheart back that she didn't offer any scrutiny when he agreed to go to church with her. She stroked his head like he was her lost puppy returning obediently to his master.

"I knew you'd come around," she'd said. "I had a long talk with Mama Rose." A tiny tear welled in her eye but didn't fall, "Mama explained how these things work and said I might as well get used to forgiving you." Shelly said this with such sincerity and affection he decided not to be offended by her last comment and to let her think she had won. Heck, he took it a step further, suggesting they have an informal church wedding, making their commitment of faith and love complete. This would cover his secret indefinitely.

Shelly wanted the wedding on the anniversary of the day that they made their pledge to be friends forever—what was he then, eleven? He really didn't care when they did it. All he wanted was to get her "mello." It didn't matter what he had to do to make it happen. Besides, the initial insult he felt at the suggestion that his love for Shelly wasn't enough for her was subsiding. Yes, that was the crux of the problem. He had it all figured out now. She needed her spiritual grounding. He got that. He'd go with her wherever and whenever she wanted to go.

So they went to church, church, and more church. They went to the Baptist church, which was where Mama Rose attended, and they went to the St. Phillips Cathedral near their home. The churches were wildly different. Mount Prospect was mostly colored with a generous sprinkling of other races. Its décor included rich wooden pews, carpet the shade of ruby, an elevated altar and a huge area behind the pulpit for the immense choir, usually clothed in white and gold robes, which sang every Sunday, and it was loud, or lively, as Shelly preferred to say.

St. Phillip's was a monumental contrast. "Fly in the ointment" came to mind. If there was one colored person other than Shelly, it was the janitor who sometimes paused in the elaborately ornamented vestibule outside the second set of doors to peek in. Mark wasn't quite sure if he was colored, but Shelly had been teaching him how to tell if a person who appeared white was, or might be, colored instead.

St. Phillips was reverent, quiet, up and down with the kneeling, for no reason obvious to Mark, and mass was rendered in Latin: who was supposed to benefit from the Latin?

When he asked Shelly how they could do that: go from the Baptist church, then to the Catholic church, then back again, Shelly looked at him and declared, "Isn't God at both places?" Again: as if he was supposed to know.

Jake had been praying, yes, praying, something he had picked up as a result of being reunited with his wife. He came on it quite by accident. One night Irene was in her prayer closet, which was really Mark's old room redone. She was in there ranting and raving in other tongues and tongues he plain old couldn't understand. Jake found himself literally walking the floor between her room and his. He was worried and frankly scared. He started talking to God on his own. "God, if you're there, what is Irene doing? Is she okay? Is there someone in there with her? Should I go in?" At first nothing happened, no answer; it figured. However, he continued to talk, to question, to converse. It was becoming part of his routine.

When it was reported in the news that his parents had died in a car wreck, the *Tribune* asserted, "under mysterious circumstances," Jake had struggled with his feelings. He hated them and was glad they were gone, but he also felt that crushing emptiness: the feeling that comes with the death of a loved one. He was confused. Irene had tried to console him. He was grumpy and sullen for days. When he started asking God for peace, no audible voice spoke to him but ease resonated in his heart. He couldn't explain it, but the bitterness seemed like wasted energy so he let it go.

A week or so after the funeral, which he did not attend, something extremely pleasant began to occur. Routinely, Irene, just minutes out of her prayer closet, was all over him: hugging him, clutching him, kissing him, touching him.

Mama Rose said that God was responsible for Irene's transformation. The blood must have drained from his face the first time he heard Rose say that. She gave him a worried expression and asked if he needed some water. He could only hope that Irene wasn't sharing intimate details of their life with Rose. It was like the woman was a fortuneteller anyway. She really didn't need any help. Jake found it difficult to believe that God would…well, it just seemed strange. But even Irene said that God was responsible for her boldness.

"This is who I was meant to be if sin hadn't corrupted me and the people around me," she'd say with a smile and a pat on his rear. Jake's constant thought was, *who wouldn't thank a God like this?*

Life was almost complete. Yet there was still the nagging matter of their not having actually consummated their marriage this second time around. Although technically they had never divorced, Irene wanted them to wait for their church wedding.

They had been living like this for over two months now: this "married-not married" state of things. By now Jake knew he'd do anything for this woman. It all started out innocently enough.

It was the night of the proposal. The lights were low. Shelly had flipped the switch off as she, Mark and Mama Rose left the house. Irene was still on her knees, eyes shimmering, holding the ring in front of him. He eased onto the floor next to her, kissed her hand and told her that he had never loved anyone more and could think of nothing more important in the world than being her husband. That was when the shift of power took place. That is if he ever had any to begin with.

"Let's get married on Christmas, Jacob. We can celebrate the birth of Jesus and our renewed love at the same time. I think it would please the Lord, don't you?"

"No, I don't," he remembered spouting, "Your God can't be that cruel. I'll give you one week, Irene."

"Jacob," she laughed, "the church needs more notice than that."

By the end of their date he had reluctantly agreed to a Christmas wedding.

"I'm going to continue living with Mama Rose until the big day," she was saying as she carried the dishes from the dining table to the sink.

He spun her around so fast that he had to remind himself that he had never been violent toward a woman nor would he. Irene looked only mildly annoyed.

"Absolutely not!" he thundered.

"Jacob, I really thought you were over that stuff with Mama Rose."

"Come on, Irene, you know that's not it."

"What then?"

"Irene, I'll wait forever for you to marry me, if that's what it takes, but I'm not waiting another moment to be with you."

Her face registered her inability to figure out what he was trying to say.

He clarified, "I mean I want you in my house with me. You asked me to marry you and I'm ready to do it today. But if you need time to plan something special, okay, but I'm not living another moment without you and that's final." The glimmer in her eyes was devastating. He could see that the only power he had over her was what she allowed. In fact, he was completely at her disposal. So when she came up with a compromise he was ready to go for it. No matter what it was.

"If I do come to live with you, we won't have sex until our church wedding."

He wanted to "shush" her. Who was this woman anyway? "Sex," for the entire time they had lived as a married couple when Mark was a baby, she had never been able to even utter a euphemism for the act. Now it rolled off her tongue as easy as saying "bacon and eggs." Living with this new Irene was certainly going to be an adventure.

"Yes, baby, whatever you want," he uttered, unable to believe he was this whipped.

*T*wo down and nine more months to go. Even Irene was beginning to doubt their resolve to make it to their church wedding day. It wouldn't be a sin to give in. She and Jake had never been divorced. But she really wanted their promise to be fulfilled in the church and to be witnessed by their church family.

Irene got up from the rug next to her bed. She laughed, thinking her knees must be chafed from kneeling so long. She had her answer. Jacob wasn't going to be able to hold out until December and she didn't want to. Her Bible lay open next to her. She had been reading the psalms and praying for patience, when she clearly heard the Spirit say: Why? She sat quietly peering at the pale white walls of what had previously been Mark's room. She closed her eyes again, making her spirit listen for something more. There was nothing more. She got to her feet and sat on the bed next to the lamp table. Pulling the black rotary phone to her lap she dialed her pastor's home phone.

"Pastor Marvin, hello, this is Sister Schultz. Do you have a moment?"

"Yes, darlin', what's on your mind?"

"I wanted to ask you about the wedding." Irene pulled on a strand that hung from the hem of her dress, while biting on her lower lip.

"I have a question for you, too, Irene. Why are you and Jake waiting so long? I appreciate your decision to remain celibate until you've recommitted yourselves in the church but you've imposed this on yourselves and I'm sure it must be difficult."

"It is. That's why I'm calling."

After a series of "ahas" and "yeahs" from Pastor Marvin, everything was set. They would be married the third Saturday in April. Jake was going to be thrilled.

Jake sat on the sofa, his brown cotton work shirt unbuttoned to the waist, rubbing his temples. Fatigue caused his head to drop on the pillow behind him. He had rooted out the pipes in Tilly Dunham's cellar and roughed-in plumbing at the Anderson house where they were building an additional bathroom. Despite the chill outside, his tee-shirt was soaked to the bone. He absolutely refused to give in to his weariness. He needed to stay awake to talk to Irene. They had to have this out once and for all. Did she think he was made of steel? He wasn't. Things were going to change. He was her legal husband: he had rights. His eyelids closed, then snapped open, closed, then snapped open again. He reached for the silver candy tray, empty. He could see his reflection. His blond curls were damp and lay flat on his head and he was badly in need of a shave.

Diversion, that's what he needed. He'd call Mark. The boy was always talking about the advertising business or Shelly's new job at Akiko Designs. Perhaps they could share some funny story from Mount Prospect. He and Shelly were becoming regular attendees lately.

Jake moved to the end of the couch, reached over the high arm, careful not to disturb Irene's yellow handmade doilie, and picked up the phone. The sound of the rotary dial lulled him into a semi-conscious state. The receiver slipped from his ear as he heard Mark's voice.

"Hello. Hello, who's calling?"

"Yeah, Mark, it's your dad," Jake said, giving his head a quick jerk.

"Hey, Pop. How you doing?"

"I'm dying, son. Your mother and me, well, we're not, you know."

"Whoa, Pop, I don't need to know this. Wait a minute; she's not making you wait until the wedding. Pop, that's crazy. You two have been married for almost thirty years."

"Crazy, yeah, well. She's worth it. But this whole Christmas wedding thing…it's so far away."

"If you were me, you might consider that lucky."

"Lucky, speak English, son."

"Never mind. Wouldn't want to spoil Shelly's surprise."

"You sound excited," Jacob said, pulling the phone from his ear and giving it an odd look. Mark never was anything less than enthused when it came to Shelly. This obvious sarcasm was strange.

Jake heard the squeak of Irene's doorknob. "Gotta go, son. Call me if you need me." Jake hung up the phone, not waiting for Mark's reply. He stood and went to the foot of the stairs. "Rennie, can you come down here for a minute? We need to talk. And no touching, I can't handle that tonight."

Irene came to the top of the stairs, a twinkling of curiosity in her eyes. "Jacob Schultz, have you lost your everlasting mind? What are you yelling about?" Holding onto the banister she sauntered down the stairs. Her pink pajamas, fluffy slippers and thick robe were hardly an aphrodisiac, but Jake found her irresistible as usual.

"Did I hear you say 'no touching'?"

"You did." Jake had meant for this to be a serious conversation but the absurdity of his last comment made it impossible not to grin. Irene reciprocated. She glided down the rest of the way and into his arms. Looking up into Jake's eyes, he noted the soft pink of her lips and the silkiness of her brows. Her smooth skin begged to be touched. He traced the outline of her mouth with his thumb.

"See, this is what I'm talking about, Irene," he said, shoving her slightly back.

"What?"

"This. This isn't working."

"I know," she said, sailing her slender nails through the hair of his sideburns.

"I can't have you in my arms, stroking me…"

"I know."

"Kissing me…"

"We can't continue like this," Irene agreed.

"No, we can't. Wait," Jake said, grabbing Irene's shoulders, "you don't want to move out? Do you?"

"No, baby, I don't. I want to move the wedding up." Suddenly off her feet and in the air, she peered down into her husband's eyes.

"Hallelujah; thank you, Jesus!" Hearty laughter followed.

Jake postponed finishing the Anderson job. Who wanted to work or supervise work on a 20-degree evening? Besides, Shelly had called a family meeting. Perhaps he had a grandchild on the way. Wow, what kind of life would his grandson or granddaughter have growing up mulatto in the sixties in Chicago? Times had changed he knew, but Mark and Shelly still drew stares from people. They were adults and had chosen this. What about the poor baby? She would have no say about who she was. One thing was for sure: she'd be his blood and that meant something to him. Nobody had better dare disrespect her and he know about it. He was getting ahead of himself. He had already given himself a mulatto grandchild that he was going to get into fights over.

Maybe Mark was starting to feel the weight of the decision that he and Shelly had made to be together. Maybe the day-to-day of it was more than he had bargained for. That didn't sound like Mark, though. He had always wanted Shelly and seemed willing to do anything to keep her. Whatever was going on, Jake would never find out if he didn't get going.

His car was on the fritz so it was going to be Big Green tonight. Not going to work would just about get him there by 6:00. He pulled his heavy wool coat from the closet and adjusted the flaps on his cap over his ears. He wrapped one of Shelly's double-crochet scarves around his face and into his lapel, leather gloves on and he was out the door. The shrill wind lifted and swirled dry and icy snow into the air. It pelted Jake's face. Late February and it felt like the dead of winter. The bus couldn't come fast enough, Jake thought, as he removed his gloves and rubbed his hands together briskly before putting them back on. "Finally," Jake said as he and two other passengers boarded the bus.

Only a few brave or desperate souls had ventured out. He had the pick of whatever seat suited him. He decided to sit near the front, which was unfortunately near the door that didn't quite close and a bus driver who was far too chatty. The wipers whisked back and forth, "Shut up, shut up, shut up…" squeaking out Jake's silent prayer. He twisted in his seat, hoping the driver—Jeremy Evans of Lilgrey Street with the twin daughters who were driving him crazy and spending all of his hard-earned money—would take the hint. Driver Evans didn't until his personal friend came aboard, and asked Jake for his favorite seat, which Jake was only too happy to give.

Alone with his thoughts, a sense of foreboding came over him as he exited the bus to make his transfer to the next, which would put him a block away from his destination. Apprehension set in. It wasn't the abandoned buildings or the drunks standing on the corner or even the worsening weather. Could Shelly have bad news? Why had she called a meeting on a day like this? He was turning into an old woman. There couldn't possibly be any real trouble between the lovebirds.

The squeal of metal on metal jolted Jake forward and signaled his stop. He got off, saluted the driver and trekked through the standing snow. It was evident that the managers—if they could be called that—didn't bother to shovel the walks in front of the buildings and houses they managed. He hadn't worn his galoshes. Didn't think he needed them, but over here where the snow was high and icy, his feet crunched right through the stiff surface to the concrete below. His ankles were freezing.

He walked up the sidewalk to Rose's tiny house where the family was to gather. After ringing the doorbell, he waited. "It's Jacob!" he shouted through the front door. He stepped in. The entryway was tiled with intricately worked red and black hexagons. Jake could tell that it had once been exquisite. It now had chunks missing and was covered with dirty slushy water. He was late. Rose was nowhere to be seen, probably off on one of her missions. Shelly sat next to Mark across from Irene, giddy and perky; she was already into her story. Mark was sitting wide-legged, one arm loosely draped over Shelly's shoulder, wearing an expression fairly opposite of hers.

Jake pretty much knew how this would go. Irene would listen to Shelly's news and then tell her and Mark their good news about moving their wedding date up to April. Girls trading stories: one happy exchangefest. He and Mark would add a few comments to show they were paying attention, everyone would share genuinely good feelings and call it a night.

"Guess what, Mom," Shelly loved saying that, said it every chance she got: "Mom, are we going to see you this week for dinner?" "Mom, will you be visiting the shop soon?" "So, Mom, I'll be bringing my new dress over for alterations on Saturday." On and on it went like this. Jake wasn't surprised that she rarely called him Dad. That had to come harder.

Anyway, tonight she was exuberant. "Mark and I are going to be married."

Jake and Irene gave each other a quizzical look and turned back to Shelly.

"At Mount Prospect," she continued. "Isn't that wonderful? We want our union to be blessed by God. Just like you and Mr...Dad. Can you help me plan it, Mom? Mama Rose is really busy these days, and anyway I feel like it should be you, you know."

Shelly was bursting with her news as Jake pulled off his coat and leaned into the hall to kick the snow off his shoes onto the welcome mat.

"Jacob, Mark and Shelly are going to married at Mount Prospect," Irene was saying as he came back into the center of the room and the conversation.

"I heard that part. So when is the big day?"

Irene twisted nervously in her seat and tilted her head oddly toward Jake, "Uh, April," she forced out quickly.

"What!"

Irene jumped from her seat. "Come with me, Jacob, I need your help with something." Pulling him by the arm, they started up the stairs. Before she could start, he did, "But Irene, we're supposed to be married in April."

"Pop, we could change our date if..."

"No!" Mark was cut off by the shrill retort of both his mother and wife.

"April it is, honey," Irene shouted, sweetly, from the top of the landing. "You know we'd do anything for you."

Jake groaned; to his utter dismay Mark and Shelly's wedding meant postponing his own. Hadn't Pastor Marvin told them that the date they'd chosen was the last available Saturday for a wedding this April? Maybe he'd make some kind of exception for their rather unique circumstance. Irene grabbed his arm and pulled him down the hall. She was undoubtedly hoping they would not be overheard again.

"Jacob, I know what you're thinking: we had the last available Saturday in April, but Pastor Marvin told me that all the Fridays in April are open. If we can wait until the kids are married, we can be married the Friday following their wedding. I'll make it worth your while. We'd only be waiting a few additional days."

"Irene, this is manipula—"

She grabbed his waist with both hands, pulled him tight to her, and kissed him thoroughly.

"Worth your while," she whispered by his lip, in his ear, at the base of his neck.

Chapter Thirteen
Mama's House

Beatrice Roslyn Brown stood quietly in a corner of the title office waiting for her escort; she knew he was dependable if often a bit late. She fingered the books, surprised to see several she had read. She watched as Joe Flannery walked slowly up the stairs. He looked to the left and to the right. She supposed he was awestruck by the building. It was elegant with its white carved columns supporting its foundation. The large mahogany door with ceiling-to-floor windows seemed regal. It had an ornate gold knocker for decoration. Joe tried to use it, ignoring the doorbell. Margaret walked heavily behind him, lifting one rotund leg after the other. She breathed deeply and appeared to be sweating. She pulled her worn handkerchief from her bosom and rubbed it across her forehead. Beatrice watched Margaret mouth the words, "Wait for me, baby." Joe turned and extended his hand. His entire frame quaked as he struggled to assist his wife up the remaining stairs. Beatrice shifted slightly to watch the couple stroll casually by.

"Did you see that uppity wench in the lobby?" Margaret whispered too loudly for a woman trying to be discreet.

Joe, who had been busy admiring his opulent surroundings: rich mahogany, crystal chandeliers and beveled mirrors, simply answered, "Who?"

"The cleaning lady," Margaret replied. To his quizzical look, she said, "Rose."

"No. I wonder what she's doing here?"

"Probably looking for a job." They laughed triumphantly as they made their way to the conference room pointed out to them by the secretary.

Joe and Margaret Flannery were early. They had all but spent the money they were about to make from the sale of 5501 Maple Street. It had become an albatross. There had been six sets of tenants in the last ten years. The Yarboroughs were deadbeats, always wanting this or that fixed and never paying their rent on time. It was time for them to go. Margaret had taken great pleasure in delivering the news.

"Mr. Yarborough, I need to speak with you and your wife."

"She's not home, Mrs. Flannery."

"That's all right, baby, we can talk this over, just the two of us."

"Mrs. Flannery, I really don't think it's appropriate."

"Listen, John, you and Louise have to be out of here at the end of the month."

"But, Mrs. Flannery, our agreement?"

Margaret had explained to Joe how she laughed in John Yarborough's face. They had a handshake agreement. Joe always told his tenants that he trusted them and didn't feel any need to get anything in writing. These people were usually so desperate to get a place they didn't mind their "no questions asked" policy. But the Yarboroughs were pushy. They never got their lease but they did get more repairs and upgrades than any other tenant. The house hadn't been in this good of a shape since Rose left it. What was she doing in the lobby?

The heavy door behind Margaret opened slowly. A large man wearing a dark navy suit and a gentle grin walked in. Margaret gave him her prettiest smile, while Joe stood to extend his hand.

"So where is our buyer?"

"Patience, Mrs. Flannery, Mrs. Brown and her counsel will be in at one. You are the most punctual people we've ever served. How long have you been waiting now?"

Before Margaret could answer, a slim redhead in her mid-twenties opened the door carefully, followed by Rose and a tall, well-dressed Negro man.

"Rose!" both Joe and Margaret said at the same time.

"I see you've met Mrs. Beatrice Roslyn Brown, and do you know Mr. Johnson as well?"

Margaret's thin red lips formed an "O" but no words emerged. Joe stood. Narrowing his small brown eyes and curling his upper lip into a snarl, he extended his narrow arm exposing his pale wrist, which protruded a full three inches beyond the length of his jacket sleeve. He pointed his long finger. "What's she doing here?" he shouted, totally ignoring Johnson.

"Mrs. Brown is our buyer," the agent responded.

"No way," Joe stated flatly.

Rose nodded and without a word she turned to leave; James Johnson held the door for her.

"Now, wait just a moment," Margaret started in hushed tones. "Honey," her voice was impatient, "the new house, the money. And don't forget we actually signed some papers this time."

"Yes, you did," James said as the door slowly started to close. "We'll be in touch about those papers within the week."

By now Joe had to feel his pockets thinning, his debts mounting, and his new house going back on the market, and the papers he'd signed for that house. Mama Rose knew he wouldn't bother to bring a lawyer to this closing. They probably hadn't bothered to read the documents they'd signed either. After all, the system had always favored them, that is, until now. And as far as they knew, Beatrice Roslyn Brown had a lawyer, a good one by the looks of him, even if he was a Negro.

"Hold it just a minute, Rose," Joe said, practically tripping over Margaret's chair to reopen the heavy door. "Miss Rose, hold on there. We got us a legally binding deal. You can't get out of it now."

Rose smiled and James had to hold his head down as to not reveal his amusement.

"Mr. Flannery, I really don't have time to deal with foolishness. Do you want to sell your house to me or not?"

"Yes, Ma'am, I certainly do."

Margaret turned to do some snarling of her own.

"What?" Joe said as he regained his seat.

"I wanted you to get her back in here, not suck up to that…" She finished the rest of her sentence in hushed tones.

"Well," said Mr. Eubanks, nervously fingering his tie. "Shall we begin?"

The only thing that kept Mrs. Beatrice Roslyn Brown a.k.a. Mama Rose, from floating away on a cloud of joy was her counsel, who secretly held her hand underneath the table. He was there on his day off wearing his suit that he reserved for official business when he had to represent his company off-site. It was true what they say: clothes make the man. When he worked at the Johnson and Johnson Moving and Storage or his auto repair shop, he wore blue overalls. They were neatly pressed but that had never bought him any credit when it came to getting respect away from the shop. When Mama Rose asked him to put on his Sunday best and meet her at this address he had no idea why, but he caught on the moment he walked into Axtell Title. Mama Rose was as smart as a whip. There was no denying it.

While signing the papers, Joe occasionally cut an angry look at Mama Rose and James Johnson. Margaret looked their way, every few minutes, with a mixture of hatred and lust. Mama Rose gritted her teeth and squeezed James' hand hard when Margaret gave him that hungry look. It was all she could do to refrain from telling the woman to act her age.

With the deal done, Margaret pushed the papers toward Mr. Eubanks and placed her round fingers solidly against the rich grain on the great wood table. With great force and effort she shoved her plump body and chair from the table. She then firmly gripped her armrests and began to stand, revealing a wilted and wrinkled pink print frock. The chair squealed under her massive weight.

Joe's flimsy limbs shook as he helped his wife from her seat. Mama Rose wondered if it was Margaret's mass or Joe's humiliation that caused him to quiver.

Mr. Eubanks extended his hand in an attempt at protocol, but the Flannery's, who were without manners or shame, left without a word or any attempt at courtesy.

Mrs. Brown rose with grace and offered her hand to Mr. Eubanks, who surprised her by kissing rather than shaking it. Seems his mother, who had refused help from her family, had accepted visits from Mrs. Brown while she was in the hospital. Tom Eubanks was eternally grateful. When Jake Schultz had formed his plan to get Joe Flannery to sell to Mama Rose, Tom Eubanks was only too happy to act as title agent charging the Flannery's a fraction of his company's normal fee. Since the Flannery's were getting a deal and saving money, they were more than happy to accept Jake's recommendation of closing with Axtell Title. Mama Rose placed her hand on his and said, "Thank you." James opened the door, led her into the waiting area, out into the lobby, out the door, down the stairs, and into his pickup truck. Mrs. Beatrice Roslyn Brown was going home and it felt real good.

Jake and Irene sat on their porch like the old married couple they were. That was, except for the sex part. Things had gotten so steamy in the house he had suggested they come outside for fresh air. Tomorrow Mark and Shelly would have their church wedding, and he and Irene would have theirs six days after. There was no use messing it up now. He could have easily taken advantage of the situation. It seemed the prelude was losing a bit of its allure for Irene. Still it had become almost a promise to God now and he wasn't about to help her break it. They were holding hands and surveying the neighborhood.

Rose was set to move back into her old house the day after Mark and Shelly's wedding. She, too, had been mindful not to overshadow the big event. Jake, for one, had thought the big event would have been a colored girl marrying a white boy, but that wasn't big enough. Now they had to do it all over again in a church, which effectively pushed back his own wedding. He wasn't bitter really. He simply wanted his own wife so badly he could taste it. Celibacy wasn't anything he had ever done willingly and if it weren't Irene he was waiting for, he was sure he wouldn't be doing it now.

"Hello, Jake, Irene." Mrs. King's son was busy arranging all kinds of flowers and plants on Rose's porch. His mother had passed away and bequeathed in her will that Rose should have as many of her flowers and plants as she could stand. What an unusual thing to leave someone. The entire community was abuzz. However, their Rose was returning. People who had been mere children when she moved were acting as if their best friend was coming home.

Irene had informed him on more than one occasion that Rose had never lost her connection to this neighborhood or the people. She should know, being herself one of Rose's protégées. To tell the truth, Jake also had a fondness for the old bird. Irene made sure he knew that Rose was the very hand of God in her life. It was she who had led her to the Lord and was in no small way responsible for their reconciliation. Rose had asked Irene if she found it strange that two people separated for almost thirty years had made no effort to divorce.

Irene wouldn't hear it at first. She preferred to believe that he was lazy, which she knew for a fact wasn't true, or that he had simply neglected it, which she also knew was not true. He was nothing if not thorough. So the only remaining explanation was that he hadn't wanted to. This was in fact the reality. He had only been in love once. And only love merited marriage in his mind. And although he had never been religious until recently, somewhere deep inside him he believed that marriage only happened once, with your one true abiding love. He had found his one love and there wasn't going to be another. Mama Rose had convinced Irene that she needed to talk with him to give him a chance to explain his actions. That she, in fact, needed to forgive him because her soul would suffer if she did not. Jake remembered asking if that was the reason Irene had taken him back. He wanted her under almost any circumstance but he drew the line at obligation.

He could still remember her hearty laugh, "No, silly," she said, making the oddest face he had ever seen—it took him a while to get used to her humor—"forgiving you in no way obligates me to be with you. I'm with you because my heart tells me it's where I am supposed to be."

"Couldn't your heart have said something sooner?"

"Would you have been ready sooner?" Her statement was both declaration and question. He knew it didn't require a response.

Irene, who had been holding his hand and stroking it with her thumb, turned to give him a provocatively sinful glare. The moonlight intensified her gleaming smile. Her deep dark hair cascaded about her shoulders and the rich bronze of her tanned arms glistened from perspiration. Jake's leg made an involuntary quiver and the phrase "six more days and counting," reverberated repeatedly in his mind.

Chapter Fourteen
The Wedding

*M*ark sat with his back against the wall, dull green stalls on his left and urinals on his right and his friend Bob standing sentinel at the door. What was he doing in Mount Prospect's bathroom with another man? Oh yeah, his church wedding to Shelly. Mark looked at his fake patent leather shoe as he sat in the rickety wooden chair tying his laces. He could see his reflection, and in his estimation "grim" was an optimistic estimate of his expression. Shelly's words intruded on his solitude, "I want you to be saved. Heaven won't be the same. Be with me forever." Like attack dogs they latched onto him from every side. He imagined himself pulling out a sword. With one fell swoop he vanquished them all. Other words soon followed, "Come unto me all of you who are heavy laden and I will give you rest." Again Mark took out his sword. It withered in his hand.

"Got to lay off the late night snacks," he mumbled.

"What'd you say, buddy?" Bob turned to look at him, "Need some help, fella? Your hands are shaking like leaves. You're never going to get those shoes tied at this rate. What are you so nervous about? You should be an old pro at this. It's not like you're not already married. The hardest part's already done."

"You're right. I'm okay, man. Let's get this thing over."

Shelly's confidence had never been more evident. She waltzed down the ruby-red carpeted aisle like an ancient princess about to be crowned queen of all she surveyed. The snugly cinched midriff of her crystal-white pearl-laced dress caused her to walk even taller than usual. Her perfect teeth made a radiant smile, and the curly tendrils that fell easily over her cheeks made her look like an exquisite brown china doll. She was lovely. Jake needed to admit it now, for his own sake. He had always been able to see why Mark found Shelly attractive, why she was the only match for his own bravado. No one had ever touched or challenged him like Shelly did.

Jake could still remember becoming instantly jealous when Mark, as a baby, became excited at Shelly's arrival. Her color, while a factor, was a convenient excuse to keep his son's love all to himself. He had been a selfish man. All of that was going to change now. He had Irene, and in six short days he was really going to have her. Rose was back and that only made Irene more generous and giving. He was glad for his own sake, too. Had he really missed the old bag? Well, anything was possible. And Mark, his once-estranged son, was back in his life. He might even have a brown grandbaby soon; that would definitely be different, but he'd love it no matter what. Jake smiled at the prospect. You couldn't tell him that people didn't change. Why he even had a fledgling relationship with God. He was happy. Who was he kidding? He was ecstatic!

Jake sat back in his seat. The end of this day signaled the countdown to his own wedding. Could she possibly move any slower? Let's get this show on the road, for God's sake. Everyone was laughing. Irene and Mama Rose were glowering. He hadn't said that out loud, had he?

Head hanging in shame, Jake contemplated his son. "Poppy, Poppy, look at the baby." His rosy cheeks beamed at the thought of her. "Pop, I rescued some girl today. A bunch of guys were ready to jump her just because…" his young voice trailed off. "But, Pop, you don't understand. Shelly and me, we have a special friendship." Then, "Don't worry, Pop, Shelly and I are not going to be so close anymore." Hum, a promise he wasn't able to keep. Jake smiled to himself. He eyed his son's shoes, perfectly shined. The boy took after him when it came to his grooming. His perfectly tailored tux fit his strong physique impeccably. The white boutonnière, one of Rose's flowers, graced his satin lapel. And his face: what the… the boy's face looked like he was chewing on last year's dirty socks, twice warmed over.

An extreme sense of panic washed over Jake. What now?

*H*er son, her wonderful glorious baby boy, was a man. And he was about to be married in the company of God and his parents and all of his friends. She hadn't been the best mother. It's hard to do the best for your child when you can't even take care of yourself. But, glory to God, she had the good sense to let Jake raise him. What a good job he had done. Mark was polite, gracious, intelligent and genuinely good. Yes, Jake had done a good job despite himself. *Look how handsome,* she thought as she took in his appearance.

Her eyes traveled his fine profile, his broad shoulders filled out his sculptured suit and his strong chin and dimpled cheek added character to his face. Where was his dimple? He wasn't smiling, not a hint of humor. He was nervous, that's all. So why did he look petrified?

Irene tried to dispel her rising discomfort as she watched her daughter-in-law proudly strolling the center aisle between the pews. She was everything any mother could want for her child: beautiful, warm and loving. The fact that she wanted to be married in the church, although she was already legally married, touched Irene's heart profoundly. They were all going to be part of the family of God. Shelly had phoned her about a month ago telling her that Mark had accepted Christ. Eternity was in their grasp. Irene felt tears welling in her eyes. She had promised herself she would not cry. A delicate smile arose as she felt the flow that told her she would not be keeping that promise. Her vision slowly cleared. She looked toward her son. He didn't look petrified any longer. He looked horrified.

"If any man sees just cause why these two should not be joined together this day…"

"Um, um. Pastor Marvin, I have a confession to make…"

Jake's body went rigid. "Irene," Jake started, his voice in a near panic.

She turned toward him, her mouth agape. "What is it, Jacob? You know something about this?" She squeezed his hand enough for him to feel her fear.

Shelly's face registered the horror she was apparently feeling. She reached up to touch the face of her beloved. Mark grabbed her hand in a way that was so apologetic, Jake could feel his son's heart breaking.

"I've been living a lie."

Jake's stomach lurched. He thought he might lose his lunch but he needed to be the rock. Everyone was going to need his strength now. He turned to his wife, whose grip had gone weak. He grabbed her hand more firmly and forced her face toward his. "Irene," he spoke soft but firmly, "I have something to tell you about our son." Her eyes met his, desperately searching them for answers.

Mark grabbed both of Shelly's hands and turned toward the congregation.

"I'm sorry, everyone." Shelly appeared faint. Mark pulled her to his side in what Jake felt was a generous gesture, considering.

"You came here for a wedding. There is not going to be one." The collective gasp was deafening. The hem of Shelly's shimmering white satin dress was two inches closer to the floor, suggesting that she was only standing at the behest of her husband, who supported her limp body. Poor thing, she was probably still a virgin. What horrible measures had his son taken to hide his true self from the world?

"My wife thinks I'm…"

"Here it comes, honey. I should have prepared you," Jake confessed, his tongue nervously going over his dry lips. Irene was clutching his arm. Jake looked about anxiously. He had long gotten past his fear of this revelation and in fact had no longer thought it necessary. But wishful thinking had not made it so. He wondered how this religious group of people would take the news. Sure they'd still love Mark. But would they respect him? Would his very manhood be challenged? Well, he guessed that came with the territory, didn't it?

The faces of the crowd were an unusual mix. The older deacons and deaconesses simply looked curious. Some of the young people looked giddy as if they were about to get a juicy piece of gossip that they'd have to ask forgiveness for, once they shared it with everyone they knew. This was going to be too good to keep to one's self. If Mark hadn't been the subject of disclosure, he'd be hard-pressed to keep it to himself.

The Johnson boy had jumped to his feet, his teeth so tightly clenched it seemed they might shatter. He was clutching the bench in front of him. Jake could hear him now, "Shelly, come away with me. You and Schultz were not meant to be. We will get this farce of a marriage annulled before all the crocuses die." To think how he himself had tried to keep Mark and Shelly apart. Now he couldn't think of anything he wanted more than for them to be together. Irony. Jake craned his neck more. He wanted to see how Rose was taking all this in. When he finally got a good look at her, she was standing, firm and stern. She took a deep breath and calmly but loudly said, "Spit it out, boy. We haven't got all day. My granddaughter's wilting up there."

Jake thought she looked a whole lot better now than she would in ten minutes. Poor Rose. The woman had no idea what was about to come.

"…a Christian." Mark stated emphatically. "My wife thinks I'm a Christian."

"A Christian?" Jake repeated loudly, again drawing every eye in the sanctuary.

"I've been lying to her. I didn't want her worrying about my eternal soul. The one I wasn't even sure I had. So this wedding is postponed until I can be properly baptized and welcomed into the family of God."

Shelly still wasn't standing on her own strength. To Jake, she looked like one of Mama Rose's flowers that had languished too long in the sun.

"Hold on a minute, son, about that baptism. If you go down a dry devil, you're simply going to come up a wet one. Have you had a change of heart?" Pastor Marvin belted.

Mark didn't answer immediately. For Jake the room went dark, the chubby-cheeked balking babies hushed their whimpering and even the yelping shepherd tied to the parking meter across the street went silent.

"Yes, sir, I believe I have. As my wife was coming down the aisle, I became increasingly uncomfortable."

Jake found himself groping for Irene's hand.

Mark continued, "I was praying for her, for our life together, for the children we will have and the difficulties we will experience. I thought about her living on without me, about my father living on without me, about my mother...anyway I believe. I have believed for some time now, but I was afraid. I didn't want to depend on anyone greater than myself. Depending on Shelly was already killing me. When I thought about what might happen if I lost her I felt sick and the thought of depending on anyone or anything else in that way was so unappealing to me that I just couldn't fathom it. But today, today as I saw my dear sweet Shelly coming down the aisle, I realized my logic was flawed. The very thing I was trying to avoid I was setting in motion: being separated forever from the one person I loved the most. I want to be with her forever. Her God will be my God because her God is God. In the face of all my brothers and sisters, I confess the Lord Jesus Christ this day."

"Then that's all that's needed, son."

"But what about the baptism?" Mark questioned.

"May I speak?"

Mama Rose. How had she managed to be quiet for so long? "I suggest we get the wedding done and proceed straight to the baptism."

"Yes, I agree," Irene said as she stood to voice her opinion.

"Yes, yes, for God's sake and for mine, can we just get the thing done?" Jake thought he was mumbling to himself again. He was proven wrong as the whole congregation broke out in hysterical laughter.

Irene sat all the way across the bench seat from Jake as they drove home in his station wagon. Usually she snuggled right up under him as he drove. If only he could read her mind. Her gaze was so listless. What was she thinking? As for Jake, he was thoroughly exhausted, tired right down to the bone. The wedding plans had been stressing and consuming Irene. Yesterday was the first time in about a month that she had given herself over to passion. Lately she was so into making sure that every detail was perfect for Mark and Shelly's wedding, she had not been her usual affectionate self with him. Their arrangement had been so unusual anyway. Since she agreed to live with him until they could be married in the church, they had been blissfully strained.

Going all the way to the threshold of sex but not consummating it was taking its toll on both of them. If their own wedding had not been planned within the week, Jake was sure they would have gone up in flames. And what was this torture for, really? He and Irene had never been divorced. Legally they were still married. And today they had nervously gotten ready for Mark and Shelly's church wedding. They were legally married, too, in a civil service; if you could call Vegas civil. Was all of this ceremony really necessary? God knew, in both cases, that they were with their soul mates. Jake thought about it. It was for the women, of course. Certain things had to be done for their delicate sensitivities. And in Mark's case, at least, the church wedding had forced him to confront his demons and deal with his crisis of faith. If anyone would have told Jake that he would have beat his son to the church to confess Christ in front of a little black congregation, he would have laughed them to scorn, but that is in fact what had happened; and he couldn't say he was the least bit sorry.

Well, they had lived through Mark and Shelly's church wedding, through Mark's baptism and their own church wedding today. Yes, he had actually done that. As they stood there about to dunk Mark in the name of the Father, the Son, Jesus, and the Holy Ghost, he couldn't see what sense it made to come back to that same church with the same people to get married again to his own dear wife. He spoke up, "Excuse me, Pastor Marvin, do you think before you dunk the boy you could say the words over Irene and me?"

"The words?" Pastor Marvin asked, his long white robe already soaked to the waist with baptismal pool water. There was a hush over the crowd, a few snickers and a loud gasp from Irene.

"Well, I just don't see why we need to come back in a week assembling the same people to do virtually the same thing, minus the baptism, of course." That drew a few more giggles and a couple of very loud "amens." Irene remained silent until the pastor looked to her for her approval, which she gave by an almost imperceptible nod. Then, with Mark standing in the water shivering, Pastor Marvin said the words over them. In less than three minutes, the pastor, who was also starting to shiver, finished with, "I now pronounce you recommitted in Christ, under the marriage covenant for life. You may kiss the bride," which Jake had promptly done. Irene gave a tacit response: her lips hardly met his as he leaned to kiss her. He stood there for a moment, letting the power of the words that had been spoken wash over him and he truly felt the difference.

Pastor Marvin, with the help of Deacon John, leaned Mark into the water and baptized him into the family of God. Between her flood of tears and legs so wobbly she could hardly stand, Shelly positively beamed with joy. Sister Big Bosoms and Sister Giving Heart came over to cool her with one of the paper church fans that pictured a happy family and advertised Watkin's Funeral Home. Mark went under and jumped out before Shelly actually swooned. His hands were flying in adulation and exaltation. "Hallelujah!" he shouted at the top of his lungs. Jake's son was a happy man. Jake could relate: at one with God and the woman he loved. Was there a better feeling?

With Mark properly baptized and dressed again in his tuxedo, the reception commenced. Irene, who loved to dance, asked her husband to take her home right away. And now she was sitting as quietly and as calmly as possible clear on the other side of his car. What a way to "start" their own married life.

This silent drive was driving him crazy, "Irene, are you all right, honey?"

"Fine."

"What are you thinkin' about?"

"Things."

"Care to elaborate?"

"No."

And so it was, Jake alone with his thoughts and his silent wife. It was a lazy Saturday evening. There was little to see from the car window, a few people strolled the sidewalks, seemingly on their way home from wherever they had been. The sky was black and starry, the moon high and shiny. Perhaps Irene was tired, too, and entranced by the brilliance above. It was the not knowing that made this the longest fifteen minutes in his recent history. Should he be glad to be finally home with Irene or not?

Jake pulled his large station wagon to the curb and got out to go around and open Irene's door. The silver of his car glowed like an extension of the moonlight: romantic. Jake hoped it was a good sign. He reached for her hand. She didn't meet his gaze. She really was upset with him about their all-too-spontaneous wedding. He wanted to be married tonight but he was also thinking about her. Did she really want to go through all of that trouble again in a week? She couldn't, could she?

They made their way slowly up the stairs, and Jake turned once again to look at Irene as he turned the keys in the locks to get into the house. Still she didn't look at him. Everything was as they had left it: neat and clean. His huge sofa beckoned his weary body but he really wanted to be upstairs with his church-wedded wife. He didn't really expect anything to happen tonight; just lying next to her in the bed would be more wonderful than almost anything he could imagine. He had blown that. He reached to help Irene off with her coat, "Rennie, I realize you're upset with—"

"Shut up, Jake." She rasped in a husky tone. Jake loosed his hold on her coat. It dropped to the floor.

"Irene!" Before he could get thoroughly upset he noticed her eyes: something was smoldering there.

"What's come over you, Rennie?" She moved straight for him, wrapped her arms around his neck and forcefully captured his mouth with hers. Jake heard the groan in the back of her throat and went right to his knees, pulling her to the floor with him. She was tugging at his coat, forcing it down off his shoulders. He let her. His suit coat and tie soon followed. Next Jake felt his shirt being ripped from his body, buttons pulled away flying in all directions. The sensation of Irene's nails scoring his chest was almost too much. His breath caught in his throat; for a minute he didn't think he'd be able to breathe, but he was no fool. This was the answer to his prayers. He tried to reach behind Irene's neck to unzip the soft ivory mother-to-the-groom dress she had purchased for her son's wedding. After fumbling with the zipper for what seemed like an eternity, he found himself repaying the favor she had done him. He gripped both sides of the neck of her dress and tore it from her shoulders.

The sight of her creamy neck, as she threw her head back in surrender, took all his self-control away. He pounced on her. The rest was a blur; shreds of clothing flew everywhere. No words spoken. None needed; a lifetime of passion and need overtook them. Jake's orderly existence twisted and turned out of control and he loved every blistering moment of it. The ornamental button-tufted accent pillows flew to the floor as Jake and Irene cleared the couch to make love there. Floral arrangements tumbled from their places as they kicked over the coffee table. Rolling near the window brought down one of the curtains, which were only closed at night, concealing the seat that he and Mark knelt on to survey the neighborhood.

He and Irene made love over every inch of his—no, their—living room. Irene's voluptuous body, which had filled out in all the right places, was pressed firmly against his own. They were wrapped tightly in each other's arms, rolling over the floor, giggling uncontrollably. Jake had never experienced anything like it. Now, this was how marriage was supposed to be.

Jake woke up with Irene in his arms. He was thoroughly worn out. Rapturous and immense pleasure had been theirs; and it wasn't just physical. Unlike when they had been together years ago, this time they had given both body and soul. There was no shame, guilt or holding back. For the first time Jake knew that Irene had given him all that was her and she had done so without reservation. And he had been freed. From the moment her hand touched his bare chest, he felt unleashed. It scared him at first. He didn't know what he might do, how far he'd go.

He still might ask Irene if he had gone too far. He had done things with her this night that he had only imagined. But she had been wild and ravenous like a stalking cat.

Irene had given him some indication as to what this night might be like while they were living together waiting for their church wedding—even though legally they had never been divorced. They were not having sex, but at times she was so lusty toward him that he wondered if she'd be able to make it till the "marriage day." Then as suddenly as the intimacy started, it stopped as she threw herself into the preparations for Mark and Shelly's wedding. He couldn't really complain. What would he say, "Why aren't you still kissing me, stroking me, and generally turning me on just to switch me off?" He knew the answer: they were waiting until their church wedding. So he bore it. There was nothing to be done but to wait. It was just that the "preview lovemaking" had been so good he didn't feel Irene could possibly live up to it when they really got together. But he was wrong, wrong, wrong; and if her moving now against his side was any indication, he was about to be proven wonderfully wrong again. They had fallen asleep with just the downed curtain over them. He was feeling a bit chilled, but if he were a betting man, he would have to say he wouldn't be feeling that way for long. Irene was becoming insistent. He rolled his body onto hers.

"What's this? Tears?" Glistening brown eyes returned his gaze. Her dark hair was splayed over her arms as he held them above her head. She gave a weak smile and turned, trying to bury her face by her upper arm. Jake used his thumb to gently wipe her cheek and then felt the lump rising in his throat. "I'm so happy, Irene," he muttered as his own vision became blurry.

"Me, too," she managed weakly. Those were the last coherent words they spoke for several hours.

Epilogue

It was another September. The autumn leaves started to turn their varied shades of passionate plum and ravishing reds. The gorgeous sun-streaked sky made it a magnificent day for the celebration. Rose's house was in an uproar; everyone was making preparations. Irene cooked. Her new passion was experimenting with varied ethnic cuisine. Today they were having a creamy potato salad and a cheesy chicken enchilada pie. The potato salad was chilly cold and the enchiladas were still simmering hot.

Mama Rose hurried down the stairs, pulling her pale green apron from the hall closet as she entered the kitchen. She plucked a huge cobbler from the oven. The aroma of a peach orchard filled the room. Gooey thick purple syrup oozed over the edge of another tin. It held a great treasure: blackberry cobbler, Jake's new favorite.

Jake busied himself hanging huge vividly colored bulbs, usually reserved for Christmas, from the archway that led from the entryway to the living room. A screech of tires caused Jake to jump from his stepladder. He switched on the colored bulbs and dimmed the overhead lights. Soon there was a small knock on the door.

"Bonpa, open the door!" a wee voice yelped. Jake lunged for the door. Three-year-old Diana jumped into his arms. He kissed his grandbaby soundly on both her chubby cheeks, while pushing her bushy brown curls from her brow so he could see her sparkling amber eyes.

"Poppy," another small voice rang out. Jake felt a tug at his pant leg. "Look, Poppy, see my gun?" Four-year-old L.J. pointed his red water pistol at his grandfather's nose. His deep brown complexion along with his extremely straight black hair made him look like he was from India or some other exotic overseas place.

His sister shrieked, "Don't shoot me, Lil' Jake. Bonpa, don't let 'im get me." The hard heels of her patent leather shoes dug into his side as baby Diana shimmied up around his neck trying to avoid her brother's reach.

"Whoa, Dia, you'll break Bonpa's neck if you're not careful."

"Sorry, Bonpa." She kissed his neck, "All better? I love you, Bonpa."

"I'm sorry, Pop." Mark was saying as he followed his children into the house, toting their overnight bags and sundry toys and accessories. "She started with the 'Bonpa' business last week, as if 'Poppy' wasn't bad enough."

"Not a problem, son. If my grand-girl wants 'Bonpa' then 'Bonpa' it is."

Mark shrugged. Shelly rushed in brushing a kiss on her father-in-law's cheek, "Hi, Pop." Her smile was brilliant. Jake still felt strange when she called him "Pop" but he loved her. He loved her for making his son's life complete. He loved her for his two terrific grandchildren and his goddaughter, Sam, Donna and Bob's daughter. Their sweet girl had adopted him as her own grandfather. She wasn't about to be outdone by her godsister and brother. If they had a grandfather, so did she. "Poppy Jake, I came along to help you take care of the babies." L.J. sneered at her and stuck out his tongue. She rolled her eyes at him and returned her attention to her adopted grandfather. "Poppy Jake, can you read my animal book to me?"

Jake plopped down in the window seat. Baby Diana was still hanging on his neck clutching for dear life. Little Jake had pulled his pockets inside out looking for coins, and Sam was in the middle of a pirouette. "Do you like my new skirt? Mama says it's a maze."

"You mean the color is maize," Irene corrected from across the room.

Jake thought she looked like a yellow sunflower. Her new skirt was exactly the color of her short-cut hair and was very complimentary to her clear green eyes. Jake was thinking about walking them to the candy store on the corner. He gloried in the looks he received as he marched his own personal United Nations down the street. His grandchildren loved him with all their hearts. He could see it in their laughing eyes and he could feel it in their tender touches. As he contemplated what it would take to get all three of them ready, Diana hopped from his lap and ran into the kitchen. She had that look in her eyes. Jake thought he should follow.

Diana tiptoed to the edge of the kitchen table. She was sniffing the air, "'mells yummy," she said. Her smile was devious.

Just as she was about to plunge her little index finger into the piping hot goo of the blackberry cobbler, her great-grandmother's voice rang out, "Diana, you'll get burned."

Jake was ahead of her. He scooped his youngest grandchild up before her hand reached the dreaded delicacy. "Thanks, Bonpa." She pretended to walk away and then ran back in the direction of the pie. Her grandfather scooped her up again and whirled her in the air. They repeated this ritual three times, Diana's laughter rippling through the house. She was a joy to her whole family.

As Diana scrambled to the floor tying to repeat her escapade for a fourth time, her grandmother interceded, "That's enough, Dia, you'll wear Bonpa out. Go in the other room and play with the other children until dinner."

"I don't want the little table."

"We don't have to sit at the little table today. It's celebration day," Samantha assured her god-sister.

"What's celebration day?" Diana questioned.

"It's the celebration of the day Mark and Shelly met again."

"Who's that?" Diana's little nose crinkled.

"Mom and Dad, silly goose," L.J. sounded. Everyone covered their mouths or turned their heads, not wanting L.J. to see them giggle at his inappropriate comment.

"Don't call your sister names, L.J.," Jake announced in his authoritative voice.

"I forgibe him, Bonpa."

"As well you should, my little one." He pinched Diana's nose—it was so like her mother's and she had Rose's wise eyes. "Always forgive as Christ has forgiven us. And don't ever, ever, ever waste your time with hatred. It eats at your soul and devours your dreams."

"Devours?" Lil' Jake yelled.

"Yes, devours!" Samantha mimicked, her hands clutched in claws as she let out a roar, chasing L.J. and Diana from the room and down the long hall that led to the back of the house.

Yes, Jake felt he was about the luckiest man alive. He lived in a magnificent palace with a gypsy princess. The queen bee lived right next door and his children adored and waited on him. He was respected far and wide—well, at least within a several block radius of his home—and his heart was filled to bursting with love. He was truly blessed, for this was the family he had always wanted, the one he always needed.